n; *Hard Loves, Ea* ... *of War*; *Long, Hot Summer*; *Falling in Lo* ... *gain*; *The Girl Now Leaving* and *Not Just a Soldier's War*, as well as a collection of short stories, *Women Are Bloody Marvellous!* She has written for television and radio and won the Chichester Festival Theatre Award. Born in Romsey, Hampshire, she now lives in Southsea.

BY THE SAME AUTHOR

Women Are Bloody Marvellous!
Jude
Jaen
Women of No Account
Hard Loves, Easy Riches
The Consequences of War
Goodbye Piccadilly
Long, Hot Summer
Falling in Love Again
The Girl Now Leaving
Not Just a Soldier's War

Betty Burton

THE FACE OF EVE

HarperCollins*Publishers*

This novel is entirely a work of fiction.
The names, characters and incidents portrayed in it are the work of the author's imagination. Any resemblance to actual persons, living or dead, events or localities is entirely coincidental.

HarperCollins*Publishers*
77–85 Fulham Palace Road,
Hammersmith, London W6 8JB

www.harpercollins.co.uk

This paperback edition 2002
3 5 7 9 8 6 4 2

First published in Great Britain by
HarperCollins*Publishers* 2001

ISBN 0 00 651044 2

Typeset in New Baskerville by Palimpsest
Book Production Limited,
Polmont, Stirlingshire

Printed and bound in Great Britain by
Clays Ltd, St Ives plc

For Russ, with whom I spent many years of pretty good life (and who always had a good idea for my next novel).

For my grandchildren and their parents – without whom life after Russ wouldn't have much meaning.

For the nursing and other staff at South Africa Lodge Nursing Home, Waterlooville – who kept me going in the last months of his life.

For Yvonne Chapman – without whose support, especially during the time of several re-writes, *The Face of Eve* might never have been completed.

For the St James Hospital Portsmouth Support Group, holding one another up and understanding the blackest humour of we who are confronted with the devastating reality of dementia in our 'nearest and dearest'.

For my many, many understanding friends and colleagues who have 'been there for me' as they say in all my strange actions and weird moods.

Russ believed that we reap what we sow – I think that I am harvesting more than I ever sowed and that I have been, and still am, a fortunate woman.

Last, but not least, my thanks to my editor Susan Opie and my agent Jonathan Lloyd for not having me sectioned.

PROLOGUE

London, 1938

The head of SIS, the Secret Intelligence Service, had been given a brief by the Foreign Office. This he passed on for action to a major seconded to SIS from the army.

The brief was this: to create a new arm of SIS – a specialist section to look in to how an enemy might be attacked by unusual means from within its own territory.

On the face of it, it was a straightforward enough assignment. Irregular warfare was nothing new. T. E. Lawrence had already used it against the Turks, and the Boers had used unmilitary tactics against the British in South Africa. The major considered the possibilities: sabotage; inciting labour unrest; use of propaganda; misleading intelligence; use of double agents; women employed as spies and couriers; anything at all that could weaken an enemy. With such breadth and complexity of the work ahead, he felt he might just as well have been given a pin and told to move the pyramids.

Who might be most useful and reliable against a fascist enemy – for it would be fascist? Jews would be; Marxists and Communists; leftist unions; socialists generally; and anarchists, as well as the cleverer sons and daughters of the army and navy.

Who had the creative imagination? Writers of popular

fiction; artists; inventors; men who had created business empires from nothing.

Who had the skills to carry out wild schemes? Actors and actresses; people with criminal records for theft or burglary; those with mental agility gained from practising acrostics and logistical puzzles; prostitutes and gigolos; fire raisers and explosives experts; known killers who had escaped the rope with the help of silver-tongued barristers – even the barristers themselves. There were many with skills and knowledge that might be used to subvert the enemy, the Third Reich.

And so The Bureau was formed.

No square-bashing, no big guns; the shiv, the garrotte, hand-guns with silencers would be the preferred weapons of these underground, anonymous recruits.

No Colonel Blimp or Old Bill of the Better Hole.

No notion of rules of engagement.

No notion of fair play.

David Hatton – politically left, experienced film-maker, public-school educated, attractive to (and attracted by) women – had spent his life so far doing what he liked best: travelling the world, recording its coups and conflicts on film. As an unashamed 'Red' he hadn't much in common with others of his background, which was old money, but saved from the fate of many old families, who have only land with which to bless themselves, by an injection of common blood and enterprise in the person of a grandmother with a past – she was a stage performer. What had recommended David Hatton to The Bureau were his numerous contacts all over Europe and in the United States, and the chums who had got their education, as he had, at the most prestigious schools in England.

By the time war was declared, most of the chums were still living within the social stratum into which they had been born. Their occupations and professions were got dynastically, their social circles were very much the same as those of their parents and grandparents. They married their own kind. But landowners, City bankers, chairmen of insurance broking companies, circuit judges and magistrates did not make the best subversives – the kind The Bureau needed.

The Bureau turned with better success to the army and

navy officers known to Hatton. Inevitably, at the start, they called upon their own kind. But there were others – academics whose careers were a sinecure and often were ready to overturn society anyway.

Bracing his shoulders against the icy December wind, David Hatton, newly uniformed RNVR officer, left the comparative shelter of the Inns of Court, crossed the Strand and made his way to Doughty Street.

Doughty Street was in Clerkenwell, which had always been a touch more Bohemian than Kensington or Chelsea. David had sentimental boyhood memories of this street composed of large, well-maintained Georgian houses. Thirty years ago, many of the entrances had been flanked by clipped bay trees in white tubs, and the sills held iron-railed window boxes. Aunt Cassie Pomfret, who had lived halfway along on the right as he now walked, had spoiled her nephews and nieces with parties, magic shows, Christmas treats, and treasure-hunting picnics in the walled rear courtyard.

Aunt Cassie had been David's grandmother's sister and, like her, had been a beauty and an actress. Both had married into stuffy upper-class families, which they proceeded to open up to new kinds of books, fashions and ideas.

As he passed by what had been the Pomfret house, David sprang a moment of nostalgia for the days when the windows were not taped against bomb-blast, and shuttered as they were now, but dressed with muslin curtains that seemed always on the move in the breezes.

His rumbustious twin, Rich, had been the one with some new twist to an ordinary game. Inevitably, there always came a time when shrieking and shouting got out of hand and they behaved like street children. With variations, Aunt Cassie always used the same kind of stratagem to gain control. 'Children, I think Mr Dickens may be at his writing, and we wouldn't like to find ourselves popping up in one of his books as the plaguy Pomdiwiggy family. Shall we go inside and play Pillows and Cushions?' Pillows and Cushions was exactly that, two sides set about one another until they ran out of puff or Uncle Pom called for order on a hunting horn.

Three houses further along, David Hatton looked up at the windows of the famous house in which Charles Dickens had created his Bumbles and Fezziwigs, and smiled, remembering.

The house to which he had been invited today looked like a family home, but within it was a gentlemen's club. The interior, which extended into an adjoining house, was new, but had the appearance and atmosphere that had not seen change in a hundred years: quiet luxury; thick carpeting; pleasant lighting; oiled hinges and wood panelling.

A few days ago, David had received a call from Linder. 'Lunch, ol' man? Club in Doughty Street. Not a gentlemen's club, so your Labour credentials won't be compromised, ha, ha. A dining club. Nice place, you'll like it.' the gentlemen's clubs that Linder's sort liked were not David's own territory; never had been.

The people he mixed with in leftish political circles believed that when the war with Germany was won there would be more than democracy, there would be equality. That was what people wanted, although David had already seen what could happen to that dream in Spain. The Spanish had thought the old rulers had gone for good. But the Republic had been destroyed, as had Rich. The old ones had returned and bombed the dream out of existence.

He had returned home from the awfulness of the Spanish Civil War dejected, convinced that he had seen there a rehearsal for the inevitable war in Europe.

It would be easy to become defeatist, but since he had

been summoned by Linder he had hope for himself. The rumour was that Linder was recruiting for The Bureau. If what David Hatton had heard was right then he wanted to be in at the beginning.

'Your coat, sir?' The elderly attendant helped David remove his well-tailored uniform topcoat. He seldom wore formal clothes, but when he did he stood out, tall, fit and handsome in a well-worn way. David thought Linder would be impressed that he had volunteered.

'If you will follow me, sir, Linder is in the visitors' luncheon room.'

The silence was as velvety and brown as the wood-panelled walls, broken only by an occasional chime of glass, and the rustle of newspapers.

Not a gentlemen's club? Well, it certainly was no Labour club.

Although he had not met Linder for ages, David Hatton knew a great deal about his recent past – if one could believe all the reports in the financial and the social press.

'Hatton! How splendid to see you.' Linder's hand was firm and warm. 'Take a pew.' He laughed genially, for no particular reason that David could tell except, he guessed, it was part of the image Linder had of himself. If others considered him to be ruthless, he considered himself to be resolute, knowing well his faults and advantages. The hardness behind his smile had helped make him a million in the City.

'Sherry?'

'Prefer a Scotch, if you don't mind. It's bloody cold out there.' The whisky appeared on the table almost as soon as it was requested – a really good single malt, warming and persuasive. 'Excellent stuff . . . OK if I still call you Lindy, or is that not on?'

'I'm still Lindy, though not many call me by that name these days. Yes . . . Lindy. They do have good stuff here, which is why I prefer to meet people here rather than that damned draughty office they've given me . . .' And pointing to the menu he added, 'Ever had "Paget's" steak pudding? Try it . . . best thing they do.'

'Sounds all right to me.'

'We'll talk and eat.'

'Fine.'

A steaming basin wrapped in stiff white linen arrived with the ceremony of a communion chalice. The steaming meat and suet crust after the whisky acted like the massage after a Turkish bath, and soon David was amiable and relaxed. For one thing, he could still see a bit of the old naughty-boy-of-the-class Linder, who used to be the bane of some tutors' lives. Too clever by half, that had been his problem – and theirs.

'The Bureau, what means that to yourself, Hatton?'

'Something Winston Churchill dreamed up whilst he was reporting on the Boer War?'

'Good! Right! Infiltration . . . undermining the other side . . . licence to commit any covert act that can wrong-foot opposition.'

'D'you mean the enemy?'

'Right, Hatton, the enemy,' Linder chuckled. 'Still thinking wearing my civilian hat. Yes! Ungentlemanly acts. Creating The Bureau isn't entirely his idea, although, as you know, Winston was never averse to appropriating an idea here and there, if it got him noticed. But he's the fellow who is forcing Whitehall to put their financial shoulder behind it. The Bureau will leave the cloak-and-dagger MI5 and 6 boys to do the thing they do best.'

David sensed that Linder might be wondering how far he might go with a known leftist – lately Linder's 'opposition'. There might be Communists in every university and cathedral in the land, but left thinkers, especially those who frequently travelled abroad, were potential trouble.

'And you are still roaming the world recording for posterity and the *Picture Post*?'

David felt his hackles rise. He had always been serious about his work, which he saw as documenting an alternative history, that of the great mass of humanity. 'Look here, Linder, if you want me in your bloody Bureau don't trivialise what I do. I take exception to that. I'm not a holiday snapshot merchant. I consider that I'm doing a better job than men shut up in their dreaming towers.'

'And *you* look, Hatton – apologies if I offended, but the role of The Bureau is going to be vital to the outcome of the war – in Europe especially. I have a lot of people to find and it's just common sense to go for people one knows and trusts. You wouldn't be here if The Bureau – meaning myself – didn't think your work is important and that you have what we want. And yes, I do want you in.'

David felt a bit foolish for overreacting. 'OK. I'm not some kind of prima donna but I hate it when friends assume that, because I never go anywhere without a camera, I will do their wedding photos.' He straightened up in his chair and dropped the chummy pose. 'MI5 and MI6 exist so why The Bureau?'

'Our secret services have been too gentlemanly for too long.'

'The secret services *gentlemanly*? Come on, Lindy.'

'Compared to what The Bureau will be.'

'There are SIS agents who would turn in their own brother but –'

'Those fellows know only how to sit in hotel rooms in Batavia and pay for snippets of gossip from the locals. You won't find SIS agents sitting on hillsides waiting for ammunitions trains to cross bridges they have dynamited. But you know a bit about that.'

'You're referring to my time in Spain?'

'Of course. Did you know that the Soviets have a virtual university for their secret agents? GPU. GPU agents are professionals, the best bar none. The Bureau will take a leaf from their book so that none of our people will go into the field unfit and untrained. Nor will they be in any doubt as to their role.'

'Which is?'

'To fight dirty with the best specialists we can muster – even if that means getting a forger or safe-breaker out of prison. The Bureau will take on very special operations. There will not be a shortage of money, agents will be well paid, but nothing is recorded. If we take you on, you will cease to exist officially,' he chuckled again, 'so you will never receive a demand for income tax.'

'Neither, I imagine, will I be insured or receive any kind of pension?'

'You're not short of a bob, old boy.'

'*I'm* not, but what about those ex-cons?'

'They'll get plenty of cash – it's up to them if they don't put some under the mattress. Are you in?'

David grinned. 'Bet your life – but you already knew that, Lindy.'

'Been a long time in the financial world, ol' boy. Pays always to have a plan, and to know who fits where. Glad to have you in, Hatton. Go and see Faludi – remember Faludi? Of course, who could forget old Fancy Pants?'

'Faludi's a decent chap.'

'Of course he is, otherwise he wouldn't be my number two.'

'Services Research Bureau' showed on the worn door plaque of offices in Baker Street, London. There had recently been an increase in traffic in and out of the dusty-looking building. It was from here that Colonel Linder was creating Winston Churchill's bastard branch of the secret service.

Lieutenant David Hatton was meeting Captain Faludi. Linder, Faludi and Hatton – similar social class, similar education, very different characters. As fellow boarders, Faludi and David Hatton had been on better terms than either had been with Linder. Linder was a snob, Faludi and Hatton were not. Now the three were officially members of the armed services – Colonel Linder, army; Captain Faludi and Flag Lieutenant Hatton, Royal Navy.

Captain Faludi's naval rating clerk knocked and put his head round the door. 'Will you want a cuppa when your visitor arrives, sir?'

'That would be nice. And try to find some sugar; that substitute stuff is vile.' Like Hatton, Faludi's voice was gentle, and his matinée-idol looks were very well suited to navy uniform.

When Linder had talked with Faludi about compiling an initial list of men he knew well enough to trust – together with a subsidiary list of any likely women, David Hatton had not been in the top dozen, but when Hatton's file came up, Faludi saw that Hatton was 'the goods'. One should not listen to gossip, especially that picked up when weekending in country houses. It was probably true that Hatton was very much a ladies' man, and that he had enjoyed a rather exotic life in the world of films and publications. Faludi had not seen him for some while – except in the way one does see old friends at weddings and funerals – and was pleased to discover that he had turned out better than most of their particular college set. Perhaps the actress grandmother had brought something lively to the old family. He had noticed that same effect upon other families – his own being one. Great-grandmother had valued her independence above everything – except perhaps her looks – and when these began to fade she married an English lord and infused his future lineage with good common Mediterranean blood.

In David Hatton, Bazil Faludi felt certain that he had found a like mind. Linder had seen him and passed him on – the seal of approval.

Faludi heard his naval orderly's cheerful voice. 'Cap'n said you was to go right on in, sir. Bring you a cuppa? Proper sugar.'

'Hatton! Good to see you again. You look well; the togs look good.'

David Hatton took the outstretched hand, then patted the insignia on his shoulder. 'Off the peg. Looks a bit new, but I'll wear it in. Good to see you too, Faludi . . . should call you "sir", of course. Thanks.' He took the chair Faludi indicated. 'Linder says you are dealing with miscreants, reprobates and oddballs like me.'

'Absolutely! Specialists in every field from safe-cracking behind enemy lines, to sleeping with the enemy.'

'Whoa, Faludi, that would be too special for me.'

'You see, Hatton? You have formidable male preconceptions. The Bureau will take transvestites, homosexuals, women and the walking dead.'

David raised his eyebrows.

'Now do you see how different The Bureau will be?' Faludi smiled, a smile that had in the past made famous actors and youths swoon for love of him. Faludi was what he had once described as 'of the Ancient Greek persuasion', which meant he liked girls and boys.

As they talked, from time to time Faludi glanced at some loose pages on his desk. David Hatton guessed that these had probably been gleaned from the file that Intelligence had undoubtedly been keeping upon his left-wing activities.

'Tell me about this woman.' The captain tapped a page. 'Her file is new, pretty sparse.' He took off his glasses and tapped his teeth with the tortoiseshell earpiece.

'You'll have to give her a name, Faludi. You know me and women.'

Faludi put his glasses on again. 'Factory girl, caused "trouble at t'mill". Joined the Party in '38 . . . popped up again in Spain with a new name . . . left in spring '39 with a Russian soldier, a GPU major, no less, and two Spanish nationals – children. There are cross-references with your own file. You know who I mean – Anders, Miss Eve Anders. Tell me what she's like.'

David felt a chill of apprehension run through him that Whitehall should already have gleaned so much about such an apparently obscure young woman. Why had they bothered?

'She has very feminist views – she wouldn't appreciate being in the same list as the walking dead. She's probably the liveliest and bravest woman I've ever known, one of the most loyal, the most dedicated to her cause.'

'Which is?'

'Which is something that will sound trite and idealistic.'

'Nothing wrong with idealism.'

'*Liberté, égalité, fraternité.* My friend is idealistic – a humanist, romantic, self-educated, articulate . . .'

'And very beautiful.'

'"Lovely" is the better adjective. Eve Anders is a lovely young woman.'

'And she ditched you for a Russian soldier.'

'She didn't ditch me. I wasn't even in the same league as the Russian.'

Faludi frowned. 'Sorry, David, I hadn't realised . . . I had assumed it was nothing serious.'

'Neither was it!'

'All right. No need to get stroppy then. You can hardly blame me; you do have a certain reputation.'

David didn't reply.

'You know her well enough to tell me that she and The Bureau might suit one another?'

'Put it this way, Faludi . . . sir, you think that you are fishing with a sprat to catch this big GPU mackerel . . .'

'That is not what I think. I am impressed by what I see on Miss Anders' file. So far we haven't many female operatives, and this young woman appears to be excellent Bureau material. What's funny?'

'If she knew you referred to her as "material", you might find that you'd caught a piranha fish. Yes, yes, I know her well enough to recommend her to The Bureau. And I know that she won't leave the safety of Australia unless the Russian gets protection from us.'

'A GPU-trained officer working for us? Oh, he'll get protection all right.'

'They rescued a couple of orphans. You'd need to persuade them that they will not be returned to Spain.'

'Go and talk to a fellow I know in the Commonwealth Office. Arrange for the children to remain in the care of whoever they are with in Australia. Make sure it's good; we don't want to have our prospects worrying about children.'

'Out of curiosity, Faludi, how did you find them?'

'We never lost them, dear boy.'

'You mean him, the Russian, don't you?'

'Major Dimitri Vladim was GPU. We want him. And, from what we know about the girl – well, we get two for the price of one.'

'She's not a girl, sir. Being young doesn't make her a girl. Eve Anders is a mature woman in experience. Her upbringing and Spain made her that.'

'Excellent. Down to business. Orders are – persuade them and bring 'em over safely. No fuss.'

The next time Lieutenant Hatton reported to Captain Faludi was to confirm that he had been successful. Miss Anders and Major Dimitri Vladim were on a commercial airline flight.

Eve Anders looked out of the aircraft's round window and saw the ground drop away below.

She had mixed feelings about going home. Leaving the children hadn't been easy, but she had to be sensible. She was no mother substitute for them, never would be. Jess Lavender, with her large family, would fill that role.

Here she was again, elated at the thought that she had been persuaded to get back into the struggle for democracy.

There had been times when Eve felt that she'd had democracy up to here.

Democracy and justice existed like things frail and sick, things that couldn't be left to take care of themselves. They prodded you and banged on the floor. Attend to me!

Why listen when nothing changed?

At fourteen she had hammered on her head teacher's door and said, It's not fair what you've done. It hadn't been fair, but nothing had changed.

At seventeen, she had stood in front of a crowd of workers and said, It's not fair the way factory girls are treated. It hadn't been fair, but the girls had been intimidated; they retreated so that, again, nothing had changed.

Then Spain – so much misery, so much blood and death, such a lot of orphans and widows, such great numbers of maimed men – all that, yet still democracy in Spain had died. Dead as mutton.

And now her own country had invited her to jump through the same hoop. Attend to me!

She had been thrilled to bits when David Hatton had made contact with her. A special unit was being formed. It was in need of women. Too hush-hush to talk about on the telephone. He absolutely knew for sure that she would revel in this new work.

'You know that I would never leave here without Dimitri.'

He'd said that he thought that could be arranged.

She knew all this was bait to her curiosity, but she was ready to go home, so she took the bait.

On this evening in early 1940, winter impresses itself deep into the flesh and bones of forlorn, hopeful Britain, at war with well-armed Germany. So it seems hardly fair, does it, that there hasn't been a winter as cold as this since Queen Victoria reigned? But, as it says in the slogan such as propagandists are thinking up daily, 'Britain Can Take It!'

The country has been at war since 3 September last year – a day when skies had been blue, a day golden and warm, and almost silent. Long before Christmas all that had changed. Now, the entire country has become relentlessly cold. Days appear shorter and darker and colder than anyone can remember. The frozen British have no one else around to warm them up with a bit of support. So they whistle in the dark, and warm their spirits with slogans and spit patriotism into their hands as they 'Go To It'.

It is over twenty years since the last war – 'the war to end wars'. Now this new generation is up in arms, the same old enemy, the same old war, going to slog across the same old terrain as their fathers and uncles. Same old bits and pieces will be left for mothers, sisters and aunts to pick up.

In twenty years and ten million deaths, the ghost of that old war travels on this train in the bodies of young airmen, sailors, ATS women, and men and women, who were boys and girls yesterday, now travelling to shore bases, airfields and army camps. Who has learned anything at all? Who would have thought, after four years spent in putting an end to all those young lives, that it would all start up again?

Well, for one, Eve Anders, travelling from London to Portsmouth on a gloomy, slow railway train, thought so. Still only in her early twenties – born just as the last one was ending – she is experienced in war; has seen its most terrible consequences; not a pessimist, but has been where Hitler's Luftwaffe and Mussolini's soldiers were practising the imposition of fascism on a decent fledgeling democracy. She was there last year, at the moment when democracy in Spain was annihilated. She had escaped by the skin of her teeth, sure that worse was to come.

Eve looks out at the cold darkness beyond the window of the London train, yawning. The man whose reflection she sees dimly and whose body warms her skinny back is Dimitri Vladim. He escaped with her and so far they haven't been parted. But who knows, now that they have left their hide-out?

They are on the last leg of their journey from Australia to the naval town of Portsmouth via London. The long journey hasn't been too bad until these last fifty miles. The crowded train slows down yet again. Dimitri rubs a circle in the murky steamed-up window and peers into the impenetrable blackness.

No moon, not a glimmer of light in the blacked-out winter landscape. They travel in the corridor, lucky to find even that space, but still shifting and sifting to make room at every gloomy station.

From here on, until the war is over, this is how train journeys will be: people in their tens of thousands packing and moving – even children. By coach and train schoolchildren remove from the security of their own familiar city streets and schools to go away to live in the country, which many of them will find empty and frightening. Eve Anders, now ten years on from that same experience, could tell you how it feels to be a city child and to see for the first time a wide landscape without sight of people.

Dimitri Vladim sees only his own bearded features close to Eve Anders' profile, and beyond that nothing but the dark.

A shiver runs through him. Eve asks if he is cold. No, he's fine; just listening to the wolves – but he doesn't tell her this. Blackness lighted only by snow. One minute he was growing up surrounded by his large, extended family, the next crammed with siblings and cousins – all of them in the charge of grandparents – fleeing ahead of trouble. Enveloped in fur covers and caps, the elders and youngers of the Vladim family skimmed across white plains. There was howling. Why had the children been told about wolves? He heard them howling in the black Russian night, but understood that he and his family were not fleeing from wolves. They were Ukrainians, but the Jewish/German blood of their ancestors was strong. The Vladims were an educated, opinionated, and well-off family. Dimitri was the first to become a Communist; first to become a soldier; enthusiastic in his belief in the brightness of a Soviet future.

That flight into the snowy darkness is a lifetime away, but the wolves still howl in his subconscious. When he hears them he becomes wary. He heard them last in Spain when he began to doubt his role as a political commissar. He has never told Eve how her body, scrambling and laughing to passionate climaxes with him, had stopped his ears to the warning howls until it was almost too late.

Fellow passengers idly watching him see an unusual man, big and broad, his voice strong. His life as a senior officer in the Red Army shows in his confident manner; his generous nature shows in his mouth, his intelligence in his eyes, and his love of life in the creases around them. Nowhere is evident the pain he has buried for loss of his own country.

Nor the added ache that the woman he assumed was in love with him is not: 'I love you, Dimitri, very much, but I am not *in* love with you.'

The result is the same – she will not agree to marriage. She will probably still sleep with him, make love with him, have fun with him, but she will not marry him, which is what he wants. Now, more than ever.

In coming to England with her, he has taken a leap into the unknown. He knows how valuable he will be to the secret service of this country – the latest pack of wolves to circle – but will they risk letting him 'disappear'? He is GPU, the most professional secret service in the world. That pack too must be out there on the dark plains following the scent of him. He knows GPU thinking only too well.

Their options are that they will finish him off here before he can do too much damage; negotiate for his return and then execute him; 'persuade' him to work as a double agent. His best hope now is that he will prove invaluable to the British secret service, who will see to it that Dimitri Vladim 'disappears'.

He doesn't really know why marriage has become so important. It is not because he wants to tie her to him – with a woman like Eve that would not be possible – nor because he wants to lay exclusive claim to her body; he has never been like that with women. He has believed, ever since he set eyes on him, that the secret service man Hatton did at some time have a relationship with her. And it is he who has arranged for them to come to England.

Dimitri has sometimes teased Eve about the affair. She always responds crossly and sulkily, insisting that it was not an affair, just an impulsive girlish romance, a crush. There is no meaning to this word.

It doesn't matter.

And he must be grateful to Lieutenant Hatton for getting him away from Australia. He felt exposed there, and knew he was easily traced.

A thought, deep in the major's subconscious, struggles to surface. If Eve would marry him, he could become a naturalised British subject, protected by that status. His conscious mind puts the subconscious down before the thought enters his mind.

His conscious says, 'Is like world outside is vanished,' he corrects his grammar, 'has vanished. In Ukraine when I was boy, we played games in the dark, in the spooky cellars of the old house, Grandmother's house. We played ghouls and ghosts. I do not remember any rules, but there was a purpose which was to scream very much.'

Eve smiles. She has always warmed to his voice, which, she suspects, he deepens and thickens because women like its masculinity. She certainly did the first time he spoke to her. Here in the corridor the lighter-toned English hardly speak and when they do it is quietly, head inclined into shoulder. In the recent past, Eve has become cosmopolitan and familiar with the traits of other nationals, but she is English at the core and she knows how curious the eavesdroppers are.

Each time the train stops Dimitri unhooks the leather strap, lets down the window and leans out. Maybe the driver knows where they are, but who else does? Peering into the dark as the train slows, someone asks anxiously, 'Excuse me, can you see if this is Guildford? I have to get off at Guildford.' Or, 'They said at the ticket office that we should get to Liss by six thirty.'

To oblige, as he has control of the window, Dimitri asks, 'Is Guildford big place? OK, this is very small railway station, but signal is red. There are trees and bushes all around, some trucks . . . I think a farm trailer and tractor. Where you think this might be, Eve?'

'It could be Liss.'

He repeated the name.

'Or Liphook.'

'The signal is now green. I get out for you and ask . . . Liss is next stop.'

The man with the strange accent is a sign of things to come, foreigners with disturbing friendliness – but likeable, this unusual man in a new trilby and three-piece suit. He tells somebody that he is Russian. He could be anyone until he opens his mouth.

When three people get out at Liss, Eve finds herself sharing the small space with a sailor who is probably in his mid-twenties. He sticks a cigarette between his lips. 'Like one?'

'Thanks.'

He gives her a quizzical smile. 'They're only Woodies, you know.'

'I like a Woodbine – I was brought up on them.'

Last year she was saving dog-ends and making roll-ups. The days of cigarette brands as class indicators are gone. A packet of five Woodbines have become quite a prize.

'What about your friend?'

'I should ask him.'

'Fag, chum?'

'Thank you, that is very kind. We have none left.'

'Only cheap ones.'

Dimitri laughs. 'We have smoked cheaper ones . . . even we have smoked nothing at all. I like very much English cigarettes.'

'Well, well, you never know, do you? I had you as a cork-tip and cigar couple. It don't do to presume things. Saw you waiting at Waterloo. Noticed you been out of Blighty . . . you know, you've had the old sun on you.'

Eve nods, wary of getting into an exchange of histories;

the suntan laid down in Spain, deepened to bronze during the weeks in Australia.

This is her first day back home and, although English newspapers have published articles about the war in Spain written by her, not much news came the other way, so that she has very little idea of what people thought about the violent takeover of the Spanish Republic by the new dictatorship. Probably didn't think about it at all.

'It won't take long to fade in this weather.'

'Worst winter in living memory, it says in the papers.'

She nods, and they continue an exchange about the great freeze and the shock it was to the South to see what a real fall of snow is all about. She is a southerner and hardly saw snow in all the years she was growing up there.

Dimitri withdraws from Eve and the soldier by leaning on the window handrail, gazing into space and smoking in his idiosyncratic way, two fingers against his lips, hinging them away only to allow the used smoke to escape. From the corner of her eye, Eve watches him – the man who had given up everything to escape into France with her.

Dimitri Vladim, though genial, expansive and uninhibited, is also very good at keeping his own counsel; an easy man with a strong sense of what was right – not moralistic, just a sense of what was right and what was not. In Spain though a political commissar whose function was to interfere when it was in the Russian interests, being also a GPU graduate, he was first and foremost an undercover agent. Eve does not realise what this means: that They will never let him go, but will track him down. He surprised that They have not done so already. There were few places he could have run to on leaving Spain. True, he has a false passport, but They will not find that too much of an obstacle. And even though he is travelling now as Josep Alier, somebody, somewhere could put two and two together and come up with Major Dimitri Vladim.

He is quite fatalistic about this. For now he will see what happens in England. Maybe the British secret service don't know about his GPU role, but he can't count upon that. Once they do know, he will become a bargaining piece. All that he can do now is to wait and see.

During the last year of the war in Spain, mused Eve, they had somehow found one another like creatures in the mating season, but unlike creatures who don't know about tomorrow, they knew that, like anyone in that war, they could at any time become pieces of flesh and bone to feed rats and crows. Those weeks when Eve had been with Dimitri, she had thought that if they were to be blown up, at least there would be traces of lovemaking on the pieces.

War gives people lunatic notions.

But, as she had thought a hundred times in Spain, what more lunatic notion is there than to go to war? When you saw the results, it was madness. Yet here she was back home, back to the same madness.

The sailor's voice dragged her consciousness to the surface again.

'Sorry,' she said, 'I was daydreaming.'

'I was only saying, do you know London at all? You know . . . seeing as you got on there.'

'Hardly at all. The first time I went was for the Coronation. Every building was decorated – Union Jacks everywhere. I thought it must be the most splendid city on earth.'

The sailor said, 'So did I – went with the Sea Scouts; got a look right up the front row in The Mall.'

Eve smiled to herself. He would have been only a slightly smaller version of what he was now – a thin, neat sailor, always shipshape and Bristol fashion about his person; would shave, and oil his hair before he went on duty. 'I went with a flock of starlings,' she chuckled, 'little schoolkids, but I think a flock of starlings would have been easier to control.'

Since then she had seen Paris – three times. And she had lived in Madrid, Barcelona and seen castles in Spain. And churches and colleges razed to the ground. Was it possible that London could end up with its ancient buildings bombed to rubble? Hitler, with his efficient Luftwaffe, would find the capital a fine target.

An airman who was gathering his bags closer to the door said, 'I was up there then too. Real show, it was. My old man never held with royals – suppose I don't really, but we hadn't never seen anything like it.' A short laugh. 'He an't never going to forgive me for enjoying myself.' He paused and gazed out of the window. 'I hope we seen the last of all that. Once this war's over, the royals is going to be finished. Who's going to miss them?'

Nobody would have dreamed of voicing such a controversial view in public a little while ago. Eve had been told that it was like this in the early days of the Spanish Republic: people spoke their minds about previously taboo subjects, being provocative, breaking down the barriers. Now they were back where they'd started. It had all been for nothing.

The train, which had been running on a single track, now rattled over the points where tracks met or diverged. This was the same track that had provided the soundtrack to her childhood, hardly noticeable but comforting. When the goods-yards closed on Christmas and Boxing Days, it was most strange, almost as though the air was empty.

She had spent the first eighteen years of her life within the sound of this railway track. And she had left meaning never to return.

Eve peered out and was thrilled to see a scene that had been such a familiar part of her childhood that she had been unconscious of it: Portsmouth's big railway goods-yard, with long engine run-in sheds with distinctively shaped roofs, white markers, signal lights and a complicated arrangement of snaking silver rails. Hardly a light showed but a yellow haze escaped the openings of the run-in sheds and was caught by the steam and smoke of the working engines. Now she could hear the clatter and chuffing that had always been there in the background of her early years.

In the clear frosty air, everything highlighted by frost and snow, she had a total picture of a bit of her own past. Ray, her big brother, had worked here. She had crossed the footbridge many times to hop on a train and skive a ride into Portsmouth Central, knowing that if ever she were caught riding without a ticket Ray would bail her out. Railwaymen looked after their own.

Although outwardly unruffled, Eve and Dimitri exuded tension. How close to one another they stood, how white her knuckles, how frequently his jaw worked.

Dimitri put an arm about her and gave her a big kiss. 'I like this place, and English people are nice.'

'I hope nobody ever disabuses you.' Eve patted his hand in a gesture old for her years, but then those weeks before the fall of Barcelona had made her that.

'I think in England we should marry.'

He'd asked her in Cape Town and he'd asked her in Sydney, Australia.

She kissed him gently on the cheek. Her tone was light and bantering. '"When the town clock is working well, do not send for the clockmaker." I got that bit of wisdom from a Red Army officer I used to know.'

He squeezed her hand. 'Don't believe everything Russian soldier tells you.'

The engine hit the terminus buffers. Passengers left their seats, unfolding their stiff, cold bodies, reluctant to face the sharp sea air.

Sea-water, oil and things rotten swilled around the station platforms and were picked up by the wind that came knifing across the harbour. Eve, her feet cold, was anxious to be gone. A couple of porters who looked shrammed in spite of home-made scarves collected first-class passengers' luggage and took it to the exit on handcarts.

A stark announcement in a voice not used to making public statements: 'Lissen, please, passengers who wasn't able to get off at Fratton or Central can find buses and trams outside. There isn't many taxis. We're sorry about this, but there's a real shortage of staff.'

Dimitri hefted the baggage of third-class passengers who needed help and shouted to people who were still unsure about leaving the train. 'Is Portsmouth Harbour station where we have come to. Some buses can go back to stations missed. Thank you. *Bon voyage*.'

This was the old Dimitri, the one who had kept their heads above water when the Republic was sinking. He would burst into the little rented room where they sometimes met, holding parcels wrapped in newspaper, announcing, 'Is ham, real vodka and best American johnnies. Don't ask where from, is not good for you to know. Eat, drink and we will use up all US navy rubber.'

He was such a good, jolly man that Eve wished that she was able to love, in the way she first believed she had. Love him enough to marry him. But love doesn't often do what is wanted – otherwise David Hatton might have said he loved her long before he offended her sensibilities and killed her spring-flower love stone-dead.

Hefting their bags Eve and Dimitri went out of the station, hoping for a place on a bus that would take them back to where they were supposed to have been met.

At the ticket barrier a woman wearing a uniform that Eve didn't recognise stepped forward. 'Miss Anders,

Major, I'm your transport.' She took some of Eve's bags. 'Sanderson, Electra Sanderson. My father – we call him The Dad on the basis that he doesn't think that there are any more – The Dad's a classics man. Don't even ask what my brother's name is.'

'Agamemnon?'

Sanderson laughed. 'Close, Miss Anders. Just wait and I'll find my porter if he hasn't run off with my thrup'ny "joey".'

The porter loaded the bags and Electra Sanderson gave him keys and directions where to find her car.

Dimitri dipped a little bow. 'This is amazing, how you find us.'

Eve knew how. Contacts, instinct, past experience, bush telegraph. Only months ago she had been a courier waiting at obscure runways for small aeroplanes carrying VIPs.

'Not so amazing, Major. The station men know me. If there's a diversion or a delay they pass it on. They're good chaps. Look, we could get a cuppa here if you're desperate, or I'll take you straight round to Griffon House – it's up to you.'

Dimitri answered for them. 'I think we should like something that will go to our toes very quick. Is there whisky, maybe? I do not hope for vodka.'

'Right, Major, let's see if we're in luck.'

The buffet was steamy from the tea urn, and blissfully warm. Private Sanderson had obviously done this before because she did not wait at the counter but ducked under and went behind the scenes, bringing a few filled rolls on a tray set with cups and a pot of tea. 'Don't look so worried, Major. Money has changed hands.' A small, thin woman, wearing a tea towel tucked into her belt, came over, plonked a milk jug on the table and said confidentially, 'No good asking for no more, Miss Sanderson. There's two good doubles in there.'

Sharing the whisky between two cups and pouring herself tea, Electra said, 'Cheers. Welcome to Portsmouth, Miss Anders, Major Vladim. Anything you need over the next few days, you can get me at this number. She handed over a piece of paper. 'But I expect Lieutenant Hatton will . . . well, you know . . . brief you . . . sort things for you.'

Dimitri tossed the whisky back and consumed all the rolls after a half-hearted offer to the women. Sanderson produced a packet of Black Cat cork-tipped cigarettes and told them to help themselves. Then Dimitri got up and, leaning over the counter, rumbled words quietly to the waitress, who shook her head sadly at him. Eve watched him out of the corner of her eye. Whatever it was he wanted, he would probably get.

He returned to the table where their driver was pouring tea for Eve. She indicated the pot to him but he shook his head and winked at her. 'I wait for more milk to come.'

'Dimitri, you really are the limit. Not in England two minutes and you're making your "little arrangements" just the way you did in Barcelona.'

Electra Sanderson showed concern. 'Was it bad?'

Eve and Dimitri glanced at one another. Eve said, 'It was bad.'

'I wanted to volunteer, but The Dad wouldn't agree.'

This woman was thirty if she was a day, but Eve said in an even tone, 'Maybe you shouldn't have asked him.'

'I know. I didn't ask him about this job. I just went to a friend and said, Can you do with a good driver, and he said yes he could. When I turned up at home in my uniform, The Dad didn't bat an eyelid.'

'Here's your milk then, sir, but honest, the cow's run dry.' The waitress grinned cheekily at Dimitri. 'Miss Sanderson, you tell him, it's no good him come here doing that charm stuff with me. One and six, sir. War-time prices, I'm afraid. Everything's going up.' When she gave his change, he pushed back a note. 'No, sir, that's too much.'

'Is for you, please.'

'No, sir, I'll take a tanner if you like, but that's a ten-bob note, you understand?' speaking slowly, emphasising as one does to a foreigner. 'Ten bob's a lot of money. Don't you never tip nobody more than a shillin', and that's too much.'

'Amy, you are not nobody, you are saviour of this poor traveller who have such a big body to keep warm. Please, Amy, you take ten bob. Buy some flowers.'

'Oh, all right then, if you insist. Flowers? Not bloody likely! They tells you not to hoard nothink, but everybody is. I'm putting a few hanks of wool to one side. And I know where I can get a couple of pounds of red three-ply. Thanks, sir, thanks very much.'

'Red is my favourite colour, Amy.'

The girl laughed, 'Then I'll knit you a pair of socks.'

He held up one large foot. 'This size?'

Amy smiled. 'Lord, sir, that's some plates o' meat, all right. I reckon I'd have to buy up the whole stock of wool – be like knitting a pair of dinghies.' And tucking the note into her blouse pocket she went smiling back to her steamy tea urn.

Charm, and more charm – Eve hadn't seen much of that from Dimitri for weeks. The decision to leave Lavender Creek had been right. Both of them were coming back to life. It was ages since they had made love with any enthusiasm. But when he'd said "big body to keep warm" she'd had a stunning recollection of its vitality, its solid virility.

Sensing that her mood had changed, he caught her eye and gave her a wink, then turned to the driver.

'Has been very nice meeting Portsmouth. Thank you, Miss Sanderson.'

'Yes, thank you,' said Eve. 'I didn't know what to

expect, coming back to England, and this half-hour has given me time to get my breath.'

They all rose from the table and Sanderson led the way with a bright torch. 'Steps here, mind the sandbags. Sorry about the train journey. We seem to get more funny ones than the regular ones these days. We all grumble, but don't like to in case it's a troop train or something that's been the hold-up. Oh good, the moon's come out again. Makes it easier to get about.'

Moonlight showed that the transport was a large car painted over in messy-looking matt camouflage. Even so, the styling was unmistakable.

'Nice car,' Eve said.

'It was The Dad's. People are asked to give up their cars, so he told me to take it. I look upon it as his seal of approval of me leaving home. He doesn't know it's been camouflaged, but he knows that I'm a depot chaffeuse. It absolutely drinks petrol so I expect it will soon have to be put away for the duration.'

Eve smiled to herself. She wouldn't bet on it. There would always be some VIP who would expect to be driven around in a car the size of his opinion of himself.

'Would you like to sit up front, Major? Plenty of leg room for you.'

Eve knew a well-maintained engine when she heard one. It ticked over like a Swiss watch, then slipped smoothly into gear and they slid away into the unlighted streets. Vehicles approaching from the opposite direction came into view as slits of light and passed by still with hardly any headlight showing. What must it be like when there was no snow and no moon lighting up the roads? Barcelona had had its streets blacked out, but it felt very strange to be back in her own home town in the same state. The last time she had seen it at night the harbour had been a-glitter with ships dressed over, and seafront and pier lighting.

* * *

Griffon House was ten minutes' drive from the station. Even in the cold moonlight Eve saw nothing that she recognised except the seashore. But then this hadn't been her stamping ground. Here there were streets of large three- and four-storey terraced villas. It was only on very special occasions that girls from her old part of town kicked up their heels here. Just one building she thought she recognised – the great lumpen hotel where she had once gone to meet David Hatton. Ages, ages, ages ago. She couldn't stop the *frisson* of thrill as they passed by. What the hell, that was all done with ages ago. What he had done – satisfying his curiosity about her early life – wasn't so bad. It was that he hadn't understood why he should not have done it. Her childhood was her own, and he had assumed that it was all right to delve into it.

The sky had cleared so that the moon was highlighting the curling tops of the waves, their sound like the shushing wind in pine trees. It was a bitterly cold sea, but its sight and sound touched the scar of a day in Spain as near perfect as Eve had known. Later, it had bled tears, and even now was tender when touched.

Sanderson flashed her lights and heavy gates were opened by a soldier wearing a red armband and white flashes, whilst another came close to the car window. 'Evening, miss. Everything OK?' he said, looking briefly at a pass she held up. 'Thanks, miss. Two more for the *Skylark*.' Torch-lighting a list on a clipboard, he peered in at Dimitri and Eve. 'Major Vladim? Right. Miss Anders? Right.'

'Yes, yes, Corporal, get a move on. My passengers' feet are cold as Sno-fruits.'

Genially, and in a low voice he said as he tapped his two stripes, 'Not so much of the "get a move on", *Miss* Sanderson.' Stamping his iron-studded boots on the stone driveway to illustrate that he was the expert on frozen toes, he waved them through. 'Now, you go careful, Miss Lec, or your dad will come to hear about it.'

As she manoeuvred the car along the narrow driveway, Electra Sanderson said, 'I . . . um . . . should explain. That sort of exchange doesn't usually go on, you understand. Griffon House security is really taken very seriously. It's just that he was in the TA – the Territorial Army, volunteers – then he became the local bobby in my village. You could trust your life to Corporal Miles. But I wish that he wouldn't call me Lec. He wouldn't get away with it in the regular service but personnel here aren't your regular people. But of course you would know that. Here we are then.'

The earthy smell of laurel hedge with tom-cat undertones overlaid that of the smell of the sea just a few yards across the road. Eve let the informal Sanderson and Dimitri off-load the bags, placing them in the shelter of a high, wide porch. This was a very grand house indeed: massive double doors with stained-glass window-lights, heavy brass knocker, a bell pull as well as a central brass door boss almost as big as a football, suggested 'Only persons of rank may enter'. Who had lived here? This must be the grandest house on the seafront in the town where Eve had lived until she was a young woman, yet she wasn't aware of its existence. But why would she be? This was not a place for a working-class girl.

These comparisons of class and rank had always been part of her thinking. I must stop it, I *must* stop it, she thought.

Easier said than done for anyone nurtured from birth in the English class structure. As a child Eve had only been able to articulate her sense of inequity as 'It's not fair!' Now she could write pieces for left-wing papers, and argue her corner.

'Thank you for your help, Major,' Electra Sanderson

was saying. 'I'll ring for somebody to let you in, then I'll be off. I expect I shall see you whilst you're here.'

The outline and features of the house were easy to see in the bright moonlight.

'Do you know who lived here?' Eve asked.

'I don't actually. Well, there are rumours that . . . well, no, one shouldn't pass on rumours.'

'Griffon House? Why *Griffon*?'

'I do know that. Come back here.' She took a few steps away from the house until she was brushing against the high, dense laurels. 'There now, look up.'

Dimitri too looked where the woman pointed.

The beast that stared down was as big as a man and ready to swoop down upon them. Snow and frost etched its folded dragon wings and talons, its patterned breast and great, hooked beak.

'Good God! It seems to be looking right at us, doesn't it?'

'Oh, he is, Miss Anders. He is carved like that to a purpose.'

'Is this a wooden thing? Or is it plaster?'

'He is a great hand-carved wooden beast.'

Eve, still looking, said, 'He? You made a point of that.'

Sanderson gave a little giggle and straightened her jacket. 'Very definitely, Miss Anders, but you would need to be in what was called a "salon" to . . . well, get the full picture. Not a thing one would want impressionable young girls to see – if you get my meaning.'

'Is not true griffon, but he *is* Bavarian, that I am nearly sure. He is a house-guard. Is not easy to rob house with such creatures around. There should be others?'

'Well, yes, Major, there are four more.'

'But not so . . . ah – virile. Hey, is right word, Eve?' He looked up at the ugly creature almost admiringly.

Private Sanderson again gave that knowing little giggle.

'You are right. The others are female, or maybe neuter. How did you guess?'

'Is not a guess. I have seen others. Big man monster guarding entrance watching who comes, like the sphinx in Egypt.'

'You're not superstitious, Major?'

'Perhaps. Just a little.'

No one answered the doorbell, but a man shining a torch before him came round the corner of the house crunching frozen snow.

'Keef?' Sanderson asked.

'You have to come to the side door.' He picked up a couple of bags. 'This way. Milord's had all the leaded windows boarded up – in the event of bomb-blast.'

'The front door looks OK.'

'It won't tomorrow.'

Electra said good night, and Eve and Dimitri followed the bobbing light along the path to the door over which an eerie blue lamp shone coldly. A series of curtains that did not slide on rings made a maze of an outer lobby, clinging and hampering, putting up a fight with any attempt at a swift entrance or exit. Then suddenly the visitors were within a warm and welcoming hall whose floor was a startlingly beautiful mosaic.

A tall, slim, splendidly exotic woman, aged over thirty but below forty, bore down upon them. She was dressed in a vivid flamenco skirt and warm jumper in Shetland wool over which floated a long fringed stole that must have belonged with a georgette tea gown. Her hair was bound with a scarf tied in a complicated knot. She was grateful; everything about her floated gracefully.

'Ah, Keef, these must be the guests from Australia. Goodness, look at that wonderful suntan. Hello, my dears.' She held out a hand, wrists jangling charms and jewels. 'Phoebe Moncke. My job is to keep this place running on oiled wheels.' She laughed generously, leading them further into the house. 'Joke. Right, Keef? Keef knows; times when it's a bit of a bear garden.'

Eve shook her firm, dry hand. 'It looks good to me. Must be a bear garden on oiled wheels.'

Again that warm laugh.

As Dimitri took her hand he raised it and brushed his lips. 'Thank you, I am very pleased to be in English house, Miss Moncke . . . is Miss?'

Ignoring the question as to her marital status, she said, 'Major dear, how sweet. Do call me Phoebe; everyone does. If you need anything and I'm not around, you can give the gong a whack and Keef will come – won't you, Keef? – like a genie from his lamp. Your wish is his command.'

Keef might have been deaf for all the response he showed. Phoebe Moncke gave them a friendly smile with her mouth and a shrewd look with her eyes. Her chaotic appearance and chatter didn't chime with the shrewdness.

'Sorry, but I have to write down some stuff about you – like a hotel, really. Come through to the warm room – we always try to keep one room liveable.'

They went on to the next room but Keef did not follow.

The room, with its decorative ceiling and embossed wallpaper, was at odds with the uninteresting utilitarian furniture. There were no curtains, but shutters were fastened across the tall windows. A fire in the marble fireplace saved everything. Large lumps of tree burned brightly.

'Take a pew and get warm. Nice G & T?' After blowing down a speaking tube, she pronounced clearly, 'Whoever is in there – bring some drinks in the warm room if you will.'

As they were warming up, Keef came in with four drinks on a tin tray, offered them, took one himself and sat close to the fire.

Eve hadn't had such a good G & T for a long time.

'Good stuff, Keef. Is this the bottle Baz Faludi brought in?'

'On its last legs.'

'Oh well, much appreciated. Cheers, my dears. Welcome to Griff. Now let's just get shot of the paperwork. The questions are quite straightforward, if you will just check that we have your name right and that sort of thing. And your passports, please. They go into the safe whilst you are with us.' She laughed. 'Safe – you should see it – more like a vault. Makes one speculate on what Milord kept in it.'

Eve opened the battered bag that had been with her since she first began travelling, but Dimitri took the bag from her and refastened it. 'I think we keep these.'

Phoebe smiled. 'Major dear, it's easy to see that you have travelled in countries where papers and passports should never leave your person – but this is *England*.'

'Of course, Miss Moncke. Is wonderful that I am at last here. I know for sure that secret police will not keep my papers from me in UK. Even so, is better if I keep them safe for now.'

A short, silent skirmish ensued in a battle of egos, which Phoebe Moncke lost – or at least made a strategic withdrawal. 'So be it, Major darling. Now, I am sure that you will want to get settled in. Keef, will you show them up? Keef, by the way, is in cahoots with me here. He's good with the paperwork, I'm more practical. You might not think so, but I am. Now, you have connecting rooms, small bathroom at the end of the landing. Be dears and don't take deep baths. We try not to bathe every day. Two overhead showers, quick and clean at the same time as being patriotic. Must save fuel as we are urged. Quite right too.'

One of Eve's dearest friends used to say of his covert homosexuality, 'It takes one to know one.' Eve knew

Phoebe Moncke was as much a put-up job as she herself was. Her approachability, eccentric dress and disarming, dotty way of speaking was acquired, as was Eve's cool poise and cultured accent. If you weren't careful you could easily find yourself falling for it.

'Chatter, chatter, that is my worst trait. Anyone will tell you so. What you need is rest and quiet, so up you go, and we will talk in the morning.'

Suddenly, after days and days of being moved from pillar to post, they were alone, standing in a room, numbered 10 by a postcard pinned to the door. An electric heater with a fan blasted welcome heat into the chill air.

Dimitri laughed aloud and flung out his arms as though to embrace the astonishing cream-and-pewter-coloured room. 'Is wonderful!'

Eve laughed. 'And amazing. I've only ever seen this stuff in magazines.'

'Art Decadent . . . is very good.'

'Art Deco.'

'No, no . . . I know Deco, this is Art Decadent.' He picked up a stylised naked nymph holding a table lamp. 'See.' He patted Eve's bottom and let his hand rest there. 'You do that same thing.'

'What same thing?'

'Toss your head when I do the things you like with my tongue. You like to try now?' He was already pulling loose his neatly knotted necktie and popping out shirt studs.

Although Eve felt the first strong shiver of desire that she had known in weeks of coolness, with it she felt anxiety, not sure that she was ready for a return to the urgent passion that they had known in Spain. Or rather, not sure that she would succeed and so they might yet again collapse into frustration and unspoken reproach. Jess Lavender, who had been their saviour in Australia, had said, 'You expect too much of yourself, sweetheart. You've had a bad time, what with the war and being starved half to death.' She had been right. Eve had had a worse war than Dimitri as far as deprivation went; his body and spirit had hardly changed.

Sitting on the edge of the gorgeous bed, she kicked off her high-heeled shoes. 'Absolute bliss,' she said as she warmed her feet by the heater and allowed her head to sink into the pillows. She felt relaxed and idle. Random thoughts flittered around her mind as she watched Dimitri undo his clothes.

How much pleasure his broad, solid torso had given her, not too hairy, but enough for the sensation she enjoyed. Narrow hips, rugged legs, and arms strong enough, when they made unhurried love, to hold himself above her until they were both ready for him to let his weight settle upon her. She had never been able to support herself on her arms for as long, but then, when she took the initiative, lovemaking was usually swift and energetic.

Barefoot and with his shirt hanging open and his trousers unfastened, he came to sit on the edge of the bed and idly traced patterns on her arms and legs. It was so wonderful to be easy together again. It had been so long.

'That's nice.' She closed her eyes and allowed other thoughts to run around in her mind.

The invitation to return to England had come at the right time.

Now they were here. Eve Anders and Dimitri Vladim, who had found each other in one war, were about to be involved in another. Ready to choose a new direction. A third major crossroads. The first had been about principle when she had confronted the factory owner she'd worked for. The second following quickly on that when she had left behind her first twenty years, become Eve Anders and gone to Spain. That had been about idealism.

Now, the secret service. This was about patriotism.

As well – she admitted to herself – as feeding her ambition. Becoming one of an élite group was a step towards fulfilling the deal she had made with herself: never let life become humdrum or domesticated. Never be defined by a man. Her assets were intelligence, fearlessness and determination; her liabilities, passion and what her brothers called 'going off in all directions at once'. Outwardly cool and composed, in the right circumstances with the right man, she had a combustible nature.

Only four men had ever attracted her in any serious way. Duke, David, Dimitri and Ozz.

David Hatton, although he had seen her passion flare up, had not had sex with her. He had been what her mother would have called 'a perfect gentleman'.

Ozz, sensitive, generous, a homosexual, had been killed in Spain.

Duke was in her life like a dark secret. They had known one another from the time when they were emerging from childhood. He was the one who knew her best, the one who, if he walked back into her life, would assume that they had rights to one another's body. Duke Barney had been her first lover. Where he was, or what he was doing now, she had no idea, except that it would be certain to have to do with horses – and money. A lot of it.

Dimitri had taken her moments of urgent hunger for sex as a bonus to his own. He became lost in passion when she was the one to initiate it. She probably didn't realise how lucky she was to have a man who accepted her as she was. Unfortunately, he had fallen in love with her; wanted them to be married.

Now, he tumbled her onto the cream satin covering a springy bed, and unhitched her silk stockings.

'Hey, that may be the last pair I'll have for ages.'

'OK, do that thing . . . roll them down, slowly like in the hotel.'

They had both loved those few days' break in the journey here. The first time since she left home that her legs had been encased in fine stockings. The first time he had seen her so beautifully clothed in silk underwear, embroidered, film-star glamorous, the stockings attached to white, satin suspenders.

'Is like unwrapping a special gift. I would like you always to wear such things.' He ran his warm hands up and down her legs, teasing her, getting ever closer to her stocking-tops. She let him, knowing that these apparently idle moments of teasing and caressing inevitably led to them reaching a climax together.

'Careful!' She saved the lamp from landing on them, then, laying back, arms flung over her head, she breathed a heavy sigh and accepted a soft kiss from Dimitri's smiling mouth.

'Is long time since I have seen you with so much happiness in your eyes.'

When had that been? Happiness had been just about the rarest commodity in a Spain short of everything except violence.

Putting her arms about his neck, Eve looked into his eyes and suddenly felt good. They smiled at one another, caressing as she disrobed him and he undressed her, and bits of their tanned bodies were revealed. It was as though the turgid flow of their recent relationship had suddenly become smooth-running again.

Eve said, 'I love your eyes. Do you remember that day when I opened the door by mistake and found you holding an inquiry into the death of that nurse? That look! You glared. GPU officer look – hard as nails. I thought, he must be an absolute pig.'

'Even so, you let me come to your room that same

night. I guessed you were not so cold as you looked. I think you were wanting to fuck with hard-as-nails pig?'

'True. I'm glad you don't give it credit for being lovemaking.'

'So true. You had no patience to wait for us to do it. I was big boss Russian Commissar; you said to yourself, I will have him.'

'Oh, so it was only *me* who wanted it.'

'I did not say that. You drive the big limousine car like it was your own. You drive . . . did drive . . . you *drove* like a man. I think you look as haughty as czarina.'

'You've never told me that.'

'I watched you all the time, and your boss-lady watched me. I think Alex was not surprised that we took such a quick fancy of one another.'

Eve laughed and shook her head, 'Oh dear, Dimitri, what shall I do when these people have knocked your English into shape?'

There was a pause, when he didn't respond.

'Have you ever wondered what would have happened if I had not opened my legs for you that night?'

For a second his eyes clouded. 'Why think of it?'

The question that she had almost asked him at other times: 'Would you have come back?'

'Yes. It was love I felt for you then. I do still. So much.'

'Dimitri, I can't take on the responsibility of being loved. You threw everything overboard and came with me and the girls. You had so much, and now you have very little. Now, you don't really have me.'

'I know. I was not forced to buy Josep Alier's papers to escape. I was not forced to disappear from army. You don't want marriage with me . . . OK. You are young for marriage. I understand. I love you. I cannot change love.' He caressed her with the expertise he had learned at the hands of the courtesans Uncle Leon had taken him to in his youth. 'I believe you. Is of no consequence . . . no damn! *Is* of consequence, but we have this thing . . . we are good lovers.'

His fingers had reached the buttons on her cami-knickers.

She tousled him, breathing in the warm wool and cotton of his new clothes.

He kissed her passionately, then grinned down as they moved together. Suddenly he rolled off the bed.

'Dimitri! What are you doing?'

'To see if next room is better. Maybe. Also I get some johnnies which is in my tooth bag.' Opening the connecting door, he let out a whistle. 'You should see. Come.'

Eve shivered as she stood looking at the amazing room. He wrapped her in his arms as they took in its full beauty. Art Nouveau at its most restrained and beautiful. Black and white and silver.

'This is a man's room, probably that of the master of the house. You must have it.'

Dimitri caught her about the waist and pressed himself close, aroused again. Grinning, his good white teeth and red lips framed by his beard, he nuzzled her neck, his hand pushing her skirt up. '*Nyet! You* must have it.'

'Oh, for goodness' sake, you crude Russian backwoodsman.'

'Crude, crude? Is not crude, is sexful, is Russian. We do not have clever wit like you English.'

'Stop talking so much. Russians will talk. Which bed?'

'No bed. Here, on floor of master of house. No, quick, stand up.'

Joy and laughter surging through her, she tickled him under his arms, which made him struggle and laugh until he stopped it with a passionate kiss, grasping her waist and drawing her close. She wanted him so much that, when she felt his erection hard against her, she relaxed and took him in. Then as they were about to move again, she twisted away. 'For God's sake, Dimitri, get those damned Durex.'

She laughed when he tossed the box on the bed. 'You buying in bulk now?'

He opened a packet, fumbling in his haste, and swore in Russian. 'I have plans to use every one.'

Taking the disc from him she expertly made him safe. He hoisted her legs around him, nearly too late, and he murmured something she didn't understand as they reached the extremity of pleasure together.

She kissed him in the uninhibited way of her old self and fell back onto the bed. 'Oh, Dimitri, that was amazing.'

Falling down beside her, he said, 'Look at you, all disarray. You look like bad woman in Kharkov red-light district. Maybe you want that I pay for you? I would like to pay, it would be some fun. How much you would charge?'

'How much am I worth?'

Pushing her damp hair away from her forehead, he looked tenderly into her eyes. 'Everything I have . . . which now is only my life.' Then he grinned, 'And a box of one hundred best Durex.'

When they were both light-hearted, Eve felt that she would go anywhere, do anything to stay with him. Although, what she expected true love to be wasn't there, no one had ever given her such contentment and fun.

Dragging themselves onto the bed, they lay with their arms about each other. 'What were you doing in the red-light district of Kharkov? Politicising comrade prostitutes?'

'Good prostitutes are valuable to the community. Young men need to learn how it is done, for the sake of the women they love. In Kharkov I was very young.'

He drew her to him. 'I love you, Eve. You know that is

true. In all my life I never loved a woman so much. How many times have you said that you will not marry me?'

'About a hundred.'

'Please, not this time. Let us be married.'

Every time he asked her to marry him, she had thought about it seriously. She really didn't know what love was. She loved the *idea* of him – the man who had given up everything for her, the romantic hero of myth – who had swept in at the eleventh hour and seen her and the girls over the border to safety.

She kept her tone light. 'Dimitri Vladim, what am I going to do with you? I'm not the sort of woman who marries. You deserve a kinder woman in your life. I am too restless and hungry for . . . for everything. I have always wanted to know everything, see everything, go everywhere and be involved in life. For ten years I saw my clever mother live and die her awful life; when she wasn't up to her elbows in soapy water, scrubbing and washing, she was peeling potatoes and making something of us children. She didn't want us – want me to live like that.'

'You are not your mother, Eve.'

'That's where you're wrong. My mother knew that she had made a mistake. She was an educated woman, and ambitious, but just as she started her career she met my father and fell in love.'

'So? Is oldest story in the world.'

'And so is the hero going off to the other side of the world and leaving the girl to get on with having the baby.'

'But your father was sailor, was he not?'

'He was. He went everywhere and saw everything that my mother longed to.' Her voice strained at the inner stress she was raising in herself. 'I should have been born a man.'

His response was to laugh aloud as he caressed every curve and hollow from her soft shoulders to her legs.

'Oh yes, I see, God made big mistake. Even so, marry me, Eve.'

'Oh, shut up or I will marry you and then you'll be sorry. Do you think that a wife would put up with this rough beard? Would Mrs Vladim always be ready to take off her knickers?'

'You like the beard.'

'I love it, you know I do, but Mrs Vladim would soon be telling you that it was too bohemian. Bearded men suit mistresses.'

His deep laugh seemed too baroque for the elegant rooms. 'This time not so quick.'

The shiny satin black bed cover embroidered with stylised belladonna lilies of padded cream silk was ostentatious.

'We can't do it on this. It's a work of art . . . and off with those prickly trousers.'

'Name of this is Harris, English gentlemen wear it.'

'Not when making love. An English gentleman would never do it wearing Harris tweed.' She felt light-hearted. Even if it didn't last, it was wonderful.

'Russians are passionate. Sex is good for the health, we Russians are healthy people.'

'And for the soul.'

'Come to bed, God rest your soul.'

She laughed. 'Help me fold this glorious bed cover. Do you know what belladonna lilies symbolise?'

'*Nyet!* But I am sure that you do.'

'The symbol of the virgin.'

With a loud whoop of derision he flicked the silk cover from her hands and tossed it behind a chair and they made love again, gently and affectionately. And again.

They rested easily, talking in low tones in a desultory fashion about the last few days of almost continuous travelling. Now, for the first time in days, they mentioned the children. It had been hard to leave them, as much for Dimitri as for Eve. Genia had grown to adore him. She still called him *el cabrón* – the bastard. To Genia, all men were bastards – she had good reason to believe that. The war had orphaned her, made her a refugee in her own country and now in exile. She had been sexually assaulted even as she fled from the fascists – by a boy she had gone to school with.

'They'll be happy with Ozz's mother, won't they? Jess is so calm and practical.'

Fleetingly Eve pictured frail little Posa, seated between the rows of vines, curiously watching the venomous little snake, and the little jump as Jess Lavender had got it bull's-eye with a rifle. Posa had not cried out; the toddler's entire life had been lived to the sound of guns. It was going to be hard not to worry about the girls.

'Have you got any cigarettes in your bags?'

He found those Electra Sanderson had given him, but it would have been better had they gone straight to sleep. Then Dimitri would not have, yet again, talked about marriage, and Eve would not have suddenly felt trapped by their situation. They would not have become tight-lipped with resentment, and Eve would not have gone back to sleep in the other room.

It was dark and cold enough for breath to show on the air in the Art Deco room. Very early, Eve heard Dimitri switch on a bedside lamp, and then strike a match. He knocked gently and pushed open the connecting door. His big body, bare from the waist up, was back-lit, and the tip of the cigarette glowed.

'I'm not asleep.'

He sat on the edge of the bed, his weight causing her to roll downhill.

'I have come to say that I am very sorry. I am sincerely sorry. If you do not love me, Eve, I have to accept . . . I cannot make you love me. I cannot help it that I love you, but it was so bad to say such things in my sorrow that I must lose you. I should not have said about the lost baby. It was cruel. But I wanted to make you hurt, because I was hurt. No, please, let me say. I cannot stop loving you. Is not possible. I think I have been in . . . is what you call fool's paradise?' He shivered.

Eve held open the covers, not as an invitation to intimacy, but so that she wouldn't have to see him sit there in the icy room.

'We had an affair, Dimitri, an affair that worked. OK, it was lop-sided . . . uneven. You love me and I care for you. Caring for somebody is probably longer-lasting than romantic love. Caring for someone can be as deep as love. You want everything to be good for a person you care for. I don't *love* Genia and Posa, they are not my children, but I care for them deeply. That's how I was able to leave them – do what was best for them. I doubt if I could have been so objective about children of my own.'

Dimitri put his arm round her and drew her to him. 'Please don't cry.' His voice was so gentle. She hadn't realised that she was weeping until she felt Dimitri dabbing her face with the sheet.

'Please don't be angry with me. I couldn't bear it if we lost one another because we quarrelled. I am lucky that such a lovely man loves me.' She felt his erection grow and harden against her hip. 'I don't want to lose you. Perhaps they will let us work together. We would make a good team; we understand one another.' She smiled, wiped her eyes and switched on the Art Decadent lamp. 'And if they don't, there's always the good sex, but only if you accept that I am not ready to marry – you or anyone. My life suddenly became mixed up with yours. Things happened *to* me. I feel that I've lost control of my own self.'

'What . . . ?'

'Just let me finish. I want you to understand without

us rowing. Your decision to abandon your career and get away was your own. You must have thought about it. You got your Josep Alier papers, the clothes, food for us – you see what I'm saying? You planned it, did what *you* wanted. I had no option but to pick up the children and run; you had the option to stay or leave.' She reached for his cigarette and took a pull on it. 'I shall be grateful to you till the end of my days that you decided to run, and I know how hard it must have been – and how hard it's going to be.' Handing back the cigarette, she breathed a sigh. 'Right, now I've had my say.'

'What it is that I must do?'

'I guess that you will be a lot more valuable to The Bureau than I. Why don't we wait and see what their plans are? I have no idea how it works, but I imagine we shall get leave the same as people in the forces. We will spend as much time as possible together.'

He brushed her temple with soft lips and she slid down the bed to give him her own.

She must have fallen into a heavy sleep, for when she awoke, Dimitri's place in the bed was empty and Eve could hear coming from the bathroom snatches of his baritone as he hummed something alien to English ears yet which had become familiar to her.

This was the first time since Cape Town last autumn that they had had any real privacy. As she listened, an intense desire grew to have his hands and fingers create scented lather on her breasts and behind, which had become firm once more, and in the hollows of her armpits and folds of her groins. Even as she thought about bringing him creatively from arousal to their mutual climax she scrambled out of bed and across the corridor.

A hand-written notice in thick black crayon – 'No more than 3 minutes *PLEASE* – and the fact that he was as ready as herself, only served to rush the last two stages of the slow seduction she had planned. The water suddenly lost its heat and they both jumped and laughed.

There was a knock on the door and a female voice said, 'You goin' tae be long doin' that? It's awfu' coold oot heer.'

Dimitri opened the door as he and Eve were donning towelling robes taken from a whole range of sizes hanging on hooks. 'Come in. We are making quick as possible, so having two showers together.'

The woman with the Glaswegian accent and light brown skin let them share her look that said 'a likely story', but she seemed to be a pushover for an oversized Russian with glowing pink skin, giving him a smile as she went into the cubicle, whisked the canvas curtain and turned the water on. 'Good think'n. Three together would save – Bloody hell! Water's coold again.'

Breakfast was a very basic affair taken in what must once have been the main reception room. There were a lot of unfaded places on the walls where pictures had been taken down. Cornices and a central boss were elaborate, as was the stencil work above and below a dado rail and around the double doors, also elaborately decorated. Even without carpets and furniture the room was impressive.

A line of people had formed. They were moving quite quickly to be served from a makeshift counter on which were gas hotplates and a steaming urn by two women dressed in wraparound floral aprons and white headscarves. 'Kedgeree or porridge, and there's toast up there with the tea.'

Dimitri flirted large helpings of both choices from the woman with the doling-out ladle. Eve settled down with him at a table with six plain wood chairs. To her great pleasure, the oats had been cooked perfectly; had simmered gently all night in water with just a pinch of salt, the standard of porridge she had been introduced to by her aunt.

A moment of such painful guilt. She had her own way of dealing with guilt – a kind of box trap in her subconscious which she could snap open and imprison anything disturbing. It worked very well – to a point, but over recent days she had forced so many bits of guilt in there and it was becoming pretty crowded now that Genia and Posa had been consigned to it too.

She looked up and, meeting Dimitri's gaze, realised that she had been staring at a spoonful of porridge halfway to her mouth.

He reached across the table, squeezed her hand and said in a quiet voice, 'I miss them too. Is better they are with Jess.'

Nodding and blinking fast against tears, she shoved the porridge into her mouth.

'You folks mind if I join you?' The woman from the shower-room, now softly speaking with a Canadian accent, put her tray of food on the table.

Dimitri at once leaped up and held out a chair. 'We are friends in shower, also at table.'

She offered a delicate, well-manicured hand, nails painted the same pink as her palms. 'McKenzie – Dr Janet McKenzie.'

In his best charming manner, he bent slightly from the waist as they shook hands. 'Dimitri Vladim.'

Eve shook hands. 'Eve Anders. I'm sorry we emptied the hot water tank.'

'Not your fault. The boiler wasn't meant to cope with a sudden early-morning rush. Anyway, maybe I should do in England what the English do . . . aren't they in favour of cold showers?'

'Only to cool our lust.'

'Hell, Miss Anders, why cool one of life's great gifts?'

'Didn't you have a Glaswegian accent just now?'

'You're sure it wasn't Edinburghian?'

'I thought Glaswegian, but I'm hardly the one to ask.'

'It's a kinda hobby, trying out voices and accents. I have a set of recordings made for actors.'

Eve had worked at rejecting her Portsmouth vowels in favour of her present neutrality and correctness. She understood what Dr McKenzie was saying.

Dimitri, still hungry and unsatisfied by the plain food, asked, 'How you get these nice eggs?'

'Ah-ha, that'd be telling, but I'll share.' She loaded half onto toast and passed it to him, and he did not protest as an Englishman might have. 'I know a nice woman who keeps hens and I have made friends with the cook. Always a good move to have a contact in the kitchen. These are very good eggs. How about you, Miss Anders?'

Eve declined.

Dimitri, eating fast and demonstrating his enjoyment with a waving fork, said, 'You think I too could become contact?'

'You might, but you would need to drop that dreadful accent. I guess you speak really decent English.'

Eve's spontaneous peal of laughter turned heads at other tables. 'He thinks it is charming.'

Dr McKenzie passed him more scrambled egg on toast. 'And do you agree?'

For a moment Eve thought about it, then nodded. 'I suppose I must.'

'If you have finished your breakfasts, I'll do my bit of business with you here.' She passed each of them a card. 'That's me, the letters mean that my discipline is philosophy, psychology and psychiatry – I am not a Freudian. I happen to think that sex and mothers are in general A Good Thing. Also I no longer practise psychiatry – preferring psychology. The times of your appointments with me are on the back. Miss Anders, as you're after Major Vladim I should be grateful if you would disappear this morning, and you, Major, must not compare notes with Miss Anders.' She smiled. 'If it bothers you not to be entirely open with one another, be easy. I am, as you say, Top Brass, here; not discussing our interviews is in the nature of an order. OK? Nice to have met you. Now I must fly. See you this afternoon, Miss Anders. I recommend Handleys, as a store and for their morning coffee, Miss Anders.' In a stage whisper: 'They have a supply of leather boots with sheepskin linings. A good investment by the look of the sky.'

She gathered her papers and files as Eve and Dimitri sat on over their near-empty cups. 'How about if we start straightaway, Major?'

Top Brass with beauty and such white teeth in a broad smile, and the soft Canadian accent – Dimitri was on his feet in a second.

'Do you drive, Miss Anders?'

'Anything and everything.'

'OK, then you needn't hang about for transport. The Griffon drivers are always busy and I don't like to ask them to take me on shopping trips, though they are ours to call upon. However,' she dropped a ring of keys into Eve's hand, 'take my little run-about. It hasn't been out of the garage for days and needs a warm-up. OK?'

'Absolutely! I love cars. What make is it?'

'A quirky little MG with a canvas top; cold as all hell, so wrap up. You'll find my hat on the seat; if it needs a crank ask Baldock – you'll find him in the stables.'

Eve beamed at the woman's generous offer. 'Oh, thank you, Doctor. You're very kind.'

The McKenzie hat was like none she had ever seen, but perfect for a car with so many places for cold air to be drawn in: a pointed sheepskin cap with earflaps that tied under the chin and a peak that could be pulled down well over the brows. This she donned over the beret she was wearing. There was also a long hand-knitted scarf which went round her neck three times and left plenty to tuck into her coat. The only unwarmed part were her legs and feet. She intended to go for the boots. Normal shopping. In a department store. She felt joyful. Yes, that was the word, joyful.

Driving in the ice-ruts was very like negotiating the hard-baked mud on some of Spain's minor roads, but there Eve had had the weight of a big truck to crush ridges; the neat little MG two-seater was as light as a moth in comparison. But being behind any wheel and revving a well-maintained engine gave her great satisfaction. The rear and side mica windows crackled like a bag of potato crisps.

She parked outside the main door of the store, and as she approached, it was swung open for her by an elderly doorman. A cloud of warm air was sucked out to envelop her in scents and perfumes, metal polish, linen fabric, warm dust and dampness from snow walked into the carpet. After all she had seen and been through, the scent of civilisation in a department store was as if St Peter had opened the gates to Heaven.

The doorman pushed against the door to keep out the offensive day. 'May I help, madam?'

The years dropped away, and it was only yesterday that she and Katey had dolled themselves up and gone 'down Town'. The Co-op had been their regular style and price range, but Handleys was beyond their territory, just an occasional Saturday afternoon treat. It was here that they stole fashion and style to take away in their minds and make up in fabric by the yard. The Co-op was good for dress fabric; you could choose it in Handleys and buy it at the CWS or Bon Marche for a quarter the price and make it up at home. She smiled to herself, thinking: Kate and I were never greeted by the doorman. I must have become posh. A woman who shops in Handleys and goes up to the tearooms. She felt happy.

'Are you open for coffee yet?'

'Yes, madam. First floor. Thank you, madam.'

Only one or two of the little coffee tables were taken, but the rest were laid ready for the ladies of Southsea to take coffee. Eleven o'clock was the time. This place had been the Mecca of what passed for Southsea society, and although Eve and her friend had been daring girls, they had never ventured into Handleys restaurant. They had scorned it . . . too toffee-nosed, too stuffy. Women did not go to Handleys unless wearing hats and gloves. Eve had a hat – the beret she had brought with her she wore close over her springy, corn-coloured curls – and she was wearing gloves, the very nice ones, hand-stitched, unlined calf that she had picked up with her coat on the journey back to England. Like the coat she wore – long, expensive cashmere styled on the lines of a military greatcoat, warm as toast, cheap as dirt – everything she had bought had been handmade and tailored. Very quick, lady. Very cheap, very good, lady. Luxury knickers and petticoats embroidered there in the doorways of open-fronted shops by little girls. She had been reminded then of her own days as a machinist. But she had been to school for nine years and been allowed to become an adolescent before she was doing similar work, and by machine.

The uniformed waitress waited patiently, pencil poised over her order-pad on a string, as Eve started to tweak off her gloves, then stopped as she remembered her hands were still in bad shape from working the Lavender Creek vineyards. 'A pot of coffee for one and some biscuits.'

'Fancy, chocolate or plain – or a selection?'

'Digestive would be nice.'

Hours to idle away until her afternoon appointment with Dr McKenzie. The receptionist in the hairdressing department said that if madam would just take a seat, she would enquire whether there was a possibility of her being seen without an appointment. Yes there was. And a manicure? Yes, that would also be possible.

By the time Eve returned to the main store, the stylist had turned the curls into a long bob that dropped over one eye. The beautician had masked and cleansed her face until it glowed beneath the arsenal of cosmetics she recommended Eve would be wise to purchase – 'This is probably the last of the luxury goods. Everybody is going over to war work.' Eve went along with it and purchased everything suitable. It was all a wonderful experience. Her worn hands and nails had been soaked and massaged and grouted into ladylike softness, a French manicure giving neat, short nails with whitened undersides.

All the while she was within the curtained cubicle being pampered, Eve was entertained by conversations on either side of her. 'Stocking up for the Duration' was the topic of the day – probably of the week too. Clients for perms, washes-and-sets, and Marcel waves – and their hairdressers – exchanged bits of information in hushed voices. There would soon be a shortage of Marmite and tinned milk, black lead and hard soap for daily women; but daily women were disappearing to do men's work. The prospect of black-leading one's own kitchen range was frightening, added to which, the domestics would soon be on the blackmail because of the higher wages they could get in the little engineering firms and welding shops that were opening up everywhere.

With Eve's experience of factory owners in this town, she couldn't envisage such a turnaround in the fortunes of Portsmouth women needing work. There were, as there had always been, 'beached women', whose husbands and or the common-law fathers of their children went to sea for long periods of time, then would come ashore, blow their pay, and leave having given the women another mouth to suckle, clothe and feed. It could still terrify her to think how close to that life she had been.

David Hatton, on behalf of The Bureau, had provided Eve and Dimitri with a decent wad of money, some of which she now spent without guilt on a fur jacket. The assistant, wearing black with white Peter Pan collar and pearl earrings, fanned out the coat showing off the long silver, silky fur. 'Car-length opossum, madam, a beautiful coat. Glamorous, madam. Only a woman with your colouring and figure can really *wear* a coat like this. It was forty guineas, but what with the problems of cold storage, it is now thirty guineas. You won't regret it, madam.'

Eve didn't need persuading. When she drew out a fifty-pound note in payment, the fur assistant needed to defer to the manager. Eve was enjoying herself. A coat like this would normally be paid by account. Perhaps they thought she had robbed a bank. But the long silvery fur of opossum was probably not the easiest to sell – a bit on the exotic side for her home town. More suited to London. She loved it. She had seen a film studio photograph of Betty Grable wearing such a coat and apparently nothing else.

Dimitri would love that.

The thought of surprising him aroused her. She had done as Dr McKenzie had asked and stayed away from Griffon House whilst she was interviewing Dimitri, but now she wanted to be back there.

This sudden wish to see him surprised her. Was it more than the anticipation of watching his reaction to surprising him in the seductive coat? Was this how people felt when they were in love?

Driving back to Griffon House she went back to playing Betty Grable for Dimitri.

Dr Janet McKenzie
PLEASE KNOCK AND WAIT

Eve did so until the door was opened by a large, youthful, balding man; horn-rimmed glasses and a nice broad smile. 'Miss Anders? Please come. Dr McKenzie will be two minutes.'

'It's OK, Eric. If you'd like to come in, Miss Anders . . . Just type up these notes, Eric, and you can take off.'

Dr McKenzie closed the heavy, panelled door behind her and indicated a low glass-topped table and two carver chairs, obviously part of the set of a dozen or so arranged around a long table covered with dust sheets. 'Please take a seat.'

The room was warm from a fire of logwood crackling and flaring close by. Eric knocked and brought in a tray with the paraphernalia for tea. 'Would you?' Janet McKenzie indicated that Eve should pour tea. 'I must get a footstool. I spent the morning with my legs dangling. Five foot three – the world is not made for us – and I need to make notes.' She settled herself. 'I love the smell of burning logs, don't you?'

Eve nodded towards the flames. 'Especially applewood.'

'That's applewood?'

'Yes. Apple and cedar are the most aromatic – not that many people burn cedar in this country.'

'But you know about it?'

'My brother used to bring home chippings from work – not often, but it was lovely.'

'Your only brother?'

'No, I have two, both older: Ray, who was more of a father to me than my own father – he was at sea – and Ken, who was fond of the girls and was good fun, except that he wouldn't do his share in the house. He could afford to have fun, Ray took on everything.'

Daylight disappeared as another heavy snowstorm piled large flakes on earlier falls. The only light in the room was from a red-shaded reading lamp and the flaming wood. The earlier wind had dropped, so that the snow fluttered down and the sound of any vehicles became hushed.

A wonderful sense of tranquillity – Eve felt it physically as it seeped into her tense nerves and muscles. As she breathed in the scent of the burning wood, she felt her shoulders slump and her stomach muscles relax.

'Sisters?'

'No.'

The short silence was filled with Dr McKenzie stirring a minute tablet into her tea.

Unaccountably, Eve wanted to tell her about Bar.

'There is a friend – since we were twelve . . . we have always said that we were sisters.'

The image came like a clear snapshot: water swirling around herself and Bar, clinging tightly to one another as they leaped into a woodland pool. 'She created a ritual to unite us – you know how girls do – she said, "We're two halves of the same whole, Lu." And I believed then that we may have been.'

'Lu?'

Eve looked up sharply.

Janet McKenzie said, 'You said she called you "Lu".'

Eve went silent. She must tell this woman, this Bureau psychologist.

'Is Lu a pet name you have outgrown?'

'No. I used to be Lu – Louisa Vera.'

McKenzie nodded encouragingly, professionally, allowing her client time to consider how to talk about something that was vital and large in her life.

'All this you see here, this Eve Anders, is a person handmade by me – a bespoke woman.' She gave a wry smile. 'Lu was born into the lowest stratum of society. She hated it – the poverty, the ignorance, the *acceptance* of it by my . . . by *her* own kind. When she was still a girl, she decided that she would get away . . . somehow.

'Eventually she escaped because she was lucky, she was clever and she had a mentor – a school head who encouraged her to aim high, to be ambitious. Before that, though, there was that whole summer of Lu with Bar – living away from the squalor that her/my mother and brothers tried really hard to keep out of the house.'

'I'd like to know a bit about Bar.'

Eve spoke quietly, staring into the flames, unaware of the conflicting messages – a soft smile and a sad look in her eyes. 'We were born six months apart, each of us on the turn of the year. She is dark, born at the winter solstice. As a girl I was even fairer than I am now. I was born midsummer. We said that we were two halves of the same person. She was very fey . . . pagan. She was everything that I was not, but I'm sure that I would have easily changed places with her, or gone to live with her. She could cast spells . . . tried to teach me all the magic of the woodlands. There was one occasion when I believe that I did almost get there.' The flames flickered wildly in her vision, though she was unaware that tears were coursing down her cheeks. 'Girls of twelve have such wonderful and simple ideas of how easy it all is.'

'But it's not, is it?'

Eve shook her head and accepted the tissues Dr McKenzie offered. Reluctantly she withdrew from the flickering sun through birch trees reflecting on the surface of a green pond.

'I'm sorry. I am not normally a crying sort of person.' She regained some composure by refilling their cups.

'Are you sure?'

'Of course I'm sure.'

'I don't mean, are you forever blubbing and snivelling.'

'I know.' There was something not right about expressing feelings to a complete stranger, yet that is what Eve wanted to do. It felt to her as though here was this doctor – an empty vessel into which she could pour the sludge of bad memories that had turned sour and frightening in the pit of her stomach – and this doctor was glad to have her do so. It was a ridiculous thought. 'Sometimes I do feel like crying, but it is not what the Wilmotts do.'

'The Wilmotts?'

The name was out. Drawing her gaze away from the fire, Eve met Dr McKenzie's quizzical look.

'Until I was nineteen, I was Lu Wilmott.' She gave the other woman a look that might have been construed as defiant – or proud. 'And then I made myself Eve Anders. That's really all there is to it.'

'Miss Anders, you realise that to me you are a complete stranger. All I have been given is the facts of your life in this slim file. I have discovered that you and Major Vladim have a relationship – and that is all. The fact of that relationship is perhaps for another time. Before that, I should like to get to understand a little about you,' she smiled warmly, 'what makes you tick, so to speak.'

Eve felt a sudden apprehension. 'I just told you.'

'You commented that crying is not what the Wilmotts do, then immediately became defensive. Is it the crying, or is it the Wilmotts?'

Again that same desire to tell. 'It is because I *am* defensive – I have a lot to defend.'

'To lock away?'

'Yes.'

'What is it about crying?'

She thought for a few seconds. 'It is crying that . . .' The words wouldn't come.

McKenzie waited patiently, but Eve appeared to have dried up.

'You are finding this difficult to say?'

'Of course I am. I am not the sort of person who . . .'

'Who?'

'Who can talk about . . . I like to be private. I don't want people to get the idea that they know me.'

Eve didn't notice the slight look of satisfaction that appeared in McKenzie's eyes.

'But you have had close relationships?'

'You mean love affairs, sexual relationships?'

'If you like.'

'Yes. I'm quite good at that.' She smiled wryly. The other woman must suppose that she spent half her life on her back. Well good. She could think what she liked.

'You can let yourself go with something as powerful as an orgasm, but crying terrifies you?'

Eve found herself blushing at her interrogator's bluntness. 'It doesn't . . .' She had never uttered the word 'orgasm'; she felt that it would come out 'organism' and she would feel foolish. 'Sex is never going to go on for long. Even when it's good, you know that it's going to stop, it is always under control. Well, I mean that it is something that has a boundary, a limit to it.'

'But not responding to a need to cry?'

'That's right.'

'Losing control?'

Eve nodded.

'How about anger?'

'The same. I don't know why you need to ask. It is obvious.'

'It is not obvious to me. Expressing anger is a healthy emotion.'

Eve didn't comment.

'I can see that you are angry.'

'Oh, really?'

'I don't mean the kind of fractiousness that you are feeling now – some authoritarian figure asking you questions that you really don't want to answer – that's not anger. Why *are* you answering me?'

Eve retained her poise and looked directly at her

tormentor. 'To be perfectly frank, only because I want to be part of this set-up. The officer who recruited me said that The Bureau was made for me and I for it. And he's right. So I'll answer any damned question you like just so long as you tell them that I am normal enough to be one of them.'

'You think The Bureau needs *normal* people? *Really?* What normal person would want to become a secret operative? The Bureau needs an appearance of normality, of course, but their best people will be extraordinary abnormal people, people with vision and a crazy kind of dedication. Normal people don't always see far beyond the ends of their noses – would you agree?'

Eve shrugged her shoulders.

'You, Miss Anders, are, I believe, far above a normal person. I still know very little about you, but the mere fact of your relationship with an officer of the Russian Army who has jumped ship, so to speak, and become a man who must be seen as a traitor in his own country, is –'

'A traitor?'

'No?'

'He is a good and loving man who gave up everything to rescue two orphans and get them away from the war.' She had said more than she intended. Maybe Dimitri had not mentioned that.

The other woman got up to balance a new log on the others, the dry, curling bark of which flared at once, giving the dark skin of her noble nose a kind of luminescence. Eve wondered about that. She had known a man in Spain with that same proud profile. He had been a doctor too, working in a bombed-out hospital; even in the midst of that mayhem he had appeared cool and capable. It was all in his narrow skull, with the skin so tightly stretched that every contour was visible. Dr McKenzie had that same quality, the haughty length of her nose exaggerated by the severely bunched hair at her neck.

Turning her head away from the fire, she said, 'You are an ambitious woman?'

'Yes, I would say so . . . very ambitious.'

'Do you think that you could forego marriage and children to satisfy that ambition?'

'Yes.' Eve was ready to blurt out the fact of her miscarriage when the log toppled into the hearth.

'You seem very positive.'

'I am.' I see where this is leading, Eve thought. They were playing cat and mouse with Eve's control over wayward emotions.

'When was the *first* time you felt real anger – I mean something so powerful that it left you feeling afraid of it?'

Another image, from an angle that looked down into their mother's grave as Ray and Ken and the bearers stood, toes to the fake grass. Ray and Ken in dark suits and ties, and white shirts with stiff detachable collars, their shoes polished to the hilt; Lu in a borrowed tam-o'-shanter and a coat with the hem altered. All the Wilmotts – except her father who was, as ever, on the other side of the world – in their 'deep black', showing grim respect that they did not feel. They had never liked Vera Wilmott because she was an outsider.

'At Vera Wilmott's graveside when Lu realised that she was never going to finish her education and that Vera didn't really die from the tumour, she died because she was so poor and Lu couldn't go to grammar school for the same reason. To get medical treatment or an education you have to make sure that you don't live in that kind of poverty.

'Vera Wilmott, my mother, was young . . . and had once been elegant and pretty . . . a student teacher swept off her feet by one of the handsome Wilmotts. She shouldn't have been dead; if they hadn't been so poor she wouldn't have been, but she had had to sit at home stitching ribbon trimmings on garments. The money hardly paid for the gas to light the room in winter. Her womb got diseased.

'You said that anger is healthy. What good does it do? Lu didn't know what to do with it. If that's right, then why did she run away, making a show of herself in front of the Wilmotts? Actually, she *wanted* to make a show of herself – throw herself upon her mother's coffin and sob her heart out.' Eve fell silent, covering her terrible anxiety by drinking tea.

'Miss Anders,' Dr McKenzie's tone was firmer now. 'I'm sure you know how this works – I cannot recommend you to The Bureau knowing that you are vulnerable. You are a really very special person, you know. If you have only half the talents that are here in your file, The Bureau will not want to lose you to the ATS or the WRNS. Your vulnerability is your past. We have to talk about it. You have to say things out loud. It won't be so terrible.'

'If we can talk about Lu . . . She was angry. She was furious. Lu wouldn't thank me for crying so long after the event. But I feel her heartache as much now as she did then. And her guilt. Vera dying let Lu down; Lu felt guilty that she was angry with Vera. Vera's womb had produced a daughter with huge ambitions and a talent for learning, the same womb that developed cancer and deprived Lu of her mother's gentleness and of the one thing they both had wanted – for Lu to get an education and get out of the poverty they lived in.'

Again Dr McKenzie leaned forward so that her noble nose was close. 'Lu probably had a mother as good as they come, and she did not deserve the treatment handed out to her. It wasn't Vera's fault that she let Lu down. Am I right?'

'Of course you're right! But she was bursting with anger, and it was centred upon the body in the coffin. She didn't know what to do about such overwhelming anger. So she ran away. She made a show of herself in front of the Wilmotts, she hurt Ray and Ken, and left them to the disdain of the Wilmotts.'

'Where did she run to?'

'Not far, but to a part of the beach that's dangerous when the tide's coming in.'

'And . . . ?'

'Lu wasn't stupid enough to do anything too serious. She tore down some warning notices – broke them up and hurled them into the waves.' Eve gave a faint, wry smile. 'Sheets of plywood don't break easily. Then they come flying back with every gust of wind. She hurled big stones at them, but the stones bounced off. Poor kid, her tantrum was so pathetic.'

'Why do you think she didn't throw herself on her mother's coffin and sob her heart out? For God's sake, this was her mother who had been dealt a loser's hand. Don't you think that the girl was entitled to rail against what brought her mother to this? Why didn't she show her anger? She was entitled to, wasn't she?'

'You don't understand people like us. This is my home town, you know. Did you know that?'

Dr McKenzie made a note.

'Eve Anders has come home to Lu Wilmott. I could take you to where generations of Wilmotts have put up with being cheap labour. But Lu got out. She knew there was something better.'

'You said "people like us" – who are they?'

'My people.'

'You mean Lu's people?'

'No. Yes.'

'Shall we talk for a minute about this?'

'About what?'

'Eve Anders' involvement with Lu Wilmott – Louisa.'

'No. She's Lu.'

'Well then, Eve Anders' involvement with Lu.'

'Must I spell it out?'

'It would be easier for me.'

'Three years ago, Lu Wilmott got on a train here in Portsmouth, and when she got off at the other end, she was Eve Anders. She/I took nothing of my old life except a couple of mementoes.'

'And it worked?'

'Yes.'

'I would really like to know what Lu's reaction was when you rejected her in favour of Eve Anders.'

'Rejected? I haven't rejected her.'

'Very well – secreted her. Go on, please, tell me something about her.'

Eve leaned back, drew a deep breath and let it out slowly. She latched her fingers and circled her thumbs one round the other. A smile lighted her face. 'People said that she was a fire-cracker, always going off in all directions.'

'And was she?'

'Oh yes. At any one time she could be the Maid of Orléans, Queen Boudicca, Ellen Wilkinson, Helen Keller or Catherine the Great. One of her last performances was in front of a meeting of factory workers. She organised them into a union . . . got a medal for it.' She breathed out deeply again and stretched her fingers, then laughed. She didn't know why, except that in the first time for months, Lu was very close. Comforting. 'And had she known you, I'm pretty sure that she would have been you as well.'

The doctor laid one finger on Eve's arm. 'She did better than that, she became Eve Anders. I can't believe that she's not proud of you.'

'You think so?'

'An idealist fire-cracker concealed in intelligence and beauty? I know so.'

'She wasn't ashamed of educating herself and using her intelligence to get away.'

'Which is what she did.'

'At a price, of course. When Lu Wilmott became Eve Anders, it had to be –' she made a sharp chopping motion – 'at a single stroke and ignore the pain.'

'And it must have been very painful.'

'Yes. But it was the only way, a clean cut.'

'How did you deal with the pain?'

'I took myself off to Spain where for a year or so I did crazy things like driving trucks up to the front line, picking up pieces of Spaniards blown apart by other Spaniards until there was nothing to do except run for it.' She saw her skinny, bedraggled self, armed with a carving knife and carrying a piece of bread and – what was it, some meat? – she could no longer remember the detail – and joining the trail of refugees as it went through Barcelona, taking a half-alive baby and a disturbed adolescent with her.

'And?'

'She ended up here, spilling her guts to a head doctor.'

'I like the idea of the fire-cracker girl. Exciting idea. You are proud of her, aren't you?'

'Yes, I am.'

Dr McKenzie gave her a warm, generous smile. 'As she must be of you, Miss Anders.'

'She keeps me on the straight and narrow.'

'You make a good pair, and I would like to get to know you better. We shall be seeing something of each other, I've no doubt.' She rose to stand a fireguard in the hearth. 'Look, I'm afraid our time is up. Would you like to straighten up and powder your nose? That door leads to a cloakroom. By the way, did you find Handleys?'

'I did, and the car was wonderful . . . thank you. I saw the store in an entirely different light from when Lu and her friend Kate used to go on an occasional spree. Hobnobbing with the nobs, showing off, getting above herself, making out that she's better than her own sort.'

'And was she?'

Positive and firm: 'Yes.' Then quieter and gentler, 'Yes, she was.'

'Why?'

'Because her mother told her that she was.'

'Did you get some leather boots?'

'Oh yes.' She smiled. 'And a spontaneous coat – a three-quarter fur jacket.' She grinned like a girl. 'I can't believe I did that. The assistant said that it was exactly what this weather called for.'

Dr McKenzie nodded at the dark swirling outside the window. 'No mistake about that.'

'But, for God's sake, that coat had nothing to do with the weather. I was already wearing a warm coat. I wanted it because it was so gorgeous. You see, she's still there, going off like a fire-cracker.'

Dr McKenzie shook hands firmly and smiled. 'Going off like a fire-cracker, or an ability to appraise the situation and make a quick decision? Now, I must fly . . . I'll leave you to take your own time. Go when you feel ready, no one will disturb you. By the way, Miss Moncke would like you to call into her office when you finish here. Best of luck with your new career.'

New career!

Implying that she was suitable for The Bureau?

The face that stared back at her from the bathroom cabinet mirror as she blotted cold water from her eyes was the face that she had not seen in months. Confident, untroubled and lively.

The spirit of Lu was strong. Eve looked her in the eye and smiled. *Stick with me, kid, and I'll show you a good time.*

'Dimitri, come and see.' There was no reply, so she opened their connecting door. The room was immaculately tidy, not even his soldiery row of brushes and comb; it felt uninhabited. A *frisson* of worry clenched her stomach as she opened the wardrobe door and found it empty.

Sitting on the bed that had last been used for patching up their quarrel, she knew that he was gone. Phoebe Moncke wanted to see her and this was why. She would put on fresh make-up, have a cigarette and go downstairs. The snow whirling past the window was relaxing; she felt very fatigued and her eyes were sore. She fell asleep but could still see the snow.

The silent, feathery flakes soon slanted into a blizzard into which Dimitri was disappearing. He wore the clothes in which he had escaped Spain; he was Josep Alier again. The guards at the border crossing looked at his papers, then pushed him around; Josep Alier was a peasant. The guards became aggressive and the girls clung to Eve, terrified at the fierce argument that was soundless. She told them to hush and be good. Suddenly the Josep Alier coat was torn from him and he was transformed back into the Russian officer Major Vladim, as she had first seen him. There was a quick rat-tat-tat and bloody holes appeared in his uniformed back. He did not move, but stood there as though the bullets had not touched him, even as his blood ran down. Rat-tat-tat again. As he began to topple she shouted, but strange, unidentifiable noises drew her attention away from Dimitri dissolving into the blizzard.

Rat-a-tat again. 'Miss Anders? Miss Anders?' It was a young woman in uniform. 'Sorry to bother you, but Miss Phoebe would like a word.'

The snow had resumed to its earlier gentle fall. The cigarette she had lit had burned out in the ashtray. She found it difficult to drag herself back into awareness.

'OK, I'll be right down.'

Phoebe Moncke, businesslike and serious, handed Eve

a single sheet of paper folded but not in an envelope. 'The major asked me to give this to you.'

'Has he left already? Where –'

'Nobody tells me anything, darling.'

'And if you did know, you wouldn't say.'

'*Couldn't* say, darling, couldn't. No, not at all.'

'Of course. Thanks for this.' She slipped the folded sheet of paper into her jacket pocket with no hope that she would learn much about where he had gone.

Back in her room, she sat in the armchair and listened to a woman humming contentedly as she moved around opening and closing drawers, taking over Dimitri's room.

Eve,

What I can think as I make you this note is only that maybe you have not seen my handwriting. How strange, but I can not think of any occasion what we have written anything. I think that you must write in large, hasty clear letters. I should be most interested in how you think of this handwriting. I expect that you must write your English words with strong strokes of *the* pen (you see I do know good grammar) for you are the very strongest woman I have known – and that also includes my dear babushka who was not afraid of howling of wolves. Also you are a good woman. I will ask to send money to Jess for Genia and Posa. *Salud* dearest of all *compadres.*

Your most loving and faithful man,

Dimitri Vladim.

Their lives had become fused, fasciated like saplings that are pressed together, growing a single trunk until there is room and then they divide.

All that about handwriting was not his message; the message was in the word *compadre* – 'friend'. Was he admitting that their affair was over?

It was very chilly in the room, and could have been warmed up a bit had she been willing to draw the thick-lined curtains, but she was loath to shut out the gently falling snow and the sea lapping against ice that had formed when the last tide had receded.

The sea had frozen.

She would bet that kids from her old school had been down there, daring one another to do something, anything, to get a bit of fun out of the novelty of frozen sea. Nothing like these weeks of Arctic weather had happened in her memory and probably in memories going back generations. Snow and ice like this never came to a coastline sheltered by the Isle of Wight and warmed by the waters of the Solent.

She hoped that she would not have to stay long here. Whilst she stayed here in the salubrious Southsea area of the town, she was unlikely to come across any of her old friends. She had moved on and could not go back . . . would not.

She would do anything rather than that.

With the departure of Dimitri, she had, so to speak, cleared her emotional decks; she was responsible for no one but herself. Whatever happened from here on, she had nothing to lose.

On day two Eve was called for interview with Captain Faludi.

They were in one of the many rooms at Griffon, transformed from costly bad taste into basic offices furnished by the Ministry of Information. He greeted her with the same kind of handshake, firm, dry and warm, as Janet McKenzie's had been, then invited her to sit opposite and proceeded with an interview that took the form of an informal conversation during which he took notes.

After about fifteen minutes he asked, 'Lieutenant

Hatton says that you appeared keen to join The Bureau. What do you know of it, then?'

'Nothing at all. But I know Lieutenant Hatton and I guessed that he would not suggest me if he didn't believe that I could do the work, or that I would not enjoy it.'

'Do you often make such snap decisions?'

Hm. That was a tricky one.

'Quick decisions, yes. A snap decision is probably not thought through.' She smiled at him. 'I'm quite good at thinking on my feet . . . quickly. Also I was ready to come home and it seemed an opportunity I should take.'

'Not because you particularly wanted to?'

'No, yes – I mean I *did* want to. I was just saying that he didn't need to persuade me.'

'You insisted that Major Vladim should accompany you?'

'I didn't actually insist, but I did think that we should stick together.'

'It does appear to be a little insistent if you –'

She felt he was needling her, and she wouldn't have any of it. 'As I said, sir, I thought that we should stick together. He had helped me escape from Spain; I could hardly come home and leave him there. He was . . . is, a refugee.'

'And absconded from his regiment.'

'He did. And his country. He gave up everything when he helped me to get out with the children – I expect you have all that on our files, sir.'

Faludi nodded. 'Probably not all. Are you romantically involved?'

She gave him a direct unblinking look. 'Is that relevant?'

'I think so.'

'Do you mind telling me why?'

He looked back at her, rather surprised to discover that Hatton was probably right. The dossier that he had provided gave a picture of a working-class girl, idealistic, clever – Hatton suggested great intelligence, well, time would tell – and loyal. Hatton, or someone, had dug very deeply into the past of this beautiful, but rather snooty young woman.

'You realise that before I even asked you to attend this interview my people had done their research?'

'Yes, I had realised that.' A small smile, mostly in her eyes. 'Not much good wasting time on unknown candidates.'

'So, how committed are you to this . . . ah, liaison with Major Vladim?'

'There has never been any commitment on either side. But I do feel loyalty, and I believe that he does too. But I can only speak for myself.'

He frowned a little at this. 'Do you mind that your life is in a folder somewhere?'

'Yes, I mind very much but . . .' She shrugged.

'But what?'

'It is necessary. If you were to accept me, I'd want to be confident that there had been a thorough check on my colleagues.'

He looked at her thoughtfully. She was so straight-laced and correct. He could not imagine her driving a supplies lorry to the battle front, or living openly and unmarried to a Russian officer. He could, however, imagine her having some sort of a fling with Hatton. Hatton's women had always been elegant and lovely.

'Can I be sure of that, sir?'

'I'm sorry? Sure of what?'

'That you don't recruit people less loyal and dependable than I am. I am, you know. Loyal and dependable.'

'I believe that you are. As, I believe, are the other candidates who have been selected.'

He turned a page. 'Tell me about walking out on your employer.'

Eve felt her neck become flushed, but luckily it remained hidden by a georgette scarf. 'What do you want to know about it?'

He shrugged and made a slight gesture with an open hand. 'You mentioned loyalty and dependability.'

'My loyalty was to the women I worked with. My employer treated his workers unfairly – he played on their vulnerability knowing they were in no position to complain. I was in a strong position. I am not badly educated, I am articulate and, as I have said, I am loyal and dependable. My co-workers depended upon me. I told him that he was a bad employer – and then I left. Also, and this is something Lieutenant Hatton couldn't have reported to you, my employer thought that he was entitled to sexual favours. Factory girls are as entitled to respect as any others.'

That's you put in your place, Faludi, he thought. She's turning this interview on its head.

Yet he didn't mind. She fulfilled his own requirements for the new kind of agent The Bureau would need. The Bureau had sent Hatton fishing for the Russian, but it appeared that they had caught something almost as rare.

'Thank you, Miss Anders. I can tell you now that you are acceptable to The Bureau, and Colonel Linder will confirm your appointment at once.'

'Thank you, sir. I am very pleased to hear it.'

On her file he noted 'NKA'. Nothing Known Against.

Eve had come up to London on the early-morning train. Yesterday, after Faludi, she had been passed on to David Hatton, a strange experience with the formality, and a clerk taking notes. His instructions to her had been that she go to London where outside the Science Museum there would be an unmarked bus. When all the new recruits were on board they would be driven to some recently acquired premises which would be used for induction training.

'I am to work in an office then, sir?'

David Hatton had looked at her over the rims of his tortoiseshell glasses and smiled. 'Did you expect you'd get your invisible ink and a morse-code ditter straightaway, Miss Anders?'

'You're making fun of me . . . sir, but I did expect that I would be sent for training or something.'

'We are all at the training stage.'

From which she suspected that The Bureau might not yet have an up-and-running training plan.

'The small group of people you will be working with, Miss Anders, are as new to The Bureau as yourself. Each one of you will have a differing task. Your own is to judge which, if any, of them would provide a risk to security.'

'Yes, sir.'

'Any suggestions as to what you will look for?'

She'd been shocked at the idea of spying on her colleagues, but she'd answered, 'Egotists, *and* egoists, gossips, blabbermouths, anybody whose drinking goes beyond sociability.' She'd paused then, not looking at him because she was pondering; said, 'I would keep my eyes and ears open for anything that didn't quite add up, accents that don't fit the picture.'

'Yes, good, Miss Anders. Perhaps you could expand on that a little.'

'Well, sir, supposing one of the group isn't quite what they appear. They make little mistakes, nothing much, a hint that they might not be everything they present to the world . . . their past is questionable.' She had not raised her eyes, but drawn her brows and held a finger to her lips as though she was still considering his question, waiting for his response. He'd remained silent. After long moments she'd slid her glance in his direction, but his eyes had not met hers as he concentrated on doodling what she'd at first taken to be hieroglyphs but then realised were notes. She had taught herself a little of the 'Gregg' version of shorthand, which was sinuous and flowing. His configurations were angular and minuscule.

'I didn't know you wrote Pitman, sir.'

He'd looked up and given her his old, devastating smile. 'I do, Miss Anders. I have always been grateful that I was persuaded to take a few evening classes.'

'I'm sorry, sir, I interrupted.'

'No, I think we have finished here. Any questions?'

'Ah, yes, sir. May I ask whether we are all compiling reports on one another?'

'I can't tell you. Suffice it to say that each of you will have differing tasks. Interview over.' He had pressed a button on his desktop and nodded to the clerk, who left the room.

Eve started to rise from her chair. 'May I go now, sir?'

'I'd like it if you stayed for a glass of something.' Once the clerk had retreated, her immediate senior officer had become David again. 'Though God knows what, Eve. Sherry? I'm sorry, but this office doesn't run to much else. Gin, but no Indian. Camp coffee, tea without milk – and that's about it.'

She'd hovered between wanting to stay but knowing she should go if she was to maintain the proper distance between them now that she would be working under him. But it was for him to be making that kind of rule, wasn't it?

'Is my response going to be written up in your Pitman notes?'

He'd got up, come over to her side of the desk and sat on its edge, his body keeping a formal distance, but the look in his eyes invading. 'I said that the interview was over.'

His behaviour had been unforgivable in Spain. Their relationship went back a long way, with highs and lows, twists and turns. He had dug into her past at the time when they had first met and she had been like Cinderella at the ball, dancing till midnight and then disappearing. When they'd met again and she had become Eve Anders, he couldn't leave it and had gone on to uncover Lu Wilmott.

Now suddenly it had seemed childish to keep refreshing her pique every time she was with him. She'd returned his smile. 'Thanks, David, I've had worse drinks than gin without.'

'Good.' He'd held up the bottle. 'Beefeater?'

'Looks good to me.'

The tots he'd poured had been sensible – generous but less than doubles. He'd touched glasses with her. 'Here's to a sparkling new career for you.'

'Thank you . . . David. Am I to take it that I'm in your sector?'

'Are you still Republican?'

'Are you?'

He'd grinned. 'I managed to swear an Oath of Allegiance.'

'Then so could I.'

'Now?'

'Why not?'

Raising his glass he'd said, 'Here's to George. May he be the last of the line. How will that do?'

Grinning, she'd said, 'I'll drink to that. Until that day, I promise I will do everything in my power to see that no fascist usurps him.'

'Nicely said, Eve. You'll make a bloody good and devious member of The Bureau.'

There had been a short silence, not awkward, as they'd accustomed themselves to the renewal of their relationship. Eve had idly followed the wire that led from the button on his desk to a black box showing a small red light. When she'd returned her attention to him, he'd been watching her. The interview had been recorded. She'd raised her eyebrows a fraction of an inch. It didn't matter. What did she expect if she wanted to belong to this maverick branch of the Ministry of Information?

Rewarming their relationship had left them only the new Spain to talk about with any ease. He'd asked about the children, and what they looked like now they were recovering. She'd told him about the generosity of the Lavender family. The naked gin hadn't gone to her head as she had expected, but she'd refused a second. He'd walked her to the door.

'David? I do know the meanings of "different" and "differing".'

He'd turned off the recording machine. His smile had become a grin as he'd put his arm briefly about her shoulders and squeezed – gently, friendly. 'That's my girl.'

She'd stiffened at his familiarity.

'Sorry.'

'That's one thing I'm not. I'm your junior officer. Different assignments mean just that, but differ-ing . . . ? This group I'm assigned to – same task but *differing* because we will all have our own version of one another. Right?'

He'd given her an unsure smile.

'Don't *ever* try to do me a favour, David.'

The bus felt damp and smelled musty, the crisscrosses of blast paper over the windows made the interior dim. There were already a number of people waiting but nobody spoke more than a polite mumble. With the last recruit on board, the driver got in, the engine rumbled and they drew away. Destination unknown.

'Hey, how are you?' Eve took the firm hand directed at her. 'Wilhelmina de Beers for the record, DB to my friends.'

'I'm OK, thanks, DB. Eve Anders. You're South African?'

'Born and bred. You recognise the accent – how come?'

'I've spent a couple of years in – working with people from the four corners of the earth.'

'Go on, see if you can say which part. Cape? Jo-burg? Durban?'

Eve laughed, trying the young woman's accent. 'Hey, min, I'm not thet goowd. Oi say maybe Ifrikawna?'

DB laughed with delight. 'Man, you're good. Right, I'm a Boer but never a bore.'

'I can imagine.'

'Yeah, well . . . I've been called worse, but only behind my back or they'd get a fist in the teeth.' She laughed again, showing almost all her whiter-than-white teeth. 'Not seriously . . . not in the teeth, hurts your knuckles. Maybe a fist in the gut. I'm quite proud of having Voortrekker blood. But, who'd ever know, it's so mixed up with my trekker ancestors – the old trekkers got on pretty good with Zulus and Bushmen – Bushladies I should say – I guess that's where I get this hair.' She didn't mention her skin colour, which was a beautiful, blooming *café au lait.*

DB removed the ski-cap from which sprang a mass of corkscrew curls shiny, black and memorable.

'Have you a clue where we're going?' Eve asked.

'Naw, I tried sweet-talking the driver, but he's been issued with a lip-zip.'

'I guess we will be too. Is Wilhelmina de Beers your real name?'

'Hey, is Eve Anders yours?'

'Touché. I just meant . . . you know . . . with de Beers being the diamond family . . .'

A young man's face appeared round the side of the high-backed seat. 'Hello there. Paul Smyth-with-a-Y, pronounced Smith – my family practises reverse snobbery.' He had a wide, open grin. Standing in the aisle he shook hands briefly, then squatted to be at their level. 'All in the same boat here. Sooner we get to know one another, the sooner we shall get to know one another . . . if you get my drift.'

He was of middle height, with a broad, kindly, open face, crisp brown hair, nice eyes with smile lines at the corners, straight mouth with a full lower lip. Not exactly nondescript, but the type that wouldn't catch much attention in a crowd. Unlike attention-catching Wilhelmina with her jet-black corkscrew hair, and dark eyes set in a striking high-cheek-boned face.

Paul Smyth pointed a finger jokingly at Wilhelmina. 'This lady is Miss de Beers all right. I'll vouch for that. I've seen you perform, Miss de Beers. It was memorable.'

'Really? Nice of you to say so. I never thought of any performance of mine as memorable.'

'Come on, don't be modest. You weren't sitting where

I was sitting. Honestly, Miss Anders, this lady's got a voice like nobody you ever heard. Well, that's not quite true. If you ever heard Billie Holiday, she's a second Billie Holiday.'

'Aw, if only that was true. She is so amazing. Have you heard her for real, Paul Smyth-with-a-Y?'

'Oh, have I! I was there in Greenwich Village the night she first sang "Strange Fruit".'

DB's eyebrows rose. 'Really! At the Café Society?'

'My God, yes,' Paul said. 'Even thinking about it, the hairs on my neck rise. Wow! That song knocked us all sideways, didn't it? I thought nobody was going to applaud, so I did . . .'

'That was you? Man, you certainly whipped up a storm. It was *super.* I tell you, Eve, you had to be there to know what it was like.'

'I wish I had been. I'm a real fan of hers, and Ella Fitzgerald's.'

Paul made a gesture that said everything. 'If you're a fan of Ella and Billie, then you will be of DB. You followed Ella the night I first heard you sing.'

'Oh yeahhhh.' She faced out both palms and wiggled her fingers. 'I sure was an acceptable nigra that night.'

These three appeared to be the only ones to have tried to get acquainted as the coach lurched through the disturbed streets of London. Along the entire route of the journey were gangs of men filling bags with sand and building them into buttresses against bomb-blast; digging out earth in open spaces to build underground bomb shelters; slow convoys of low-bed army lorries bringing anti-aircraft guns to the centre of London.

Eventually the coach came to a halt, and all heads were turned to the windows. A voice from the front of the bus said, 'I say, what d'you think. They've brought us to the Scrubs.'

There was an apprehensive silence, then everyone scrambled to a window.

'Good God!'

'I say, driver, are you sure this is where you are supposed to be taking us?'

Not even bothering to turn round, the driver just nodded.

Wilhelmina de Beers kneeled in her seat and looked out. 'What's the Scrubs? Looks like poky to me.'

Paul Smyth answered, 'You're right, it *is* – has a reputation for being hard.'

The bus door opened, and a tough-looking man in army uniform came aboard and asked for names. 'All present and correct, driver. You can go on through. Return to your seats, ladies and gentlemen. And before anybody asks, yes, this is Wormwood Scrubs Prison, and yes, this will be where you'll be working for the next number of weeks. Make the best of it, 'cause let's hope this is the last time you'll find yourselves in jug. Leave your bags and cases on your seats, they will be delivered to your accommodation. Anybody not got tied-on labels? Good, good, you followed instructions . . . let's keep it that way.'

Inside the dour building, where electric light was on but poor, the entire complement of ten were gathered and kept waiting for five or more minutes in a reception area where at one time, presumably, new inmates had checked in. DB, Paul and Eve stuck together.

'Hey,' DB said, 'what a lark if they fit us out in uniforms with arrows!'

Eve, infected by her new-found colleague's unwillingness to be sober, added, 'And give us bags marked "Swag" to keep our possessions in.'

'And hob-nailed boots,' Paul added.

From somewhere behind them a woman's voice said low, but clearly meant to be heard, 'I don't know about you, but I would say that merriment is inappropriate in the circumstances.'

Nobody appeared keen to agree.

DB said, 'Somebody's got a donder up her backside.'

Paul and Eve giggled with restraint, but it showed in their faces and drew them further into cahoots with DB.

'What the hell's a donder?' Paul asked.

'A Zulu staff of office – big stick with a ball on the end. You can donder your enemies with it.' She demonstrated with a rolled-up newspaper, biffing Paul on the head.

'Thank you kindly, miss. I'll store that gem away for the day when I need a six-letter answer to my clue – "A Red nod for a twack."'

Eve and DB looked at him sideways questioningly.

A young woman standing close by said, 'That's good . . . *really*. I've never met an anagrammatist as fast as you. Frances Haddon, known as Fran – glad to meet another addict.' Her voice was a lot like Eve's, low and gentle, her speech clear, good elocution. She touched hands briefly with the other three, who at once made room for her in their small circle.

DB asked, 'Just what are we all on about here?'

Paul said, 'Crossword puzzles, anagrams. Not a very good one.'

Frances Haddon remarked, 'Off the top of your head like that? I'd say it was very good.'

Soon they were taken into the part of the Scrubs where they were to start the induction process. They were to work round the clock. Two shifts of three people and one of four. The groups were self-selecting, Eve, DB, Paul and Fran being one.

Overseeing the Scrubs 'operation' was a most attractive woman called Vee Dexter. A story did the rounds that she was waiting for confirmation of her appointment as personal assistant to Colonel Linder with whom it somehow became known she was having a love affair,

Linder's wife and children being safely tucked away in Suffolk.

Where such gossip started was impossible to decide. The problem was, true or not, gossip was valuable: it was from such sources that truth emerged, a picture built up. But ought such chit-chat in their midst be reported? The on-going problem was how much was planted. Eve decided to take note and leave decisions to the end of the induction.

Mary-Rose Toffler was another whom Eve found hard to place. She was an older woman in a shift group comprising an older man, Mel, and Stan, most likely Greek. On Saturday mornings when they all received lectures and talks, Mary-Rose always appeared to continue taking notes afterwards, and to intrude upon any little gathering. Maybe she was just socially inept, or overeager. Or maybe, like Eve, she wasn't sure she was getting it – getting what was going on here. Eve wondered whether any of them did. What was important and what was dross?

Working in a building with permanently blacked-out windows, they found that the actual time of day was apparent only when they came off shift. They sorted paper, entered lists, filled requisition forms and were asked to redesign them for clarity.

Paul and Fran loved this work. Their mind sets were suited to dissecting a problem, looking at it and making something of it. Neither of them could understand others who didn't think in that way. Paul defined it as being 'those who could, and the rest', meaning those who couldn't do the *Telegraph* crossword puzzle before breakfast. Eve and DB were quite contented to work under such giant minds.

Vee came and went between the Scrubs and The Bureau offices in Baker Street, one of which was that of the chief, Linder, who would occasionally come into the Scrubs to look around, missing nothing.

The old prison was believed to be temporary accommodation for the recruits, but soon it appeared that The Bureau was settling in very well. All the bits of carpet in the world wouldn't give any kind of comfort to their working place, but they were a cheerful bunch, enthusiastic at their acceptance into the War Office. Even the most curious of friends and families would be impressed to hear that they must not ask questions because it was 'the War Office'. Hush-hush.

Knowing this gave the whole group a sense of their worth. Not that they could see much of it in the work that many of them found tedious. Where are the cloaks and daggers? they would jokingly ask over their beer glasses at weekends when they were free. Where is the invisible ink?

Often, on Sundays, all ten of them would just roam around. Nothing better than walking, they agreed, to get to know London. Then they tried the trams and trolley buses, and then the underground, and within a short time had learned the best and quickest routes, as well as the most interesting and picturesque destinations.

First-aid posts were being created in alleyways and church porches. Everywhere Londoners seemed to be practising: lowering 'injured' volunteers down ladders. On end walls yellow-painted letters 'SWS' indicated where water could be had if the mains were blown up. Along the platforms of some of the main underground stations, wooden bunk-bed frames were being erected. Fire engines without warning bells tried out narrow side streets for use in emergencies.

Some Sundays the Bureau recruits caught a sombre mood as they saw Londoners battening down the hatches in preparation for the inevitable. The weeks since Eve came back to England had been dubbed 'the phoney war' because of all the restrictions and preparations that seemed so much fruitless labour when both day and night the skies were quiet.

People grumbled, but nobody gave up.

The Bureau trainees gained more information from their evenings in the pubs than from reading newspapers, none of which said anything about London children returning home from the safety of the country.

'My gel Alice went and got her kids back. They was more scared of all the bloody cows and horses than the chance of a bomb.'

'Our young Nobby said it put the frit up him. "It's all empty, Grandpa," he said. "Ain't nothing there except empty fields." He's right. What do you reckon they do with theirselves . . . all that empty space with nobody there?'

'Only time we ever saw the country was hop-pickin'. You wouldn't get me living there. Same with me, their nan went down Sussex way to see the little'ns. They wanted to come home with her. She told them, people pays good money to have holidays, go camping and that in the fields. My son says they should come back.'

'Schools is all closed.'

'If enough comes home, they'll have to open up again.'

Considering none of them had met before they arrived at the Scrubs the recruits got on well – friendly, easy to talk to and eagerly listened to; ordinary, likeable people of whom Eve guessed she must be the youngest. All were as earnest as herself to make good, to be accepted to go on to the next stage of training. She paid attention and watched the ways other than in words they expressed themselves. It was rather like her journalist experience all over again. For a while, whilst she was in Spain, she had written some columns for some of the more liberal journals about ordinary lives, trying to give readers more than a report; people in their variety and with all their quirkiness was what she tried to give.

Sometimes Eve and DB went around together, roaming the London stores which Paul and Frances Haddon found boring, leaving those two talking maths too advanced for Eve and DB to comprehend. Other times they went out as a foursome.

Occasionally they were allowed a day off in the week and decided to have breakfast at the Lyons Corner House at Marble Arch, which still served decent food, and this simple fun together affirmed their friendship.

DB was always entertaining – 'good sport', she called it. 'I'll tell you what would be good sport. Let's all go to Joe Lyons at Marble Arch, go in disguise, and see how long it takes to find one another.'

Eve went for simplicity. She got Vee to find her an old mac and hat, and wore her own shoes muddied up a bit, then queued for a cup of tea and a bun in the basement brasserie. By midday, the appointed time, she had detected none of the others. Then she saw how people were looking up, but, as the English do, trying not to watch as Paul, with a greasepaint Groucho Marx moustache, and copying the famous bent-kneed walk, carried a cup and plate to her corner and sat at her table.

A waitress put some coins by his plate. 'You forgot your change, sir.'

'Thanks, Fran.'

'Oh, damn you, Paul, I went to such lengths to get them to let me do this.'

'How about me?'

'Oh, you were good, Eve. If I hadn't bribed Vee to tell me about the old mac and hat, I think I'd have taken ages to get you.'

Fran went off to the manageress's office to return her borrowed uniform.

'DB's the winner. Let's join forces and find her.'

But although they went to every floor of the Lyons Corner House they couldn't.

'Come on then,' Fran said, 'let's go buy her a trophy. I saw a lipstick chap on my way here.'

Even this early in the war, everyday things were becoming unavailable in shops. Small-time street-traders appeared from nowhere with little cases containing unobtainable objects of desire, selling at speed until crowds gathered and policemen approached, when the traders would vanish.

'Vi'lets, dearie, lovely sweet vi'lets.' Although she was disguised by only a shapeless hat and shoulder blanket tied across her bosom, a truly unrecognisable DB thrust posies at them. 'This is my friend, Kath, who has let me stand with her all morning. You're a sweetie, Kath.'

'Don't you want your flowers, dear?'

'Naw, you just sell 'm again.'

With Paul still wearing his Groucho moustache, they went off down Oxford Street. 'You cheated, DB.'

'Of course I cheated. What did you all expect? We're Bureau people, I thought we would all cheat.' She thumped Paul playfully on the arm. 'As for you, you silly bugger . . .'

They had become a foursome – unlike the other six, who hadn't been able to find the trick of working as a team in the same way.

On the last Saturday of the course, after yet another lecture about surveillance, Vee congratulated them all and said that although Colonel Linder couldn't be with them, he had arranged with the landlord of The Star and Garter to have a round of shorts on him.

The shorts turned out to be generous doubles of whisky. The Scrubs contingent drank and played darts noisily against the locals until closing time. The landlord had no idea what these rowdies were doing at the old prison – although he told his regulars, in confidence, that they were doing emergency planning. He was shrewd enough to guess that they might not be the last, so he put up with their loud voices because they didn't seem short of money.

Afterwards, the Bureau recruits went back to the Scrubs to take a look at the telephone exchange that was now installed. They felt pleased that the place they had worked on finally looked important and complete. The ten gathered in the kitchen, which contained only an electric kettle and a tiny electric oven with two rings. They stood around, sharing the few bottles of stout and beer they had persuaded the landlord to part with, drinking from their coffee mugs.

Mary-Rose, now rosy-cheeked to suit her name, stepped out of character and raised her voice. 'Listen a minute. I know I've had too much to drink, but I want to say something before I get any squiffier. All my life I have been a solitary and studious person. I shunned social contact, believing myself to be self-sufficient with my books and studies, but here, with all of you, for the first time, I have learned what it is like to live and work close to people. I expect it's gone to my head, but I want to tell you before we all go our separate ways that I would never do or say anything against any of you. I have found you all to be good and nice people and I was brought up never to say anything behind a person's back that I would not say to their face.' She bowed her head shyly. 'That's all. Could I beg a cigarette?' Offers came from all round the table.

Mel, the most senior of the men in terms of age – probably in his early forties – squeezed Mary-Rose's hand. 'That's really sweet, Mary-Rose. We've all enjoyed ourselves, haven't we, gang?' They clinked their mugs and agreed. Eve guessed that 'gang' wasn't a word he would have used in his past life. There were little things about each of the others that didn't ring true.

Maybe they felt as she had done when she had cut

herself loose from home, joined the Communists and gone to Spain – they were experiencing an entirely different game; an entirely new set of rules; a strange kind of freedom.

Mary-Rose looked at each of them very seriously. 'I don't just mean *enjoy*, I mean . . . you have become more to me than . . . well, pals. Mel, would you do the honours?' She took a bottle from her shoulder-bag. 'It's good stuff . . . the best.'

Mel held up the bottle. 'And you're not kidding there, Mary-Rose.'

They drank well into the early hours, then dispersed when Mel said, 'Well, gang, I'm off, got things to do, places to visit.' There were no goodbyes, no references to when they might see one another again.

Paul, DB, Eve and Fran came out into a gloomy, foggy, London, and started to walk in the direction of their digs.

Fran said, 'Blow this for a lark, I'm not ready for bed.'

'Me neither,' said Eve.

'Good,' said Fran. 'You want to know what I think?'

'Yeah, we deserve a treat.'

'I absolutely agree,' Paul said. 'I'll stand one if anybody knows were to go. No pubs open. How about Joe Lyons? What time do they open, Eve?'

'Not for a couple of hours yet.'

Paul shrugged his shoulders. 'That's my entire knowledge of London high life. No use asking the lad from the sticks.' He often referred to himself like this, but if he was once a country boy, it had been some time ago. Eve thought he might be an army man.

'Come on,' Fran said, 'I know where. Top secret, no questions asked.' And, guided by her, they walked through backstreets, ending up at an all-night cabbie stand from which came an enticing aroma of tea stewing and bread frying in lard.

'Oh my God,' Paul, always ready to eat, said, sniffing the air. 'We've died and come to Heaven.'

The prospect of food made them feel hungrier and even more cheerful, and their long walk had dispelled tiredness and cleared their heads.

The stand, sheltered by a tarpaulin and lit only by an oil lamp, was underneath arches. A few London cabs without lights were parked close by. The only places to rest were a couple of benches made of empty drums and scaffolding planks. Cabbies, after stretching their legs, warmed their hands on steaming mugs, leaned against Thames Embankment wall, and sorted out the war strategy and a government who didn't know nothing. Trains rattled overhead.

Fran said to the other three, 'Sit you down, this is my shout,' and went straight to the stand. 'Four sweet teas, Herb, and eight well-done slices.'

The vendor peered. 'Lor love us, miss, it's you. Where you been keeping yourself?'

'Here and there, coming and going . . . war work, Herb.'

'Aw, miss, don't say that. Don't say you ain't going to give your loving public no more –'

Fran interrupted, 'Now, then, Herb, you know better than to ask. Walls have ears. Don't you know there's a war on?'

'So they keep saying when I try to get a bit of extra sugar. Sweet tea's total necessary to my blokes – keeps 'm going. And not just cabbies. Now there's the wardens and ambulance girls as well as the night-shift safety gangs off the lines.' He pointed to above the arches where trains clattered and rattled over points. 'But will the Min'stry a' Food listen? Will they buggery.'

When Fran returned to the others, carrying a tin tray holding four large mugs and a pile of thick, fried bread, their expressions were eager and curious.

'Don't ask! Or you'll get none of this. I mean it.'

'Fair enough,' Paul said as they fell upon the bread, murmuring and groaning with pleasure as they bit into the crisp, lardy outer layer and munched the soft, steaming centre. 'We won't even ask how you come to know this amazing place and what it is Herb thinks he's not going to get any more of.'

DB whispered, mock conspiratorial, 'Maybe it's one of Lieutenant Hatton's tasks.'

Eve agreed. 'It just might be – do you think this is what it might be like if it was a real operation?'

'Oh yeah,' Paul answered lightly. 'Herb just passed Fran a secret message, under cover of fried bread.'

DB slapped Paul on the back, making him splutter into his mug of tea. 'Oh my God, Paul! You just swallowed the message.' Everything they said made them laugh like schoolkids.

Herb leaned out of the serving hatch and said genially, 'Oi, miss, watch it, or I'll have to give you the old heave-ho for lowering the tone of my establishment.'

Paul said, 'DB, give Herb's place a bit of style . . . sing.'

'OK. What?'

'"Strange Fruit", DB. It has to be. Give Eve and Fran something to remember.'

'And leave them crying?'

Paul put his hands on her shoulders and looked her straight in the eye. 'Hey, lady, you sing da blues, sure we gonna cry.'

DB sang, stopping Herb's customers in their tracks.

When daylight came and Herb had rinsed his last mug, the four hired one of the cabs which took them back to pack their bags.

After she had packed her things, Eve sat down to write her report, which was quite long because there was much she thought worth mentioning, though not in detail. She ended: 'It is my opinion that Toffler is already working within The Bureau and was a plant to induce reactions from us on our last day, as was the rumour that there was a clandestine relationship between the Chief and his assistant. E. Anders. 25 February 1940.'

Then, just as they had parted from the others, the four walked away from one another. There were no goodbyes and they did not look back.

When Eve returned to Portsmouth, it was not to Griffon House, but to WRNS quarters in a requisitioned building with high ceilings and hollow-sounding floors. There a surprise met her in the person of Phoebe Moncke, smart in a WRNS officer's uniform that was the very opposite of her shawls and scarves at Griffon.

'Sit down, Miss Anders.' Phoebe smiled broadly and indicated her new look. 'Surprising what a good scrub up will do, isn't it?'

'You look very good, Miss Moncke. I guess I should call you ma'am.'

'Yep. For the present I am your senior officer. Poor Miss Anders, I dare say the place looks top heavy with brass. Some of us need rank to get on and off the Portsmouth shore bases – they're like ships: civilians not allowed on board. This gold lace gives me clout. The same will go for you, although it isn't likely that you will need to wear uniform. You will be kitted out, and given all sorts of passes.'

'Right. So I am a WRNS officer too?'

'Officially. I understand from Captain Faludi and Lieutenant Hatton,' she tapped a manila file – different colour from the one David had had. How many files on her were there? – 'that they agree you are right for The Bureau and that you have sworn allegiance.' Eve didn't show her amusement at the allegiance she had sworn before David with a G & T in her hand.

Eve nodded.

'How does your conscience sit on the oath?'

'I'm not sure exactly what you mean, but this is my country, I could never be anything other than loyal to it.'

'Yet you would have stayed on in Spain?'

Phoebe Moncke's manner was disarming. Eve had not yet sorted out her ideas and strong emotions for the two countries she loved. Phoebe's velvet-glove questioning, her gentle manner and soft voice, forced Eve to put her thoughts into words.

'Had things turned out differently, I would have stayed on,' Eve said, 'because I believe that I could have contributed – no, that's not the right word . . .'

'It's not bad.'

'No, "contributed" sounds pious. I'm certainly not pious. I could have done something worthwhile. As regards loyalty, I suppose that I'm just honest to my ideals . . . or something along those lines.' Eve ventured a smile and shrugged her shoulders. 'It's no wonder politicians sound so false. It's hard to put into words something you feel strongly about.'

Phoebe nodded, tilting her head to one side as people do when they are being noncommittal. Eve realised that it would be prudent to watch her words, but if Phoebe was to be her senior officer she should be straight-up with her.

'You see, if the fascists hadn't won the war, then I might have been of more use there than here.'

'Why?'

'I was working in a kind of refuge for women and orphans and I had managed to scrounge food, and we did bits of rough work for a fish or a few vegetables.'

'Tell me about the children. I have one of my own.'

She smiled. 'That's classified information. I keep her well away from my own front line.'

Eve hadn't envisaged Phoebe in the role of a mother. 'I may well finish this with tears in my eyes. I hope that they won't count against me.'

Phoebe leaned across and touched the tips of her fingers briefly on Eve's wrist. 'Tears may well count in favour.'

'I used to write the occasional column, which some magazines published.'

'Nothing much The Bureau doesn't know about its people.'

'In one item, I used a phrase said to me, I think, by a Scottish woman: "This is not just a soldiers' war", meaning that almost the entire adult population was involved. Women and girls went to the barricades after work to give a bit of respite to the soldiers. I used to see them; they wore these soft espadrilles, caps and bandoliers, walking arm in arm five abreast through the rubble. They were super . . . *they* knew what they were fighting for. But the children didn't! The very little ones who were undernourished couldn't fight off the ordinary infections, and bombs and shells aren't selective about who gets it. Some kids just wandered around until somebody took them in. There was one instance that really got to me. What was left of the population of an entire village that had been razed to the ground started walking north . . . I'm sorry . . . once I get started . . .'

'No, go on. You're the first person I've met who saw it first-hand.'

'This refuge . . . a woman I had known through the International Brigade helped some Spanish women start up shelters. I went to work in one. It was devastating. These kids were lost and scared out of their little minds. What could we give them? Damned all, except a drop of milk from our scrawny nanny goat, and what could be scrounged.' She drew breath and took a long drink of water. 'You see, I said there might be tears.' Looking up, she saw tight lines around Phoebe's mouth and wretchedness in her eyes, but Eve ploughed on because she wanted her to know that she wasn't some young woman who merely liked the notion of becoming a Bureau agent, who thought it might be glamorous. 'We had two good sources of food: people on the fish quay and a Russian officer – whom, of course, you now know. They kept us going right to the end.'

'Thank you, Miss Anders. I quite see why you would have been on the horns of a dilemma if that war had gone the other way.'

'Ma'am, I will be a damned good agent, given half a chance. I could be very useful. This is where I was born and brought up. I see England from the underside. Not many Bureau people I have met so far are working class.' She paused. It seemed that whenever she needed to say what made her tick, she couldn't do it without the old devil 'class' coming into it. But that was how it was now that she had pulled herself away from her roots.

'Can you see it from both sides? You are no longer the factory girl you used to be. I have read Dr McKenzie's report.' Phoebe made a kind of beckoning motion as though to draw words from her mouth. 'Can you?'

'You know about the factory girl; she's still here, ma'am. The factory girl made Eve Anders. The factory girl's view of England was, *is* of its underside. I may have put this protective Anders shell around her, but when Anders looks at the world, it is through the eyes of a factory girl with the added experience of Anders.'

'"To thine own self be true"?' Phoebe gave Eve the gentlest of smiles, mostly with her eyes.

'Yes, yes, that's the Anders philosophy in a nutshell . . . even if it sounds like godalmighty clap-trap.'

'You went to Spain on the side of the Republic – would you wish to see Britain go that way?'

'Eventually, ma'am, yes, but we have a lot of obstacles before that day comes. To be quite honest, I object to being a "subject". It's demeaning.'

'How would you feel about going back to Spain?'

'You mean now?'

'In a few weeks.'

'A few weeks! Well . . . I'd feel apprehensive. I became quite well known in some areas.'

'The Bureau needs a woman in Spain. Lieutenant Hatton thinks you're the one for the job.'

Spain! A dozen conflicting thoughts swept through her.

'You think he's wrong?'

'No, ma'am, no. I was just surprised that it would be Spain.'

'Fancy a walk along the seafront? We shall be working together for a while, so let's get a bit better acquainted.'

The front was just a short walk from Phoebe's temporary office. As soon as they reached the open common a chill wind gusted, carrying sea-water smells. A gang of council workers were attaching coils of barbed wire to the handrails where Eve had often leaned over with the girls from school. Two blonde little girls, obviously sisters, dressed alike and holding buckets and spades, were peering through the web of barbs at the shingle and sea.

'Look at them,' Eve said. 'How can you possibly explain *that* to a child?'

'Maybe we can save them from worse.'

'Maybe they will end up dead!'

She didn't trust herself even to apologise. The sun broke through the grey mass of cloud. The tide was surging out towards Chichester, the sea now flashing silver sparkles, moving as though fingers were dabbling the surface. It surged around the stanchions of the pier, the ebbing water sucking gently as it revealed bright green weed.

'Oh, sunshine, just what I needed.' Phoebe took off her tricorn hat and shook out her hair, very different now from the exotic tangle that went with her Griffon dress.

'You appear quite a different person from when you took us into Griffon,' Eve said.

Phoebe laughed. 'I was trying her on for size. I like to do that sometimes. I used to play characters on the stage.'

'Is this the real you, then?'

'Will the real Phoebe Moncke stand up?' she laughed. 'You see, nobody did.'

They walked on. Phoebe pointed across the water. 'Look, the sun has picked out that town just like a floodlight.'

'That's Ryde.'

'Beautiful, isn't it? I expect you know the Isle of Wight well?'

'Only as part of the scenery, a hump on the horizon. I've never been.'

'Yet you have been to Europe and Australia.'

'Oh yes, Paris, and a few nights in Cape Town and Hong Kong and Singapore on the way back here.'

'When were you in Paris?'

'On my way in and out of Spain, but I had been there before . . . to do with my old job. It will be somewhere in my file. Lieutenant Hatton knows about it.'

'You are just the cosmopolitan lady to live it up at the Madrid Ritz.'

'Madrid?'

'David Hatton says you can do it. Sophisticated lady.'

'Hardly sophisticated.'

'After we've finished with you over there,' she pointed to the Isle of Wight, 'you won't say that. I shall be asking you, "Will the real Miss Anders stand up?"'

*   *   *

At last Eve Anders got to set foot on the Isle of Wight at Ryde, just opposite where she had been standing with Phoebe Moncke only two days previously. The weather was springlike – clear air, an azure bowl of sky and sunlight bright enough to penetrate the sea and turn it blue.

With the sun on her face, the smell of engine oil wafting by, and the thrum of engines shuddering the soles of her shoes, Eve leaned on the rail and watched as the old steam-paddle ferry made its way across the short treacherous span of the Solent that flowed between the island and the mainland, directly across the busy shipping lanes. Filling her mind with moving pictures, she drew in the busy traffic slipping in and out of Portsmouth Harbour: grey top-heavy battleships low in the water; grey, nippy Royal Navy corvettes; grey warships, unmarked and with unfamiliar outlines that came up or disappeared over the horizon; vessels painted with zigzag patterns that could suddenly leap into view when eyes adjusted to the distraction of the camouflage.

Eve Anders knew her local history and it was an awful history to contemplate. Portsmouth was a naval town, which thrived only in time of war. Time and again it had risen like a phoenix from the ashes of peace. She had been a young child throughout the last period of peace, and had grown up with unemployment and poverty blossoming all around her. Now, the phoenix of war was rising again and with it Portsmouth's fortunes.

As the ferry turned, its paddle thrashing the water, she felt a thrill, as she always had when starting out on something new. Unknown territory: the Isle of Wight, a tiny landmass cut off from the mainland when the sea broke through millennia ago; Ryde, until now a cluster of buildings in the midst of dense trees. This was still England, still Hampshire, her own county, yet the couple of miles of sea she had just crossed gave her a strange feeling of liberation. She held back from disembarking until the crowd had cleared, enjoying her light-hearted mood.

I'm back to my old self, she thought.

Her eyes sparkled with health, and the enthusiastic spirit of Lu as she had been on the day when she stepped off the train in London on the first day of her new life as Eve three years ago. Now she stepped onto the quayside at Ryde, looked at the endless stretch of pier, and was glad to have worn slacks and flat shoes.

'Miss Anders . . . over here, Miss Anders.' A voice that she had heard before.

'Miss Sanderson! Electra! Fancy you being here.' Eve shook her hand warmly. 'Is this coincidence, or are you here to waylay me again?'

'The latter. Not such lux transport this time.'

'Never mind the transport, it's good to see you. Are you well?'

'Oh, absolutely! Never better. Give me one of your big bags – they'll be picked up later today. Just bring your tote. Cup of tea? Ah, I know what you'd love. It's absolutely special. Minghella's, ice cream for the angels; can't buy the stuff on the mainland.'

They sat with little dishes. 'Isn't this the most heavenly stuff?'

'Delicious, but how long can they continue to make it?'

'The big factories are all closing down. I have an absolute passion for ice cream. I caught it in Italy as a child and its never gone. The real stuff is hard to find in England, but here it is. I've been coming here every day.'

There was something so disarming and naïve about Electra Sanderson's chatter that Eve was reminded of her childhood friend and soulmate, Bar Barney. Bar's enthusiasm had been so infectious that it was impossible not to be carried along with her.

'What's happened to your FANY uniform?'

'I'm between jobs, as you might say. Not exactly between, but on a different tack. I'm not sorry – all that explaining to people . . . friends behaving like lewd schoolgirls. "I say,"' she mimicked, "what do you think, old Lec's a FANY!" I mean, a joke's only a joke if you've never heard it before, and I got fed up explaining that I was proud to be a member of the First Aid Nursing Yeomanry – somebody was certain to say, "Show us your bow and arrows, Lec." So, I've become a Bureau PA – that's personal assistant to Commander Kiefor, "Keef". You know, of course, that he's Commander Kiefor now?'

'Yes, it was he who gave me my orders. Said I should wear flat shoes.'

'Did he ask if you could ride a bike?'

'Ahh, so that's it. No, no he didn't.'

'Can you?'

'Well, yes, if I can remember.'

'Nobody ever forgets how to ride a bike.'

Two sit-up-and-beg cycles were propped against a wall at the pier exit. Each had bountiful baskets back and front, and old-fashioned lamps attached front and rear.

'Don't take against them because of their appearance. They're absolutely well maintained (by yours truly) and very kind to the derrière. Put your bag in mine, just in case.'

'In case of what?'

'That you wobble when you get going.'

'I'll take a turn or two along here, if you don't mind.'

Eve hadn't been on a bike since her elder brother had taught her on a borrowed errand-boy's bike – all the kids in the street had learned on it. It was a wonderful feeling; the tyres were springy and the chain and cogs clean and oiled.

'There! I told you. Not a single wobble. Come on, let's get going.'

'Where?'

'A couple of miles to the east of here. We follow the shoreline.'

The lane was narrow and not well surfaced. Electra went ahead, calling back over her shoulder from time to time, pointing out across the water to where Portsmouth lay.

'Here we are,' Electra called back as she turned sharp right and then sharp left again. 'How was it? Not far enough to make you stiff. Not even out of breath.'

'But perspiring like mad.'

The bikes were left propped against a brick outhouse, and, swinging Eve's tote, Electra led the way round to the front of the house.

Eve said, 'Wow! What a smashing house!'

'Absolutely genuine Lutyens.'

Typical of Lutyens' architecture, the house had tall fancy chimneys and broad stretches of narrow windows that looked out over a wide stretch of neglected lawn to the sea.

'What's the house called?'

'Just The House by the Sea.'

Eve laughed. 'Oh, I like that.'

'Come on in. I'll show you where you'll be putting up. Hardly anybody here at the moment; it's just been opened up.'

Although the downstairs rooms were almost empty, and the floors were bare polished strip-board, the house had a feeling of being lived in. If this were mine, I'd never want to move, Eve thought. Then, as she went to the upper rooms overlooking the Solent with its constant movement in the shipping lanes, and the distant natural chalk buttresses beyond which, as she well knew, was the exit from her home town, the road to London and beyond, she settled for: If this were mine, it would be the perfect place to come home to.

It was reaching midday. 'Something to eat – outside?'

'Smashing, it's warm enough. Can you tell me about the others who will be coming?'

'Of course. Grab a tray. Rosehip wine? The Dad's a whizz at country wines.'

'They're called hedgerow wines where I come from.'

Electra looked for a moment as though she would ask, 'Where's that?' but, like Eve, she had become part of a world where you didn't ask those questions – unless it was your job to do so, and then you could call up one of the personal files.

Eve covered for her. 'Wines like this, if they're made by an expert, are so good you wonder why you bother with vinos.'

'Cheese roll . . . almost sans cheese?'

'Sounds good to me.'

They settled on the untended grass facing the sea.

'What has Keef told you about this house?' Electra asked.

'Very little, only that it's for specialist people who are going . . . "underground" is it called?'

'What it is really is a kind of rehearsal room for a big production. Not many parts, all those ones involved will be stars. Keef and Phoebe's jobs are to see that you are word-perfect.' Electra grinned. 'WRNS Officer Moncke.'

'I know, I know, what a turn-up for the book.'

'Out of the Scrubs people, there's you and Wilhelmina de Beers, and a Paul Smyth.'

Now it was Eve's turn to grin. 'Smyth-with-a-Y. He's a really nice chap, so's DB – Wilhelmina. I suppose we must have done something right at the Scrubs.'

'I wouldn't know about that, but I guess you're all good Bureau material.'

'You seem to have picked up quite a lot since I last saw you.'

'The Dad's in the know, which is why Keef got me out of the FANY and into The Bureau. Now, what else can I tell you? Well, Peter Follis – he will be here. He's a magician. He can transform a person so that their own mother wouldn't know them. Ever heard of him?' Eve shook her head. 'Brilliant. Worked back stage for years. Mostly simple stuff, like a chap with a bald head and limping on a walking stick can transform his appearance in a trice if he ditches the stick and dons a cap and a pair of spectacles and strides out. Phoebe explained it to me. That's the simple stuff.' She hunched her shoulders and smiled like a schoolgirl telling a secret. 'Actually, that's about all I know about him.'

'According to Keef, that is what he is going to do to me – transform me.'

'Peter and Phoebe Moncke, according to Keef, have worked together for years. They have – or used to have – their own theatre?'

'Oh, is that what she was talking about?'

'A small place. I think they call it "experimentational" or something . . . ad-lib . . . Dada theatre, the sort of place The Dad wouldn't approve of as "intellectual and foreign". Strange though, The Dad knows Keef and doesn't mind him at all. It's my opinion that Keef went to The Dad's college – most of the men he approves of came from there. Of course, Keef's a different generation, but an old boy's an old boy for ever.'

'What about *Commander* Kiefor and *WRNS Officer* Moncke? Are they colleagues or what?'

'Oh, colleagues, I'm certain.'

Eve waited for her to go on, as she was bound to. Electra was a superb gossip, like a gently babbling warm stream. The thing was, Electra's stream wasn't as shallow as it appeared. Like the previously 'potty' Phoebe, there was a lot more depth to her than first appeared – had to be, or she would hardly have been taken onto the Bureau staff.

'I believe that Keef was the money behind "Solo" – Peter Follis and Phoebe's theatre. You might not believe it, but he's the younger of the two.'

'Keef?'

'Yes. Quite smitten by her – but in a purely platonic way, even though they are quite prepared to share a room. Very queer set-up. But that's theatre people for you. Look, I have to go down to the town to pick up supplies, and meet the ferry. Ration books complicate things for us. We have to register with local shops, otherwise there would be too much curiosity. We couldn't be registering everybody who comes and goes here, so we put in some permanent cards and the rest is sent over by ferry from the RN stores. Lieutenant Hatton has left all this to me, and he's really pleased with me. He's nice, isn't he?'

'Really charming.'

'Some of the girls who saw him at a local hop – local as at Griffon – well, they called him my lover boy because he kept dancing with me until I had taught him to jitterbug. I'll have to take the brake down, pick up our supplies, your luggage plus Miss de Beers and Mr Smyth.

'You hang around here, open kitchen cupboards, find out where stuff is. Somebody might drop in with a tray of eggs – just leave them on the dresser. Lovely bit of sun, have a walk along the shore if you like. By the way, how is your delicious Russian – or shouldn't I ask?'

Eve gave her a wry expression. 'I think I just might take that walk along the shore.'

Electra winked. 'Good idea.'

Eve sat as close to the lapping waves as she could. Much of the time she had spent strolling along the shoreline path she spent thinking of Dimitri. Where *was* he? Their new situation disturbed her. She hadn't bargained for missing him quite so much. The Bureau had whisked him away at speed, leaving no trace. The only thing she had to prove that he had ever existed was the short note. She shouldn't complain, because it was the way she had left her family. Once before a man had been chopped out of her life – Ozz Lavender. Even after all these months, she still missed him. Now that Dimitri was gone – true, with a cleaner cut – she was hurting. He was a great comforter. If he was here now he would draw her onto his generous lap and wrap his arms around her, making soft comfort in Russian. Watching the ever-increasing circles from a stone thrown into the sea, she tried yet again to analyse her feelings for him. Why couldn't he just –

'Loo-loo-loo-loo!' The high-pitched ululating call carried along the coastline from the left. Eve's mood lightened. She had heard that Zulu call before, carrying clearly across the River Thames. DB. What sport!

Eve ran towards the sound and arrived at The House by the Sea to see DB and Paul coming towards her.

Paul wasn't a man who found it unmanly to give hugs and kisses. He threw his tweedy arms around Eve's shoulders. 'Come here, you thing, and be warmly greeted.' Their pleasure at meeting again was obvious. 'Miss Sanderson said we would know our third colleague.'

'Evie Anders, hey man, it is good to see *you*! The old firm . . . only Fran missing.'

'I saw her again, just for a minute . . .'

DB linked arms with both of them and they set out towards the sea. 'Who'd have thought it? We must have done something right at the Scrubs.'

'That's what I said.'

'Played a pretty good game of darts.'

'Nothing else I can think of.'

'Oh, *there's* modest.'

'You saw Fran, and . . . ?'

'It was just for a minute. I don't think she wanted me to see her.'

'Fran?'

'Well, she wouldn't, would she, if she had got her posting? She was boarding the Aberdeen train, and I happen to know that The Bureau is starting a cipher department in Scotland.'

Dimitri! That was the likeliest place for him to be sent.

'A cipher set-up there – Fran's just the woman to be part of it. It's where I hope to go after . . . um, after this operation.'

'What else do you know about it? I'm not just fishing, I really need to know . . . It's personal. Would there be a . . . I don't know . . . a Balkans . . . Eastern Europe . . . Soviet section?'

'Maybe a Polish section. I'm just guessing. I was waiting for interview, and met a Pole,' Paul chuckled. 'He was doing the "Ximinies" crossword faster than me, so maybe there will be all kinds of ciphering and decoding going on there.'

'He's the guy for the gossip, Eve,' said DB. 'Hey, will you just look at that view. Is that where we've just come from – Portsmouth? I don't remember all those tall houses. It's pretty.'

Eve looked across. 'Technically, that's Southsea. People there don't like to be included in Portsmouth.'

'It's the same all over,' Paul agreed.

'Tell me something I don't know. In my country, it's not only the whites knowing they're better than the blacks – the blacks often have shades of black: yellow blacks, with light skins, who think they're better than the real darks, but not to the Cape coloureds. They're real class, almost white, but not to the whites they're not. To the whites, they're all niggers, and it's only that my nigra blood goes back so many generations that I'm not a problem. I'm all washed out. Except for my hair. The girl used to keep it oiled down and in tight pigtails so that no one would ask about Great-great-grandpa.'

Eve said, 'I love your hair.'

DB laughed. 'After I was transported to Italy, I set it free.'

'Do you suppose we'll be working together?' Eve asked.

'I'd feel OK about that,' Paul said.

'Me too.'

'Either of you speak Spanish?' Eve asked.

The other two looked sideways at her.

'Like a native,' Paul said, 'about the one thing I can do. French, Portuguese, Greek – Ancient and Modern, German – High and Low, Swedish, Italian, a lot of Low Country dialects, and I can get along in Icelandic and Inuit. Got me a Masters and a PhD, said he, showing off. I don't know how I came to be able to do it. I just can – a gift like some people can do maths at six years old.' He squeezed Eve affectionately. 'So, to answer your question, yes I speak Spanish.'

'What's Inuit?'

'Eskimo. So, I guess you speak Spanish too, which is the link, and you wouldn't have asked if you didn't already know something about your operation. DB?'

'I speak it pretty good, but I'm better at Portuguese. My mom was my auntie's Portuguese maid, and my pa married her. Is Paul right? You speeka da language?'

'Not like a native, but I have a good ear for picking up speech, and I picked up my colloquial Spanish on the hoof.'

They stopped and squatted on the stony beach beside a clump of scrub, which sheltered them from the late-afternoon breeze.

'Nothing personal, Eve, but how old are you?'

DB said, 'That's personal, Paul, but, hey, man, who

cares, you're a sweet mate. I'm twenty-six and I'm a lesbian. I like black girls, which doesn't go down that good if your community is Dutch Reform. Minds as closed as a bull's ass in autumn, which is why I was packed off to Italy to have my voice trained professionally. Not many Cape coloured girls in Milano.'

The other two didn't immediately respond.

'Hey, man, have I shocked you?'

Paul laughed. 'No, but I was only asking Eve her age because of what she said about learning colloquial Spanish on the hoof. I guessed you meant actually *in* Spain, Eve?'

Eve nodded.

'You look too young to have been there.'

'And you look like a jolly chap in your tweed jacket and bad haircut, except that it's a disguise for a razor brain. First time you spoke to us you picked an anagram out of the air.'

DB said, 'Will somebody tell me what you two are talking about?'

Paul said, 'On the hoof means that Eve was in Spain long enough to learn the language. Colloquial means she learned it from people and not in classrooms. There's been a civil war going on there. From my guess at her age, it means that she must have been only twenty or younger when she went there.' He looked at her questioningly. 'I assume you were helping the right side.'

'You mean the left side?' When Paul nodded, Eve added, 'Do you solve murders in your spare time?'

DB said, in oddly accented Spanish, 'So we're the chosen.'

'But for what?' Paul asked.

'I say, man, what sport if we are sent undercover together.'

'You must be joking. Can you imagine the three of us together being unnoticed?'

'What about separately?'

'In Spain? If you went as a volunteer, Eve, and you weren't a nurse or doctor, then you must have carried The Card.'

'Paul!'

Communists ever only referred to the Communist Party as 'The Party' and the membership card as 'The Card'.

Ever since Phoebe Moncke had talked about the undercover operation in Spain, worry had been gnawing at Eve. If her cover was blown it would be bad enough, but to be discovered as a card-carrying Communist would mean, at best, incarceration in one of the terrible traitors' prisons; at worse elimination. If she were to be recognised as the woman who used to drive a truck carrying supplies, it would hardly matter that she held a UK passport . . . no, a forged Irish one probably.

If she let her thoughts go in that direction, she would become jittery.

'Sorry, Eve. Don't worry, I've carried The Card since I was a student. No longer actually in my pocket, of course.'

'That doesn't mean it's a good idea to tell all and sundry.'

'DB's not all and sundry, are you?'

'I'll tell *you* something, you wouldn't be welcome in my country. God's Own Country.' DB cupped her hands round her mouth and shouted across the water, '*Neit roi. Swartz verbotten! Lesbians don't come home!*' For a moment a crack appeared in her 'What sport! What a lark!' casing, allowing Eve and Paul to see the sores. 'Hey, man, I'm starving. Is there a kitchen we can raid?'

Paul said, 'Electra said we can help ourselves.'

DB nudged him. 'Oo it's "Electra" now. He was really keen on her straightaway, Eve. She'd be just right for you, Paul.'

'I know. D'you think I have a chance there?'

'There's no one else,' Eve offered. 'Go get her, Paul.'

'What, with you two watching?'

'She taught Lieutenant Hatton to jitterbug. You could try that tack.'

'The fair Adonis in a naval uniform. Oh dear, the competition *is* strong.'

Eve said, 'He's too old for her, Paul. You're just right.'

'Not too old for jitterbugging.'

DB said, 'It's probably just his bait. I mean, how much closer can you get to a stranger than dancing?'

That was the way she and David had started: two strangers in a tango embrace. 'It would do for a start, don't you think?'

The two young women linked arms with him. He was *such* a super man.

Phoebe Moncke arrived during the evening with Keef and Peter Follis in tow. Including Electra, seven of them sat round a table to a meal that was a plain but delicious vegetable stew followed by a batter pudding, plenty of eggs and milk, but unsweetened. Electra apologetically said, 'I could have used saccharin, but I think that's worse than unsweetened. When you get used to no sugar, many things taste much better.'

Paul said, 'I think that's about the best batter pudding I've ever tasted.'

'Oh, Mr Smyth, how nice of you to say that.'

'I'd rather be called Paul . . . is that all right?' His eyes swivelled between Keef and Phoebe Moncke.

Keef answered, 'I don't see why not. Everybody refers to me as Keef.'

Phoebe leaned across and patted his hand, 'That's because you are and always will be Keef, darling.'

Over cups of Camp coffee substitute, Phoebe said, 'The three of you will be on the same operation – namely to be in place should there be a sudden exodus from

France of the Duke of Windsor and Wallis, both of whom I know quite well, but whom, I'm afraid, have become bothersome. Whitehall no longer has time for their childish pique. At the moment they are comfortably ensconced in the South of France, but it can only be a matter of time before they decide to leave. The Germans, as you will know, have been wooing them. It would be a great coup for Hitler if he could persuade them to line up with him. He has made them such promises.'

Paul asked, 'Are the rumours true that they are pro-Nazi?'

'They have been fêted and shown the new face of Germany, the roads in particular. The Prince of Wales – as he was then – was impressed. When he said his famous "Something must be done" to Welsh miners, he had roads in mind. He saw himself putting all those unemployed men to work making a British autobahn network. But it is probable that he hadn't realised that the famous German autobahns have been laid out so that the great army of the Third Reich, with its convoys of heavy guns and tanks, can move fast.'

Phoebe Moncke, with her fluffy pose dropped, was a formidable woman. Eve liked her better like this. 'Any questions?'

'You said I will have two roles here . . .'

'Right! Let's talk about Mr Smyth. Miss De Beers' agent, Mr Smyth of London, will travel with her to Lisbon, where she will give recitals. You will be carrying messages – the sheet music. Messages will be secreted within the notes.'

'Brilliant!' Paul said. 'But if the notes are encrypted, won't that produce some pretty weird sounds? Also, there are only seven letters.'

'You've probably heard of dots . . .'

'Microdots – messages on miniature film?'

Keef nodded.

Paul went on, 'But that's incredible. I hadn't realised that things were so advanced. Messages on music notes? Wow!'

Phoebe said, 'Wow, yes. You and Keef will be working on that, as well as you working with Miss Anders' Spanish – she's supposed not to speak the language and refers to a traveller's guide. It's mostly a question of getting her to answer questions in the phonetic Spanish a non-speaker would get from the guide.

DB asked what Peter Follis' role was.

'You and Mr Smyth will not need much of his attention; you are who you are. You spend your time here singing away to your heart's content and learning to be a bit of a prima donna who leaves everything to her agent.

'Miss Anders needs Peter. If she were to return to Spain looking as she now does, she would be in jeopardy – in fact, we would not send her. You may or may not know that Miss Anders was in Spain right up to the end of the war there. She knows the country well, and there may be people who will know her. So, she is about to be transformed by Peter into a wealthy socialite who is indulging her fancy that she can produce a book of photographs of the flora of the area. She doesn't have to justify what she is doing – she's rich.'

'How will we get in?'

'Miss de Beers and yourself from Shannon to Lisbon. Miss Anders same air route, then from Lisbon into Spain by road. One of our people will drive you across the border.'

'Aren't border crossings difficult?'

'Not to any extent between Portugal and Spain. It is at airports that the new government is a bit edgy about who comes and goes – mostly who goes. There are still a lot of people who were involved in the war trying to escape. Many have prices on their heads. Remember, it is always the detail that makes for a successful operation.'

It occurred to Eve that Phoebe might be new to The Bureau, but not the work of agents.

'Dr Janet McKenzie, whom Miss Anders already knows, will be joining the team here at The House by the Sea. You three are the first of many who will pass through here on short but intensive courses, on their way to a career with The Bureau's Special Operations. Miss de Beers and Mr Smyth will leave here ahead of Miss Anders.'

Next morning Eve went into her first session with Peter Follis. Peter, who had said very little the previous evening but had made copious notes, now had the floor to himself.

He began by asking her to stand up. 'Walk to the door . . . right! Now walk back without purpose. You have all the time in the world. You drift aimlessly, languidly, wiggling your fingers to dry nail-varnish . . . Not bad, not bad. It's a beginning. Now, Eve – OK to call you Eve? – let us consider this hugely wealthy butterfly who believes that she has great talent as a photographer. Can you think who would take the part in a Hollywood production?'

'Myrna Loy?'

'Not quite, too dizzy, not young enough . . . Don't worry, we'll have a bit of a think about the right model later. Then you must pull her over your head like a second skin, step into her body and soul as you take her over.'

'Vivien Leigh?'

'A blonde Leigh? That *would* be good. You have that same snooty look . . . don't bridle; in all real beauty there's an element of snootiness. If not, they are brought down to the level of the rest of we mortals. She's about to receive an Academy Award for her snootiness. "Mammeh, oh, Mammeh".' Peter Follis' mimicking of the Scarlett O'Hara voice and the big dramatic gestures, made Eve almost fall around laughing.

'Why can't I be myself but,' she smiled, 'adjusted to suit?'

'You sound confident – d'you think you can do it?'

'It won't be the first time.'

'Really? Good. So let's do it! Dr McKenzie will be here to help you, but I believe that when we have made the physical change, much of the rest will fall into place.'

'Physical change?'

'We start right away with banting.'

'What's banting?'

'A particularly effective regime for the loss of weight. You didn't suppose all Hollywood stars' svelte bodies are God-given?'

'I never gave it a lot of thought.'

'Banting is nothing strange like eating only cucumbers and swallowing tape-worm capsules. You may smile, but actresses – actors too, the vain bunch – can become desperate. Anyway dear Mr Banting has been very effective with his theory of food – plus a little good red wine. When you are undercover, you may dine sensibly and remain stick-thin.'

Eve looked down at her generous breasts. 'Stick-thin?'

'Yes, Eve, those are a minor problem. Don't concern yourself, they will spring back when you return from your sojourn in the sun. Banting only disperses adipose.'

'I have been stick-thin before, and it wasn't attractive.'

'There is a great difference between starvation and scientific nourishment.'

Electra went to the pierhead with the brake and returned with a smart middle-aged man with jet-black hair and a scarred but handsome face – Ronalde, a hairdresser and make-up artist who had worked with Peter, making ageing actors and actresses appear thirty years younger. He was extremely courteous, asking Eve if it would be convenient for him to start with her hair directly he had changed his 'attire'.

DB and Phoebe couldn't keep away from Ronalde, who, as he worked, asked Eve questions which she answered as well as she was able in her new identity.

'Your new style must be very different from the previous time when you were wherever it is that you are going. How did you wear it?'

'Haystack. Then close crop because of the head-lice. God, how I hated that.'

The other women made gruesome expressions. Ronalde said, 'Not many actresses keep clear of them. It's not very hygienic back stage you know.' He applied sulphurous-smelling bleach, which was kept steaming beneath a towel, then massages of sweet-smelling creams, finishing with a foamy shampoo that smelled of rosemary.

When Eve emerged from the bathroom, her hair was platinum blonde and almost straight. Ronalde had strained it back away from her face. 'There, madam, sleek as a seal, no electric driers, let the air do it. You must always find the best professional to do the recolouring. Go to the most exclusive and expensive man, and be very positive.'

Janet McKenzie arrived at The House by the Sea three days after Eve's hair was bleached blonde, bordering on white, by which time Eve was used to her new reflection. Her eyebrows had been narrowed to a fine line, but there was no apparent change to her figure, although Phoebe Moncke insisted that the scales showed a twenty-ounce reduction.

'I don't think I shall reach stick-thin.'

'Be patient. By the end of the month there will be a difference.'

Janet greeted Eve with obvious pleasure. 'So, my dear, how have things been since we last met?'

'I've been really well. A Special Operations agent is exactly me. I'm loving every minute of it so far.'

Janet opened one of the bunch of string-fastened files that lay on the table where they sat one on either side. 'I thought things went well at our session together at Griffon House, and you did well at the Scrubs induction.'

'I guess I must have. They haven't thrown me out.'

'Let's talk for a bit about how you feel about these sessions? I guess you don't have any experience of hypnotism?'

'No.'

'Are you wary of it?'

'Not wary, but I can't believe that I shall be able to do it.'

'Intelligent women make very good subjects. How about if we make a start now? In the armchair, feet raised on the little stool, hands on the chair arms. The picture facing you is that of a gerbera. When we begin I want you to look at its centre as you listen to me, until I ask you to close your eyes. You will not fall asleep, you will always be aware that you are in this room and that it is me who is talking to you. You may open your eyes at any point, but I would prefer that you did so when I suggest it. Are you warm enough? Good. I will slip off your shoes and put a nice warm little blanket over your feet. Ready when you are . . .'

And so began daily sessions with Janet McKenzie. After the first two Eve began to look forward to gazing at the flower and being lost in time until she heard Janet say, 'Three, two, one. You may open your eyes.'

Janet McKenzie was helping Eve to submerge her utopian ideals and the urge to talk politics. 'Eve is bored, bored, bored by what might be happening in the world – except as it affects her directly.'

'You mean I have to be a self-centred rich bitch then?'

'Exactly so. For the period that you are there you have no opinions except the frivolous ones – whether the Paris style or the American style is the better, not even a comment about Paris fashion disappearing; nothing about the war. Your "Irish ancestry" helps there.'

The transformation of Eve and the running of her as a Special Ops agent in the Madrid Ritz was going to cost taxpayers a pretty penny. She only hoped that The Bureau would think that it had got its money's worth when it was over.

They were out walking together along the shoreline when Eve mentioned this to Janet. Janet gave her a lecture about doing what she was best at and leaving the Treasury to worry about value for money.

'They've been spending money for as long as anyone can remember, keeping men in comfortable hotels in the Far East, and paying out for dubious intelligence. You'll be good value, Eve. Running this place alone would pay a soldier's wage for a lifetime. So shut up and think like a woman who never thinks about the cost of anything.'

There seemed to be a lot of hanging about, so, as she would be purporting to be a photographer of nature, Eve asked Phoebe for a camera and as they walked she took photographs. In the house she learned as much as she could about the technique from books and practising.

'How d'you feel about your man now that you have had this space around you – this emotional space?' Janet asked one day on one of their walks.

'I miss the lovemaking.' Eve smiled, crinkling her brow.

Janet rolled her eyes upwards. 'We all do, and it's likely to get worse for the faithful types. Are you one?'

'No, I don't have anyone to be faithful to.'

'This one's a serious question. How do you cope?'

'With not having a man?'

'Yes. You're not a lesbian, so what happens when you want it – sexual gratification – I mean *really* want it so that it's like a thirst, but there's nothing to quench it; worse, nothing likely to be around?'

'I don't know that I want to answer that.'

'Why?'

'Oh, come on, Janet, it's a bit personal, isn't it?'

'It isn't curiosity. I really need to know as much as I can about you – what makes your clock tick, your pendulum swing, how likely you are to fall into bed with somebody. Y'know what I mean?'

'The sort of people I come from don't talk like this. It's kind of embarrassing.'

'But you are no longer the sort of people you come from. Men masturbate all the time – they know it, their friends know it, it's accepted that they like to do it, so they do. You know that, don't you?'

'Of course I know it.'

'But you think it's kind of embarrassing for us women?'

'For it to be a topic of conversation, yes. Maybe you're used to it – I'm not.'

'I'm your psychologist, Eve, and I know that it's a bit unprofessional to talk to you away from the room – but I know you.'

Eve felt niggled with herself. She hated to be thought prudish – she didn't like prudes – but until now she had never expected to be questioned about how she conducted her private life.

'Young Lu Wilmott, she is the embarrassed one. Am I right? Or am I right?'

'Lu *is* me . . . is Eve.'

'So who are you?'

'Eve Anders née Lu Wilmott.'

'Lu is a child . . . a girl, she ceased to exist three years ago. The team is giving you another face and figure to take with you to Spain; I must give you a new character. OK, it is a *pseudo* character, but you cannot take this child along.'

'She is not a child. Lu is the absolute nucleus of Eve.'

'How can she possibly be the nucleus of this intelligent woman?' Janet McKenzie moved in front of Eve and spread her hands wide. 'For God's sake, Eve, let the child go. Give her to me if you don't feel that you can ditch her.'

Eve felt a terrible danger, as though a foothold she had been sure was secure had come loose. She turned away from the path and towards the shoreline, and sat on the strand just above where the tide had withdrawn.

Janet McKenzie squatted beside her, touching her lightly on the shoulder. 'Eve, you're an intelligent woman. You have been amazing in what you have done. You're brave, resourceful, and an ardent mature woman. You're twenty-two – you have lived your life more fully than most young women I know. Give yourself a chance, Eve. Be yourself, be the woman you've chosen to be.'

The threatening attack of panic began to subside. 'If I give up Lu, I will have deserted my own class – my ideals, if you like.'

'Isn't it a bit arrogant to believe that somebody like me can't share those ideals?'

'I shall never forget what it felt like to be Lu and not get a grammar school place because she came from the wrong end of town.'

'And I shall never forget what it felt like to be *Janet* and not be acceptable in any school because she is black. So I left and found a place where what counted was my mind and not my skin and hair. I shall never forget, but I have moved on down the road since then, though I am still Janet McKenzie, I am still black.' She sat close to Eve and reached out for her hand. 'This is the friend, not the psychologist.'

Eve looked down at the fine, long brown fingers, fingertips painted fire-engine red, and ran her own fingers over Janet's pale pink palm. 'You are black, aren't you . . . isn't that strange? That's never occurred to me. I don't mean that I think about you as being white or anything like that, I mean that I just see Janet . . . Dr McKenzie.'

'As it should be in a perfect world. And I see Eve Anders. Quite by chance – because of my professional relationship with you – I happen to know that you have this immature little person you keep lugging around with you.' Janet put an arm lightly round Eve's shoulder.

Eve smiled and gave Janet a light kiss on the cheek. 'Come on, let's walk.'

DB's delightful voice could be heard every morning as she did her exercises, but mostly she was preoccupied and serious. Paul was his usual likeable self, trying out a bit of cussing and learning how to get on in a Roman Catholic church, what working men ate and how they ate it. Most days he went off with an instructor to learn the techniques of handling a tiny fishing boat.

DB and Paul left the island before Eve became suitably stick-thin.

When Eve was thin enough, Electra drove Peter and Eve to London for a few days. There, Peter introduced Eve to some exclusive fashion houses, where they selected a stunning wardrobe down to the last comb and scent spray. A small amount of jewellery – paste but good – handmade shoes, and gloves and suitcases.

Eve, letting the Treasury worry about the cost, revelled in the anticipation of wearing these beautiful clothes.

She had anticipated that she would return to the island, but Phoebe Moncke appeared at the hotel in which Eve was staying and gave her everything she needed to fly to Shannon airport and from there to Lisbon.

David Hatton, who had found some reason to be going to Eire, travelled with Eve on the aeroplane from England. He felt it necessary to reinforce in a low voice what Janet McKenzie had impressed upon her many times. 'You don't know Spain; you don't understand any of the languages, but you will pick up useful phrases as any visitor would, and you go about with a little English/Spanish dictionary in your pocket.'

She gave him an arch expression, and said in the languid, amused tone she had adopted, 'David, darling, I shouldn't dream of mistreating any pocket of mine . . . you see?' And slipping a hand into a fine leather pochette, she retrieved a slim volume, and a pair of fine gold-rimmed glasses, which she donned, turning to look directly at him.

He raised his eyebrows and gave her a pleased look. 'Is this another of Phoebe's ideas?'

'Actually, no. I do have a minor defect, so these are perfectly genuine.'

'Whoever said "Men seldom make passes/At girls who wear glasses" was an idiot. You look stunning.' He put his hand over hers and squeezed it in a friendly way, so that she didn't retreat from it immediately.

'David, please tell me what happened about Dunkirk.' Even as she had been leaving for Eire, she had seen in the newspaper the first of Portsmouth's 'little boats' returning from France with troops who had retreated as far as possible so that there was only sea left behind them. 'How will I know . . . ?'

'Pick up what you can. You are too much of a spoiled society lady to care much about some little battle that's hundreds of kilometres away. You'll be asked whether you would like morning papers with your breakfast. If you just say OK, you'll get something, but days late because the English papers have to be flown in. Just don't read them avidly.'

'I'm well aware that "the devil is in the detail" – Peter Follis hammered that into me.'

'Madrid will be buzzing with regular SIS agents. If you think you spot any of them, report to Electra.'

Electra would be stationed in Eire for the duration of the Windsor surveillance operation. She would be Eve, DB and Paul's 'Aunt Maureen', to whom Eve would book regular calls.

'I have a wager with a chap in MI6 that we could run one of ours right under their noses and they would never know who it was. So I'm relying on you.'

'You really are all just a bunch of schoolboys.'

'I wish I were coming with you. I'd love to see the place now. Take me a lot of photographs.'

He walked with her to the steps of the Lisbon plane. 'I wouldn't dream of wishing you good luck. You'll be too good to need it.'

She kissed him lightly on both cheeks in the French style, then ran the tips of her calf-clad fingers lightly from his ear to his chin. 'Thank you, David darling.' And then in a whisper, 'Just you get Electra to tell me about Dunkirk – not the full story, just about how it went for us.'

As she boarded the aircraft, she could have staked anything that his eyes would be following her silk-stockinged ankles, high-heeled court shoes and peach-coloured barathea skirt as she mounted the steps. She gave him the whole film-star departure, and loved it. Just as she reached the top of the steps, she turned and waved a fingertip kiss at him. He touched the peak of his uniform cap and left.

He was more handsome now than when they'd first met five years ago. On the flight, she allowed herself to think a little about him. It was weeks since she had made love. She still wondered what it would be like with him.

Waiting for her at Lisbon was a highly polished motor, an enormous Buick convertible, cream with green trim and crimson upholstery, huge chrome headlamps and foglights. A real motor – but with a false chauffeur: Mendoza. He was Portuguese, and one of Colonel Faludi's 'people' who had had experience in some other branch of the service. He was Eve's senior, and she supposed that he would also be advising the Chief on how she performed.

She felt nervous. Her hands were cold and shaking; she stilled them by holding tightly to her clutch bag tucked under her arm.

Keef and Phoebe had kept saying that it would be a pretty safe operation. Spain was a neutral country where warring countries could mix and watch one another.

Of course, if the new right-wing government were to enter the war, it would be on Germany's side. But it wasn't likely, as the last thing this country needed after its own devastating civil conflict was another drain on its resources. And the people? Franco's government might support the fascist side, but what sort of army could Spain recruit? Concentration camps were full of men and women who had fought to hang on to their republic. Many had fled the country or been killed in a bloodbath of cleansing the new state of opposition. Thousands just kept their heads down but would be loose cannon in this war between Britain and Germany.

Spain wasn't going to war with anybody.

As Switzerland had proved in the last war, neutrality had value which Spain needed for its restoration. This was how it was possible for Eve to be able to enter the country and travel in it – provided she had good credentials. She had Southern Irish papers; Eire was no friend of the British. Her documents were false – but perfectly false. Who would question that she was not Eve Anders, the young woman who had been born in Eire and brought up in England but had returned home at the start of the war? Eire was in much the same state as Spain: its own civil war had left it spinning. Eve Anders, whose photograph was fixed and certified on her passport, would bring welcome currency to Spain. Pounds, punts, dollars – she could pay in any of them. Even so, she was apprehensive.

True, her appearance was changed, but Janet had advised keeping her name.

True, she would be moving in high society, mixing with those who had been in exile during the war.

True, most of the Spanish people she had met on a regular basis never knew her name – often she'd been called the American Girl – but throughout the war there had been what General Franco had named his 'fifth column', meaning those who were loyally awaiting the overturning of the Republic. If they were discovered, they 'disappeared'. In the new Spain, tables were turned, old scores were being settled.

There was always the chance that some small thing might give her away. It was the risk she must take. Peter Follis had said that the better the actor the worse were the butterflies in their stomach, sometimes retching right up to the time when they stepped into the spotlight. She hoped he was right, but it didn't feel like it at the moment.

'You are comfortable, Miss Anders?'

'Thank you, Mendoza, yes. But I would like to have the top down.'

'It will be windy.'

'I know.'

It *was* windy, but with a scarf round her head, Eve luxuriated in the extravagant motorcar.

'It is a long drive. I will stop at suitable places for you to have refreshment and walk a little.'

This he did. From the way he was greeted, Eve guessed that he knew the inns very well. Always polite, always the servant, he left her at small tables to be attended by the owner, and conducted to the primitive 'facilities' by the wife or daughter.

It *was* a long journey but Mendoza was adamant that he was not fatigued. 'You must not concern yourself, madam.' The only time that either of them relaxed role was when he said, 'When we reach the border, I will deal with the guards.'

Eve was following their route on a map and knew that they were nearing the border with Spain. She began to feel almost sick with apprehension. Perhaps he sensed that.

He pulled into the side of the road and got out. 'I have *café au lait* in a vacuum flask. I think you would like some?'

It was here for a few minutes that their roles reversed. Removing his peaked cap, Mendoza poured two beakers of coffee. If he had looked forty in his cap, now, with very black hair receding on both sides of his head, he appeared to be nearer fifty. 'The border is no more than three kilometres ahead, Miss Anders. There should be no problems, but this is how we will do it. I shall open your door for you, you do not get out. The guards ask for the papers, I shall interpret for you. *You* do not get out, you hand me your papers and I shall give them to the guards.'

'OK.'

'Border guards have boring work, and they sometimes like to make their work appear important. However, they will find a beautiful woman more interesting than her papers; these are perfectly good, but if they ask too many questions, you may get out of the motor to walk around a little. Their eyes will follow you. You understand?'

'A bit of silk stocking?' she smiled. He did not. It had worked for Mata Hari, the famous seductress/spy of the last war, but she had gone a great deal further than a bit of silk stocking; in bed with the enemy, she was supposed to have beguiled secrets from them.

'Never address your chauffeur as "mister" or "*señor*". We are a little at ease here for a few minutes, but we are not social equals, *ever*. Assistance from a chauffeur is taken for granted, at the most a nod of acceptance, no more than that.'

'Thank you.'

'If you wish, maybe you should call me by my given name. It will serve the purpose in all circumstances. My name is –' The pronunciation he gave was 'Heysoos'.

Eve repeated it. 'Isn't that Jesus?'

'It is.'

'I have never known anyone with that name, except in the Bible. Isn't it a responsibility . . . I mean a kind of burden?'

'No, Miss Anders, it isn't so unusual in my culture. The Christchild wasn't the first Jesus, and there are many, many Marías.'

'Actually, I like the name as you say it – Heysoos.'

He stood up, replaced his cap and his seniority dropped away.

They entered Spain without incident.

In the sun, the Ritz's terracotta façade was impressive. Domed and balustraded, the hotel glowed in pale blue neon. Mendoza brought the motorcar to a halt, opened the door for Eve, then a uniformed doorman conducted her inside. Mendoza, with a porter on board, drove off to where the expensive luggage could be off-loaded.

Eve was surprised at how quickly the hotel had recovered from its wartime experiences, ready to welcome the return of patrons who had not ventured into the country until the General was safely installed.

Mendoza and the car disappeared and suddenly Eve was on her own, floating free. Her anxiety disappeared. The rush of adrenalin was something she recognised and welcomed. It made her alert and quick-thinking, and gave her the stimulus she loved. Eager, and in love with life. She was determined to work as much as she was able without the car, without Mendoza around. Peter had been right: her butterflies disappeared, but she remained tense and alert.

The well-turned-out manager appeared, expressing his pleasure. 'Allow me to attend to you myself.' He beckoned the reception clerk, who dealt quickly with Eve's papers.

'I shall conduct you to your suite, madame.' He led the way. 'As you requested, we have provided for you a personal maid, Nati, who has very good English. In the past, she was a tutor in department of languages.'

'Why would she leave a good post like that?'

'Since our recent difficulties, there are some things no longer quite as before.'

Eve said, 'Oh, really?' with convincing disinterest. Then, giving him a coy look: '*Gracias.*'

'Ah, you speak our language?'

With a touch of silly affectation she gave him a smile. 'I have a few words, and I have a dear little dictionary in my bag.'

With urbane graciousness, he asked, 'May I ask what is the second word madame has learned?'

'*Por favor.*' She pronounced it 'favour'. 'Is that right?'

'Almost, almost, madame – ff-*vor*.'

She repeated the word.

'That is very good, madame. Perhaps you will like for the maid to help you learn a little more.'

'Well, *gracias, señor*,' She made a show of being pleased with herself. 'What is your name?'

'Ah, madame, my name is my burden. It is Quixote.'

A little pause. 'Why is Ke-hotay a burden?'

'Quixote is the hero of a book, who, with his servant Sancho Panza –'

'Oh, you mean *The Man of La Mancha*! I just loved that book as a child. I always thought he was called "Quicksote".'

He was all affability. 'You see, madame, now you learned a little more of our language.'

A mental image flared in her mind of the blue fields of La Mancha, and the smell of lavender. In a second she had doused that little flame of memory.

The manager opened the door with a flourish appropriate to Eve Anders' accommodation. 'Your suite, madame.'

'It's delightful.' She went to the balcony where there were loungers, and a small table under a deep awning. In direct line of sight was another hotel, equally splendid and restored. She gave it no more than a passing glance although she knew from her briefing that it was likely to be a source of great interest to her. The Hotel Royale was the preferred hotel of German officials.

Within the sitting room, Quixote was giving orders which were acknowledged in a woman's voice: '*Sí, señor*', '*Lo comprendo, señor*', '*Sí, señor*'. The voice was quiet and cultured, and had what Eve thought were the accents of a Catalan. When she withdrew from the balcony, Quixote was standing waiting with a woman who could have been any age. Her face had the exhausted look that Eve herself had had when she'd first arrived in Australia, and there were a few grey streaks in her hair, but her chin and neck were still firm, indicating she was probably no more than thirty. She wore the neat uniform of a maid and held a folded towel over her arm.

'Madame, this is Nati.'

Nati gave a little bob of acknowledgement. There must be thousands of such women, Eve thought, now being knocked into a post-war humble shape.

Eve nodded her acceptance of Nati through Quixote. 'She can begin with my trunks straightaway and pressing any creased garments.'

Nati nodded and disappeared.

'She understood that OK.'

'You will find her very useful, madame.'

At last left alone, Eve poured a glass of fresh, chilled citrus juice and carried it to the balcony. The sun was well up but the awning shed a restful light. A radio that had been broadcasting classical guitar music now turned to news items, mostly concerning Spain's internal affairs, but there was an item concerning France which, it was said, would capitulate to Germany at any time. She would have liked to order her car to be sent for so that she could talk to Mendoza, but having just arrived she couldn't do that. 'Nati.'

Nati appeared, '*Señorita?*'

Eve was glad not to be addressed as 'madame'. 'Run me a cool bath and lay out some cream linen slacks and a short-sleeved jacket which you will find in my trunk.'

'*Sí, señorita.* Do you like bath salts?'

'Thank you – *gracias,* Nati.'

'Undergarments, *señorita?*'

'Anything you like.'

'The temperature is rising very much. Cotton would be best for you. Your country is cold?'

'Not in summer, but there are summer rains.'

Nati nodded and disappeared, and Eve heard water

thundering into the deep bath and smelled the evocative scent of oil of lavender. Having soaked for half an hour or so, she put on a cotton wrap and dark glasses and went back to sit in the shade of the green awning. At once her attention was caught by a flurry of activity outside the Hotel Royale. Three black, highly waxed long-bonneted limousines drew up and were immediately attended by the equivalent of Quixote and the rest of the other hotel's special guest entourage.

Her weeks of training held her in her relaxed pose; she might have been asleep for all the movement she made. But her eyes were open and her brain was active and memorising the men and the order in which they emerged from the motorcars. The first three were in formal but lightweight suits, the cloth of which, Eve guessed, contained a high proportion of silk. At this distance she could not see detail, but the high old-fashioned collars of the shirts were those favoured by well-off Germans – as were the motorcars.

The passengers of motors two and three were splendid in uniforms of dark blue and of grey. Flash illustrations of German military insignia memorised at Ryde told her that one was a general, one a navy commander, and four of lesser rank whose insignia were too far away to be certain.

She thought that this was something worth reporting to Electra, added to which she wanted to test her line of communication with 'Aunt Maureen'. She called the hotel exchange to book a line. When one became available she stood back in the darkened interior of her sitting room and watched the Hotel Royale whilst she told Electra that she had arrived safely and that the hotel was very satisfactory.

'I'm just sitting around on my balcony wearing only the smell of soap and Chanel, watching the world go by . . . Of course I'm wearing a bathrobe, you are funny . . . No, nothing of interest, just the odd cat and dog, and some very posh soldiers . . . How should I know what rank? . . . Very high, I should say – lovely military caps, grey and very shiny peaks . . . I'm not out here to find a husband, I'm here to do my book. Actually, I was more interested in the lovely cars . . .'

That banal conversation should have satisfied any eavesdropper of her bona fides. She hooked the earpiece on its holder and went back to her chair on the balcony.

Dressed for the part with flat shoes and carrying a camera, Eve spent the latter, and cooler, part of her first day exploring the area surrounding the hotel. It was so strange being here again, seeing the city from a new perspective, walking the streets instead of manoeuvring a big truck through them. Inside the hotel there was an atmosphere of quiet luxury – easy to be seduced into the life.

At dinner Eve chose a table where she could watch who came and went in the dining room, without being easily seen herself. As far as she could tell, the guests were mostly Spanish, a few Portuguese and an aristocratic-looking Frenchman. If there were SIS agents here, she couldn't pick them out. David had said that it wasn't likely that there would be. But how would David know? The regular secret services, being suspicious of The Bureau and its radical methods, weren't likely to jeopardise their own operations because of some mistake made by a raw recruit to the maverick branch. That Winston Churchill had seen the success of irregular agents used by the Boers did nothing to recommend The Bureau and its special operatives to MI5 and MI6.

Eve spent an hour in the lounge, reading a novel and sipping a brandy with ice, a mix which made the waiter assume that she was American, then went to bed feeling tired, but did not sleep well – her mind working on dreams of being suddenly naked in a well-dressed crowd.

The next two days went well. She settled into the routine of the hotel, the food and wine were good, the waiters attentive. If she would be remembered by anyone, it would more likely to be by kitchen and domestic staff.

The third day was hot well before noon, so she bathed and sat on the balcony wearing a headscarf and beach-wrap and a pair of dark sunglasses. She had had another bad night when she had even more vivid dreams of being seated at dinner and the whole restaurant erupting in laughter at her nakedness except for custard dripping from her face. She had called Electra, who wasn't much comfort. 'Egg on your face, Eve. Don't let it worry you, I never do.'

What happened while she was sitting there was a bit unnerving. A sporty motorcar was driven slowly past the two hotels a couple of times, and was then parked a hundred yards or so past the entrance to the Hotel Royale. A woman wearing very dark sunglasses and in a dark dress, with a kerchief tied loosely around her head and neck, got out of the driver's seat and leaned against the bonnet. After a minute she lit up a cigarette. After another minute, propped against the wheel-guard, smoking her cigarette, the woman reached into the glove-compartment, brought out a large hand-held camera, and took several shots of the Ritz, including where Eve was seated basking in the sun. Eve remained in her dozing position until the woman drove off. It was easy to misread situations. Perhaps the woman was a journalist? Tourist?

Eve dismissed the incident from her mind until late that evening when Nati brought up a large envelope on which was written 'By Hand. Miss Anders, Ritz Hotel'.

What the envelope contained was quite chilling: an enlargement of a section of photograph obviously taken by the woman in the sports car. It might have been a photo of anyone. But not anywhere. In one corner was a small portion of the distinctive entrance to the Madrid Ritz. Eve turned the picture over. 'There is a little-known but delightful English tearoom (it is no longer known by its old name) in Montefiore Square, close to a very photogenic little church. 16.00 hrs is a good time to be there. Perhaps tomorrow? Un-English street tables in shade.' There was not even an initial, and the handwriting was not familiar. Eve ordered Mendoza to bring the car round early in the morning.

Oddly enough, that night she slept soundly.

Mendoza examined the photo and the message.

'Were you aware that this was being taken?'

'Yes, by a woman. I had a moment of wondering if it was me she was photographing, but then I thought I was being paranoid.'

They had driven well out of the city and had stopped where it was quiet. He had brought iced *limonada*, which Eve drank gratefully as the sun was already up and drying. 'There is little between suspicion and paranoia, Miss Anders,' Mendoza smiled. 'One doesn't need to look under the bed at night, but it is reassuring to know that there is no one there.' He smiled.

'I'll remember that.'

Tapping the photo he asked, 'What did she look like?'

'About my height, quite elegant in her movements – no, not elegant, I'd say languid. What I mean is that she wasn't surreptitious. Dark frock – probably green. She lit one cigarette from another. A large wristwatch on her right hand – could be a man's watch. The headscarf she wore was tied loosely under the chin as an English woman walking her dogs would; probably not American, they usually tie at the back of the neck . . . certainly not tightly under the chin as Spanish women do. I think the car was an Español Suissa. I couldn't see the registration number. I think the car was wine-coloured.'

'Not green, and you are not colour-blind?'

'No, I'm not. But I *was* wearing dark glasses. And I could hardly take them off once she started taking photos.'

He nodded. 'So I am to take you to Montefiore Square.'

'Yes.' Not what he said, but his tone made Eve feel tetchy. 'That's all right with you, isn't it?'

'This is your operation,' he smiled. 'I go with you for the ride.'

'I'm going to take Nati. So please turn round and tell them to send her down.'

'Why?'

She was feeling edgy and uncertain; couldn't interpret Mendoza's mood. Perhaps because she had spent too little time with him. He shouldn't have asked her 'Why?' This was her operation.

'She could be very useful. She speaks good English and I am supposed not to understand Spanish, so I want to take her about with me as my interpreter. How honestly she interprets will show how far I can trust her. If you take her round to the kitchens or whatever servants are supposed to do whilst they are waiting around, it will give you a chance to talk to her, see if she tells you the same as she has told me.'

'Which is what?'

'Nothing much.'

'You don't trust her?'

'I don't trust anybody.'

He looked at her briefly as he turned the car, and smiled. 'That is the first rule of secret work.'

Mendoza knew Montefiore Square.

'Will you please stop the car right here, bring my photographic equipment and follow me? Nati, you stay where you are.' As Eve stepped out, the heat rose up from the stones and hit her a blow that was almost physical, only deflected by the shade of an ancient fig tree. When Mendoza reached where she stood looking up into the dark green canopy, she almost snatched one of the bags from him and began to adjust the mechanism without looking in his direction.

He started to say something but she stopped him. 'Just shut up and listen . . . please. Now, d'you see that car? That's the woman's car or its twin.'

'It is not a very feminine motor, not at all a lady's choice.'

'Really? It could be my choice. Maybe you don't know modern women, Mendoza.'

'True, madame.'

Mendoza was beginning to irritate her. She had met the type on too many occasions: put a woman in even a slightly elevated position and they couldn't deal with it. He might be her superior within The Bureau, but he didn't like the reality of taking orders from a woman.

There were few people at the outside tables, which wasn't surprising as it was hardly out of siesta time and shops were only just opening up. So Eve chose a table where no one could come and sit behind her. The buttoned chintz-covered cushions on the rattan chairs were warm and had probably been in use since the days when English tourists frequented Madrid. A waiter, with black hair taken straight back and slick with oil, came and said '*Señorita,* you lake to order tea?' His attempt at a man's hairdo made him appear younger than the boy he still was.

'You speak English.'

'I am learning, madame. If you will order in English, *por favor*, it will be bad for me . . . Sorry, *señorita,* will be *good* for me. I am José. English is Joe.'

'All right, Joe, what shall I have?'

'You lake Earl Gay? We have him, also teacake, also Shelsea bun, also fruity cakes in slices, also small pretty cakes in papers. You understand OK?'

'Absolutely, I do. Small pretty cakes in English are "iced fancies".'

'*Sí*, madame, iced fantasies white and . . . ?'

'Pink?'

'*Sí, señorita.* Very sweet, weeth . . .' He struggled for the words but Eve guessed that there would be glacé cherries.

'Then I would like those and some Earl Grey tea.'

She sat back, enjoying the dappled light that gave the illusion of cool air, and lighted a cigarette. This was very nice. In a past life she had often stopped at some small café like this which the war had seemed not to have touched. It was surprising, though, to find one so close to the city.

'*Señorita?* Excuse me. Perhaps you are expecting to meet an English lady?'

Eve's smile faltered; she shook her head. 'Not me. Give my driver and maid some refreshment, *por favor.* You understand, José?'

'I do so, *señorita.* Very well I understand. *Gracias, señorita.*' Joe zipped smartly off, his small bottom tight as he tried to stop himself from running.

From behind her sunglasses Eve watched from the corner of her eye as a woman in a spotted frock and a large shady hat came out from the tearoom. This, Eve guessed, was the one she had come to meet here.

The woman took the seat opposite Eve and looked up from beneath the brim of the straw hat. 'Hello, Eve. Bet you a G & T you never expected it would be me.'

Eve didn't need to look at the woman. The voice was memorable, resonant of her entire war experience, of the lorry depot, the driving, the refuge, of Albacete, of Barcelona, of Madrid. Of the rare G & Ts, mugs of dreadful coffee and unexpected English tea, and of rare shared American cigarettes, smoked to their ends which were saved and rolled again. Helan Alexander. Eve's heart leaped with joy, then again with unease.

As coolly as she could, she smiled and shook hands, then pulled the glasses down her nose. 'Helan Alexander? Alex! I'm so pleased . . .'

The woman smiled and helped herself to a cigarette from Eve's silver case. 'Were you going to say, ". . . of all people"? Here, have one. I'll give you something to do with your hands.'

Eve laughed lightly. 'I expect I was going to say that. But I suppose I might have guessed seeing the Español Suissa.'

'You noticed?'

'Bet your darned life I noticed.'

'I move in exalted circles these days. All the right accoutrements are essential. Here, José, put the teapot on my side and then you can go. Just look at you, Eve. You look a million dollars.'

'Isn't it amazing what a bucketful of money will do?'

'I have a good many bucketsful, as you know, but I can never turn myself out like you.'

'You said they would allow you to stay on, but I didn't really believe it. You were supporting the other side.'

Helan Alexander – Alex – had been in charge of a depot that got supplies trucks fixed and out on the road again. It was an unusual job for a woman, until you saw Alex at work. Her husband had been Max Alexander, a coloured man with a Swiss passport, an intellectual revolutionary. Her family, the Poveys, were second only to the German Krupps in the manufacture of armaments. Alex had inherited the majority shareholding and become a wealthy woman by any standards. She had met Max and had caught all his revolutionary fervour, which was how she had come to be supporting the Republic against the invading fascists. Eve had heard all about Alex's guilty wealth.

And here she still was, large as life, living in this new fascist state.

'I might have the majority shareholding, but my grandfather, having seen the possibility that one day there might be an "unsuitable" Povey inheriting, saw to it that all decisions relating to the company who made machine guns and other death machines should be made by a board of managers. Nice move: he could rake in the profits and keep his hands clean.' She paused and drew deeply on her cigarette. 'And I'm a chip off the old block.'

'No you're not. You put money into those refuges.'

'A drop in the ocean, Eve. You wouldn't believe how many millions I have.'

'Even so . . . you worked openly in support of the Republic.'

'Just another upper-class rebel. Unity Mitford's back in the bosom of her family, isn't she?'

'Oh yes, she's back,' Eve said ruefully. 'Months ago. "The Storm-Trooper Maiden" who sat and gazed worshipfully at Hitler until he invited her to his table.'

'Well, that's it, isn't it? Lord Redesdale's wayward daughter, infatuated, misguided, led by the nose to follow a charismatic man. Silly girl. Isn't that what they say?'

Eve smiled. 'I suppose they do.'

'So I am the silly girl who fell in love with a black Communist. Same difference. If you are high-born enough, wealthy enough, you are without doubt a silly girl. When I wanted to buy my land, a couple of officials came to see me. All that was necessary was to eat humble pie and say that I was young and silly, and I was in love with Spain itself. I didn't really understand any of it, I just wanted a bit of excitement.'

'They obviously bought your story.'

'Of course. They hope that my family will open up a new factory in the industrial North. *And*, as I told them, my role here was just fixing lorries. I wasn't really involved.'

Eve knew that that wasn't true. She had been chauffeuse to Alex and the two Russian officers when they had come up from Albacete to Madrid on some inquiry.

'You don't have to justify yourself, Alex.'

'Is that what I'm doing? Yes, I suppose I am. Anyway, they now like me, and I can stay here as long as I like. Just don't get involved in any more silliness, Miss Povey. So I don't.'

Eve raised her eyebrows. 'So we met here quite by accident.'

'Of course. I come here whenever I am visiting Madrid, and I happened to see you and recognise somebody I once met at a skiing resort in Switzerland. Remember that? I expect I helped you fix your skis, and you sort of remembered me when you saw me today.'

'But, Alex, I don't know one end of a ski from another.'

Alex laughed, looked up and held her hands out to the sunlight. 'I doubt if you'll be put to the test here.'

'Do you live in Madrid?'

'No, much further south, on the coast of the sun, it's known as the "Jaws of Hell", or the "Frying Pan of Spain" – I prefer the "Jaws".'

'Seville?'

Alex Povey raised her eyebrows. 'Close. Ten out of ten for geography. Hot as Cairo without the people. I love it. You must visit. Now,' with mock fierceness, 'if Joe hasn't turned to stone, perhaps he will go tell his mother that a young friend from way back has suddenly appeared from nowhere and we want a proper English tea. *Comprendes, José?* Take away the pink cakes and we will have English fruity cake and then figs and cream.'

José jerked his attention back from the interesting scene. '*Sí, señora* . . . Alex . . . madame . . . *señorita* . . . at once.'

'When did you have figs and cream for tea in England, Alex?'

She smiled. 'If and when I go home I shall introduce it as a standard at Fullers.'

The serving of the two English ladies was taken over by a middle-aged woman whose lips looked tight and sore from any number of small scars. 'Carla, this is Miss Anders, who was a schoolgirl when I last saw her and look at her now. Carla is José's mother.'

Carla smiled with her eyes, holding her painful lips together, nodding acknowledgement as she laid out some delicate china and a whole Dundee cake cut into a fan of slices.

'Carla is bringing up her boys alone and wants them to learn English and French.' Carla nodded. 'So that they will be able to work in the best hotels.'

Carla put her head on one side and shrugged a little as though not counting any chickens.

Eve said, 'Your son does very well with his English. Has he been learning for very long?'

'About three months,' Alex said, momentarily touching the woman's hand. 'We are very pleased with him, aren't we, Carla?'

The woman nodded and brushed Alex's shoulder briefly, tenderly, and went away indoors as silently as she had come.

'Is she dumb?'

Alex nodded.

During her service with the International Brigade, Eve had seen any number of silent women, and men, in states of nervous collapse, empty-eyed and often as uncommunicative as Carla; the difference here was that Carla did have expression in her eyes. Alex had spoken only in English and the woman appeared to understand perfectly yet never responded at all, even though they appeared to have some kind of tender friendship.

Alex took over the tea table. People around lost interest. Now she spoke in a much lowered tone and smiled wryly. 'Are you still a men-only woman?'

Eve laid her dark glasses on the table and looked directly at Alex, who had once made a pass at her. 'Not even one man at the moment, but I'm still not interested – except as a friend, Alex.'

Alex laughed. 'I don't think I was serious at the time, but I was missing Max so much and I didn't really want to get involved with another man. What happened to the Great Bear?'

'Dimitri?'

'You certainly went overboard for each other.'

'Wartime romance.'

'They never last, Eve. They've either got a wife or they get themselves killed. But I do have a very interesting man in my life again.'

'Here? I mean, in Madrid?'

'No, he's bought the property adjacent to mine, down in the "Jaws of Hell". We have a lot in common – horses and sex.' She fanned her mouth and blew. 'Hot as Hell also. The strong, silent type. Nothing like the Great Bear.'

'Does he share your love of cracking motors?'

'Of course, though it's still horses for me. Now I have the beginnings of a stable. My ambition is to bring some great horses back into this country. Why don't you come down and visit?' The cigarette she had been smoking lay in the ashtray, but she absent-mindedly lit another. Eve noticed that her hand trembled slightly as she held the lighter. Alex saw her watching. 'I know,' she said, 'I *am* going to cut it down,' and gave a short laugh. Beckoning José, she said, 'How about you, Eve, a nice icy G & T?'

'I can never fancy it before evening.' Which of course wasn't true.

Carla, probably used to the way Alex liked her gin, sent out a tall glass, well filled. 'Thanks, José. Tell your mama she's a love.'

With a straight uncompromising look, Eve asked, 'Who told you where to find me?'

'You really don't need to know, Eve. Only that it is somebody who has your wellbeing at heart. Who else but me is going to get you into high society?'

'I don't like it, Alex. It's cloak-and-dagger stuff. You appear to know something about why I'm here, or at least how I came to be here, yet you get in touch with me in such an idiotic fashion.'

Alex sipped her drink appreciatively. 'I thought it was rather good. I thought you would appreciate it.'

The only likely person to have informed Alex was David Hatton. They were old friends.

'Don't be like that, Eve. I'm here to help. With me introducing you, it won't look like infiltration. Madrid's high society is very tight, which is why they are so pleased with the goose-steppers at the Hotel Royale, new people with plenty of money and the right ideas.'

'What about your old *left* ideas?'

'That's the past, my dear. If anyone is curious, I was a silly young thing whose head was turned when she fell in love with a dissident.'

Eve remembered how devastated Alex had been when Max was killed and she started drinking too much of the plentiful local wine. 'Also, they can't afford to throw you out,' she suggested.

'That's right. They need the Povey guns and bullets. *Everybody* in the world needs the Poveys.'

Eve remembered that Alex was the only Povey left.

How far could she trust her? After all, Alex had stayed on.

A little way off, away from the area of the visitors to the tea-room, of which there were very few, Eve could just see Mendoza and Nati, who appeared to be getting along very well.

Eve understood the old Alex, who had gone against all that her family stood for, a woman who had been on the side of the Republic during the war, had married a black man, a Communist.

'I'm out of my depth here, Alex.'

'You don't have to worry.'

'I'm not *worried*. I would just like a few explanations.'

'I can understand that. I think you should not have had me sprung upon you like this. Maybe somebody wants to see how you handle it.'

'Handle what?'

'This situation, an unexpected event. An important one.'

The only explanation to the 'situation' was that Alex was working for either The Bureau or MI6. Let it not be MI6.

'It's your own situation that concerns me. You seem to be living here quite as easily under the fascists as you did under the Republic.'

'I have to live somewhere, Eve. I think I'm needed here, both for my plans for horse breeding, and other things – like helping you, as I've been asked.'

'That's not what I mean.'

Eve attended to refilling their cups, hoping that this intense conversation would not be obvious, though Alex appeared relaxed enough. 'Why should these people trust you? They were the enemy, for God's sake.'

'Money, Eve. That and the fact that my family still trades in the armaments that helped get the fascists back into power is in my favour. Then there are the orphanages

– they are still thriving. There aren't many who are even curious about me. I'm a wealthy woman washed up on the shores, and I'm good value for money . . . people like me.'

'Of course, I like you too, Alex. I'll like you a lot more when I know who asked you to contact me.'

'You know I'm not going to tell you that. Be patient. What are you doing with yourself all day?'

'Taking photographs for a special book on flowers.'

Alex gave a derisive snort. 'Just what the world wants now, a book on flowers. That certainly puts you on the fluffy-headed girl list. Perfect. What we now have to do is to get you into Madrid society. You can meet my new man – he's not exactly *mine* but we make a great partnership with our Lipizzaners,' she lowered her voice, 'and he's *wonderful* in bed. Not only is he amazingly beautiful, but young, young, young.'

Eve smiled. 'I'm pleased that you've got a nice man in your life.'

'Oh, he's not *nice*, Eve. He's an arrogant bastard who is equipped like his own stallion, and is just as much a thoroughbred. And he's a better businessman than I ever met.'

'He sounds like a Swiss army knife.'

'You can laugh. He had it figured out that there wouldn't be many decent horses left when the war ended.'

'So, you and the arrogant bastard have a common aim to replace the ones that went in the pot.'

'Spaniards love their beautiful horses. My man sees his fortune here.'

'He's Spanish?'

'Don't ask me. He says he's Egyptian. He's some kind of dago, the beautiful kind. He *says* he's come here from South America, where he picked up his string of mares and the stallion, Diabolo.'

'But you don't believe him?'

'No. His stallion is a Trakehner. It's my guess that he smuggled him out of Poland before the Germans laid hands on him. Worth his weight in gold.'

'I'm not sure whether you're smitten by the man or the horse.'

'They are an extension of one another. His hair is longer than the horse's tail, and he binds it like Diabolo's. They look down their long noses at the world – you'd think they were posing for an equestrian sculptor. But then I unbind his hair and it all changes. He becomes . . . oh, not feminine . . . different. You'd have to sleep with a man with long curling hair to know what I mean. His name is Paulo Fuentes – so he says – but I call the both of them Diabolo – the dark devils.' Alex smiled, pleased with herself.

Eve found herself thinking of Duke Barney, her own dark devil, who was always there, somewhere in her subconscious. 'I really think I should get back to my camera, or the light will be gone.'

'Will you come and visit me?'

'Of course I will. If only to see Diabolo and his beautiful master.'

'Hands off. He's not your type.'

Eve rose to leave, and as Alex bent forward to give her the double cheek kiss, she said quietly, 'You know that I've known David since we were kids. I also know Baz Faludi. It was Baz who told me to contact you.'

'Oh?'

'I'm Bureau.'

'Damn it, Alex, you always did like a bit of drama. Did we have to go through all this rigmarole?'

Alex laughed aloud. 'Oh yes, the Poveys love a bit of drama.'

'What happens now?'

'You will start receiving invitations to parties.'

The next few days followed the same pattern as those before Eve met Alex. Mendoza wasn't needed to drive, so he went into the city to keep tabs on the German party as they went about Madrid. Eve began taking Nati with her to interpret any request to take photographs of the flowers in private courtyards. They were always back in the hotel by the time the sun became unbearable, and Eve spent the hot hours resting or relaxing on her balcony, poring over the prints that Nati collected from a little specialist studio. Certainly the work was very good. These prints and what Eve gleaned from reference books drew her into a more genuine interest in the subject, so that it was not boring to spend so many hours at the Ritz.

Before dinner she had a drive out with Mendoza, but neither of them had much information to exchange.

The Germans, however, seemed to be having a high old time. Beautiful women in expensive clothes came and went and were often taken for drives in the big black cars. Theirs was as much a routine as her own and Mendoza's.

What were they all waiting for?

Was it really only to be on hand if the wayward ex-King of England should choose Spain when he fled his luxurious bolt hole?

But that was exactly why they were there: waiting to

persuade him to declare his support for the Third Reich, as he had done before Britain and Germany went to war with each other. Behind closed doors on both sides, it was believed that given half a chance he would try to make a pact for peace which would leave France, Poland, Belgium and Holland in the hands of Nazi Germany. If he was returned to the throne, civil war could easily break out in Britain, giving Germany good cause to step in and become the peacemaker. Hitler would have won the war that he'd started with hardly any cost to his people.

What a waste of resources. What a self-centred, self-indulgent couple the Windsors were. Old enough to be her parents and behaving like spoiled brats.

It couldn't be long now before they knew one way or another what they were going to do. The supposedly impenetrable fortifications protecting France had remained impenetrable – the German army had skirted round them and pressed on, towns and cities capitulating as it went.

Just a matter of time.

Occasionally, when she saw one of the Germans leave, Eve would grab her camera bag and follow in the direction he went. Mostly – as Mendoza too had discovered – they went to a place in the old town which was festooned with flags and swastikas, a propaganda office where Eve presumed they could send and receive messages with impunity. She did not hear from Alex, nor see the Español Suissa motorcar.

One day Eve was preparing to go out when Nati answered a knock on the door and said that Señor Quixote himself was asking to see her.

Señor Quixote was obviously extremely pleased with himself. 'Señorita Anders, there is an important emissary, Señor Hernandez, who is asking for you.'

'Oh?'

'Señor Hernandez is an official of the General's household in Madrid.'

Eve guessed that emissaries didn't come more important than that, so she asked that he be brought up. 'Coffee, juice maybe, Señor Quixote? I leave it to you.'

'Of course.' He bowed out, obviously very impressed that Eve should have such a visitor.

The visit was short and sweet and quite formal – no coffee or juice – just an invitation for Señorita Anders to view the restoration work of the gardens of the General's Madrid home that was being carried out under the supervision of the General's wife. Señorita Anders would probably wish to bring some cameras and film.

'That's wonderful, Señor Hernandez. Please say that I am honoured and will be delighted to see the new gardens.'

'It will be the General's pleasure to send a car for you. When is the best time – I mean for the favourable light?'

'Morning is best. Some flowers fade in the sun.'

'Would tomorrow be convenient to you?'

'It would.'

'Thank you, *señorita.* Tomorrow at seven?'

'Seven would be fine.'

Soon after the emissary left, Eve received a telephone message that her driver had brought her car up and was awaiting her. Mendoza had instituted this himself, so she went quickly down, festooned as usual with her photographic equipment. Mendoza sped away, taking a road to the south where they had not yet been, and, at a suitable place, parked.

'You apparently heard about my invitation.'

'No, what is that?'

'To photograph in the General's garden.'

'When did this happen?'

'Just before I learned that you were waiting. I thought that's why you arranged this drive.'

'That is excellent. I think you will not need me any longer. Bureau contact is working. I have orders to return to Lisbon.'

'Why?'

'I don't know, probably because I have given you a good report. I would not expect to know. The English do sometimes tend to treat their non-British agents with less understanding than they might.'

'How about the way I'm being treated? I didn't know a thing about them moving you. What are they doing, chucking me in at the deep end?'

'You may not have experience in the field, but you have been well trained. Your performance is excellent. I do not know anything about your true identity but Miss Anders is everything that she is supposed to be. You are not in at the deep end, as you say; you have been swimming very strong, and will continue to do so when I am gone.'

'Why do *you* think they're pulling you out?'

'It is possibly to do with the lady in the sports car. She mixes in the new high society. She has been forgiven her old ways. She is reformed and a friend of the new State. And she's one of the Bureau's trophies, I would think. It is probable that Miss Povey is a sleeper. You know what this is?'

'An agent who does nothing until they are awakened for some special work?'

'It is possible that London thinks that I am superfluous because they have awakened her – so I am recalled to Lisbon.'

'OK, but I've been glad to have you as a guardian angel. Out of curiosity, Mendoza, how have you been receiving your orders here?'

'You have an aunt in Ireland, I have a grandfather in Portugal. He is old and sick. I telephone him at night to make sure that he is no worse, and there is a mail delivery.' He gave her a flicker of a smile.

'What do you do when you are not being a Bureau person?'

'I am always a Bureau person. At home, we have a family business, taxi and car-hire. It excuses me when necessary. Also a bar – quite nice, respectable, an excellent place for exchange of information.'

'Why do you do it?'

'For God and my people. Fascists are anti-Christ. We, my family, believe in an old-fashioned ideal that Jesus of Nazareth preached: one world, one people, equality. He was the first Communist. I believe that. I live by that. What else is worth anything?'

'Should you be letting me know so much about yourself?'

'No. But there are times when one must put down a marker and let one other person know: this is me, this is where I stand, this is what I would die for.'

'Thank you.'

'And now, Miss Anders, you must dismiss me for some misdemeanour. I am to leave the car for you. Will you be able to drive it?'

'I could drive a tank given the chance.'

'Good. I think that you should drive yourself back to the hotel, make a show of anger, leave the car for the porter to take to the garages and stomp off in great indignation to change your clothes, because you will – or I will – have spilled coffee over them. You will not want to talk about what happened, only that I am dismissed. As far as you are concerned, I shall disappear, and you will not know or care.'

'OK.' And without warning she jumped out of her seat and into the road, sending the flask flying out of his hand with the coffee spilling over both of them.

He jumped back and saved the flask from falling. 'Well done, Miss Anders – without spilling a drop on the Buick's upholstery.'

'That would have been desecration.'

She drove back into the city and did not see Mendoza again.

The expedition to the General's gardens was a start to something Eve could never have instigated herself. Having spent a couple of hours being taken around the lovely grounds of the house, and photographed so many exotic climbing plants that she could have based a book on them alone, she was invited to join the aide to the General's lady, who was taking coffee on a beautiful veranda shaded with lush vegetation.

Here she was, in the lion's den. Supping with the devil.

That morning she had looked at herself in the mirror and wondered how she could do this. She hated everything the General and his regime stood for – their self-importance and arrogance in believing that they had an absolute right to rule. When Spain had gained democracy, the generals, bishops, judges and aristocrats had taken their wealth and abandoned Spain. The war had been about them – about their wanting to put an end to Spain's young democracy. And, with the aid of the fascists, it had happened.

Eve apologised for not having learned enough Spanish to converse, but the aide said that he did not mind because he liked to practise his English. When Eve was asked why she had chosen to stay at the Ritz and not the Hotel Royale she replied that she'd had no preference, other than that she had stayed in the Ritz in London.

'But the Ritz is out of fashion, not a very jolly place for such a pretty young woman, Miss Anders,' insisted the aide.

'Actually, I'm supposed to be working.'

'You must have parties. Too much work will give you lines before you are old. Maybe you British are too sober?'

Eve laughed. '*Señor*, I'm not British, but Irish.'

'No? But as far as I can judge, your English is very good.'

'We speak English in Ireland, and I was brought up in England.'

'Ah, is Ireland then not part of Britain? I am quite an ignoramus beyond my own country. Only Portugal I know.'

Of course. Portugal was where many of the old families fled when Spain became a republic.

'No, *señor*, it is not. The part I come from is not.' Here Eve's subconscious helped her to steer clear of the word 'republic'. 'Irish people love parties. We call them ceilidhs and we hold ceilidhs at the drop of a hat.' The setting up of a tripod camera to photograph the veranda was the most useful prop to hide behind. '"At the drop of a hat" means that we will take any excuse to enjoy a party.'

'Then you would like the Royale. There are always parties there.' Eve almost heard an invitation coming, which is what she had been hoping for since her arrival. It was obvious now that the Ritz was intent on keeping its dignity, whilst the Royale provided for a less stodgy clientele. 'I often hear the band playing.' Eve laughed to show how much she enjoyed the music.

Janet McKenzie had said Eve was a good actress because she could get inside the character. I am, she thought. I'm living this part. Loving it. If he starts talking politics, I will agree with him.

'Germans too will have parties "at the drop of a hat". This evening I shall be hosting a small cocktail party for the various visiting internationals. I think you would like it, if you care to come. Just cocktails, but we do like to . . . What shall I say? Men love their uniforms and the ladies their fine dresses. In recent times Madrid has seen no such occasions.'

'I love to dress up. Thank you, *señor*, I should really like to attend.'

'Then you shall receive an invitation. Probably the first of many.'

And so it was that at six o'clock, Eve, dressed to kill by Nati, and accompanied by her, walked the short distance between the two hotels. Almost the first person she saw on entering the lounge where the chatter was only outdone by the laughter, was Alex Povey. She looked stunning, wearing a shade of blue that offset her glittering necklace and drop earrings – sapphires, every one. Nor were Alex's jewels alone in the room; they were in the good company of diamonds, emeralds and rubies. Eve's rented fiery opal drops, as with her plain cream-coloured, short, flimsy chiffon frock, were all the more noticeable in comparison to the gaiety of the dresses worn by other women. She stood out as very modern.

Alex was the only person there who could have seen the slightest resemblance between the Eve of Barcelona and this one. In any case, it wasn't likely that any of this company had even been in the country at that time. These were people who had fled with their wealth, or been kicked out of the Republic. This was the new, same old gang of the right-wing.

McKenzie's voice in Eve's head turned her detestation to delight. A party . . . a party. A challenge . . . a challenge.

As the smart equerry who had called upon her at the Ritz came forward to welcome her, she took in the entire room. Her training came into its own: she fixed all the main points in her mind, especially the German military in resplendent uniforms.

This cocktail hour was not going to be easy, but it would be exciting, even fun.

'Miss Anders.'

'Señor Hernandez, good evening.' Then the aide who

had escorted her on the tour of the Franco gardens approached, and a waiter appeared with a tray of drinks. Eve chose an ungarnished pink gin, sipped it and nodded her appreciation of the flavour. London gin. The best. David Hatton had been the one to teach her about the many and varied gins, long ago and far away, when she'd been living another fantasy quite as bizarre as this, and entirely carefree.

'Let me introduce you to a few people. We Spaniards are very sociable people, we want visitors to enjoy our country. A young lady such as yourself must have a social life whilst you grace our city.'

Grace our city? It was all so Ruritanian and musty.

'To be working in Madrid, as I am, should be enough. It is so beautiful.'

Conducting her through the glittering gathering, the aide stopped at a group who were obviously dressed to go on to some grand occasion. 'Miss Anders, may I introduce Baron von Pfitzer.' The baron took her fingers as Eve had seen actors do in films set in old Austria, and barely brushed them with his lips. Von Pfitzer was as handsome as hell. Contempt for his politics was no protection against sexual response. She saw his eyes lower to her breasts.

The baron undertook to introduce Señorita Anders to some of his many acquaintances. Eve having apologised for understanding neither Spanish nor German, he said that they would start with only those with whom she could exchange gossip.

'Baron, I have no gossip.' She smiled prettily. 'I am a hardworking woman. I have a deadline to keep.' This he translated into German for a grand and mature lady as, 'Frau von Mentz, may I introduce Miss Anders, from Ireland. She says that she is a working lady who does not speak any language but her own.'

Observing that this was someone special, Eve gave a

tiny bob of a curtsy, inches short of what a duchess or princess would expect but sufficient to acknowledge that this woman had status.

'I speak some English, Miss Anders.' Frau von Mentz had a very clear and beautiful voice; perhaps she had been or was a singer. 'I vass in England many times when I vass a girl.'

'Did you like England?' Eve put two fingers over her lips in an innocent or apologetic gesture. 'Or maybe I shouldn't ask such a question now that we are at war with them.' That 'we' had come as inspiration. If Eire was not at war with Britain, it was not supporting it.

Frau von Mentz raised her eyebrows and pointed conspiratorially at Eve, leading her away from the group she had been with, taking en route another apéritif and indicating that Eve should do likewise. 'You don't tell no one. In the old days I loved it. When I vass young. You guess what my profession was?'

'Frau von Mentz, what do you mean, when you were young? If you don't mind me saying so, your complexion is wonderful and your figure very lithe.'

It was true. Only the confident way she held herself and took command gave her that air of maturity Eve had responded to.

'My dear working lady, how sweet of you to pay such compliments – you who have the face of an angel and the figure of Venus – well, a Venus that a woman might have painted or chiselled. Have you noticed how so many of these marble women have the thick, heavy body of the male with a delicate head and pudding breasts as an afterthought?'

'Oh yes, I've always wondered whether Greek sculptors preferred male bodies or had never studied a woman's body.'

Frau von Mentz's laugh was so hearty that it drew

glances. 'My dear Miss Anders, I can see that you and I will get along famously.'

You and I, von Mentz, most probably will. You, Frau von Mentz, will be a safer entrée into Madrid society than Alex Povey, Eve thought. As far as Eve could judge, Alex had not once glanced in her direction. She was in a circulating group who, by the amount of banter that seemed to be going on between them, looked on pretty friendly terms.

'I am told by the General's lady that you are interested in flowering trees?'

'Flowering climbing plants, actually, but really anything that is exotic and unknown back home.'

'Perhaps you would care to see my collection. Not climbing, but mountain and desert flowers grown in pottery.'

'I should like that, thank you.'

'Not that such plants would have much success in your country – so damp and green.'

'Gardeners like to look at what they cannot have, and they try. Many Victorian ferneries have been turned into cold houses for growing alpine plants. I can see those same people wanting to adapt with heat and light.'

'I will tell my husband that you are to be sent for at your convenience. I rise very early, if you would like to be out in the cool air of morning?'

'It has always been a time of day I like, even though mornings back home can be black and wet and cold. There is something about being up before the world starts turning.'

'I have never thought of it in those terms, but that is how I feel also. Perhaps you would like to join me very early one morning, and we could watch the sun rise?'

Hell! I could really like this woman, Eve thought. The liking appeared to be mutual. Useful to have a foot in the enemy camp. What could she do with it? She had, at present, not much idea.

Frau von Mentz looked around. 'The General's lady is not here.'

'I thought that it was her party.'

'It is, but not always is she able to leave the house. A pity.'

Why not always able to leave the house? Eve was keen to gather more information about the circle of high society she was infiltrating. If the Windsors did flee to Madrid, then this was the very society for them, and with the friendship of Frau von Mentz she could be well established by then.

'Have you worked out what I was doing in England all those times?'

'Are you a singer?'

'You are almost correct. I was a Shakespearean actress from when I was sixteen. Ophelia at almost her true age.'

'You gave it up?'

'I thought that I should before I was being offered the part of one of the witches.' It was a joke. Eve smiled. 'In fact I married the man who financed many of the productions. It was true love. I was soon widowed and I miss him.'

'How dreadful for you, and you so young.'

'He, alas, was not. A marriage of spring and winter, people said. We were very happy . . . and I have my present husband, who I would not miss quite as much. Come, my dear, let us join this noisy little crowd.'

The group was of mixed nationalities – two of them Italians, apparently adherents to Mussolini's cause – same brand of fascism, different coloured shirts.

This little group bewildered Eve, as only one of them spoke anything that she could understand, so she wandered out of that circle but away from Alex.

Frau von Mentz came up behind her and said, 'I

know who would like to meet you. She does not live in the city, but she is an English woman. Come.' She took Eve's hand.

'Miss Povey, I have brought you this intelligent and delightful speaker of English, I have taken a great liking to her, and so, I am certain, will you. Miss Eve Anders. I will not tell you about her – you must discover that for yourself – but I tell you, she knows a good statue when she sees one.'

Alex, who was standing with a group of fair and dark men, threw up her hands, one holding a cigarette, and kissed Eve on both cheeks. 'Ah, we meet again. Frau von Mentz, this young lady I knew when she was a titchy little thing learning to ski. Two days ago, she wanders into the English tearoom, a grown woman. I recognised her at once.' To Eve: 'I thought you would have moved on by now.'

'No, no. Look at this place – why would I want to move on? And, Frau von Mentz has invited me to watch the sun rise.'

'So, Miss grown-up Anders, tell us all. How did you come to impress Frida von Mentz with your knowledge of art?'

'Neither of us care for Venuses with the shoulders of discus throwers.'

'You hear that, Mikos?' She glanced at the short dark man beside her. 'Mikos is Greek. I could tell you the names of the rest of them, but you won't remember them – sauerkrauts and spaghetti.' She poked one or two of the men clustering around her in the chest.

They liked it, responding to her outrageous stereotyping. One, pointing back at her, said, 'And what are you then, Miss roast biff of England?'

'No, darling, I am an English crumpet. Don't you dare, Tietze, I said *cr*umpet.'

Tietze asked if Eve spoke any Spanish at all.

Alex replied for her. 'We aren't good at languages. We wait for you to learn ours. If you don't, hard luck, you'll never know what we are talking about. From now on, I shall talk to Miss Anders in our own tongue.' She captured a passing tray. 'Have another glass of wine, darling. It's the best. I'll bet you thought the Spanish can't make wine. They can, they do, but it doesn't travel. Spanish wine should be drunk only in this country. As you can see, Eve, these lads have been confirming this for an hour.' She raised her glass, 'To Señorita Anders, who must be welcomed into our circle because she knows a good statue when she sees one.'

Eve couldn't tell whether Alex was really tipsy, or was playing up to it. Then from behind Eve's back came a man's voice that stopped them all in their tracks. In Spanish, with an accent she did not recognise, he said, 'Stop it, Ladybird!' A sinewy, suntanned hand in a ribbed white cuff within a sleeve of fine black cloth reached across and removed Alex's glass from her hand. 'Excuse me.'

Eve was so unnerved, not only by the autocratic demand, but by the look on Alex's face, that she did not turn round, but side-stepped back into the company of von Pfitzer, who smiled warmly.

'Ah, that man, he is outrageous,' he said.

Somebody said something in Spanish about gypsies. A split second of icy silence was almost at once covered by the urbane Hernandez, chiding a little perhaps, who said in English, 'Señorita Povey's companion is a noted Argentinian horse-breeder. Spain welcomes him for that.'

As Eve allowed von Pfitzer to offer her a cigarette, she could still overhear Alex's whispered tirade: 'You've got a bloody cheek. I drink what I bloody well like, and as much as I bloody well like.'

'You know that you're going to be sorry. But you'll do as you please, like always.'

Eve didn't dare turn round for fear that Alex's horse-breeder might actually turn out to *be* Duke Barney, so entirely did this sound like him. If not very likely, it wasn't beyond the bounds of possibility. Life was always a series of coincidences.

The cocktail hour was over, so Eve dismissed Nati, who was waiting discreetly to chaperone her across the road, and allowed von Pfitzer to escort her back to the Ritz, where she left him as politely and quickly as she could.

Duke Barney *again*. The idea that he had leaped so clearly into her mind shook her because she believed that her complex feelings for him had, in Janet's terminology, been 'dealt with'.

If she could just have a few minutes with Janet McKenzie . . .

But that wasn't possible. Janet had helped in teaching Eve how to be calm in a crisis, but if all their work at The House by the Sea had not suppressed Duke Barney, better accept that he had greatly influenced her and that her first lover was still laying in wait round every corner.

Well, that was all right. She decided that the best treatment now was to enjoy a spectacular dinner with a great wine, and take her unquenched passion for Duke Barney to bed with her.

The maître d'hôtel was at his best when a guest asked him to suggest every course.

Quite late, as she was drifting off into sleep, the answer suddenly came to her. Duke! The Duke of Windsor. It was this one who must be playing with her subconscious.

It was a pleasant feeling to know that she had resolved something 'deep' on her own. She would let Janet McKenzie know when she got home.

Over the next days, Eve began to exchange her photographic project for the social life of Madrid, which was often centred around the Royale. This suited her purposes perfectly, as the people she was keeping watch on were very much part of that glittering socialising – the same people meeting one another at various venues. The baron took it upon himself to escort her if she needed an arm. Formal dinners, rather bohemian parties, which the Germans loved, even opera – Señorita Anders was included in everything that went on in Madrid.

Then, one day in July, her 'aunt' in Ireland telephoned her.

'Eve, darling, I've heard that the Castles are thinking of holidaying in Spain. I'm sure that you remember them.' 'The Castles' – Edward and Wallis Windsor.

'Of course I do, Aunt. Do you know where they are thinking of staying?'

'No, darling, but it was dear Bazil who told me, and you know Bazil – he's the first with all the gossip.'

So, now that the German army was closing in on the Côte d'Azur, the troublesome ex-king had chosen Spain.

Nati came up from the maids' quarters full of the gossip. The King of England was taking over several rooms at the Ritz, and storage space was being made ready for his belongings.

'He is coming here?'

'Yes, Señorita Anders, it is true. I have seen the porters making some secure space with locks. You think he has jewels to bring?'

'Probably.'

'They say that he is king, but his wife is not queen – is that correct, *señorita*?'

'He used to be king, but he is not now. He left England and went to live in France. His wife is not queen because she is American, and she has been married before. Kings can't marry divorced women.'

'But England is not a Roman Catholic country.'

'It's not, but the English bishops don't like divorced women any more than the Pope.'

'Thank you for explaining. You like more bath towels before the King takes all of those?'

Eve laughed aloud. What a good idea, to have a stock of towels against the invasion of the Windsors. 'I think I would like that, Nati.'

'Madame? You speak *inglés*, but you are Irish. Is that correct?' Eve nodded. 'Then what is your king's name?'

'There is no king of Ireland . . . not now.'

Nati continued almost obsessively with the neatness of the pile of towels. 'Then, *señorita*, is it that your country is a state . . . or maybe republic?'

Eve hesitated, momentarily curious as to Nati's response. 'Yes, it is a republic.'

'Spain was a republic for too little time. Then there was war.'

Eve's natural instinct was to respond to the young woman, to say something to show friendship. But who knew who or what this woman might be? There may be points to be won for snippets of information about guests. 'Oh yes, I know that, Nati, but that's all over now. Now do get on with those towels, and go and see if you can get in a stock before the honoured guests arrive.'

The Duke and Duchess of Windsor arrived in a huge motor – a Buick, same year as Eve's, but black bodywork and no retractable hood. The thin, peaked-face couple looked to Eve as small children do when playing at being big growns-ups in their daddy's motorcar. However, the proportions of motor to luggage went the other way, the vehicle being weighed down with leather valises, hatboxes and other cartons. In addition, there was a van, which appeared laden too.

It didn't seem that they were willing for any of it to be taken through the trade entrance.

The Duke's voice could be heard at a distance, high and petulant, whilst the Duchess's was unexpectedly soft for an American socialite. As it rose to where Eve was seated on her balcony, she stood to lean against the balustrade, indulging her curiosity about the new arrivals.

Across the way, she saw others do the same. Some of the Germans, now drinking long drinks and smoking cigarettes on a ground-floor veranda, she had got to know. Baron von Pfitzer appeared and waved to her; she waved back and picked up her camera. Planning to take the initiative and not wait to be invited, she went over to the Hotel Royale, passing the Duke and Duchess, standing by their car, discussing or arguing about which boxes should go where. The Duchess kept saying, 'We mustn't lose sight of them, David.' To which he replied in variations of, 'Of course not.' Neither of them took the slightest notice of Eve.

All the Germans stood formally as she walked into their territory. 'Baron, I know it's a bit of a cheek, but you have a much better view from here, so would you mind if . . .' She indicated her camera. The men shuffled chairs so as to give her the best position. At once she took several shots of the Windsors.

'May I?' Von Mentz held the camera tenderly. 'The very best.'

'Is it really? I hope so.'

'German, of course. Precision made.'

'Oh, then it must be the best. I asked a friend to choose. He said there was none better. Would you mind . . . ?' She pointed the lens at the group of high-ranking Germans she had seen arrive in uniform. They affably closed ranks by moving their chairs closer and posed cheerfully.

Then von Pfitzer asked her to take his seat so that he could photograph her with his friends. This was tricky, making her feel nervous, but being a flirty girl she wouldn't say no. She hoped that none of them noticed that when the flash bulb went off she moved her head so that the picture would be blurred. You never knew who might one day see it.

Eve's first time in the company of the famous couple was not in the Ritz, but at a formal dinner given in their honour. It was almost a matter of course that she was invited and was partnered by the baron. It was the most glittering occasion Eve had ever known in the short time she had been a visiting socialite in Madrid.

The jewellery she had brought with her was paste which, as Peter Follis had said, was acceptable for a woman travelling abroad; no wealthy woman would trust her real diamonds to a foreign bank, even less to a foreign hotel. The long-skirted gowns were adaptable, jackets and blousons could be swapped around, fashionable long scarves transformed. The colours were neutral: cream, ivory; the styles simple, which suited her spare figure and her near-white hair, which she usually controlled in a French pleat. She could never be accused of attempting to outshine the complicated fashion that cost the earth, but she could be charged with elegance.

The occasion was very formal, and seemed to Eve as stodgy as usually only the British and French could do, the latter with a touch more style. But now that Spain was being reformed as a dictatorship, the Spanish too were in the running for obsessive protocol. And like that of the Germans, because there was no democracy to temper them, the unwritten rules of the new regime were sinister.

A hush fell over the guests when Edward and Wallis entered the room, and all Eve's old feelings about the monarchy began to surface. If she had been twelve again, she would have gone and banged on her headmistress's door and told her it wasn't fair. But, oh, how well she had learned in those years. Now she could direct her protestations into a productive conduit. But it still wasn't fair that such a self-indulgent man should be able to hold more power than the people. Parliament could not declare war, but must tell the monarch that it needed permission to do so; only the monarch had the power to decide whether or not the country should be defended – and against whom.

Had he been crowned king, who could guess what kind of pact he might have wanted made with Hitler? Even the present king was cousin-close to Germans.

The baron, on whose arm Eve's hand rested, patted it and said, 'You are very silent, Miss Anders. You are nervous?'

'I am. I haven't ever been to such an important occasion.'

'And to meet the man who was once your king.'

'No, Baron, not *my* king.'

'Of course . . . but I am afraid that I have never been able to know one of those provinces from the other – what is British, what is Irish.'

'I should need paper and pen to explain. Anyhow, he's not anybody's king now.'

'I should like to know what he is doing here.'

I'll bet you would! she thought. Did he think he might prompt some speculation from her? She feigned ennui. 'Because this is a neutral country?'

'Then why not Switzerland?'

Now that Eve was in Spain for a real purpose, she was even more alert to every possibility, even that the playboy baron might be – what? An informer? A collaborator?

'Don't ask me, Baron. I'm not the type that takes much interest in that kind of thing. I leave that to you men.'

'You are a very beautiful and charming lady, Miss Anders – it is enough.'

'How sweet of you.' She gave him a lovely smile.

So, here at last was the purpose of the previous weeks of

waiting with nothing to report but high-ranking Germans and Italians racketing and – she supposed – plotting.

And here was the man whose love life had caused her country so much trouble and expense. Seeing him in the flesh, it was hard to believe that he had had the guts to stand up to so many powerful people, not least of whom were his imperious and cold mother and aloof father.

To put it kindly, he was not a substantial man, nor a man who looked at ease. His features were boyish – no wonder he liked to dress in impressive military uniforms.

The Duchess was very thin, perfect for the bias-cut, long-sleeved gown of sapphire blue. Artful gathers from neck to below the bosom gave Wallis a femininity that surprised Eve. As Wallis Simpson, the seducer, divorcée, snatcher of kings, she had been given hell by the newspapers. But Eve didn't see this now; the Duchess had a warmth in her eyes that revealed a very different woman from the harlot. Maybe Eve warmed to her because they had both chosen to wear the most simple of dinner gowns, and wore their hair stretched back so as to reveal the bones of the face. Hers were strong. As she passed by, the Duchess turned and nodded formally. This woman was no fool – Eve guessed that she had taken in every detail of the cream gown and white hair – and the paste earrings.

Seeing the couple here being fêted with such energy, the thought suddenly occurred to Eve that instead of castigating Wallis Simpson for her part in destroying her husband as king, the British people should acknowledge her as the woman who saved them from a fascist monarch.

Seeing the wooing of this couple in real life, she understood why the Germans would move heaven and earth to persuade him to be their trophy. Now she understood how important her role was.

That evening was the first of many when she was in close contact with the celebrated couple. They adored parties. And so did Señorita Anders, who was never short of an invitation or an escort.

It was soon accepted that the reason she hardly touched alcohol – except a little champagne – was that it ruined a woman's complexion. Certainly nobody minded; she was no less fun without it. She allowed people to teach her a little Spanish, which she picked up amazingly well. All in all, Eve had become part of the social set.

Being entertained was all that she now knew.

Her refuge was the suite at the Ritz, and her growing like of Nati.

Nati was a wonderful source of information. Gossip it may have been, but Eve, who as a girl had worked with dozens of other girls, knew that a snowball of gossip was always centred around a stone of fact.

'Madame, you know what it is said about these people you know . . . this royal people?' Nati said one afternoon while Eve took her siesta and Nati manicured her nails.

'Oh, Nati, do tell. Is it scandalous?'

'Not in such a way as naughty bad, but not so easy to believe. These guests are making a fuss about – you will not guess.'

'Not in a million years.'

'Is about sheets, bed things.'

'Bed things? The linen here is excellent – always fresh and clean. What can they have to complain about?'

'No, Señorita Anders, not the hotel linen. You know that the auto they arrive in is really *so* big, but even so, it could not take any more things . . . they have their clothes and all that stuff . . . so they must leave behind them damask sheets and covers. The Duchess is very, very cross; she is shouting and telephoning and calling people names. The King too, he has made some English important people come to their suite and tells them that they *must* rescue the linen.'

Eve was fascinated; servants seldom got it wrong. She had known old ladies who had been in service. 'If you're there in the room adding coals to the fire, or handing round tea, they don't even notice you.'

'Juicy gossip, Nati, keep me up to date. The story of the missing sheets is fascinating.'

'Señorita Anders, I hope you will not be offended if I say this. As with the King and his wife, I too was forced to run – when the war was here. I ran with my children to my mother and father who live here. I could bring nothing; but, you know, it is good enough that we are not killed by bombs. We are alive. Sheets! Hey, what for do they want sheets? They can buy more.'

Eve Anders could have agreed. Not so Señorita Anders. This rich lady would have more in common with Edward and Wallis than with Nati. Nati had aroused her curiosity and she wanted to know what had happened here after she and Dimitri had escaped, but she had to show only casual interest. 'Where is your husband, Nati?' She concentrated on Nati's buffing of her nails.

'I don't know. It is possible that he is in a prison camp.'

'What did he do?'

'Julio was a soldier.'

'But the war finished ages ago, didn't it?'

'Not so long, *señorita*.'

'But surely, if he is in prison, he will eventually be freed, when he has served his sentence? What has he done that is so bad?'

'There is no sentence, Señorita Anders. He was a soldier, a leader. He is a danger to our new government.'

'Nati, nobody is imprisoned for ever. Come on, look on the bright side, he might walk in at any time.' It was hateful to Eve to talk in such a shallow way, when she knew that a leader who was a danger to the Franco government had a slim chance of walking anywhere.

'I am sorry, madame, I should not talk about any of this.'

'Nonsense, Nati. I really do want to hear about you. Please tell me. Who knows, maybe I can ask somebody about him?'

Nati suddenly went pale and wide-eyed. 'No, Señorita Anders, no. Please do not. Please, I have already said more than is sensible.'

If Nati *was* a hotel informer, then Eve must be extremely careful that Nati was not working towards an exchange of confidences. After all, Eve's position here was not invulnerable. It would not take too many telephone enquiries to demolish her cover. But the mere suggestion that Eve would try to help had put a bolt of fear through the woman. Nobody could fake that.

Eve didn't show any further interest in Nati and Julio for the moment, but left it for a few days until a morning when Nati was massaging almond oil into Eve's shoulders. 'Nati, tell me about Julio. I too have had my heart broken because my man has gone.'

'He is dead?'

'No, but as good as to me. He has found someone else.'

'He must be *un imbécil*.'

'Thank you, Nati, I am glad you agree. Never mind, I'm much better off without him.'

'You will find a better man.'

'But there isn't a better one for you than Julio.'

'No. We have two children together.'

'That must be a great comfort.'

'Except that *mi padre* . . . my papa wants to take them from me.'

'Why?'

'Because of Julio. I fell in love with him. He fell in love

with me. I was a student teacher in Barcelona. Julio is *socialista*, a lawyer – I think that is the right English name?' Eve just murmured, not wanting to break the intimate spell. 'Our home was in Barcelona, it was bad, but it was our home. I thought that if I stayed there with the children, we should not get lost from one another. You understand?'

'I think so. Julio might not know where to find you?'

'It was terrible chaos. How could I say where we were? I did not know where he was fighting. Everyone knew that the end of the Republic had come. One day Julio telephones me. "Nati," he says, "the people are leaving. Go to Madrid. Your papa will protect you for the sake of the children."'

The people are leaving.

Four words that for a moment plunged Eve back into that same city of Barcelona. The tension as the battle-front came to the very outskirts of Barcelona, then the depression of defeat and the end of Spain's few years of democratic government. *The people are leaving*, and Eve had been one.

'Didn't Julio say anything about himself?'

'Of course not, Señorita Anders. If I do not know what he is doing, I cannot tell. My husband was good lawyer; he would have enemies.'

'So why are you not teaching? Why work as a maid?'

'Believe me, *señorita*, it is only because my father has friends who have obligations that I work at all. My father believes that if Julio is against the General, then I shall be also. My father is CEDA – which is the Catholic *confederación*. In my country everyone joins a party, even a religious one. This causes trouble, as with Julio and my papa.'

Eve could feel the harsh and the gentle emotions through Nati's massaging fingers. At the mention of CEDA her fingers became rigid. Then, as she mentioned her children, she wiped the oil away gently. 'Please turn to lay on your back.'

It was hard not to put arms around the worn-out woman. 'Tell me about your children, Nati.'

'My children are boys, two. My father will keep them with him to continue the Alcane name – not Julio's name, but my father's. And what can I say? I have nothing, I need to work. The *confederación* cares for its own. I married a man who loved the Republic and would fight for it. My father? He wanted the old days to return. And so . . .' she shrugged resignedly, 'they have returned – and I can no longer be a teacher. My father gets me work as a personal maid. I am better off than many.'

'You can do better as time goes on.'

'True, I am a useful English interpreter, am I not? Which is why Señor Quixote let me work here. I also know German and some French. I think Spain will keep out of European war. If my country is neutral, it will be useful to all sides . . . as you can see now. The English king comes to Ritz and Germans entertain him to dinner at Royale. Maybe we shall prosper with the war all around us.'

Eve sat up, pulled the bath sheet around her, and perched on the edge of the bed, her 'not fair' attitude barely under control. Eve the socialite was a strait-jacket. She disputed with Eve the feminist, who disputed with Eve the undercover agent. The three Eves compromised with a mildly spoken question. 'Is it all right for you to tell me about Julio? For goodness' sake, sit down or I'll rick my neck.'

Nati looked down at the knuckles of her hands, clasped in her lap. 'Julio would approve, *señorita.* My father was proud Catalonian, always opposed to the Republic. My father has olive presses, is petit bourgeois. He cannot help what he is, he cannot change, he was Falange.'

'What is that?' Eve knew the Falange all right. They had been the fifth column – clandestine, sniping, picking off their neighbours whilst they waited for the old order to return.

'Opposite way of thinking from Julio. When my husband was a student, he was against all that. You will not know of FUE – *Federación Universitaria de Estudiantes*, but it was union of students to be against dictatorship.'

A silence fell between them.

'Señorita Anders, I did say that I do not need help, but, truthfully, I must know about Julio. It is hell . . .' Nati's voice began to break, but she cleared her throat and continued. 'It may not make sense to you, but if I know what happened to him, no matter what it is, I can think of the future for my children and for me too. Children need to know about their father.'

'Yes . . . yes, I understand that.'

'Do you, madame?' Her tone was sceptical.

'Yes, Nati, I do. My father . . . I really don't see how I could . . . I mean, if Julio is in a prison camp, how can I . . . ?'

'Maybe you could ask a friend.'

'I don't have that kind of friend here.'

Nati drew breath, and said exhaling, 'You do, madame. The *señora* wearing the big hat you sat with at the English tearoom, if she knows the woman with no tongue, perhaps she could –'

Eve's stomach turned in fright. Nati thinks Alex could . . . She made herself calm down.

'What do you mean, the woman with no tongue?'

'Carla. She is the one. Her tongue is gone.'

'The woman who runs the tearoom?'

'You did not know that? I thought that you must know.' She paled and covered her mouth with her hand.

'Nati, this is hard enough as it is. What in hell's name are you talking about?'

Nati hesitated, then plunged in. 'Carla! You went to Carla's and you met the other lady, the English one. I could see that she knows Carla very well. I too know Carla.' Nati indicated with a fingernail zipped down the centre of her own tongue. 'Her man, he split Carla's tongue as she had split the Party and she could no more make speeches.'

Eve looked stunned.

'I see that you did not know this?'

No, Eve did not know this.

She was now confronted with a dilemma. If Nati suspected that she had gone to the English tearoom intending to meet Alex, and Alex knew Carla, then she, Eve, was not who she appeared to be. Cover blown.

She had to think quickly if she was to divert Nati from the truth of what she had seen. 'No, Nati, all that I know about the woman you say is Carla, is that the other woman, who I *did* know from when I was a girl, said I should say hello to the woman who made the cakes. How should I know about what was done to her? I just assumed she was being polite. I just thought . . . Oh hell, Nati! I thought she didn't speak because she couldn't understand what I was saying, or was being polite or something.'

The telephone rang and Nati jumped to answer it. 'There is a gentleman who asks to see you, *señorita.* He does not give his name.'

'Ask Reception to say that I am not available, but will be in thirty minutes, though I don't see why I should be if he won't give his name. Go down and ask if he would care to wait, and what he wants.'

When Nati returned she said that the man would wait in the writing room.

'What do you make of him, Nati?'

'Only that he has very good looks. Dark. Maybe he is from across there – Cairo, North Africa . . . His accent is bad. He is very correct and polite – but not stiff like the baron.'

'Wipe off the oil and help me get dressed. I'll have a

think about what you've said, but honestly, Nati, I don't see what I can do.'

Nati looked very nervous and anxious.

'It's all right, Nati, don't get yourself in such a stew. You don't have to be afraid. But what *is* all this about at the English tearoom.'

'*Señorita*, forgive me, I have made a mistake. It seemed so clear that if your friend knows Carla so well, then maybe there is a way to discover about Julio – because of the connection, you see?'

'Not really, Nati.'

'What is the English phrase – "holding on to straw"? I think that is what I am doing. I am forever thinking up devious ways of getting information. My father is once important in political affairs, but he would not move an ant to find Julio. He has Julio's sons – he does not want Julio.'

Eve was full of compassion for Nati, but as Señorita Anders she was supposed to be a stranger here.

'Nati, I wish that I could help you. I have to see who this man is who doesn't mind waiting. We can talk about this another time.' She took some notes from her purse. 'It is so sad for you, Nati. Will you buy your little boys something with this? Or will you have to explain to your father?'

'No, madame, he will be pleased that I am well thought of.'

'Good. You may go now. Take the rest of the day off – I will fix it with Señor Quixote. I'll get straight and go down to see who this mysterious man is.'

As soon as Nati had gone, Eve dressed, poured herself a large gin and tossed it off quite quickly, enjoying the woosh of the alcohol through her bloodstream, washing away the stress of the last half-hour. Then, picking up her pochette and camera, she went out to see who was calling.

Bazil Faludi, David Hatton and Dimitri Vladim were in Scotland, at the secret code and cipher department where Dimitri had a small section of his own, known as the Polish Sector.

'I have just heard from the PPS,' Faludi said. 'His Minister is very concerned. He's saying this is not something his Minister could possibly countenance; he means: "Fuck the Russians. They can't have their soldier back."'

Neither David nor Dimitri liked the joke – David because of the dozen possible repercussions, and Dimitri because he knew that, if he had really been discovered to be in Britain, the Russians would go to any lengths to make him return, whereupon he would be shot as a traitor or, if he was lucky, sent off to the Urals to dig for whatever dangerous mineral needed to be extracted.

Faludi said, 'I told the PPS that whatever the Minister says, I say, for the record, and with respect, that I don't care that we haven't got a leg to stand on.'

David didn't actually know whether Faludi was capable of being so forceful to a Minister's representative, but the matter *was* serious.

'There is no way that the bloody Russians are going to get their hands on a code-breaker as valuable as Major Vladim. He *is* the Polish Sector. Possession being nine-tenths of the law, he's ours. He's pumped full of information about The Bureau, he's loaded with our techniques and secrets and he has developed his own system . . . and in any case they have no *real* evidence that he ever came here. Last heard of, he was crossing the Spanish/French border, only to be lost in the fog of bureaucracy. They're fishing, Hatton; trying it on to see if we bite. He's not here, never was. Our answer is, "Never heard of him."'

'What concerns me, sir,' said David, 'is what if the Russians were to become our allies? An incident like this might blow up in our faces . . . not *ours* but in the FO's faces.'

'Is there anyone at the Foreign Office who expects them to come into the war on *our* side? Be sensible, Hatton. Germany and Russia are already winking at one another. Next thing you know, they'll be in bed together.'

David was becoming angry. Faludi had ordered him to come up to Scotland, not a clue what it was about, only to find Vladim already in the ante-room waiting, as ignorant of what was going on as himself.

Dimitri had sat through all this as though he wasn't one of 'the bloody Russians'; but now his heavy voice intruded. 'You gentlemen are . . . arse'oles, I think is the word. What do you think is on this chair, something you brought into the room on your shoe? Something you are ignoring? Do I smell? Am I an embarrassment to you? This pat-ball you are playing is with me. All that you have said is "Good morning". Lieutenant Hatton asked me why I was here. I have said that I did not know, and that is all we have said.'

Faludi looked disconcerted. 'I say, Major, no offence intended. It's just our way of getting down to things.'

'Is it so? Is not my way; I am courteous.'

'It is simply that speed is of the essence here.'

'Can you not be quick and courteous? I can be.'

'We are concerned for you, for your safety and welfare.'

'You are concerned for The Bureau, and not so much for this man here. I am valuable to you. I hold information you cannot get anywhere. In few months I have set up the Polish encoding and decoding section, now I work with others on encryption. I am not "bloody Russian". I have been senior officer in army, I was two years trained by GPU. In your country you have nothing like GPU. You are amateurs. Not worth the name secret agent, special agent, undercover operator.'

'You're right, Vladim, damn bad manners. It is because we *do* value you that we are pulling out all the stops to see that you cannot be used to bargain with. Now, I apologise. Let's start again. You have the gist of it from what has been said.'

'Gist of it? Why do you think I want a gist? I want entire information. How did this happen? Who has been loose with information? Only few people know who is Major Vladim. To all others, I am Lec Podsadowski, Polish refugee.'

David Hatton said, 'Look, Dimitri, I think the boss is right. Your people are just fishing. They will know by now that you went to Australia – we found you fairly easily – and I suspect that they've been fishing there too. They've nothing to lose by saying that they know where you are. I suspect that they don't.'

'Because I will not go back there does not mean that you people have hold on me. I am man who makes his own mind. I did not have to leave Spain as refugee, I made up my own mind. I know that when Lieutenant Hatton asks Eve to return, it is not so much her that you come fishing for, it is ex-GPU officer. A major in the Red Army with secret service training is a big fish for British. I know how it works, you see. It is what I would do myself. Shall I tell you?'

'Please do, Major,' Faludi answered.

'You know that the English woman and the Russian have close relationship. And you, Lieutenant, know her nature; you know she is idealistic woman; she has rules for herself which she cannot break. She would not leave those children to their fate – she *could* not. It is not in her nature to do so. Do you know what she had with her when she left Barcelona with the children? Some bread and a piece of fat meat – and she had a long kitchen knife that she had sharpened like a razor.'

Faludi and David let cigarette smoke drift through their fingers unnoticed as they pictured this young woman trying to escape from the awful dregs of the lost war, taking with her a disturbed girl and carrying a sick baby. What would she have done with that knife?

'One of the rules which she cannot break is that she must be loyal to her own people – I mean people with same beginnings as herself. She understands that my family in Ukraine is of high social standing – intellectuals . . . and accepts this has made me what I am now.

'My family always argue philosphy; I join army with ideals – Communist ideals. A political commissar – as you know – is what I was in Spain, sees everything, knows everything. On the fascist side, the Luftwaffe was practising blitzkrieg. On the side of Republic, my country was providing arms and some men, but we were stealing away raw materials. Spain needed those materials . . . May I have cigarette, please?'

The others hastily offered packets and lighters. Although there were files on the Russian, information was bald and speculative. But this narrative was like a newsreel; no, more than that, it was a reliving.

Faludi listened as the Russian continued, and for the first time saw how important to them all this man was. Red Army, GPU-trained, multi-linguist, and disillusioned with the Stalinist brand of socialism – Vladim must be kept out of Russian hands at all costs.

'Señorita Anders, your visitor has moved to the small sitting room, which is now cool and unoccupied. The afternoon waiter will take an order.'

Entering the room, she shivered, stopped in her tracks.

Duke Barney!

So different from the man of her dreams and day-dreams and memory. This Duke stopped her heart as much as he had when she saw him for the first time.

Adrenalin surged through her body, but she went gracefully towards him – dry-mouthed, pale, but steady on her high heels.

He stood as she approached. Well, he had learned some decent manners at last.

He took her hand. Then, cupping her face, he kissed her on both cheeks. 'Hello, Lu,' he said quietly, close to her ear.

Brief, formal kisses, his lips only just brushed her skin, yet all sensible thought and action was knocked out of her, as it had been that November night when she'd had her first experience of sex – passionate, lustful, greedy – better than anything she had known since.

Just as quietly she answered, 'Hello, Señor Fuentes.'

A boy waiter hovered.

Duke asked her, 'D'you want something to drink? Some juice or something?'

A deep breath. 'I'd like some orange juice, in a tall glass, with ice and vodka.'

'Bit early in the day, isn't it?'

'Have you become a white ribboner? Saving women from the demon drink? I'll order.'

'I'd like to buy the drinks. OK?' He smiled.

Who had taught him to do that?

'Not OK. I just sign for things here so, please, let me do it.'

'OK.'

She ordered, adding, '*La cuenta, por favor.*'

He shrugged; as when he'd worked on her aunt's smallholdings, he had no problem about taking money from a woman. In those days he would decide with 'toss you for it'.

It was approaching the hours of siesta, so the hotel was quiet and they had the shaded lounge to themselves. Weighing up one another, they sat so silently that the sound of the barman dropping ice into glasses could be clearly heard. Eve chose a small table where she could look across at the hotel opposite.

He even waited until she was seated. She smiled at him. 'Duke Barney, you're in danger of becoming a gentleman.'

'Brings in a better class of woman.' His eyes challenged and teased. 'Well, us two have been and got ourselves all grown up. What d'you think?'

'Of you?'

'A 'course.'

Eve, with her head on one side, allowed her eyes to scrutinise him from head to toe. 'You'll do, Duke Barney.'

'Will I do for you?'

'For me? In what way?'

'Any way you like.'

'I never took you for a flirt.'

'I an't no flirt.' He gave her a lop-sided smile. 'I'll

admit to bein' a bit flimsy about women who wants to pin me down.'

'Oh? Have there been many who have tried?'

'Ladybird – she'd like to, but she calls it going into partnership, pool our land and share our 'osses. Duke Barney in partnership, can you imagine that?'

'I assume you're talking about Alex Povey. So the answer's no, especially not with the *señora*. I've known you a lot longer than she has.'

'And that's a fact. You have to have grown up knowing that kind of side of somebody . . . like I know you wouldn't want to be seen wearing a weddin' band either.' He grinned. 'Hellfire, Lu, I just about bust through my pants seeing you there, all dolled up like the Queen of Sheba. You pay for dressing.'

'Well, thank *you*.'

'Oh, don't go getting all steamed up, it was supposed to be a compliment. I always used to wonder what you'd be like . . . because you always had the makings of a lady, even when you was a schoolgirl.' He sipped his drink, then laughed. 'Hellfire, you didn't half used to look down your nose.'

'That's good, coming from you. "King of the Gypsies"?'

'That's as far as I could see then. I never knew there was anything higher than that. But there is, Lu. There absolutely is.'

'Go on then, start telling me what you've been doing since I last saw you. *And stop calling me Lu!* God above! You must realise that I'm not here on holiday.'

'I know that.'

'Well, be sensible. Tell me what you've been up to.'

'I will if you'll stop looking across the bloody road. I don't know what you're looking for, but I an't sharing your attention with any bloody Krauts.'

He knew. He damned well knew. How much? It could only have been Alex.

'Mostly I've been in Argentina. You should see that place if you want to see the best of the best horses. What breeders there don't know about bloodstock isn't worth knowing. So, I bummed around there until I had done deals with half a dozen owners – all of them my own people a' course – and got a string of beautiful mares and my stud horse.'

'Diabolo?'

'Ladybird told you . . . she would. When she's had a drink, she never thinks. Telling *you* about my stud don't matter that much, but I got business rivals.'

'She must have told you about me.'

'When I dragged her off that evening when I saw you there . . . Bloody hell, Lu, I can't tell you what a shock that was. I didn't know what to do. Ladybird had had a few too many. I thought, if she wants to show me off to you . . . She likes to do that; I'm a sort of prize. Well, I an't going to look a gift horse in the mouth, and when she's not on the booze, she's all right. So I reckoned if I got her back up, she'd turn on me and you could get away.'

'I didn't even realise that it was you.'

'Just as well. I'd a' picked you up and run off with you.'

'You were telling me about your stud.'

'He's as beautiful as they come. He's not easy, but he's got the sort of spirit I need to start getting good horses back in this country.'

'You must be rolling in it.'

'I will be, mark my words.'

'I don't doubt that for one minute. I haven't forgotten the car you had waiting in our street the last time I saw you.'

Squaring his shoulders and half smiling, he said, 'That impressed you, didn't it?'

'Not only me – everybody in Lampeter Street.'

'I sold it straight after, made a better deal with one car

than with three horses – enough to get me to Argentina for six months – but hellfire, Lu, can you imagine making your money buying and selling lumps of metal?'

'But you got money to buy your new horses.'

'Not that easy. Come on, Lu, you seen my people doing their deals down in Wickham Square. Not easy, but fair deals; nobody cheats on their own.'

She nodded. Yes, yes, of course she remembered. The gypsy community horse trading. Duke's father, Eli, a gypsy who had married into the village and settled, was recognised by many in the travelling community as the one who was holder of the knowledge. By the time Duke was fourteen, Eli had taught his son everything there was to know about trading.

'Go on.'

'Don't tell Ladybird, but this breeding stock I got isn't entirely mine – except on paper. I went round all the best breeders I could find and said did they realise that because of the war the old Spanish stud-farms had gone to the wall. Well, some of them did, so I worked with them. So, I've done some deals where I bring some of their stock here and start breeding and selling. It's what the legals call a consortium. You heard of that?'

'Sort of, but I don't know how one works.'

'It's really just a bunch of people putting something into a pot and skimming off the cream when it comes up. They put in cash and stock; I put in cash and work, and experience. They know a good deal when they see one. One of the Argentine stockmen has already been to see, and he was pleased as punch. I reckon they'll be falling over themselves to put in a lot more. We can't lose, Lu. All that money that went out of this country has come back again.' He grinned over his drink. 'And don't these old Spaniards love their thoroughbreds.'

'So you're not a millionaire, then?'

'Not yet.'

'I believe Alex thinks so.'

'Let her think. If she knew I was part of a *ring* she wouldn't leave me alone. And I don't want nobody here on my doorstep having anything to do with it.'

'You mean to stay here?'

'While it suits me, a' course I do. I'd be a fool not to – cheap land, cheap labour, good contacts, open market.'

'It's a dictatorship, Duke, a fascist dictatorship.'

'So what?'

'So it believes that Spain would be well rid of gypsies and socialists and homosexuals.'

'I'm an Argentinian – it says so on my papers. Paulo Fuentes, born in Bahía Blanca twenty-seven years ago – give or take a year.'

'Give or take a place of birth. Bahía whatever-it-is is a long way from Hampshire.'

'So are you.'

'I'm not planning on staying here.'

'I never thought so. What's it all about . . . *Eve*?'

'Right! I'm glad you've got that. I stopped being Lu Wilmott years ago.'

'So why are you Eve, and why are you here flouncing around as though you owned the place and . . .' he stretched his neck and looked down her cleavage, 'and sweet and juicy and ready for pl-ucking?'

Ignoring his tweaking gesture she said, 'I'm working for the Government.' Leaning close, she whispered teasingly, 'I'm a spy.'

'I know that, woman. You're here watching the Germans, but you're not after their state secrets.'

Although she was shocked that he knew, she returned the ball casually. 'I thought you'd be impressed.'

'You're not half bad at it. When Ladybird turned on me and you walked off, I watched all the muscles at the back of your neck, and you stretched your neck like a horse that's about to get ghosted. But you settled yourself.'

'So you *were* impressed.'

He raised his dark eyes to meet hers. 'I've been impressed by Lu since I first saw her. Lu and Bar going down to the Swallit Pool to call up the spirits, all gold hair and white skin.

'Well, now she's working for the War Office. Listen, Duke, don't let's play fencing. Alex must have said something, so it's no use denying it. I have to trust you.'

'I hope that don't mean you think you can't. I'd kill for you, Lu.'

'No, I didn't really mean that. It's just that if I'm not telling you everything, it doesn't mean –'

'You don't need to tell me everything. Whatever it is, is costing them a pretty penny. Not that I mind. This is how you should always be dressed; if you belonged to me, it's how you would be. I'll tell you what I think. You're keeping an eye on what's going on over there, and Ladybird's keeping an eye on you. I don't care whether I'm right or wrong, only it's me now that's going to keep an eye on you.'

'No, Duke! Absolutely not! I don't need you or anyone else doing that. For God's sake, that's so patronising. You still don't believe that a woman can be your equal.'

'Ladybird need watching. It's why I turn up at those stupid dos with her. She thinks she's bullet-proof. Because she's got herself in with these people, she thinks it's all water under the bridge what she did in the war here. But if she gets found out they'll cash in her chips and it won't matter who her family are.'

'Oh, I know that all right. I spent the last two years of the war here.'

'You what? You was here in the war? Ladybird never let on about that.'

'Yes, yes, I was here.'

'My God, woman, if you don't take the cake. Go on, tell us.'

'It's how I met her – not at some skiing holiday when I was a girl, which is the story she's giving out.'

He laughed. 'There wasn't a lot of skiing in Portsmouth at the time.'

'I don't really want to talk about it.'

'You said you trust me.'

'You're about the one man in the world I do trust.'

'I should bloody well hope so.'

'I don't want to talk about when I was here in the war, because the end of it was so sickening and awful and I was scared to death.'

'OK, OK. All the same, you came back.'

'I have, and I won't make any sense to you because we see things differently. I've become a Red in my old age.'

'I heard about you rabble-rousing at the factory.'

'Duke, I'm a Marxist, if you know what that means.'

'No, nor do I want to. They're all the same to me.'

'Of course they're not.'

'You go and ask any of my kind anywhere in the world – England, Spain, America, Russia – they all think the same: Gypos get out.'

'Our country's different. Everybody can vote, *that's* what makes it worth keeping the fascists out.'

'You be a Red if you like. Me? I'll take the money.' He laughed out loud. 'I an't putting you down, Lu. It's that nice side to you I wish I had, but none of that washes with me.'

It was amazing to be sitting here with him, some of his rough corners a bit smoother, but essentially, the same amazing youth who had taken on any job to dig himself out of the disadvantages of his beginnings. What next? She didn't want to let him go. It was as though she had made a wish and it had been granted, except she hadn't *known* this was what she had wished for.

'My ma foretold that you and me would keep coming together.'

'She would have said it was the Fates. Or in the runes, or the stars. I always half believed what Ann told me.'

'Ma was right more often than not. Can I come upstairs with you?'

Eve tried not to hear that, concentrating on fixing a cigarette into a holder. 'It wasn't the palm-reading or the runes, Ann knew people – especially those around her.'

'I want us to do it again, Lu. Proper. In bed, with no clothes on. I want to see you like you was when you was that little spirit at Swallit Pool.'

This time she looked across at him.

'I'll even remember to call you Eve. My ma saw it as our Destiny.'

'Come off it, Duke, the little spirit of Swallit Pool grew up years ago.'

He laughed. 'And near broke my balls she had grown that lustful.'

He hung the 'Do Not Disturb' sign on the door to her suite and turned the key. Then, not giving a glance at the room, he put his arms round her and stood with his body pressed as close to hers as it had been the first time they had made their fierce kind of love.

She held him tightly, so that she could feel the pressure of his erection through her thin skirt. He opened her lips with his tongue and felt his way gently about her mouth. 'Bloody hell, I've died and gone to heaven. This is Lu Wilmott's mouth, nobody else's.'

'No it's not, it's Eve Anders' – get used to it.'

'Lu Wilmott's.'

'Is this a battle?'

'No. We got nothing to fight over.'

'You came here under false pretences.'

'You know me, woman, I'm damned good at not telling the whole truth.'

By now he was sitting on the bed, holding her between

his knees whilst undressing her, having no trouble with buttons and hooks, then moved her arm's length away. 'Now let's have a look at you.' She stood in the shadowed sunlight with a pool of warm silk garments about her ankles. Careless and willing, feminine and feeling desired to the limits of desirability, she let this lover of lovers run his hands over every inch of her, every mound, every valley, holding her breasts like fragile prizes, and running a fingertip through her pubic hair. 'This has changed, more of it, and darker red, thick as a fox's tail. I could come just looking at it.'

Madness. Eve Anders the idealist and feminist enjoyed this macho appraisement. She was her own woman, yet she wanted to be perfect for him, a man with no ideals that were like her own. She had never felt like this with Dimitri. Dimitri approved of her unconditionally. 'You used to have nice hair under your arms.' At once, she wanted to have hair grow there for him. Stepping towards him again, she said, 'I'm sorry, but that bit really *is* Eve Anders. She is a very modern beauty.'

He laughed. 'Now change places. You on the bed. You can lie back if you like.'

When he too was undressed he took a step back and with an open-handed gesture said, 'This all right for you now, Señorita Anders?'

His body was perfect and masculine. His skin, where it was kept screened from the sun, was pale olive colour, not as pale as she remembered; very sparse chest hair; large, dark nipples, their tips hard and prominent; a deep bellybutton from which a straight line of black hair went directly to the nest in his groin from which his slim, smooth erection protruded. She kept him standing there a full minute, then she lifted his testicles as he had lifted her breasts. 'Never a time when it wasn't all right for me, Duke Barney.'

In almost one single movement they were together and

in seconds had become the wonderful complete creature with two heads and eight limbs, that each separate half searched for constantly. Maybe they made a lot of noise, maybe they could be heard in the adjoining suites. Maybe the only sounds were those gasps of joy and gratification made close to one another's ears. They wouldn't know, absorbed as they were in one another.

He stayed for another hour, during which time they bathed one another in warm water, smelling of pines and coloured green. It was as near as they could get to the pool in which they had first looked at one another.

He dried and collected his clothes as she watched from the still water.

'Do you have to go back today? It's a long, hot drive.'

Sitting on the edge of the bath he fondled her gently. 'Don't tempt me, woman. I have people to see. Rich ones who want horses. In a few weeks' time more stock is coming in and I shall have every stall full and every mare served.'

'What will you say to Alex?'

'What do you want me to say to her – that we tried to make up, in a single afternoon, for all the years when we should a' been doing it to each other but didn't?'

'Be sensible. Will you tell her you've been to see me?'

'Why not? She don't own me.'

'I shall see you again before I go back home, when I visit Alex. It will be the winding up of my work here.'

'Stand up and I'll dry you off.'

He did so in long strokes of a hand towel. 'You comes up as good as gold. If I had a currycomb I'd give you a real finish.'

She gave him a little push. 'It will take a long time for me to get used to a good-humoured Duke Barney.'

'I don't often indulge openly in light-heartedness, miss, but I feel pretty good just now.' He slipped a hand between her legs. 'And so do you.'

'Either stop here, or stop that.'

'I just want to make sure you'll come down to my place. Anyways, you can't resist me, can you, Lu Wilmott?'

She reached round his neck and pulled his head close. 'Lu's safe enough – it's Eve Anders who has the problem.'

'Then I suppose I'd better get her name right.'

'Go on, get dressed if you're going to. Is it really "Jaws of Hell"?'

'Not half. It's why I like it. Land's cheap and so's labour, but don't go thinking you can get my workers into a union.'

'I'm over all that.'

'I want you to stay at my place. I'm proud of it. I want you to see it. Ladybird will understand that I knew you before you went on that skiing holiday.'

'You had better let me tell her. She's a good person, Duke.'

'I know that. But she can be bloody stupid. One night she'll have too much drink and she'll cry on the wrong shoulder.'

'Why don't you do what she wants, and join your two stables . . . businesses? Then you'd be there to keep her on the straight and narrow.'

'I'd have to be mad.'

'You need more capital to expand – she's got it. She'd be good for you.'

'She'd stop me wearing Durex and start knitting booties. She's a broody hen, Lu.'

'Why do you call her Ladybird?'

'First time I took her clothes off, she was wearing red knickers with black spots.'

'What's she like?'

'In bed?'

Eve shrugged her shoulders.

'Why do you want to know that? It don't mean anything.'

'I've heard that before – "It don't signify" – when you gave me the opal.'

'Nor it don't. What signifies is how people feel about each other. She's very good, but she's always thinking about old Max when we do it. She gives. She's generous. Not like you, *señorita*: when you wants it you take it. Never mind the poor bugger that takes your fancy.'

He held her in a close, tender embrace that she hadn't known he was capable of. 'Come on down. We've got to do something about ourselves. We've got to keep tabs on one another. I can't trust to Ma's Fate and Destiny. I do best with addresses.'

'I don't know, Duke. I won't know where I shall be.'

'D'you go home to Roman's?'

'No! I can't go there.'

'Why? Your family's there.'

'I haven't been in touch with them since I left, just the odd letter to let them know I'm still alive.'

'That's bad, Lu. You shouldn't a' done that.'

'That's only *your* opinion. Mine is that it was the only way I could get away from being held down by being a Lampeter Street factory girl.'

'I'm not going to let you go out of my life again. I don't care what you say. Will you just write a note sometimes and send it to me care of my ma? She won't tell nobody but she'll post it on.'

'She knows where you are?'

'A 'course she knows. We an't much for letter writing, but she knows I'm set up here.'

'I suppose you aren't going home to join up?'

'What do you think? England never did a thing for the likes of me. I'm not getting my legs shot off because some bloody officer can't read a map the right way up. Haven't you read what happened to us lower orders in the last war? Both sides the same. No fear. If they wants a war, let them get on with it. Look at that lot you were hobnobbing with the other night. They took their money and cleared off until it was safe to come back.'

She laughed delightedly. 'And Duke Barney is going to relieve them of some of it.'

'A lot of it.' He held her gently. 'Please come. I want to show off my place.'

'I want to. But I'm not my own boss now.'

'Are you married to somebody, Lu?'

'No. I simply meant that I take orders from the Government.'

'I meant who's been teaching you to fuck like that?'

'Duke Barney, how like a man to think that women need men to teach them.'

After he had gone, she sat on her balcony thinking of the promise she had made to look at his place.

She had obligation and loyalty to Dimitri and David Hatton, but it was Duke she wanted to be with.

But, not all the time.

Via the Electra grapevine Eve arranged for Janet McKenzie to telephone her. When she did, her Scottish accent was well evident. Some time, Eve would ask her whether this switch of accents had any significance.

'What d'y actually want from me, Eve?'

Eve related about meeting Duke, but couldn't find a secure way of talking about her concerns with Alex, only that she was worried about the health of a mutual friend of hers and David Hatton's who was drinking.

'It seems to me that you need y'r friend David to talk to you. I'll let him know at once. Y're doing well, Eve. Don't forget to keep up with your relaxing exercises. Out of interest, Eve, how *was* the sex with your man?'

'I'd need more superlatives than I can think of to tell you.'

'What a Glasgow man would say was a "guid seein' to".'

Eve laughed. 'Janet, you might be wearing your Scottish bonnet today, but that's coarse.'

'I know . . . but it was good, I can hear it in your voice. Don't you worry any about your risky friend.'

Later in the day, Eve received a note handed in at reception which Nati brought to her. The envelope was sealed with a small blob of wax. Nati watched with interest as Eve opened it.

'Is not bad news, *señorita*?'

'No, no.'

'It looks official, which to me is always bad news.'

'It is from the British Embassy. They have a query about my motorcar.'

'You need to go at once?'

'Perhaps I need permission to drive now that Mendoza has gone. I never thought.'

Nati believed that Mendoza had been overfamiliar. She had seen the coffee-stain on the skirt and thought it was the kind of thing that chauffeurs got up to. Below stairs Eve had, according to Nati, gained some cachet for throwing him out on the highway.

'Tell a porter to bring my car round to the front in fifteen minutes. I don't want to be arrested for driving illegally.' That was for sure.

Did fifteen minutes make it appear that she had been summoned to the embassy? Might it appear that way to people with nothing better to do than to watch what guests did and where they went? *Was* any member of the Ritz staff a potential informer? Eve worried. Perhaps she should have said that she would go after her siesta. There was a stone of anxiety in the pit of her stomach. It was probably nothing, but she wanted to know. Maybe it actually *was* about the car or her ability to drive. She carried a driving licence with her home address – in Ireland.

She hopped in the car and drove away too fast. Then

she remembered her yoga breathing exercises, which calmed her.

The letter got her into the embassy, then into the small room of an official who greeted her politely with her name only. 'Use my desk, Miss Anders. Your call will come through in about fifteen minutes. May I get you tea?'

'Thank you.'

'And biscuits?'

'Just some tea, please.'

She was more nervous here, on what was legally British soil, than mixing with the people at the Hotel Royale.

'Do you know . . . ?'

'No, Miss Anders.'

The tea was very good. It was more than likely that there was an expert tea maker in every British Embassy. She smiled inwardly at such levity. When at last the call came through, the shrill bell made her jump. She unhooked the earpiece and leaned towards the mouthpiece. A woman's voice. 'Miss Anders?'

'Yes.'

'A call from Portsmouth. Connecting you now.'

'Hello? Who is that?'

'Eve, it's me, David.'

'Right . . . oh good. Is it safe for me to talk?'

'Yes, on this line. Janet seems to think that you have a problem.'

'I have, *sir*, and it's of *your* making. What did you think you were doing including Alex in this?'

'Alex Povey?'

'Of course Alex Povey. She says she's Bureau and that you recommended her.'

'Oh God! That part's true. I've known her a long time, Eve. She's exactly the person to keep us posted on what the new regime is up to. So we regularised her situation and made her Bureau. As far as your op is concerned, she was supposed to let you get on with it. *Then* if you weren't getting into that set easily she would take you to one or two occasions.'

'Then why send me out here?'

'To be in Madrid. She's a hundred miles away. What she and you do are two entirely different things. She stays there quietly gathering information on the new government.'

'She's not quiet. She contacted me in a very weird way.'

'How, weird?'

Eve told him about the photograph and the outing to the tearoom.

'Oh God. I'm sorry, Eve. Yes, she would have got you into Madrid society if it proved necessary, a short cut, but it wouldn't have been done like some comic-book spy.'

'So part of it is true? She *is* Bureau?'

'Sort of . . . yes, Eve, but –'

'No buts, David, I'm furious. Only you could have told her that I was here. She may have put me in danger. Alex Povey's a liability. She's playing cloak-and-dagger stuff. *And* she's unravelling. She talks to her lover about being undercover, she drinks, she is unstable. I don't want her round me, David. She's too dangerous. I'm in with the people as you wanted. It's going really well, but I could have done it without Alex Povey's interference. You have to get her out of the picture until I can get home.'

'I don't –'

'Call her to London. If you plan on keeping her here somebody needs to read her the riot act.'

'She has all those horses.'

'I know she has, sir, but don't you think that I come first, before her damned horses? Her lover has a stud-farm, just along the coast from her stables – he will look after them. Sort it out, David.'

'All right, Eve. I can see the problem.'

'Move fast, David. Get the Embassy to call her in here

as you did me. And something else: by calling me in here I'll bet you that Intelligence will know who your Bureau agents are, but I won't have a clue who they are. You can tell Mr Faludi from me that I could do a better job than the ones doing it now . . . sir.'

Slamming the phone down, she sat back and heaved a sigh. Then wondered who might have been plugged in to the embassy switchboard.

The party was over. SIS men would know about Alex as well as herself. A bunch of schoolboys. She only hoped that if SIS here had been listening to her tirade, there was none resentful enough of Winston Churchill's cherished Bureau to put a spoke in its wheel.

She must watch her every move now, as they might be watching too.

A day later, Eve received a call from Alex.

'What do you think, Eve? I've been asked to visit London. David wants to see me. Exciting, isn't it?'

'What will happen to your mares?'

'Paulo will take them on, it will only be for a short time. He jumped at the opportunity. Anyone would think that he was interested in breeding Lipizzaners. It will do him good to do without me for a while. Hot him up again.'

Eve was gratified that Duke had not gone home and into the arms of Alex, nor had he told her about his visit to the Ritz.

'You'll be all right without me?'

'Yes, why not?'

'You aren't very responsive.'

'It seems rather sudden.'

'Afraid that I'll run off with David?'

'David Hatton? Not interested, Alex.'

'How did I get the impression that you and he –'

'I have no idea. He's just not my type. Have a good time in England.'

There now being no royalty in Spain, the great and rich, who had been in exile during the years of the Republic, found Edward a gift to grace their dinners, luncheons, fountain-pool parties, gatherings in some of the great houses that had been ill-used during their owners' absence. Society wanted to eliminate the bad years and bring back life as it had been.

Although she usually carried a loaded camera, Eve had all but given up her photographic expeditions. A glamorous and smiling woman will always get invitations to occasions such as these, and they put her right where she needed to be – where the Germans took every opportunity to renew their acquaintance with their Royal Highnesses, which was the title they were honoured with here.

The entourage staying at the Ritz was made up of close friends of Edward's, who had supported him during his short reign, and, Eve assumed, some SIS men. She began to spend breakfast and dinner times when she was there, trying to pick them out. Occasionally she met direct eye contact, from which she slid away with the disinterest and boredom of a pretty woman who gets too much attention from too many men.

The tension around the exiled couple was often electric. One way and another, Eve's path crossed theirs.

There must be no trespass on the neutrality of the new regime because of its value as a place of contact between enemies; yet it was clear that the Windsors were being courted by emissaries from Germany, and corralled by their British protectors. When they were in public, Edward appeared always to have the same friend hovering at his elbow, and another man who appeared to be perhaps a secretary to the friend. Maybe British Intelligence? Maybe.

Frau von Mentz was always willing to gossip. She was very promonarchy but, of course, under the circumstances of accepting the hospitality of the Spain of General Franco, she only barely hinted at this. She could, however, be a supporter of the rightful King of England. And the position of the von Mentzes as part of Madrid's exclusive set meant that they were always invited to any event His Royal Highness might attend. Herr Rudolph von Mentz was not as sociable as his wife, and was usually found on such occasions in a huddle with a number of cigar-smoking men.

'Who *is* that man?' Eve asked Frau von Mentz. 'He is everywhere.' Eve nodded in the direction of the man who seemed to have the ear of Edward. 'And the other man? I see them in my hotel.'

'He is a titled Englishman, a friend of the king from student days. I am told that he was the one who made the negotiations, he was always a supporter for Mrs Simpson to be Queen of England.' That referral to 'Mrs Simpson' might be an indication that von Mentz didn't entirely approve of 'the king's' wife. 'Who the second man is, I do not know. I do not know even his nationality. Probably British. He looks solid enough to be. A joke, my dear.'

Eve was a perfect ear for a gossip. She played dumb, knew nothing of the deviousness of kings and governments. 'Is it right that she wasn't allowed to be queen because she was American?'

'That was the least of it. She had been married twice – and was *still* married when she became his mistress.'

'She was his mistress when he was *king*?' Eve looked amusedly scandalised. 'How do you know?'

Frau von Mentz laughed and shook her head, then confided, 'My dear, the only people in the whole world not to know were his own people. The British have a most heavy-handed state censorship. This is why the people were so shocked when he announced that he would abdicate rather than give her up. Rudolph and I were living in Portugal at this time, and the American, French and German newspapers were all full of the Great Royal Scandal.'

'And that man – the one who is always with his Highness . . . ?'

'My opinion, for what it is worth, is that he has still the role of go-between.'

Eve, wide-eyed and eager to hear the gossip asked, 'Between whom?'

'Why do *you* imagine they are all here in Spain, my dear?' Frau von Mentz patted Eve's hand, and then indicated the room filled with her new-found acquaintances.

'I didn't imagine anything . . . enjoying the beautiful sun.'

'You would not do for the world of intrigue. The baron tries to persuade him – the friend – that the war between England and Germany could be ended at once in a settlement between both countries which would put King Edward back on the English throne.'

'Really? How do you know all these secrets?'

'They are not really secrets. All these people know why they are here – the king, the baron and his Austrian and German friends, and all those who keep close to His Royal Highness. And Rudolph, my husband. He has entertained them all at our hunting lodge. When His Royal Highness is in company, away from the eyes of the public, you know, he is drinking a lot and he likes to boast. He imagines himself making treaties and returning to his kingdom as the hero. They all encourage him. He is their trophy.'

'It's all very dramatic. It must be exciting, being so close to what is going on . . . at your hunting lodge and that kind of thing.'

'Oh no, not me. I refused to go. Rudolph is the one who likes intrigue and machinations.' Frau von Mentz laughed. 'Perhaps he sees himself as a king-maker. And after what happened, I am most pleased that I was *not* there. I hate hunting and all this stuff.'

'What happened?'

Von Mentz put a finger to her lips and raised her eyebrows conspiratorially. 'There was an incident.'

'With the Windsors?'

'Rudolph refused to say what happened. I believe that he . . . What is it you English say? He has eggs on his face? After two days they returned to the Ritz. Did you not notice anything?'

'Nothing. I didn't even realise that they were away from the hotel.' Eve lowered her voice. 'Was there trouble between them . . . you know . . . the Windsors?'

'Oh no, he is as besotted as a youth, and afraid for her safety. The baron was more forthcoming than Rudolph. It appears that a shot was fired – through one of the lodge's windows – not from a hunting rifle.'

Eve raised her eyebrows and allowed her jaw to drop. 'Are you saying that . . . ? Good Lord, how awful.'

'The bullet was found embedded in a dresser – Bavarian, rustic, but I do love it – definitely *not* from a hunting rifle, but from a different sort of firearm. The baron did explain to me, but I did not truly understand. A large window in the room where we eat has a hole in it.'

'Does the baron believe that it was an attempt at assassination?'

'He does not believe so. A serious attempt at assassination could have been achieved whilst they were on the terrace. He believes that it was meant as a warning.'

'Against what?'

'None of them appears to know. There *is* a rumour that London has decided that Edward is to be Governor-General of the Bahamas. The baron believes that the episode at Rudolph's lodge is the British secret service warning His Royal Highness that he must stop fraternising with the likes of Rudolph and the Austrians, and take the position.'

Eve drew down a worried frown and said nothing for a short while. Then: 'Can I ask you something?'

'Of course.'

'Some of the people who have been so friendly to me since I have been here . . . they don't all understand that being Irish – as I am – is very different from being *English.* My country is not part of the British Isles. I shouldn't like them to think –'

Frau von Mentz took Eve's hand between her own two cool palms and held it. 'Oh, my dear young friend, do you think that you might be in danger because of that one shot?'

'Could I be?'

'Not for a single minute. Politics and intrigue we leave to the men. We have more worthwhile lives to lead.'

So, at last Eve had something for The Bureau. No doubt there had been secret service men in the hunting party, but would they share the information with The Bureau?

The chatter in the room stopped and the little string orchestra struck up 'God Save the King', as was usual when the Windsors entered a gathering.

'Ah, here they are,' Frau von Mentz said, rising to her feet. 'You see? He has already been at the bottle.'

'Perhaps he needs Dutch courage. After all, his life's

not his own. I might need a stiff drink if I was under constant watch of everybody in the room.'

'I think not. You would behave as the Duchess does, in control of herself. Of course, she must be in control of HRH too.'

Together they watched as Edward accepted a cocktail. The Duchess was smiling at him, but Eve bet that she was signalling a look.

'I cannot but feel a little sorry for him,' von Mentz said, drawing Eve to another part of the room. 'His mother should never have had children. I knew her before – whilst she was still Princess May of Teck – a cold girl even then. May and the act of loving . . . one could never picture her with a man or a suckling child.'

Eve smiled; von Mentz was right about that. 'From her pictures she is very poised.'

'Men marry their mothers.'

'I can't see the similarity. Queen Mary has an hour-glass figure.'

'My dear, it is more subtle than that. Men want to be told what to do. In their ridiculous "no-women-admitted clubs", they eat nursery foods, especially the English and the Germans.'

Eve laughed delightedly. 'Oh, Frau von Mentz, you are so amusing to be with.'

'Thank you. I like youthful company. These rich old *señoras* are *so* stodgy. I think they must only tolerate my bohemian past because of Rudolph. He is *so* respectable,' she whispered close to Eve's ear, 'and wealthy. Now you must excuse me, I must remind Rudolph where we are dining, and you must run along and talk to some young men. You like the baron?'

A little taken aback, Eve replied, 'He is charming.'

'Don't you see these gatherings as strange? England and Germany are at war, the Germans have taken France, yet here we are all good friends.'

'I suppose you're right. I hadn't thought about it till now. I hope that Spain won't join in.'

'In *that* war? Oh, never. They have so much to gain by offering the two sides somewhere to talk about treaties. I hope that you decide to stay here for some while. These are interesting times.'

Before running along to find some young people, Eve wondered whether she should go back to book a call to Electra, or stay a little longer.

Frau von Mentz was a professional actress – perhaps she could tell that Eve was giving a performance. Maybe she had been feeding her all that gossip about the goings-on at the hunting lodge. Across the room, Eve saw her speaking to her husband, and they both looked in Eve's direction. Eve's immediate reaction was to transfer her gaze away from them, but instead she held her moment of consternation in check, and waved. Rudolph nodded a little bow and his wife gave a friendly little finger wave. Then they left together.

A mist of perspiration had sprung around her mouth, so Eve walked out of the room and up a short flight of stairs to the ladies' cloakroom, which was, thankfully, unoccupied.

She was seated at a dressing table cooling her face with some orange-blossom cologne on tissues, when the Duchess – accompanied by a companion Eve had seen before – came in and sat fanning herself with a pretty fan. Eve smiled and said, 'Excuse me . . . sorry . . . I'll make myself scarce.'

'Don't go on my account,' the Duchess said in her soft, warm American accent. 'It's a deal too hot to move fast. Maybe I'll try some of that you're using, it smells really great. Come on, sit down, I don't bite.' She patted the seat of a silk-covered antique chair next to her and nodded to the companion, who left. 'She'll make sure nobody disturbs me for ten minutes. She's a real good egg.'

Eve, not believing her luck, smiled and took out a lipstick to give her hands something to do. 'Thank you, Your Highness. I never thought you might bite.' And Eve sat down next to the Duchess.

'Not "Your Highness" – "Duchess" is OK. I've noticed you.'

Eve raised her eyebrows. 'Goodness. Have you really?'

'Sure, at the Ritz. Eve Anders, I'm told – you remind me of myself when I met my second husband.' She smiled, one of those faces that changes completely when the corners of the mouth turn up. 'Quite a few wrinkles ago now. But you have the kind of poise I had – still have, I hope.'

'Oh, absolutely, Duchess. It is what I admire in you – if you don't mind me saying that.'

'Oh, I don't mind at all. I'll tell you something for your diary – do girls still keep diaries?'

Eve was trying to balance enthusiasm with overeagerness. 'I do.'

'I still have my girly diary in which there's a quote from a "Real Woman" – my title for her – who I thought could give me a handle on womanhood. So you can have it for free. She told me, "Come hell or high water, hang on to your dignity, keep fit and your spine always in the vertical" – as you obviously do. You are beautifully slim. Only slim women can be stylish.'

'I think I could easily run to fat. It's not easy.'

'Of course it's not. I've never found anything worth having easy come by. But you shouldn't worry about becoming fat. You won't, you love fashion too much for that. One of the things I just might do when I am moved on from here is to design fashion. I have my favourite designers, but half the time it is my ideas they use. I think I might be quite good at it.'

'Why not try? You are so clever with clothes and

jewellery. A touch of class. Didn't you once say, "You can never be too rich or too thin"?'

The older woman smiled broadly. Her mouth was wide and generous, and her teeth very American – cared for and even. Too many photographs showed her appearing straight-faced and tight-lipped. 'You may be right. I say things and they are quoted; then again if I don't say anything I'm still quoted.'

'Does it worry you?'

'No point in worrying. Journalists are so powerful these days. Nobody to stop them. People in the spotlight will say, "I don't care – if they're writing stuff about me, they're not writing about somebody else." But that isn't true. The press will write anything about anyone for a buck – and it stinks.'

'Doesn't that make you feel that you can't trust the people around you?'

'I say, we are getting serious . . . but you're right.'

'I'm sorry. It is just so amazing sitting here with you. I want to ask you a hundred questions.' Eve put two fingers to her mouth in an ingenuous way. 'Not for the scandal sheets, I promise.'

The Duchess moved to one of the chairs at the dressing table and dropped orange-blossom cologne onto a tissue with which she patted her wrists.

'It's OK. You just can't let it get under your skin.' She touched her high, unlined forehead reflected in the mirror. 'Gives you lines.'

Eve gave a little laugh. 'Then you must practise what you put in your diary.'

'If you suspected that you might be kidnapped . . . ah . . . yes, kidnapped perhaps sounds a touch dramatic. Let's say *pressured* or *persuaded*, by being held in a remote place such as a hunting lodge, to high status and big, big bucks in return for being a kind of trophy to wave at the enemy – at the same time, the enemy (in more ways than one) had the power to whisk you off without the option *but* to a quiet life in the sun that was unutterably boring, which would you choose?'

'Some choice. If it actually *were* me *I* would be on the next passenger steamer or aeroplane to America.'

The Duchess gave her own reflection a faint smile and met Eve's eyes. 'Why America?'

Giving her a wry smile, Eve said, 'It's where you would fit in. And we *are* talking about you and His Royal Highness. It's all right for *me* to say that, but I guess you can't do it, can you, Duchess?'

'His Royal Highness has been offered Governor-General of the Bahamas. We would live in an exalted state there, but with nothing to do except entertain boring dignitaries. I know there isn't really a choice, but I wanted to hear myself say it aloud.'

The Duchess handed Eve a little greetings card, which Eve read aloud. '"Beware of the machinations of the British secret service. A Portuguese friend who has your interests at heart."' Eve read it again to herself, to commit the exact words to memory.

'This is not the first. There have been others which I destroyed. And recently a shot was fired.'

Eve did the same jaw-drop that she had done for von Mentz. 'Not at you?'

'No, but as a warning.'

'By the secret service?'

'I don't know. So many people are trying to influence us. I really didn't intend to get this far with you . . . but now you know.' She stood, as did Eve. 'Great to have met you, Eve.'

'Aren't you afraid?'

'Only of dying of boredom as wife of the Governor-General. I need people, friends, things happening. I need a *life*.'

'I'm so sorry.' Eve almost felt that she was.

The Duchess smiled. 'Don't ever fall in love with a king, Eve.'

'I think all the best ones are taken, Your Highness.'

A wry smile crossed the Duchess's face. 'You're a lovely girl, Eve. You're not looking for a position as a companion, I suppose? I guess we had better let Tish come off duty. I do hope there's another powder room, or the ladies will soon be peeing their pants.'

Eve laughed delightedly. This selfish, pampered woman was causing a lot of people a lot of trouble – and yet . . .

'Thank you for trusting me.'

'It was very kind of you to listen.'

'I really do hope that things don't turn out too boring for you. I wish that I could call you Your Royal Highness. It's such a grand title.'

'I'm forbidden that honour. My husband has it, but they wouldn't give it to me. It's the one thing he most wanted me to have.'

Eve said, 'I'm so sorry,' and left.

As soon as Eve got back to her room, she asked for a call to be booked to Ireland.

When it eventually came through, conversation with Electra was short and sweet. She asked whether Aunt Maureen knew when van Gogh would call on her. 'Van Gogh' dropped into a call was the code 'urgent'.

It was all very well for the Ryde tutors to be confident in her ability to live as a different person, but they weren't surrounded by all these fascists with whom she socialised on a daily basis. When she first began to live as Eve, who cared if she had changed her name? She'd been just a truck driver. Here in Madrid, there would be undercover agents – particularly German ones. Wouldn't they see through her? Again and again she examined her demeanour, her conduct and manner but couldn't find flaws. Yet she didn't feel safe. It was no more than a feeling in her bones, but she had learned to respect those feelings.

Who knew what the MI6 agents, and the Germans and Portuguese undercover agents and the Spanish watchers might think? Being closeted with the Duchess wouldn't have gone unnoticed. Many of the watchers would be here for the sole purpose of watching the Windsors, and the Duchess had been away from their scrutiny for fifteen minutes, secreted with a woman who had charmed her way into the German circle.

When she'd returned to the cocktail party, Eve had enthused to von Pfitzer and Frau von Mentz about what the Duchess had said about American fashion and the loss of the Paris couturier houses. Was that believable? Eve thought so. It was obvious that they were dressed by fashion houses that the other, overdressed ladies had never entered.

Would I be curious about that myself? she wondered. But she couldn't be objective enough to answer.

The message on the note and Wallis's talk about kidnapping must be important. But would The Bureau think so? Eve had learned the rules of communication from Keef and Phoebe; at the time she had found it slightly amusing – cloak-and-daggery. But now that she had something she needed to get quickly to London, it didn't seem such a bad idea.

How long would it take for 'van Gogh' to make contact with her?

Not long as it turned out.

It was early evening and velvety dark when she received a call from a man who simply said, 'Van Gogh. Pull over at the flower stand. I shall be carrying flowers.'

She ordered her car to be brought round with its hood up, and walked to it with as much casualness as she could muster, even pausing to pass the time of day with the doorman.

'Van Gogh' stood at the kerb holding a bunch of bright yellow daisy-like flowers. She laughed at the sight of him.

She leaned across and wound down the window of the passenger-side door. He raised his hat and offered her the flowers. 'Miss Anders, Linder, Faludi and Hatton thought you would like these.'

'All right, Mr van Gogh. Get in. Tell me where to go.'

'Away from the centre. A café. I know a good one – Bassilo's.'

'Is it still going?'

'You know it?'

'Absolutely.'

'A bit downmarket for a society lady.'

'In a past life, Mr van Gogh, I spent many an enjoyable hour there.'

'Which means we can't go there now. Portillo's?'

'Don't know it, so direct me. You mentioned three names which I took on trust of you being genuine. What else?'

'I could tell you about your outfit.'

'Go on.'

'It is now called the Special Operations Executive but we know it as The Bureau, late of Baker Street and recently of Wormwood Scrubs.'

Eve relaxed. He must be genuine.

'Park away from the café.'

Eve smiled. 'It is a bit noticeable. I know where to go. One of my new-found friends lives close by. It's a very select area.'

Close by was ten minutes' walk to Portillo's, and it was good to walk with somebody with whom she didn't need to be on her guard.

The early-evening air was still very warm, and candles burned on every table, many of which were already taken. Eve loved the ambience of street life. These street cafés were where she and Dimitri had spent so many evenings together. In memory of that she chose to drink the unbottled red wine.

A carafe was brought. Guitar music and scores of people chattering was good cover. Van Gogh raised his glass and Eve did the same.

'Would you like to smoke?'

Eve accepted. Possibly awkward situations always seemed easier with tobacco smoke curling up between two people.

'I have something that needs to be passed on very urgently – but not so urgently that I would hand it over without a bit of digging into you. What is your outfit, and can you show me anything in the way of an ID?'

'Special Branch. We don't carry IDs like Scotland Yard.'

Eve paused before asking, 'You were a detective before SIS?'

He drew deeply on his cigarette before answering. Playing for time?

'What makes you think that?'

'Why would you even mention Scotland Yard?'

He shrugged his shoulders noncommittally.

'What's the harm? You know who I am and I want to know who you are.'

'OK, I am a detective. Seconded by the Met to Secret Intelligence Services for this one operation.'

'Which operation?'

'The same one as yours, except that I am a kind of investigator, until His Royal Highness and his wife are safely away.'

'Where do you stay to do your investigating?'

'I have lodgings and I sit around in places like this, especially those favoured by volunteers in the Nazi propaganda rooms. Have you seen them, the rooms?'

Eve shook her head.

Van Gogh smiled. 'You should. Take home some souvenirs, swastikas on everything. Pictures of blond youth and autobahns. Lots of copies of *Mein Kampf*, and in translation. I hang around there. They're trying to convert me. I no longer have to buy their tracts, they give them to me. They have no problems with me sitting around trying to understand. The partition between shop and committee rooms is thin. It's easy to listen, one-sided conversations are revealing. They believe that I'm a dumb Basque a long way from home. The Basques are an oppressed people the Germans plan to free. But they don't want the General to know.' He grinned. 'We have this secret, the low-order Krauts and I.'

Van Gogh steepled his fingers at his lips and leaned forward. 'Well? Can you trust me with whatever information it is you have?'

'Earlier this evening I was at a cocktail party.' She went on to relate the episode with the Duchess of Windsor. Van Gogh listened intently. '"Beware of the machinations of the British secret service. A Portuguese friend who has your interests at heart." That's a message sent to the Duchess. There have been others, warning of kidnap plots. A hunting trip apparently, where she believes they would be held in the belief that they would be persuaded to go to Germany.'

He raised his eyebrows and blew out his cheeks. 'The Duchess told you this?'

'Yes. I know it sounds implausible, but she said that she needed to tell somebody quite unconnected with her own circle. Maybe she thinks they really are going to be kidnapped. Maybe she wanted some unbiased person to know, if she suddenly disappeared – I may be wrong.'

'Did she mention Schellenberg?'

Eve shook her head.

'Schellenberg owns the hunting lodge where the Windsors spent some time.'

'I know about that, von Mentz gave me the impression that it belonged to her husband.'

'Rudolph von Mentz has use of it, but it's Schellenberg's.'

'A bullet was fired into the lodge.'

Van Gogh raised his eyebrows. 'Go on.'

'She hates the idea of being put out to grass . . . the Bahamas, she said. Is that right, do you know?'

He shrugged noncommittally. 'What about de Silvo – Dr Ricardo de Espirito Santo de Silvo?'

Eve smiled, shaking her head. 'I'd have remembered that one, who is he?'

'A wealthy, outspoken Nazi supporter, and he owns, among others, a well-placed villa on the coast of Portugal that he has made available to the Windsors.'

'Will they go there?'

'It would be useful if they do.'

'How?'

'The resort is Cascais, not far from Lisbon. If the king and the government can put enough pressure on him to do the decent thing and clear off to the Bahamas, we could have him out of there and away pretty damned quick.'

'Things are coming to a head, aren't they?'

'They have to, it can't go on like this. We need all our energy to fight the war at home. All this is piddling around . . . I'm sorry.'

'It's OK. I feel the same.'

'I guess what you got from the Duchess this evening will prove invaluable. Lets the ministry know how she's thinking, and what she thinks, he thinks too. I'd say they aren't thinking of going over to the Germans?'

'I got the impression it wasn't even a consideration. Her problem was with not having her own kind around her. Make him King of America and everyone would be OK.'

'Was I wrong to get you to meet me? It appears you know everything already.'

'No, no. We knew nothing about these notes. They're

important. All the rest falls into place. Now it's just a question of watching and waiting. If you need to pass on anything new, I'll give you a number to ring here rather than go through that rigmarole with the Irish connection.'

At last, Eve thought, she was doing something useful.

On the surface Nati was her old useful self, but Eve was cautious, not certain that she had convinced Nati that she knew nothing about the English tearoom. Also, Eve was watchful. Nati said things she must now wish unsaid. Both women were in insecure situations.

Yet another invitation. A musical evening for the Duchess, who was known to be a lover of blues music and jazz bands. After all the cocktails and soirées in a variety of places, Eve really looked forward to something different.

It was as the sun went down. Chairs were set out on a stone terrace, lanterns hung in trees and were strung on lines from the house. The scent of lemon oil helped to keep at bay the evening insects, but the women still covered their heads and shoulders with light shawls against the pests. The party was quite informal, and a buffet would be served later.

The programme started with traditional music of southern Spain. Eve loved the plaintive guitar, and she sat propped against a stone balustrade, absorbed and feeling the pain expressed through the instrument. Tietze, the Austrian, came to stand beside her.

'It is moving, is it not, Señorita Anders?'

Eve nodded, cross at his intrusion, but smiling. At the end of the recital she turned and answered him. 'Very moving. Neither your country nor mine could make music like that.'

'I agree, one must be born with the compatible emotion. My emotion is stirred by Wagner as I am sure that your own is by the compositions of Ketèlbey, both touching the hearts of their people. Would you agree that Ketèlbey could never have written *Das Rheingold*?'

'Probably not.' Who the hell was Ketèlbey?

'Can you think of two such contrary styles?'

Eve sensed that he wasn't interested in her opinion, but wanted to show off his knowledge – and probably to score a point or two.

'Wagner is so strong, I think he could never conceive of Ketèlbey's sombre music *In a Monastery Garden*.' He looked pleased with himself, as though he had primed himself with a little gem of superiority. 'Yours is a gentler heritage.'

'No, no, *my* heritage isn't gentle. Irish music is all fast drums.'

He laughed. 'I think that I am teasing, but if you speak English, then you are English. It is very ill-mannered of us, but I expect to you Austrians and Germans are the same.'

'Point to you, Herr Tietze.'

'Please, Frederich.'

'Shh, listen, Frederich.' She held a finger to her lips.

'Ah.'

Eve sat as she had been, on plump cushions, propped up beside Tietze with her back to the stone balustrade of a terrace surfaced with beautiful old terracotta tiles.

The voice was deep for a woman's – blues sung with sex and wantonness.

Her ears pricked up like an animal's. A suppressed thrill kicked her in the solar plexus.

That amazing voice.

Since she had last heard it flowing out into the spring air of the English countryside at The House by the Sea, it had gained power.

Her heart bounced.

DB.

Something was about to happen.

What happened was that the aide who had invited Eve to take pictures of the Franco garden pushed his way through the crowded terrace looking so pleased with himself. Whispering in Spanish he said, 'Here she is, the lady I mentioned . . . someone to speak to in your own language.' Then in English, 'Miss Anders, I thought that you would care to meet Señor Paul Smyth, who is . . . what, Mr Smyth? Manager?'

'Jack of all trades, *señor.* The agent who plans her appearances, and stops her when she would go on all night. I'm glad to meet you, Miss Anders.'

'And I you, Mr Smyth.'

'I will leave you to get acquainted.'

Tietze, who was still hanging about Eve, offered his hand to Paul. 'Tietze.'

'Pleased to meet you.'

Eve whispered in Tietze's ear, 'I am going to take our visitor into the garden where we won't interfere with the Duchess's pleasure.'

She rose and sauntered away, Paul in tow, until they were well away from anyone else.

'Oh, Paul. If there weren't people up there I'd give you a big hug and a kiss.'

'You look amazing. How's it been? Not exactly my idea of a worthwhile job. So far I haven't done anything except have quite a good time with DB.'

'Sit down here, there's nobody within thirty feet of this bench. Keep your polite distance. How about you and DB?'

'Don't you think she's come on in a few weeks?'

'Oh yes. What's she been doing to get that voluptuousness into her singing?'

'Nightclubs and bars and whatever Lisbon could offer that was full of cigarette smoke and drinks in small glasses. There have been times when she could have set the curtains alight she was so hot.'

'Come on, applause. Sounds like an interval.'

DB was surrounded by people wanting to congratulate her. Señora Franco's aide led DB to where the General's lady was seated with the Duke and Duchess.

'Who is that fellow running everything?' Paul asked.

'"Señor Fixit", he's one of General Franco's own; looks after Señora Franco's affairs. This is his place. It's a coup for him to have the General's lady and the Duchess on his terrace. How did you manage to be here?'

'Mendoza . . . you know Mendoza . . . he took us over. You probably know that he's got a bar. The day before yesterday he offered us a booking, and in a word told us to get the hell out. He must have spoken to your Señor Fixit and here we are.'

'Where are you staying?'

'Nowhere grand like you, but it's not for long.'

'How do you know?'

'Mendoza. I think it's all fixed for the Windsors to move on.'

'It is, but they're moving on into Portugal.'

'Does the left hand know what the right one is doing?'

'Who cares for tonight?'

The evening broke up.

Eve made no attempt to speak to DB, but as she was about to go to her car, the aide touched her shoulder.

'Señorita Anders, Her Royal Highness has asked Miss de Beers to sing for her at a private party in her suite at the Ritz. She asks if you would care to join her.'

'Of course. Will you please say that I shall be delighted?'

'In about one hour.'

Well, Eve thought, if they're on the move, I'll be in at the kill.

It was a small gathering in the Windsors' suite. The Duchess greeted everyone with poise and graciousness, and Eve thought, not for the first time, that she had everything the Queen of England did not have. 'Please excuse my husband. He would join us if I asked him, but he would only fidget if he were forced to sit through *my* kind of music. Miss Anders, I'm real pleased to see you again. Everybody here speaks English, isn't that just great? Have you met our entertainer? Come on over, Miss de Beers. Meet the only person who knows my plans for the future.'

DB shook hands with Eve and said all the right things. The Duchess gave a delighted laugh when people looked concerned. 'It's to do with a sewing machine.'

Eve, playing up to her, said, 'Oh, Duchess, don't give it away. When people start to talk about your venture, I want to be able to say, "I knew all about that, the Duchess told me." Of course, no one will believe me, but I will know.'

'Y'know what, Miss Anders, I do believe you've given me the confidence to do it.'

DB sang for about an hour, after which Eve invited the two newcomers to visit her suite for a nightcap.

It was as well that Nati had pulled the heavy curtains, for as soon as the three of them were safely in the sitting room, they clung together and danced a jig.

'Oh my God, Eve,' DB said, 'this bit's as fun as can be.' She roamed around, opening drawers and cupboards, smelling bottles and soaps, trying on scarves and earrings. Paul poured drinks, lighted their cigarettes and sank into one of the overstuffed armchairs, looking hugely satisfied. 'All we need for perfect pleasure is Fran.'

DB, who was fascinated by the luxurious bathroom, whooped and came out holding up two condom packets left behind by Duke. 'Oh, you bad girl. You've been doing things with men.'

Eve felt her colour rising. 'If I had been, they wouldn't be unused, would they?'

'Hey, come *on*, that's a poor excuse for an excuse. Who's been sleeping in *Eve's* bed?'

Paul just shook his head. 'Have you any idea at all what it's like to be with this woman twenty-four hours a day, seven days a week?'

'You wouldn't need any of these, that's for sure.' Unrolling one, DB blew it up like a balloon, patting it about until it landed on her burning cigarette.

'Come on, mad woman. Let's find our hotel.'

Eve said, 'It's late. Stay here.'

DB put her arms around Eve's neck and kissed her hair. 'You making us both an offer we can't refuse?'

'This place is half empty. I'll ring down and get you rooms. The Bureau can afford it.'

'You're not kidding. The Bureau should have made a nice little profit out of us,' Paul said. 'I really think I'd make a good agent – of the other sort.'

'A double agent.'

There were rooms available for Miss Anders' guests. Her own felt empty once they had gone. These days she never seemed quite to be free of anxiety.

Had she been too spontaneous in arranging rooms for two people who were supposed to be strangers?

But then, they *were* English, so it would be natural for her to want to have their company.

One of the things Janet had said was that stress kept you on your toes. Anxiety made you careful.

Before Eve went down to breakfast next morning, DB and Paul had gone, leaving a formal 'thank you' note for Miss Anders' generosity.

Then there was a phone call. 'Ladybird's gone to London. She wouldn't say what's up, but I don't care. It means that you can come down and stay at my place. If you don't come, I'll fetch you.'

'I'll try. Ring you back later.'

Then came a note on crested paper saying the Duchess

and her husband were going to stay with friends, and how she hoped that she and Eve might meet up again some day.

Then came a phone call from van Gogh. 'I hear that you are planning a trip south, Miss Anders. Would you mind giving some friends a lift?'

'Who?'

'A Miss de Beers and Mr Smyth.'

Eve told Quixote that she planned to spend a little time with some friends in Seville.

He was sad that she would be leaving. Maybe he could arrange a little farewell cocktail party?

She was touched by his sweet thought. She hated goodbyes . . . they made her melancholy.

Eve was anxious enough without Nati being agitated, fumbling with the packing, dropping things, jumping when porters brought in trays or the telephone rang.

'For goodness' sake, Nati, take ten minutes and sit down. Here, have a glass of tea.'

'Thank you, no, *señorita.* I must get the packing finished.'

'There isn't that much left to do.'

Suddenly, Nati was standing before her, hands knotted tightly and her face a picture of apprehension. 'Excuse me, Señorita Anders, now that you are going, I have to tell you this. I think we have met before.'

'I don't think so, Nati.'

'When you came here I wondered how I could have seen you before. It seemed impossible; you had not been to this country. I ask Señor Quixote if you are famous, I might have seen you in a magazine, and he says not famous but very rich.'

Eve looked up and saw that Nati was almost rigid with anxiety. Deep breath . . . relax. Deep breath . . . relax.

'Come on, Nati, spit it out. Sit down, do as I say. Here.' She poured another glass of iced tea.

Nati sat, perched on the edge of an armless chair. 'Barcelona, *señorita*, you know that I was in Barcelona?'

Eve drew on her subconscious to achieve a relaxed state but to appear a bit irritated and impatient.

'Yes, you told me that. You were a teacher. And your father brought you here for the sake of the children.'

'Yes, that is true. Please be patient.'

'Of course.'

'Julio was workers' party.' Nati looked directly at Eve, not expecting an answer. 'There was always trouble between POUM and others. Each accuse the other of betraying. When the end was near in Barcelona, old adversaries settled old arguments with the gun. My husband went out to deal with anarchist but tables were turned. I have not seen him since then. I am sorry, but I and my children are never out of danger because of Julio.'

Eve felt herself at risk now, but all that she could do was to sit still and say nothing and let Nati talk.

'After that time, it was very dangerous. Perhaps they would come looking for me and the children. What I did, *señorita*, I change my appearance from teacher to very poor person. Ha, that was not difficult. I went to my uncle, who lives in the old streets. He did not recognise who was this ragged lady. He is my mother's brother. He was simple fisherman, never in the world of revolution and politics; he lives and works only for the family, you understand? He was family and he took us in and did not ask why.'

Eve shrugged noncommittally.

'At first I was no good, because I did not know the different fishes, but my cousins were good teachers and in one or two days I was sorting and helping with the catch. Meat was scarce, *pollos, pavos*, all plucked and stewed weeks before. There was a joke which maybe you have heard: "We have eaten the last *cerdo*, but we saved for you the grunt" – the pig, you see. Which was true – the only meat was fish. The sea was dangerous to be in. But my uncle went out every day. He was not a man for churches, but he was good in the way of bringing back as much fish as he could.'

She paused, perhaps waiting for Eve to say something, but she still did not comment.

'Every day the same woman would come. She would not push but wait till the good fish was gone and ask for small things that were left. Cheap. My uncle said I must always put one good fish at the bottom of her bag and she must pay only for the bits and pieces.'

'Why?'

'*Señorita*, I am still feeling guilty. My uncle did not say why she was his favourite. I took the wrong reason. You can guess what I thought of him . . . and of the woman. No one would have blamed her. I too might have gone with a man to keep my children fed. But I did not think that my uncle would be a man like that.' She looked down at her hands as she twisted a dusting cloth.

'I am so sorry, Señorita Anders. When I discovered the truth, it was too late. My uncle asked, "Where is the English girl? She has not come here maybe for three days." He sent one of the little boys to find what has happened. I did not know that she was English, because she spoke our language well. When the boy returned, he said that the house was empty, and people said that the English woman had gone with the refugees. My uncle crossed himself and asked the Good Lord to protect her.'

Eve felt boxed into a corner. Blackmail? To gain time, she walked across the room, took out a new pack of cigarettes, fumbled the opening and the lighter and perched on the edge of the bureau. 'I expect there are many such stories. You should write them down for when your children are grown up.'

'Madame,' Nati sounded a bit scornful, 'I have no need to write. It is all here in my mind, very clear. I could describe the English girl's eyes, which I would say are very like your own. It is one thing that we cannot disguise, also the fingernails. You remember the day when I was putting cream into your hands? I commented that these parts were very large and white, and you told me that in English the word was "moons".'

Money. She had plenty of cash. She held her fingers out, inspecting them and said smiling, 'You are a good manicurist, Nati. Maybe you could set yourself up offering that service to guests.'

'Until that time, I had not seen such clear moons except for the other English woman.'

'The fish woman.'

'*Sí, señorita.* Also, the fish woman had a scar. My cousin had shown her how to use a filleting knife, it had slipped and taken a small piece from the woman's finger bone of the left hand, the first-finger knuckle. Also on that same finger was a small bump, an old wound of some kind.'

Eve didn't look down at her hands, but remembered the shock of realising that the needle of the industrial sewing machine had gone right through her left index finger.

'So you see, madame, if I write this story, I can easily bring the English woman to mind. Eyes, teeth, hands. To remember these details it is not difficult to see the bones of the face – the profile. That is the word I have been looking for. If I one day should see this lady, madame, I would tell her that I feel bad why my uncle was giving her good fish and she pays only for leavings.'

'Oh, Nati, stop feeling guilty about something that is in the past.'

'But, *señorita*, the *end* of this story is not the past. I will help you pack everything.'

'I may not want everything. I have arranged with Señor Quixote to store things until I return.'

Nati got up and stuffed the duster into her pocket. 'I think you may not, *señorita*.' She looked so serious and determined that Eve felt threatened. Nati began removing Eve's collection of summer frocks off their hangers, folding them neatly and pressing them into one of the soft-top cases. Then she stopped and came face to face, holding Eve's elbows firmly. 'Please, Señorita Anders, your time in Madrid is over.'

'Nati! Who are you, the *Guardia*?'

'*Señorita*, it is possible. Listen, please. You know when I first come here with you, I told you how I was able to get work because of my father and his dealings with Falange? OK, I understand that you are worried that my stories may be tricks for you, so please let me continue. You need say nothing, but I should like it if you could trust me.'

'OK, Nati, five minutes and then I have to leave.'

'My father is so sure of his position now, that he no longer bothers to talk quietly and in private. I learn things without listening. Since the General's return he has been renewed, people talk to him. He was fifth column – it was these people who kept silent until the General invaded, and then they helped him – small acts of sabotage, a few murders, harvests set to fire.'

Eve knew those small acts very well – dynamiting mountain passes so that lorries carrying supplies of ammunition to the front were blown to smithereens.

'Last evening, my mother and I were sitting listening to the crickets and drinking juice. My boys were asleep. It was quiet. My father was in his room where he works talking by telephone – it is the thing he is proud of, his telephone. It was impossible not to hear. He mentioned the Ritz. Then I did listen. It was to do with the singer who came.'

Eve nodded.

'He said, "Nati is maid to an English woman, perhaps she is the one." Then he was listening, then he said, "I have placed Nati in the Ritz," and he laughed. "Now it is time for her to do something for me." Then he listened again, then he said, "Ah, daughters – they are trouble. Did your mother think that she had a right to attend university? Girls were not meant for universities. All troubles start with students. Now she is down a peg or two, and I have the next generation under my roof. There will be no more *Comunista*, no FUE students in this family."'

'So what do you think your father wants you to do, Nati?'

'I don't know. I thought that maybe if I come early, before he is awake, he cannot tell me what I must do. I am sure it must be something bad. Because the person who was talking to him knew something about the singer, and then my father says that I work for you, I became so worried. I made a bad mistake about the English girl in Barcelona. I should not like to make another.'

Eve wanted to believe that this was not a trick, but everyone was capable of double-dealing. Maybe the story was bait to see if Eve could be flushed out.

Trust no one.

'I'm sorry, Nati, I really can't make head nor tail of the poor girl story. I would really like to know more about her, but, honestly, I really do need to start soon before it gets too hot.'

'I am sorry to take your time, madame. But, please, go at once.'

'That's all right, Nati, you have had a bad time. I do hope things are better for you soon.'

Nati took Eve's hand and looked at the two old scars. 'Please go at once, *señorita*. Please.'

Eve nodded and kissed Nati on both cheeks. 'Your uncle was a good man. Without him, children would have starved.'

'I do not believe in God, *señorita*, but may He go with you.'

Having hastily picked up DB and Paul, Eve took her leave of Madrid.

DB eyed the motorcar. 'I'm glad you found a nice little unnoticeable car if we are stopped at the border.'

'We have to take it. It belongs to a friend of Mendoza. I don't suppose his Bureau expenses runs to a new Buick.'

Paul said, 'It's just the thing, DB. Goes like a bullet out of a gun.'

'Don't talk about bullets, Paul.'

'Stop being so wet, woman. You've been seeing too many gangster films. The Duke and Duchess are on their way – if Eve *has* been fingered by the maid's father, nobody's going to send a posse after her.'

It was very early in the day, the sun coming up, the wind blowing over the windscreen, fluttering the women's scarves. Paul, who almost lost his linen cap, turned it back to front as racing drivers do.

DB made the sounds little boys make. 'Brrrm-brrrm. Look, Eve, he wants next go at the car.'

In everyday circumstances it would have raised no more than a smile, but when Eve started to giggle, the other two caught it. There were dust goggles in the glove compartment, which Eve tossed to Paul, and when he put them on, another bout of shouting and giggling started. They might have been three carefree rich youngsters out for a lark.

Which for now is just how they felt.

About ten kilometres out of Madrid, Eve turned off the main road south.

'I hope you know where you're going, missie,' DB said.

'Just shut up, DB, and sing to us. This is my patch. I want you both to see it.'

DB started singing something about 'bein' in the belly of the whale'. The wind carried the words away but not the melody and the chanting rhythm. They climbed. The road was dusty and winding. From time to time, Eve would slow to a crawl and wave a hand at some magnificent vista.

Once DB said, 'Hey, man, I'm sorry but I need to pee.'

'It's OK. I know all the best places.'

'She's right, man, not a burr or thistle in sight. Will you just look at this view – seems to me I've seen it before, back home. You never going to believe this, but when I was a kid I had a pet ostrich, and she'd let me ride her, and I'd take her out to some kopje a bit like this, and tell her all the things nobody else wanted to hear.'

Paul put an arm round DB's shoulder. 'That's sad. Poor little kid.'

Eve blew out cigarette smoke and mimed exaggerated violin playing, grinning at DB.

'You don't believe me?'

'A goat, I might believe. An ostrich . . . ? On rocks like these? Nah.'

'Ah, sweet, Paul. You're such a softie, you'd be putty in the hands of a lady spy.'

'She's right, Paul. You're one of the nice people.'

'So are you two. I just love you both.'

'I make up stories like the ostrich as a kind of gift to people – like Eve is giving us this gift of showing us a neck of her own woods.'

'A gift? Wilhelmina de Beers, that was such an outrageous lie.'

'No, sweetheart, not a lie – a story. If Eve hadn't given

me away, you'd have a good story to tell at a party, or get in good with a date . . . "I used to know a girl who talked to her pet ostrich . . ." Y'see, it could be a happy or a sad story: "There was this girl I used to know . . . she would ride it up mountains" or "She was so neglected that the only one who would listen was her pet ostrich."'

Paul picked DB up and swung her round, laughing. 'I'll never understand women.'

'Don't try, Paul. We're not here to be understood,' Eve said, and put an arm round his waist, and for a few quiet moments the three of them stood, taking in the grandeur of Toledo.

She would lose these friends, Eve thought. It was a reason for not allowing people to become too important. It hurt when they went.

David Hatton. She had lost him twice over. The hurt had exploded in anger.

Ozz Lavender, killed on terrain like this. It still hurt.

Dimitri? Well, she had told him to get lost. He had been closest for the longest time.

And Duke. He was too 'flimsy', as he had said himself, to make any kind of commitment. They were two of a kind. Afraid to allow anyone too close in case they let you down or went away.

Back in the car, Paul studied a map. 'After we've had the grand tour, where are we headed?'

'Find Cádiz.'

'Got it.'

'Well, we're not going there. And before we don't go to Cádiz, I'm going to call on two lots of friends. At the first, you eat everything put before you and enjoy the wine – whatever you think of it. They will have made it themselves.'

The village hadn't changed, of course. If it hadn't changed in three hundred years, it wasn't likely to have done since Eve was last here – even the tethered donkey outside the inn to draw up water from the artesian well deep in the rocks, and the goats munching the herby verges from which strong cheeses were made.

By the time the three arrived, word had gone out as it always had in Eve's previous life, that strangers were coming. Nobody actually came out of their little houses, but stood in the open doorways. Those tending small vegetable patches leaned on their hoes, sharp as razors.

Eve eagerly went towards a house with her arms stretched wide in greeting. The elderly woman in the doorway, who had been watching suspiciously, suddenly sprang into life, ran out and clasped Eve to her, wiping her eyes with her apron, and doing the same for Eve. Others joined them, spreading their arms in wonder, walking round Eve and laughing delightedly.

Paul and DB sat watching from the car. DB said, 'I don't understand a word of Spanish, but I know what they're saying: "Look at her, look, she's come back. Hasn't she got thin. Ah, but just look at those slacks, just feel that scarf. And will you just look at her hair." Am I right, or am I right?'

'You may well be right. It's not my kind of Spanish. This is a kind of bastardised Castilian, I think. They call her "American Girl".'

'What knocks me for six is that Eve can chat away with them like this.'

'She's full of surprises.'

'She did say something about being out here in the war, but, hey, I don't know what to think about this.'

'What you think, DB, is that she's their darling.'

Eve had been showered with kisses and discs of goats' cheese, a stone jar of wine, and a fat *chorizo* which Eve had said was a favourite of the friend they were going to stay with. When she said that the favourite sausage was for a young man, the long wooden table at which the entire village seemed to be seated to dine was pounded with fists and the ragged awning above seemed to flutter from the raucous laughter and innuendo.

It was very late in the day when they got back to the lower, greener terrain of Córdoba and then Seville and then Jerez – by which time they had calmed down, and Eve had satisfied a bit of the others' curiosity about how she used to take medicines and other supplies to small villages like that one.

Paul and DB were so enthusiastic about the visit that they said when things were different they would go back. 'I wonder how many people can drop by for a visit and the entire village comes out? They absolutely loved their American Girl.'

'Not half as much as I love them. They're just as you see them. I like that.'

'What did they think about you turning up in a gigantic motorcar?' Paul asked.

Eve laughed. 'Not much. It was just what I happen to be driving today. I didn't always turn up in a truck. Sometimes it was a gigantic Mercedes. Nobody was impressed – it was just the transport I used for bringing in supplies.

The other two guessed that this was about as much as they would get from Eve about her past life.

But they were wrong.

When they eventually arrived in Jerez they were met by Duke Barney.

Eve got out first. 'Isn't this Ladybird's car?' she asked, eyeing the sports car he was driving.

Duke nodded. 'Keeping it run in while she's in London having a time of it.'

Eve doubted that.

To the other two she said simply, 'This is Señor Paulo Fuentes – an old friend. You can trust him absolutely. He knows what we are doing – but *not* from me.' Duke gave a minimum of acknowledgement, but quite affably.

'You sorted it, Eve?'

'Yes. If it's OK with you we'll put up for a night or two until we get word from London.' She turned to DB and Paul. 'Señor Fuentes will drive us to Lisbon when it's time for us to leave. Captain Faludi agrees with me that we should stay together.' The authority in Eve's tone left the other two in no doubt that they should go along with her. This was a very different face of Eve from the Scrubs Eve, the Madrid Eve or the Córdoba village Eve. This one was authoritative, and Paul and DB, knowing nothing of the larger picture since they arrived in Madrid, took what she said without question.

Duke, opening the doors of the sports car, said, 'I've got a stablelad with a truck to take your bags. I got plenty of stuff at my place, soap and flannels and that. Anybody wants a nightdress, I'll get one of Ladybird's. Come on, then.'

DB asked what was going to happen to Mendoza's car.

'One a' my blokes is going to give it a going over, then get it up to Lisbon whenever you like.'

'We will be going on in Señor Fuentes' car?'

'Not so much of the *señor*, Eve,' and, holding out a hand, he said, 'People call me Duke, just Duke. Only time I'm *señor* is to my monkeys there.' He jerked a thumb at the men loading luggage onto the truck.

DB ran over to them and took some things off the truck. Giving short, quick orders to his 'monkeys', Duke started the engine, idling it until DB came back.

'Eve, wasn't this *chorizo* supposed to be for . . . Duke?' she asked.

'When did I say that?'

DB, putting the package on the dashboard, said, '*You* didn't, but the old ladies did.' Eve and DB burst out laughing.

Duke, addressing Paul, said, 'What's all that about?'

Paul said, 'Don't ask me, chum. I never understand women.'

'Nor me,' Duke said.

He drove them down to his place, 'the Jaws of Hell', driving at a much more sedate speed than Eve.

Eve was quite touched at the trouble Duke had obviously gone to. Two women were waiting to serve at an outside table surrounded by torches giving off the scent of lemon-peel.

'D'you want to wash or anything? There's a bathroom and a couple of WCs. Another one round in the yard, Paul. I make the monkeys keep it nice and clean. Rita, show them the way.'

Eve and DB followed the wide-hipped woman, who laughed and chattered, indicating to left and right the many beautiful things Señor Fuentes owned – not pictures or ornaments, but woven fabrics hung on poles, and large groups of stones that could have been from an artist or from nature. The bathroom was plaster over-painted with a pale terracotta, and furnished with a stone hand-basin, and ceramic water closet and bath that must have cost him a fortune to have plumbed in.

When they returned, Eve met his eyes at once. He wanted to know whether she approved.

'What I've seen so far, Duke, you have a lovely place here.'

Offhandedly he said, 'It's nowhere near finished, but it will be OK.'

'Where did all the ideas come from?'

'I travelled around a bit, picked up bits and pieces from here and there. Come on, sit down. I got you a nice baked fish. We have a lot of vegetables and macaroni and sauce stuff, but I went out and caught this today.' Rita, proud of the dish, placed a long fish, slit-sided and brown-skinned, before the *señor.* 'Come on, I don't stand on ceremony. Help yourselves.'

The four of them ate and talked for more than an hour. Eve was overwhelmed by his generosity and care. Nothing was too good for his guests. He got DB talking about the difference between singing blues and singing jazz.

He told Paul of his own plans for stables and asked about Paul's future. 'The immediate future? I think I should apply to join the code-breakers,' and he explained what they did and how he was suited to the work.

Duke said, 'I reckon that's blooming clever. I never did learn to read and write much sense – 'not apologising or explaining – it was a fact that's all. I can figure pretty good, though. L – Eve knows that, don't you, Eve?' He placed his dark hand over her pale one.

It was then that she wanted him to herself. 'It's been a long day, Duke. Maybe you ought to show us to where we'll be sleeping.'

'A 'course. I ought to have thought – it's just so nice having somebody who speaks proper English. I heard the monkeys take the truck round the back. You'll find your things in your rooms. Anything you want, tell Rita or the other one.'

'Duke! Doesn't she have a name?'

'A 'course. Rita, both of them. Just say Rita and somebody will get you what you want – well, if it's in the store. G'night, DB, g'night, Paul. I get started before dawn, but you just do what you want. Eve, you going to let me show you the other rooms?'

Taking her by the hand, he led her straight to his high-ceilinged bedroom where they made love at once.

'Jesus, Lu! I scarce thought of anything since I come home from Madrid. How about you?'

She shut his mouth with her tongue and kisses. She didn't want to tell him the truth; neither could she tell him the lie that she had not thought about him and what they had done together ever since. Lifting her off him, he sat up, back against the wall. The bed was little more than a wide mattress laid directly on rugs, and piled with pillows and cushions, everything covered in fabric woven in multi-coloured stripes.

'When you got back here, how was Alex?'

'I don't know. She started to hit the bottle again, and I told her if she didn't stop, I would report on her. She just laughed it off, she thought she was bullet-proof, being in with high society. It was a game to her, thinking she was in with everybody that mattered. She kept coming over, saying she needed things for her mares, asking me to look at them. Then she started to say I'd been with somebody else.' He kissed Eve and put one arm round her shoulder. 'Well, I had, hadn't I? Then, she come round here spitting fire. "Who was it, you fuckin' dago?" she says. Well I been called a lot worse than that. Still, I smacked her – only because she was getting hysterical. She calmed down. She asked for a glass of brandy, but I wasn't born yesterday. So I got her a cup of water and asked her what it was all about.'

While he was speaking, he put Eve's hand between his legs and held his own hand over it. In seconds he was aroused again. Now he put a hand between her legs, searching her face for the response that was there.

'So, to cut a long story short, she said she had been called back to London.' Leaning on one elbow he looked down at Eve. 'There's not much of you these days, Lu.' Eve tweaked a groin hair. 'Aow! I never said there wasn't enough of you. The most I ever wanted in my whole life is this. Lu Wilmott under me.'

'No, Duke, Eve Anders – on top.'

'All right then, missie.'

'Duke . . . ?'

'No, Lu. I know what you're going to say, by your voice. Ladybird never slept in here. I got all this up for you. And when you go I shall set fire to it down on the rocks. All right?'

There was no one else in the world like Duke Barney.

They both slept for a while. Then Eve was disturbed by hearing him grunt as he pulled on riding boots.

'Are you going out?'

'Coming? I don't know what you're going to wear. Those trousers you got here looks way too pricey to be up on a horse.'

'They're only trousers, Duke. Their time's up.'

'Better wear your shoes against the sharp stones.'

'Where?'

'Taking Diabolo for a swim.'

The sky lightened sufficiently for Eve and Duke to see the surf where it broke. She had learned to ride bareback, as he had on Eli Barney's land. The fast, black horse took the two of them, Eve in front, both holding the reins loose, letting the horse gallop in the warm sea.

When they had first become lovers they had struggled together in fierce passion.

This time, Eve was certain, must be the last. It was almost mystical.

This time there was no tree to support them.

This time there were no tar-barrels burning and rockets shooting into the black night.

This time, as Eve held herself to Duke with arms and legs, the sun rose and the Jaws of Hell began to live up to its name.

It was on 1 August that the Windsors boarded a ship to begin their journey to the Bahamas – very different refugees from the ones with whom Eve had fled, a year ago.

In the hold were fifty-two pieces of luggage. Among other trophies: a set of golf clubs, four baskets of old Madeira and port wine, a brand-new limousine. And a portable sewing machine.

Eve set out early in her little red car, to drive through the New Forest. It would be the last time she would be able to get petrol, so she savoured the moments. So, when she came to the Hampshire moorlands, where purple heather reminded her of distant views of La Mancha, she drew off the road.

She had been chauffeuring a big-wig American through the saffron crocus fields. 'Hell, young lady,' he'd said, 'I reckon the Good Lord must have had a pretty good day when He dreamed up this place.' And, although there was a vicious war going on, she had agreed. There had been elation and a sense of utter freedom. Free to be herself. No ties.

Then, as now, she could take risks because she had only herself to answer to.

Yet she already had strings attached. New ones. How stupid! Dimitri. Sex, not love had accounted for a large part of their relationship. She hadn't wanted him to fall in love with her. There wasn't a thing anyone could do about love. At times she almost wished that she *had* fallen in love with him.

No, no. Not really.

The only true love she ever had was for the old one: independence. For that, she was paying the high price of cleavage from people she had once been close to, and of refusing to be loved by Dimitri.

She ate a sandwich she had scrounged from Griffon kitchens.

What changes were going on there. The house was coming alive again. Shuttered windows were now draped with sumptuous Eastern fabrics and the plywood partitions had been removed.

A WRNS officer in the mould of Phoebe Moncke, before she was transformed, Petty Officer Jo Glasspool, had taken her to see what was being done.

'If you say it looks like a tart's boudoir, you won't be the first.'

'I rather like opulent furnishings. Have they kept the black and silver room?'

'Oh yes, and the one next to it. Very classy, those are.'

Eve hadn't time to see much of it, but PO Glasspool said to come in when she got back to Portsmouth.

'Who's having it done?'

Glasspool had shrugged her shoulders. 'Can't say, but it's somebody who had the cash to buy it, and ship in all this stuff. Some Indian chap is the rumour.'

Baldock, the handyman who had cared for her MG, was still there.

'I can get me hands on a drop of petrol, only enough to do you less than a hundred miles.'

Eve gave him a generous tip. She only wanted enough to get her to the New Forest and back.

Now, she was not far from her destination. The Priory, otherwise known as the Finishing School, was where undercover agents of every kind were trained in the art of dirty tricks, and skills that were criminal in civilian life. Skills to use in Them-or-Us situations, often in enemy or enemy-occupied territory – France, Poland, Holland, Belgium, Czechoslovakia and, of course, the neutral countries, Spain, Portugal, Eire and Switzerland.

Although everyone there at any one time was not

expected to undertake all of the training, most were taught how to use binoculars at night, to operate a signal lamp, to fire handguns and rifles, to send and receive morse, to wire a fuse-timer, and to detonate TNT. These were the 'hardware' skills.

Equally important was health and fitness, and the softer tricks of the trade – simple disguise, living off the land, melting into the indigenous population, and, more sinisterly, how to loop fine electric cable round a throat and throttle; learning where were vulnerable points on the body such as the carotid artery, and how to keep out of the way when it was severed. All very practical skills for SOE agents.

At the stage Eve was now – contemplating her independence and the New Forest ponies – she didn't mind what she was expected to do. Anything. Anything at all.

Every time she started anew, it felt as though she was being given an opportunity to do better than in the past.

Now, she leaped to her feet, startling the scavenging ponies. Remembering something from long ago, she clasped her hands above her head and began spinning on the spot. A childish thing. A wonderfully light-hearted thing.

She had learned how to spin until she felt herself joined to the sky, ages ago, when she was twelve. Her friend Bar had initiated her into the 'dervishing'. It had been magical, and the magic had been natural and wonderful. Bar, wise in the way of magic, Lu, city child, had spun themselves into ecstasy. And that was when Duke had appeared.

Now, before an audience of suspicious ponies, she began turning, at first gently, then speeding up. Then, raising her hands above her head, she re-enacted the graceful, dervishing spin. Off-balance with vertigo, she tumbled onto the ling, dry and crisp with last season's flowers, breathless and laughing. This was the closest she had ever come to it – not ecstasy, but joyfulness, gladness. Happiness.

She lay there on her back, looking straight up at the clear sky, brimful of all her old energy and ambition. Everything that had been troubling her since the recent entanglements with Duke and Dimitri, and had been holding her spirits down like stones in the pockets of a suicide, dispersed.

She got back in her car and drove on, ready for the challenges of the Priory.

'You are here at the Priory for a number of weeks, depending on which of the courses you are here to attend. Priory estate, as you will be aware, is for the most part given over as a centre in which you people may train and learn from older hands. There are six other houses here; only the one allocated is for you to be interested in. You will ignore anything you might see or hear. You will hear other languages spoken, but these are not your affair.

'We had hoped that women could be given a house to themselves, but as there are so few of you, and there is a group of men undertaking the same training, then it's sharing – the house, not the beds. You will need to give all your attention to training.

'The course of instruction is intensive. Map-reading, morse code and weapons training are central. Fitness and mental alertness are, of course, what is required in an agent. Special Operations! Those of you who complete the course and are successful will become operatives with very special skills.'

The candidates had not been introduced to the suited man who addressed them. His eyes roamed the room and alighted here and there on a rookie.

'You have each been selected for some attribute, craft or knowledge that SOE requires. Each of you has something to offer. Suffice it to say that whatever your field of expertise you have a limited time in which to learn other strategies and techniques. Less than perfection is not good enough and you will be OUT.

'You know all about the Official Secrets Act. The safety of the realm is at stake and we are at war. What goes on here is highly classified. You will not use the telephone; you will not leave the estate *at all* until your training is complete; all letters in and out will be read – censored if necessary. The Priory is a very pleasant place in which to train, but, but, but,' his forefinger fired shots all around the room, 'the Finishing School is not a resort. However, the accommodation is very good and the food is plentiful and excellent.' He straightened his uncreased jacket. 'Any questions?'

'Sir, those who are successful – what happens next?'

'No leave, if that is what you are wondering. If appropriate, you will go on to other short intensive courses, e.g., use of parachute. Not all successful candidates will be required to undertake this. It would be poor use of manpower; those of you who propose to sit out the war far from the madding crowd, engaged on cipher and encoding work, will not need to know how to jump from a moving aircraft.'

Before he could be asked any further questions, the anonymous man left the room.

And so the training started.

The women in Beauchamp House were Eve, Elizabeth Carstairs, Catherine Pugh, Cilla Haddington, Anomie Nash and DB.

DB arrived after the rest. She came up quietly behind Eve and caught her in a bear-hug. Eve's reaction put DB on the floor.

'Hey, man, what will you be like when you're trained?'

They had a joyful reunion.

Liz Carstairs and Cilla Haddington had 'come out' together.

'What did you come out of?' DB wanted to know.

Liz and Cilla looked at one another. 'Out of girlhood and into the big, wide world.'

'We were debutantes.'

'What must you do to be one?'

Liz and Cilla grinned conspiratorially, 'Have the right sort of mummy and daddy.'

Eve said, 'And plenty of money.'

'Oh, yes,' Cilla confirmed, 'one needs to be of a certain set.'

Liz said. ' "Coming out" is being presented to the King and Queen. When you have curtsied to them in your virgin-white gown, you become a debutante.'

'And somebody gave you a ball.'

'And that was where you were supposed to find a young man to marry.'

'You're not joking, are you?' DB said.

'No, of course we're not joking. It is the system.'

'Don't take me wrong if I laugh, but I've never heard of such a rotten way of parents getting daughters off their hands.'

'I know. I can remember standing in this long line of girls in white satin thinking to myself, this is pathetic. I would rather be a virgin in a pagan ceremony.'

'For God's sake,' Cilla said, 'I *was* pagan. I felt as though I was being paraded before potentates who were choosing girls for harems.'

'It's the ball that starts you off, gets you into the marriage market.'

DB thought that very funny. 'What's the price of a girl in a virgin-white gown these days?'

'No price will get you a couple like us,' Liz said.

Cilla linked arms with her coming-out partner. 'Not in marriage. We rebelled – told our people we were going to become pros.'

Anomie said, 'Streetwalkers? You two? Your accents alone would frighten the clients.'

'Oh, we didn't plan to do it on the streets. We thought maybe a flat in Mayfair, and only take the ones in our own set.'

'We thought it made better sense that instead of marrying them and letting them get it for free, we would pick and choose the best and charge them for it.'

'Good scheme, eh?'

'Did you try it?'

The two girls burst into laughter. 'We're still virgins and got picked up to come here.'

'To become pros?' Anomie asked.

'So why didn't you just jump ship like I did?' DB asked.

'Oh, we did.' The two young debs laughed. 'It's a long story, but we ended up here. Cilla has a second cousin Bazil who thought, with our corners rubbed off, we might do something worthwhile.'

An earlier Eve – one without her own corners rubbed off – might have thought: There you go. Their type always knows somebody to fix them up. But this new, happier Eve liked their cheek and honesty.

Four out of five had 'jumped ship'. Maybe Anomie Nash had too, but during the first days, she was as much an enigma as Eve.

DB's family was newly rich and she didn't mind who knew it. 'The Debs' families were on close terms – their brothers were known to one another – so that Cilla and Liz would reminisce about Spiffy, Old Tosh, Bobbity and Jay without realising that they were being exclusive of the others. Not that any of them appeared to mind; true or not, the family stories were jolly and kept everyone entertained.

There were five men – 'The Chaps' – in Beauchamp, whom Anomie described as 'interchangeable', which wasn't a bad description as none had any particularly striking feature except for accent: a Geordie, who had a language all his own for the first couple of days and the rest learned it; a 'posh' chap, who spoke like Liz and Cilla; two who spoke with London accents – one white and one black, both named John; and a fifth who slipped between accents very much as Janet McKenzie did – 'Tommy', but only because his chin was as elongated as that of the popular comedian Tommy Trinder.

So as well as Tommy, there was Geordie, Posh, Jim and Johnny. A sixth was expected later in the course.

The sergeant PT instructor – known to the girls as Pecs, in honour of his extraordinary pectoral muscles – had to forget Aldershot where he had knocked a good many concave-chested young recruits into shape. The Finishing School teams were to be exercised into a state of fitness but not put into hospital with strained backs and torn ligaments. It went against the sergeant's athletic grain but he was secretly glad to heed the directive because he was pushing forty and preferred the life here to Aldershot. Even so, the press-ups, arm-swinging and bicycling on their backs soon proved his warning about the evils of tobacco to be valid, and he organised a ritual disposal of 'coffin nails' in a fire pit he lit on the slipway at Bucklers Hard where they had all flopped down breathless after a very long trot.

The weapons training sergeant instructor – 'Finger' in honour of his ability to swing a shooter in Hollywood cowboy fashion – handed out ear plugs and threw the trainees in at the deep end. On the first morning they were shown almost every automatic weapon and handgun known to man; and by the time they went off duty with ears ringing they were able to put names to Schmeissers, Lugers and Colts, to make a good fist of taking weapons apart and putting them together again.

That same afternoon they were required to fire several of the weapons. Eve, who had fumbled a lot with the concealed weapon, redeemed herself by proving to be a crack shot with a rifle. Having spent a good deal of her early years in the country, where she had learned how to take rabbits and pheasants, she now found shooting at a man-sized target easy. Cilla and Liz had been taken on shoots with their brothers, and they too were well practised.

Small arms were another matter.

'Concealed weapons – it's one movement: one . . . one . . . one. Hand in your shoulder-bag or pocket, release safety catch, double-handed grip, aim, fire. Bang, bang, you're dead! But you, Anders – you woulda been dead first. You ain't looking for your lipstick. You're about as quick as a pickpocket wearing motorbike gloves.' Finger was right. Eve resolved she wouldn't want telling twice. Whether it was learning to drive, learning a foreign language, understanding 'difficult' plays and books, her attitude was, 'If other people master it, so can I.'

Weapons training was followed by signalling, followed by jujitsu, the art of throwing people.

Here a jujitsu champion – known as 'Mr Wham', whose accent was as far from oriental as a London East Ender's could be – repeated over and over, 'Fall soft, you lot. You ladies might have a bit of fat on your arses, but you got to learn to fall bleedin' soft. Fall relaxed and recover in one movement. Soft and gentle. There won't be no bleedin' rubber mat when you're going to need this.' The fall bleedin' soft technique took hours to perfect. But the ten of them glowed with satisfaction once they had learned the trick of tumbling hefty soldiers – seconded from Aldershot – to the floor.

Liz said, '*Now* let's see what can happen to a chap with a stiff goose finger.' Her eyes quite glittered with enthusiasm.

Each of the instructors had some reservations about the females, but treated them as honorary men as they would be expected to perform as such.

The trainees became so caught up in the speed and variety of learning new skills that they hardly thought about the reality of killing, until one day Cilla Haddington, apropos of nothing that was being discussed at that moment, said, 'I would never be able to do that.' The others knew she was referring to methods of removing human obstacles by stealth.

Anomie Nash pooh-poohed Cilla's lofty comment. 'It isn't going to be for real, it's just that we are supposed to do everything the chaps do. In any case, at five foot three, I could only reach the neck of most chaps.'

The other four laughed at their bouncy colleague, but Cilla wouldn't let the matter drop, 'OK, Miss Shortass, how *would* you take out a border guard?'

In a second Anomie had removed the long, tortoise-shell clip she always wore to keep up her abundant red hair, and flipped back the bar. The blade she revealed was as fine and as sharp as a scalpel.

'Go for the throat so they can't shout, and then slash on to the carotid artery.'

'It'd be bloody messy. The neck crack is how I'd do it.'

They could joke about it now, but it was essential to master the techniques of silently stalking the enemy, taking them from behind, arm tightly around the throat, and a quick jerk of the head to break the neck.

'Heads are twenty per cent of body weight, so you've got help there. Weight helps you: knee in the back, then crack, it's over. Easy as breaking a chicken's neck,' their tutor explained.

'Can you imagine how you'd feel when you heard that crack and you knew that you'd broken a guard's neck? I think I'd be sick on the spot,' Eve complained.

'No you wouldn't, Anders,' the tutor insisted. 'Me or him – that's what it comes down to. You'd be as capable as me of taking the arm-lock to its final stage.'

'Trouble is,' DB said, 'none of us is ever going to know until we're in the "me or him" situation.'

Later, sitting drinking tea as they often did at the end of the day, the ten of them together, Anomie asked, 'Do you chaps have problems with this arm-hold and garrotte thing?'

'Why would they?' DB said. 'Chaps don't have doubts about themselves as we do. "Break that guard's neck, Geordie." "Yes, sir, which vertebra would you like?"'

'Get away with you,' Tommy said. 'Geordie's a big softie. He'd just sit on his face and wait for death.'

'His own or the guard's?'

'Both.'

Geordie was known for his placid nature.

Macabre humour was a way of dealing with the brute facts of the kind of work they had volunteered for. Not surprising – the entire situation was macabre. It was drummed into them every day – 'No mistakes', 'No second chances', 'Self-preservation'.

Gradually they were becoming hardened: 'Don't think human being – think Evil!' 'Think jackboots on babies' heads!' 'Think No right to live!' 'Think, Bastard!'

Even though she was aware that her attitude had changed totally over the last two or three years, Eve still wondered how well she would perform now in a real situation. They all wondered that about themselves, and seeing the others in action at the firing range led all of them to believe that they were the only ones to have doubts.

Often they surprised one another. DB made no bones about her sexual variance. 'I just prefer girls to boys, and I don't like washboard chests. But none of you have to worry that I'll put my hand up your skirts. I was fixated on black skin since I was nursed by my Swazi nanny.' The Chaps nicknamed her the Black Pussy, which DB rather liked.

Although it was not desirable that groups of trainees formed bonds, it was inevitable under the circumstances, especially with the five women. Not only did they have menstruation, with its physical and emotional disturbance to deal with, it had to be endured without the men being aware.

Pecs was the only one to embarrass them. 'Nash! What the bloody 'ell's wrong with you today? Got your rags out?'

Anomie flared red with embarrassment and rage, then left the rest of them drop-jawed with wonder. 'What's it to you, you fucking pervert? Give you a kick? Like to dip your wick in red – if you've got one to dip?'

As soon as it was out her face drained of colour, and she continued the exercises as though the incident hadn't occurred. But she had turned on the bully and respect for her was raised a few notches, to say nothing of curiosity about her past – such language from a nice girl like Anomie.

After weeks of practising the same things time and again, the recruits all began to feel their spirits slump.

DB complained, 'It's boring, boring, boring. I thought it would be more exciting than this.'

Cilla, always confident, said, 'What did you expect, Puss, that you would be sent out in the field half-cocked?'

Eve, feeling as irritated as DB, retorted, 'You're so bloody sure that your big brain is headed for a cipher team next – what if it doesn't come off.'

'I've got it screwed on the right way.'

They laughed like schoolgirls at the flimsy joke.

An evening of boredom almost got them into deep water. It started out light-heartedly, playing a variation on the game of charades in which each of the ten would enact what they had been before Bureau, or, to save face for any of them who didn't want to reveal it, what they would like to have been.

Tommy played it for laughs, and did a fair mime of Tommy Trinder on stage.

Liz and Cilla did a double act, walking with simpering faces, curtsying and then going into a wild exhibition of waltzing together.

Geordie brought Johnny into his mime, having him kneel. Geordie made the sign of a cross with two fingers and then on Johnny's forehead. It seemed easy. 'A priest.' Geordie shook his head whilst the others went through the various nouns that would describe his calling.

It was Cilla who said, 'It's to do with Johnny . . . because he's black. You were a missionary.'

Geordie nodded. They knew instinctively that this was the truth.

Then Johnny rose to his feet and stood before Geordie. 'You think you did good for us blacks, Geordie? Making good little Christians of us, saving us from our own nice, black gods?'

The few seconds of confrontation seemed long minutes until Geordie said, 'Naw, Johnny, I never did no man good except me. I got the call – big white man taking the message to Africa, when you had your awn damned message. The best I can say to you now, Johnny, is that I was no damned good at it. But can you understand being so full of wanting to do something good, that you never asked, did anyone want it done?'

'We all have . . . well, I have,' Eve said. Eyes now swivelled to her. 'I once tried to form a trade union that people were afraid to join.' The heat was suddenly off Geordie and Johnny, and the group all turned to her with puzzlement.

'Go on, then,' Liz said. 'Do what you were at the time.'

It flashed through Eve's mind that she might be honest and act out factory work, but she couldn't bear that they should know that. She might have done driving a heavy truck, but there again she didn't want the same curiosity that had come Geordie's way – wanting to do good to people. But she had once been taken to Paris by the factory manager to model one of the latest corselets he had designed. In the end she opted for the modelling.

Jim said, 'Do models have trade unions? Or was it a model trade union? I say that Anders modelled women's fashions and tried to get the others to get into a union.'

Eve gave it to him by saying cheerfully, 'The pay was so poor, but starvation kept us thin.'

Then Johnny said, 'If you'll just hold a second, I have to get my props.' When he returned he went to Geordie and asked him to unbutton his shirt. 'Maybe you'll feel better about yourself when I've finished.' Then he hung a stethoscope around his neck, took Geordie's pulse, and proceeded to put a thermometer under his tongue. He was so practised in his actions that he had to be a doctor.

'I'm not saying what you did was good, Geordie, but my grandfather went to a mission school – and here I am. You think my bedside manner is OK?'

Nobody quite knew what to do or say. Johnny lightened it by saying in a fair go at the cadences of a Tyneside accent, 'Y'know, mon, me grandfather never did stop reading the chicken bawnes.'

DB was last. Aware of what she could do to them, she opened up the lid of a dusty piano that no one had yet tried out, and played a few chords. Starting with a low, clear note, she began to sing.

There was total silence when she finished.

A soft voice from the shadows of the unlighted kitchen broke the silence. 'Hey, man, never heard you better.'

'Paul!'

His entrance into what was becoming a highly charged emotional group stopped the game.

Eve, DB and Paul sat up till the early hours of the

morning, connecting, laughing and letting down their guard; no dynamic gestures, but small, reassuring hints that suggested here was strong friendship.

'Keep a secret?' Paul asked.

DB at once said, 'Cross my heart and hope to die.'

Eve said, 'Who would ever think *that* voice came from *this* wit?'

'I'm going to be a father . . . a dad.'

Eve leaned across the sofa and gave him a hug and a kiss. 'God, Paul, what a thing to spring on us. Does that make us aunts?'

'Oh, *you* . . .' DB said, 'I didn't know you had it in you. More to the point, who's got it in *her*? Anybody we know?'

Paul grinned. 'Give you a clue. I'm going to be the next "The Dad".'

'You're joking! Electra! Really? Electra Sanderson?'

'Soon to be Electra Smyth.'

DB added, 'With a Y but not an E. How does she feel about it?'

'Ecstatic . . . so am I. I can't believe my luck, finding a super girl exactly suited to me, and she says I'm suited to her.' He held on to his friends, one to each hand. 'A small light in a dark world, eh?'

'Small?' Eve said. 'To me it's a blinking great search-light. I don't know when I've felt so pleased with things. I've got two friends whom I love with all my heart, and one of them is going to be a dad . . . an absolutely super dad.'

'Go on,' DB said, 'I'll be the one to ask. When is it due?'

'Just after Christmas.'

DB held up her fingers, emphatically counting. 'You have to add on three to the expected date due. Eve, the dog! He was doing it to her whilst we were working away undercover on the Windsor op.'

Eve ruffled Paul's hair. 'No wonder Electra was so giddy at times. Riding that bike and singing her heart out, a Deanna Durbin song . . . "Can't help singing, dah dah dah on the crest of the wave with the pleasure that April is bringing." Wasn't it just?'

DB said, 'Come on, we need to celebrate . . . put our night training into practice. I've got a flask of brandy, and I know you've got some cigarettes stashed away. Let's break bounds and go on the razzle just for the hell of it.'

'It's three o'clock in the morning.'

'So what?'

It wasn't really very difficult to get out, and they didn't go far, only as far as where there was a slipway where a few dinghies were beached, and there the three of them sat in a cocoon of closeness.

Paul swigged from DB's flask. 'Apart from Electra and me – this is as good as it gets.'

Eve took a large mouthful of the brandy. 'Cheers. I don't make friends easily, but what we have is such a special thing to me,' she gave a nervous little laugh, 'I honestly don't know what to do about it.'

For once, DB didn't hop in with a witticism to cover her vulnerability. 'I was going to say we should bottle it.'

Paul said, 'You just did.'

'I've had lovers galore, but because I was a white, and known as a nigger-lover even before I knew about sex or nigras, I could never keep a friend. Sooner or later some mother would tell her kids, "You keep away from that de Beers girl," or some father would come to the door and tell my mom that unless she taught me what was what, and what being white meant, then I should keep away from his kids. The irony was . . . *is* . . . most trekker families have got black blood somewhere along the line. They couldn't keep me out of school because it's the law that white kids get an education, but I can't say it was much fun. Best I could do was to make the kids laugh, make a fool of myself for them. But friendship? Nah, man. Never. Singing in American clubland isn't that conducive to making friends, either. So I never had one. Not till I met you guys and Fran. Those days working in the Scrubs when we went about London together – I wished to hell I could have sent a picture home to my pa and told him, "This is civilisation, Pa. These are my friends, they don't care if I like black pussy." Oh sod it! I'm going to cry.' DB sobbed for a long time, then cupped water from the lapping shallows and splashed her face.

On the way back to within bounds, they walked slowly, mostly talking about Fran and possibly trying to get in touch with her again. Eve offered to try. 'I know somebody who is in one of the coding departments. I'll write and hope he gets the letter.' Like DB, Eve felt almost overwhelmed by the tenderness and loyalty she felt towards three people who, had it not been for the vagaries of war, she would never have met. War had brought her Dimitri too; but this friendship was something quite different – built on a thousand small acts and gestures, looks, intuition, insight, trust, shared experience, exposure, plus happiness being in their company.

'Tell you what,' Eve said, 'we'll give the others a surprise tomorrow. As it's our last day I think we should have a treat,' and she told Paul and DB her plan.

Next morning at breakfast, envelopes containing travel documents and orders were given out and lists went up on the notice board.

Eve had applied for air training, but instead she had orders to return to London and report directly to Colonel Linder.

DB leaned across the breakfast table. 'Hey, man, have you been told to swallow your instructions – or wipe your ass with them?'

'You can see them if you like. It's not fair! It's just not bloody fair! They know I'm right for air training. I'm a natural.'

Liz, Anomie, Tommy and Paul were the selected ones. Paul, of course, knew already that he'd been selected, which was why he had turned up now at the Finishing School.

Incensed, Eve went rocketing off to the administrator's office. 'Why have I not been included in the piloting tuition, ma'am?'

'The list was not made up by me, Agent Anders.'

'But, ma'am, it is exactly what I should be trained to do. I have years of experience of driving any vehicle. I would make a very good pilot. Please, ma'am, please, put me on that list.'

'I will need to speak to your immediate superior.'

'Please do that, ma'am. It's Lieutenant Hatton. He knows that I can handle anything that has an engine. I can even repair engines.'

'Leave the matter with me, Anders, and I will let you know. By the way, I understand that your house is going to Boscombe Down airfield today. Nothing to say you can't have a flight if you can get someone to take you up. Sergeant Musgrave will bring the transport out front at 09.30 hours – tell the rest of your group, please.'

The idea of an outing together before they split up had come from Liz saying what the rest must have been thinking: 'Do you think that we shall ever see one another after this?'

Cilla had said, 'If you are going to suggest that we might all meet up again ten years from now, don't even *think* of it!'

Liz, whose suggestion had been going to be just that, had said, 'Oh, come on, Cilla, you know me better than that. Am I likely to suggest such a sentimental gathering. And even if I had –'

Her friend had almost growled her response. 'You useless deb, would you *really* want to stand there waiting at some prearranged spot on some prearranged day, and none of us turning up? Or at best one of us limping up on a wooden leg or, worse, somebody's sister coming with a message? Really, if any of you get yourselves captured or injured or dead, I just don't want to know.'

Jim had said, 'OK, then let's have our reunion before we leave, and the rest of you go flying off. I can arrange for us to go over to Boscombe Down and probably get us taken for a spin in the planes they're working on.'

Boscombe Down airfield was not far from the Priory, but halfway there the group stopped, scraped a pit and brewed tea just for the hell of it. As well as a kettle and mugs, Pecs had brought a box of jam tarts. 'Peace offering, girls and boys.'

DB then produced a box she had been hiding under her seat. 'Ta-raa!' It contained an enormous cottage loaf and a basin of the most delicious-smelling beef dripping.

'Oh my God,' Geordie said. 'If I got captured and an interrogator offered me this in return for my secret, I'd have to take the bread and dripping.'

Johnny, dipping a chunk of bread into the brown jelly, said, 'And, oh my black monkey god – I'd be just as weak.'

'Where –'

'Don't ask, Jim.'

'Eve stole it.'

'Miss Butter-wouldn't-melt et cetera *stole* it?'

'Where –'

'Shall I tell them, Eve?'

'Let Paul. He's less likely to be hauled over the coals.'

'I don't even know what it's called – the big manor house . . .'

'Where the Dowager lives?'

'I'm impressed.'

'Her guards have become complaisant. It was a doddle.'

'So,' DB said, 'we girls are a success then – eh, Pecs?'

'I never heard a word of that.'

Inevitably somebody said, 'Where do you think we'll be tomorrow?'

Cilla said, 'On my way to cipher school. I'd like Liz to come too, but you haven't the brains, have you?'

Liz flicked a dough-ball at her friend, which started more let-out-of-school behaviour until Pecs called a halt.

'I went to a half-ass school near Southampton Docks where we was taught better manners than you society ladies.'

'Pecs darling,' Anomie said, 'I'd have put a skirt on if I thought we were going to be ladylike.'

'I'll tell you something – and if you repeats it I'll put in a report on you. But when I heard that I was getting a bunch of wimmin to train up, I asked them what the hell they thought I could do to get a bunch of tulips as fit and hard as my men. But you have . . . By God, girls, you proved yourself as good as the blokes. I'm proud of you – honest to God, I'm proud of you – and I reckon I deserve a putty medal for doing it.'

They joked and jeered, but his praise was sincere, which made them all feel good, so that when they reached Boscombe Down airfield, Jim's friend who had organised the visit joked about them being the entertainment from ENSA.

In ones and twos, they went up for short spins and came back full of enthusiasm. When Eve heard that a Tiger Moth would be coming in, she asked if she could go up in that. The Moth landed shortly before Paul and Tommy were taken up in the training aircraft in which they would soon be learning.

The Tiger Moth pilot was willing to do a quick turnaround for somebody as enthusiastic about the plane as he was himself.

'Why didn't you want to go up in the trainer?' he asked Eve.

Helmeted and goggled, Eve smiled broadly. 'Just because . . .' indicating that her reason for wanting the Moth must be self-evident: flimsy-looking, double wings, open cockpits, with what looked like pram wheels on sticks.

The pilot sat in the rear cockpit. The take-off was quick, the little aeroplane rocking a little from side to side until it was clear of the airfield, when it became as beautiful and well-behaved as any of the more stable-looking training craft. After five minutes of flying straight out over the sea, the pilot banked, turned and flew in the direction of Boscombe Down.

Ahead, Eve saw something she couldn't at first quite believe: a column of thick, black smoke.

Turning to the pilot, she indicated what she was seeing and he put up a thumb, indicating that he understood. Even before they approached the runway, Eve felt a terrible feeling of dread.

It could only be Paul and Tommy. They were the only ones in the air when the Tiger Moth took off.

Lower and lower Eve and her pilot came in. First she saw an indistinct mess of smoke from which protruded an upended tail and one bent wing. The crash was encircled by little figures. Then she saw a green fire engine and a white ambulance with a red cross. And fire. The pilot landed the Tiger Moth on a runway well away from the accident.

Eve tried to scramble out. In her hurry she managed to get herself caught in the safety harness. The pilot climbed out and helped. 'Stay here.'

'It's my friends . . . my friend.'

'You can't do anything.'

'Don't be so bloody stupid, of course I can't. They've crashed.'

As she jumped to the ground she was violently sick, the one time in weeks that the rejection of what she had eaten was spontaneous. The pilot, a burly, middle-aged man, held her tightly.

'Hold on there, girl. We don't know yet what happened.'

The white ambulance moved away, its bell ringing. When Eve tried to run, the pilot still held on to her. 'No!'

With the foul taste of bile in her mouth, and her limbs weak, she was glad of his strength. 'He was going to be a father at Christmas.'

'You don't know . . .'

She nodded but she knew all right. It was just the kind of card Fate dealt. Think for a moment that you are happy. The ace of spades is flicked at you.

An RAF driver took her back to the Priory alone. The others had been taken away to be treated for shock and to give evidence of what they had seen. There would be an inquiry. Two passengers together should not have been allowed to take off.

Tommy and the pilot were badly burned. Paul had been killed.

WRNS Petty Officer Glasspool stood at the top of a flight of steps that led up to the front doors of Griffon House and watched as a dark blue Royal Navy lorry backed up to the building.

As the driver drew up directly in front of the steps, two able seamen jumped down and let down the tailboard, from where three more seamen appeared. The driver, holding a bunch of papers attached to a clipboard, saluted Glasspool and mounted the steps.

'Morning, ma'am. Delivery of crates.' He consulted his clipboard. 'Furniture and fittings in the name of First Lieutenant Prince Raffi something or other.'

'That's near enough. We've been expecting these things. Unload the large crates and carry them up to the first-floor front. Make sure you all wipe your feet. Get a move on. The carpenters and fitters have been here since 08.00 hours.'

'Sorry, ma'am, unexploded bomb. All the streets leading to the seafront is closed off. Had to come a very circuitous route. Not making no excuses, that's what made us late, ma'am.'

The four carpenters and fitters were not navy men; they were obviously too old to be called up. They sat silently watching as the ABs toiled up the two flights of stairs leading to the first floor.

'Are you Figs? Don't know what's in these but, I tell you, they're a pretty solid weight.'

'Fi-gees.'

Mr Figes, a local craftsman running a small private company and employing only the best tradesmen, knew what was in them – at least he thought he knew: some sort of panelling and a grand sort of sideboard – 'Mahogany fittings, with engraved glass lights and brass trim', which, according to his work sheet, was to be re-erected with extreme skill and in the strictest of confidence. 'Also furniture and furnishings – to be delivered in tandem with the panels and fittings.' Mr Figes had been granted this contract because he was a member of the local grand lodge, where reliable businessmen with sealed lips and a liking for cash contracts were likely to be found.

Mr Figes, who took the strict confidentiality seriously, would not allow his men to take nails out of the packing cases until the RN transport had left and the large gates were closed. PO Glasspool was below, unpacking a crate of the most beautiful drapes and hangings she had ever seen in her life, and Glasspool had attended art school.

The removal of the sides of several wooden crates and much straw and hessian packing took the workmen until morning break, and when they had poured dark tea from Thermos flasks and unpacked the treat of a Ministry of Food recipe rock cake provided by Mr Figes' joiner's wife, the four of them – Figes himself, the joiner, French polisher and glazier – sat on upturned boxes and stared with confusion and English disbelief at what they had laid out on the floor of the large, sea-facing room.

It wasn't the place of any of the craftsmen to speak, so it behove Mr Figes to tackle the matter head on. 'First thing we have to accept is that we're all men of the world, and not schoolgirls.' Gestures of bravado accepted this as read. 'And while we might not see a deal of this kind of thing around here, it's commonplace in some places – especially hot countries and the like.'

'Didn't you say it was some Mufti or Mogul who had it dismantled and sent down?'

'Look, Bert Froggat, that was given to me as confidential information, and I told you in confidence. It isn't something to be blabbed about. Specialised work – that's only one reason why we were chosen. The other is my reputation. Over the years I've seen the insides of a lot of grand houses. People of that ilk don't want all and sundry knowing that their new WC pan and hand-basin have got roses climbing up them. And that's how it has to be in Griffon House.'

Bert Froggat, like the others, had no need to be told yet again. They had worked for 'Figes, Established 1896' for most of their lives. They knew as much about WC pans with roses under the glaze as he did. But he owned the business, got the contracts and paid the wages, so if he wanted to talk, then let him. Even so, the glazier Bert could not resist saying, 'This lot isn't exactly roses, boss.'

Mr Figes smiled and wagged his head. 'Well, no, not your average roses.' They enjoyed a few minutes of quiet amusement of a kind that not every morning break brought. The boss was right, such things were commonplace in hot countries, but here on the South Coast of England, with its clear light that rebounded from the cold sea, the images and carvings lost something of their mystery and eroticism. Surely, breasts like those on the figures carved into the uprights had never seen the light of day outside India, and for sure, no English woman would hold them out and push them at you as though she was selling melons.

The French polisher ran his professional hand over a few buttocks and breasts. 'A classy bit of workmanship.'

'Think it will ever take on, George?' The glazier held up one of the smaller panes of bevel-edged frosted glass on which was a finely etched image. 'What do you think she's supposed to be doing? Looks like she's being got at fore and aft.'

'That's what she is.'

'Don't look comfortable.'

'It isn't supposed to be comfortable, it's supposed to be . . .'

'What?'

'Well, fair dos all round for the blokes, I'd say. They can have two husbands in some of these countries, so I suppose if both wants it at the same time, she has to do the best she can.'

'May I say something, ma'am?' Glasspool was fortunate in having such an approachable senior, otherwise she might not have mentioned the work at Griffon House. She herself appreciated any bit of information that came to her by way of shore-base gossip; it sometimes kept you one step ahead of the field. She had already achieved her first move towards her ambition to wear a tricorn hat and gold lace. She was a firm believer in the maxim about the way to the top being as much about who you know as what you know.

'Of course, Glasspool, speak away.'

'Well, ma'am, that assignment at Griffon House – I wondered whether you were aware of its actual . . . well, nature.'

'Straightforward. Covered by the paperwork. Delivered to Griffon House by the men's navee . . . fixtures and fittings. Local businessman contracted to install. Something wrong?'

'No, ma'am, I think I coped very well in the circumstances, and I must say that the workmen were very proper. They hung dustsheets over the offending pieces.'

'Glasspool, I haven't the faintest idea what you are talking about.'

'I imagined you might not. The fittings turn out to be a cocktail bar, plus easy chairs and occasional tables and drapes. Must have cost a bomb, all hand-carved and etched glass. But, to be frank, ma'am, it's a whole lot of dirty pictures and carvings.'

PO Glasspool observed as queries raced through her senior officer's mind.

'I see. There was no way that anyone here could have known that, of course. I supposed the cloak-and-dagger stuff with the C&E was that Customs didn't want any hassle with the top brass whose furniture and fittings these are. The carpenters – just the local men, you say; no service types there?'

'Only the RN transport – driver and three. I oversaw the off-loading and then completed the paperwork.'

'Good. From here on, Griffon House receives top security on all counts. For that reason you have been hand-picked to liaise and oversee as I was.'

'Yes, ma'am.'

'The workmen must be briefed appropriately. Leave that to me. These things have a way of escaping into rumour, which is the last thing Griffon House needs.'

'Yes, ma'am.'

'You replaced the dustsheets?'

'And locked the door. There are still workmen in the house. The air-raid shelter work is still going on in the basement.'

'Two days more and that will be completed. Three days to make the basement comfortable, and then we can get in and complete the furnishing.'

'Yes, ma'am. I must say, I'm rather keen to get going on that.'

'I'm not surprised, opportunity of a lifetime.'

'Absolutely, ma'am. My father said that taking a course

in fabrics at art school would always come in useful to a girl, but I rather think he meant running up curtains in suburbia.'

'These carvings . . . how crude are they?'

'Actually, not crude at all – in fact, very beautiful works of art, Eastern erotic style, sexually explicit, but not as one sees clumsily done in some of the plain-brown-wrapper type of manual. Not that I am an art expert. Maybe you should give the room the once-over yourself, ma'am.'

The only response was a pursing of the senior officer's lips and a smile invading her eyes.

A lawyer, a naval officer and Mr Figes met in the lawyer's chambers. Mr Figes – being the only one to have seen the artistry, as well as having installed it in a first-floor room in Griffon House – had every reason to be indignant that it was thought necessary to, in the words of the naval officer, ensure that he and his men 'zip your lips', and then went on to dangle promises of contracts for work on other buildings in the vicinity of Griffon House to the 'right sort of discreet and reliable local businessman'.

'I, sir,' said Mr Figes with dignity, 'have never been otherwise. Even when working on the most menial of establishments. My reputation has been built upon skill and sensitivity.'

But he couldn't take on the navy alone so he signed an agreement to keep quiet none the less.

As ordered the day before yesterday – that appalling last day of the Finishing School course, when Paul had been killed – Eve was heading for London, due to report to Colonel Linder in the morning. David Hatton had telephoned the Priory to ask if she would accept accommodation for the night with a friend of his who had been a volunteer with the Abraham Lincolns. 'He just wants to hear how things are now from someone who's seen the aftermath.'

The train on which she was travelling was delayed. It had dragged itself very slowly along the last three miles of track. Although there was a bit of desultory grumbling and bored sighs among the passengers, Eve, in her withdrawn state of grief over Paul, and concern for Electra and DB, did not notice.

By the time Eve had left the Priory, DB had not returned from Boscombe. None of them had. It had been dreadful. She'd gone to see the Duty Admin Officer, hoping to get some news of them, but all that he'd said was that they were still making reports and that Eve should leave at once.

'It should have been me, sir, in that trainer. Paul Smyth was expecting to be married soon.'

'It's like that – a roll of the dice – so don't have any sense of guilt because you are alive and others are not. What have you been doing here these past weeks if you haven't learned that?'

She had learned that. Bureau people needed to be able to walk away from death in a way others could not. That was the theory.

Now somebody on the train said quietly, almost like a moan, 'Oh! Oh!' and suddenly, all Eve's self-centred thoughts were dispelled. Everyone in that compartment seemed to draw breath simultaneously. The train was moving sufficiently to reveal a panorama that was shocking.

Only weeks ago, in Spain, Eve had walked amongst some of the blitzed buildings that time was beginning to make into historical ruins as they gradually acquired a covering of weed and regrowth. The rubble that had been in the streets had been cleared, and repair and rebuilding had started. Madrid's wounds had acquired healing scars.

But this was the raw wound.

Here she was on a high embankment, an audience for last night's blitz. It was chilling. She had been able to cope with the blitzing of Spanish cities and towns because she was engaged in helping, doing something, carrying the injured, bringing in supplies.

To be stuck up here, looking down, was appalling. She had eaten very little since she left the Priory, yet she felt sick. Sweat formed around her mouth and her heart beat fast. She closed her eyes. *Deep breaths, deep breaths.*

Under collapsed buildings there could be people still bleeding and dying. There could be mothers down there, shielding babies with their own dead bodies; fathers tearing at rubble with bare hands, being pulled off by rescuers who knew that the rest of the building could fall any second. There were trails of smoke where timbers, deeply buried, were smouldering now, but any draw of oxygen could make them flare again.

The worst time for Eve in the civil war had been when,

out of a clear blue sky, the centre of a small village had been blown apart. Children waiting at the bus stop, women out marketing, men doing fieldwork – there had been so much raw flesh, so much burning. She had been so absorbed in the mayhem that she hadn't noticed the utter silence because the blast had deafened her. But the screams and cries were there, if anything worse, in her imagination and nightmares.

Those same sounds could be going on down there. Again she was deaf because of her remoteness.

She had given up God years ago, and wondered again why people still clung to the belief that they were being 'watched over' by a supreme being. How many times had she seen a man put a ribbon around his neck whilst he anointed another human being in dying agony? It had always made her anger rise, yet the person dying still hoped for the best. Recently she had become more accepting of such irrationality. Let people do what they liked if it helped them.

The train jerked forward a few feet and stopped again – a 'better' view. Firemen and street wardens were risking their necks clambering over the wreckage of streets that only yesterday had been terraces of homes. There was an amazing mantelpiece clinging to an exposed wall with an elaborate wedding-present clock balanced upon it; there was roses wallpaper, bright pink distemper showing dark patches of damp mould.

These were Eve's own streets. Mile after mile of them had been thrown up quickly to house workers. One bomb on Lampeter Street, and the entire jerry-built lot would come down, just like these. Best thing that could happen so long as nobody was hurt. People in Lampeter Street grumbled to one another when yet longer cracks appeared in the brickwork, and the mortar turned to sand, and the bricks themselves became eroded, and frames rotted. 'Best thing they can do with this place is put a bomb under it,' they said. But in wishing for a bomb to be put *under* Lampeter Street, nobody ever thought of bombs raining down.

Again the train jerked forward, this time inching its way into the terminus. Turning away from the destruction, Eve looked to her left, anticipating the sight that thrilled her anew every time she came into Waterloo station – the Houses of Parliament: Victorian gothic, substantial, sure of itself, looking older than its few years, reflecting its image in the brown water of the River Thames.

Her mind jumped the points from Paul, the Blitz, Lampeter Street and her future self inside the Houses of Parliament.

Stepping out into the gloom of the blacked-out roof through which not even afternoon sun could penetrate, she deposited Paul in her own Pandora's box.

'I heard about the crash. It must have been pretty dreadful for you.'

Even though the train was an hour late, David Hatton was there to meet her.

'For me! For Electra Sanderson and her baby – yes. Not for me, David. I was the one that got away.'

Without rising to her retort, he guided her to a London bus.

'I'm glad that you agreed to visit these people. You'll like them. He's really hungry for news from Spain.'

The bus should have taken them to Soho, but the stumbling journey was so tortuous that, having been constantly rerouted, they eventually decided it would be easier to walk.

Eve was pleased with how she looked wearing her sub-lieutenant's uniform. Tailored on masculine lines, it suited her slim erect figure. All she carried was a black shoulder-bag and a canvas grip. David was in civvies. They were both subdued. They had walked less than a mile before her navy serge and his dark trilby were powdered with grey ash and rubble dust.

It was late afternoon by the time they reached Soho.

When, before the blackout, the neon sign 'Archie's' had flared, it must have appeared incongruous against the old brickwork and timbering of the Carvery and Grill. Only a few square feet of striped awning remained but that might not have been due to war damage. Pasted to the entrance was the ubiquitous notice 'Business as usual'.

'Is this it?'

'It's better than it looks.'

A big man with greying hair came out from behind the bar and clapped both hands on David's shoulders.

'Davey, Davey, how're ya, kid? You look pret-ty good to me.'

David returned the greeting. 'I am pretty good. Tim, *salud*! Eve, meet Tim Redding. Tim, this is the friend, Eve Anders.'

Tim stretched out his left hand, and caught hers in a firm grip, his right remaining heavily in his jacket pocket, 'So you're the one? Truly glad to meet you. OK, I call you Eve? Good. Should call you "comrade" according to Davey, right?'

This wasn't the first time Eve had seen a pocket weighed down like Tim's. Maybe the fingers were missing, or even the entire hand, resting the arm in the pocket a way of appearing almost normal.

'Actually, I was never that,' she replied. 'I was a kind of *ad hoc* volunteer.'

'Same difference, Eve. We were all on the right side. C'mon through, I'll get Nancy to mash us some tea.'

He called to an older man with the physique of a wrestler gone soft, 'Scottie, take over the bar for an hour. Put up the blackout. Don't forget.

'Hey, Nan, meet my old buddy Davey and his girl, Eve.'

Nan was probably fifty. She had a sharp profile of long

nose and high cheekbones, and an amazingly beautiful head with long, long hair, more grey than black, hanging free down her back.

'Davey. Eve. Welcome to Archie's. Not that there's much left to welcome. Will I do as himself says and mash you a pot of tea?' She fisted Tim gently in the ribs, and he curled up as though she had floored him. The warmth of their feelings for one another exuded from their every expression.

The four of them sat at a kitchen table covered with patterned oilcloth as was used by respectable poor people in Eve's old neighbourhood. Potato scones and strong tea were passed around.

Tim asked, 'How'd you manage with the buses – getting here, I mean?'

'We didn't,' David said. 'We abandoned it and came on foot.'

Nan said, 'All Hell broke loose last night.'

Tim leaned over and took her hand. 'And when she arrived home, she looked as though she'd been in Hell.'

'Did you get caught in it?' Eve wanted to know.

'Not caught,' Tim said. 'She goes out in it.'

'Not a deal of good ambulance drivers sitting at home when there's a raid on, is there, you damned Yankee?' She gave him a tight smile. 'Not much good if we wasn't there with our vans.' Explaining, 'That's all they are, grocery vans with the insides taken out and a few stretchers on rails. Last night there was a chap went four times into a blazing building – a council home for old people – he wasn't much of a physical specimen, but by God, he'd got some guts. Each time, he brought out one of the old folks. Then he went in a fifth time and the whole place collapsed on him. One of our girls got her leg broke by a flying drainpipe.'

Eve easily visualised this grey-haired woman doing the same kind of runs to and from hospitals or dressing stations as she herself had done. The difference was that Eve had been twenty, but Nan Redding was old enough to be a grandmother.

'Have another scone, Eve. You've not got a deal of flesh on you seeing as you're in the forces.' She dabbed an extra bit of butter on one for Eve and winked. 'Being a publican has its advantages. It's all, "I'll scratch your back – you scratch mine." Not that we go a lot on the spivs and black market, but our currency now is *things*.'

'It's how it used to be Out There, isn't it, Eve? You'd know,' Tim said. 'It wasn't too bad for me – Nan used to send me bits and pieces. Trouble was, I never wanted to part with any of it for barter.'

Eve really didn't want to talk about that war – or any war. She just wanted to see Colonel Linder and be allowed to get on with her Special Ops work. But this man needed to speak about his experiences.

'When I was coming in to Waterloo today, I saw all those houses on the south side of the Thames . . . just piles of rubble – Spain all over again. But things are already looking different in Madrid.'

'The people will still see what was there.'

'I'm not sure that you're right. Human beings are very resilient. We have to be.'

'Even under Franco, that s.o.b. fascist?'

'Especially under a dictator.'

'Then it was all for nothing?'

'I don't know, Tim . . . I wasn't in a position to judge.'

David asked, 'What about this area, Tim? I see a lot of broken windows and your "Business as usual" notice.'

Tim heaved his shoulders and breathed out heavily. 'You want to come and get a gander at the back? C'mon, I'll show you.'

As Tim Redding opened double doors, a beautiful setting sun shone directly into the house. 'On Monday there was a whole street there, on Tuesday only the hole.' An inadequate word, 'hole', for an enormous area laid waste.

After a period of shocked silence, David said, 'It's a miracle that this place is still standing.'

'If Archie's was some kinda church or chapel, it'd be a miracle, but it's probably science. Archie's and the rest of this side of the street were the only good buildings in this whole part of Soho – the rest were trash without a foundation to their name. Add to that the scientific fact that blast has its limitations – it's got to stop somewhere, and Archie's and our street was its limits. Next time, it will have a clear run. But we came through, didn't we?'

'What was there before?'

'Some street-girls and their kids, some of them with their mas too; skid-row apartments for throwaway guys and girls. Eel and pie shops, newsagents, a lot of little pubs and bars. OK, the bars were dives, girls would fuck in doorways and the guys would pee in the streets . . . so what do you say? Hitler's done what the borough shoulda done years ago. Betcha that's just what people *will* say.'

'That's what they'll say about the place where I was born and grew up.' Eve stared ahead but was aware of the men turning to look at her. 'It was the rough end in a rough town. Nobody asked to be born in those streets – nobody should have *been* born in those streets. Little girls don't want to grow up to fuck in doorways. Boys don't ask to be half-starved street urchins. I got away by the skin of my teeth. It wasn't easy, and I've lost touch with my own kind because of it.' She turned and gave David Hatton a wry smile.

Tim went back into the bar, and David offered his and Eve's help.

Nan said, 'I get to bed early on good nights for bombing. You can pretty well guarantee that with skies like this there'll be a big raid. I'll get my head down by nine o'clock and have about four hours. Take the front room upstairs if you like, but I'm going into the cellar. Archie's is lucky: the cellar here can take practically everyone in the entire street.'

Tim said, 'Raises the temperature of the beer, but who complains? At least we got beer.'

'Come upstairs, I'll show you your room.' Eve and David's bags were standing side by side where Tim had placed them. Eve was nonplussed and looked from the bags to Nan. Nan gave Eve a sheet to cover her uniform and a pair of dungarees and a top. 'If you have to move fast, just grab these and you're dressed in thirty seconds. I sleep in mine.' Then she read the uneasiness on Eve's face. 'Tim thought that you and David . . . You're not, are you?'

Eve shook her head. 'He's my superior officer. But we have known each other for a long time. I thought he had arranged bed and breakfast.'

'I'm sorry, Eve. You don't think . . . ?' Nan stopped and helped Eve hang her jacket.

'What, Nan? That David thought he might get me into bed?'

'I'm sure not.'

'So where was he expecting to sleep?'

'I'm sorry, Eve. Tim must have assumed . . .'

'That I was yet another of the Hatton girls? Don't worry, Nan, I know all about his reputation.'

'Tim got the impression that you were the one.'

'I am.' She smiled delightedly at Nan Redding. 'But *not* the one for Lieutenant Hatton.'

'OK, I'm glad we sorted that out before Tim put his foot in it.'

When Eve had stowed her bag and changed, she and Nan sat at the table, ripping some beautiful damask banqueting-size tablecloths into strips and squares, and rolling them into bandages and slings. A clock somewhere chimed the half-hour.

'Half-past nine,' Nan said. 'Time I got my head down. You could come down in the cellar with me, if you like.'

'I would.'

'Did you hear that?'

Eve listened.

'Big guns, a long way off.'

Tim came in with David. 'I've called time. Not that there's anybody drinking. Scottie's collecting up. Did you hear the guns?'

'Yes, I was just saying to Eve . . .'

'Dover guns. You can always tell. That means we're for it again. Put the light out, Davey.' Tim opened up the door to the big space. The sky was as clear as could be, with no lights showing in the whole of the great city, stars were shining brightly. A good bombing night. 'There! You heard that.'

As he said it the warning siren began to wail.

Eve was glad that she had changed into briefs, shirt and dungarees. Now she slipped on her rubber-soled navy-issue brogues. Nan, in the back room, wearing a tin hat marked 'Ambulance', was thrusting a flask into a khaki shoulder-bag.

'Can you do with another pair of hands, Nan? I've done it before.'

'You're on. There's a tin hat in the bar . . . somebody left it. Take that, and here . . .' She handed Eve a generous-sized jacket. 'It gets cold around dawn.'

'How about me, Nan?' David asked.

'Thanks, love, but you'd only be in the way. Eve knows what has to be done. See you when we see you, Tim.'

Eve grabbed her gas-mask case and gave David a sloppy salute. 'I'll see you when I see you . . . sir.'

Nan was off almost before Eve had slammed the door of the converted van. 'I have to check in at the emergency station and say who you are. You'll get a tag to wear.'

It had been nine thirty when the siren had sounded. By eleven o'clock, Nan and Eve were collecting injured people on the canvas stretchers and taking them for minor emergency treatment at Red Cross stations, or to hospital for the more serious injuries.

No time for the dead now; they were left for later.

The two women scarcely had time to speak except about what they were doing.

At some point in the night, the van's engine went dead. Before Nan could finish 'Oh shi –', Eve was under the bonnet.

'Spark plugs oiled up. Got any spares? OK. In my gas-mask case – spare knickers and a bottle of perfume.' The only light was from a torch held close by an ARP warden. 'Try her now, Nan.' The engine sparked into exquisitely perfumed life, Eve thrust the black-oiled knickers into her pocket and they were off again. Into the intense flare of incendiary bombs, and the endless thump and crump of high explosives, and the hiss of water gouting from hoses, and the balls of orange flame that burst through tinder-dry timbers of old roofs.

Dawn came so clear and beautiful that it was almost impossible to believe that the sun would be rising on the city that had just been through a night of such black and red terror. Yet it was not the same city. With every night of the blitz, London was changed for ever. Acrid fumes from steaming old bricks and mortar, escaped gas, burst sewers, a terrible stench of burned fur from a furrier's still smouldering – when the all clear sounded after a raid that had lasted nine hours, Hell had come to London.

Nan and Eve passed a trail of Archie's neighbours who had been sheltering in the cellar. Nan wiped a hand across her tired and blackened face and kissed Eve roundly.

'You're the best mate anybody could wish for, Eve, and don't let anybody tell you different. This place is yours any time you want to stay – always supposing it's still standing.

Just remember to keep some satin knicks and a bottle of French perfume in your bag.'

Nan's neighbours must have wondered about her and the grimy woman grinning at one another in the cold dawn light.

Tim had sandwiches ready, and a pot mashed as Nan liked it. The two women plunged into the thick bread.

'Davey went off with his camera just after you left,' Tim told Eve.

She nodded. 'I guessed he might. He's good at that. One picture and the whole world understands.'

'I'm going to get my head down for a few hours,' Nan said. 'If Tim's done the boiler, there should be enough hot water for a bit of a bath. Take no notice of the four-and-a-half-inch mark Tim painted on. That's for high-class folks who bathes every day.'

Eve half filled the Victorian bath and slid under until only her face was above. She imagined that she could still hear the jangle of bells that had gone on all night – ambulances, police, fire brigade; the sharp crack when a wall split from its support; the rumble and crash as roofs fell in; shovels scraping rubble; ARP and first-aid volunteers calling for quiet, then listening for response from someone buried beneath the rubble.

After fifteen minutes of relaxing, she shook out her uniform, put on a clean white shirt, and went down to say thanks to Tim Redding. He looked up expectantly as she stood her things by the door and put her hat on. 'Far to go?'

'North side of the Thames, by Waterloo Bridge. My meeting isn't until later this morning, but I want to drop off my stuff at left luggage.'

'You'd best go by the underground. Buses will be all to hell. Want me to tell Davey a message?'

She grinned. 'He knows where to find me – he probably knows my movements better than I do.'

'He's a hundred-per-cent good guy.'

'He's my boss, so who am I to argue with that?'

The city tube stations were used as deep air-raid shelters where every night Londoners went down to get a night's sleep. Some went down early – families with blankets and bags of food and drink, others came in from nightclubs and theatres, still in their glad rags, some in uniform. Early morning saw a double flow of people – those going up to see if their houses or rooms were still standing; those going down to get the tube to work and see whether their office or shop was still standing.

The long escalators weren't working, so that the people who had sheltered underground had a long steep climb.

Today, a dowdy, bedraggled mother, carrying baby and bags, was trailed by a toddler still half asleep and grizzling. A woman in a smart Chanel suit picked up the child and carried him, his tousled head snuggled against her pearl earrings.

Then, on the platform, a naval officer, still the worse for wear, was being helped to his feet by a man who might have been a paper-seller in the Strand. Eve's mind played with the possibilities. If the entire population suddenly found itself living and working and fighting alongside people they would never have come in contact with before – except as boss and floor-worker, mistress and maid, shop-girl and society woman – perhaps the old class war was done for.

Having deposited her bags at left luggage, Eve walked out from the terminus into the surprising golden morning and down to the Thameside walk: sun glittering on the peat-brown water; tugs hauling cargo; a few boats dragged along by staid, grey-painted and camouflaged vessels that must belong to the navy; small dinghies crisscrossing to pontoons and landing stages. Buses and trolley buses passed back and forth over Waterloo Bridge, Westminster Bridge and Vauxhall Bridge.

Hell might have come to London last night, but the city was up and running this morning. Eve leaned on the Embankment wall, counted her blessings and discovered there were many.

She still had plenty of time to cross the river to the building that housed some of the secret services offices. She chose Westminster Bridge to cross. From her induction time at Baker Street and the Scrubs, she knew her way about London. She thought: after the war, I could come to live in London . . . or Spain if things change . . . before I retire to Ryde. She smiled. The problem for her was that she easily fell in love with places.

All part of the excitement of being alive.

Once on the other side, she went again to look at Queen Boudicca who, it was supposed, would soon be in some subterranean safe house.

Eve liked Queen Boudicca. She had discovered the stone statue during her induction weeks. It didn't really matter whether the queen was mostly legend, she was symbolic of Ancient Britain and of the strength in women that modern times had obscured by hats and feathers and lessons in frailty.

Why did we let ourselves become such pathetic creatures? I'm strong, the girls in the factory were strong, the women who fought in Spain were strong, the girls at the Finishing School were strong. So, why are we at such disadvantage? Maybe the war would change that. Women were taking over men's roles everywhere. Nan, like the women going to the front line in Barcelona, did their day's work and then went into the battle.

Boudicca was an awesome, voluptuous woman attacking in a war chariot whose wheels carried blades to scythe through the legs of the enemy – an aggressive, bloody, ancient queen yet essentially a woman with firm breasts bared to face the enemy. How glorious the woman was. The angle of the head tossed nobly back made it impossible to see her expression, but her whole story was in the steadiness of her figure as she grasped reins controlling the racing horses and the dreadful war chariot. How limp Eve's own beliefs seemed in the face of this warrior woman who was prepared to take the fight to her enemies.

Eve hoped that the ancient queen would not be removed to a place of safety. It would be too demeaning.

When Eve arrived at Colonel Linder's office, she found Phoebe Moncke and Janet McKenzie there. No Colonel Linder.

Phoebe was brisk. 'Take a pew, Lieutenant Anders. Relax, first names until we come to some conclusion.'

Eve saluted, then nodded and said hello to Janet. Janet – dressed in neat pale peach linen that could only have come from America – looked good, her brown skin shining with health.

Phoebe leaned back in Linder's leather chair. 'What we have here today is a bit of a rum situation. Understood, of course, that nothing said here goes out of this room, even if the idea is dead in the water?'

'Of course. Why is it necessary to tell me?'

Janet said, 'What Phoebe means is that this is a wacky idea and whether it works or not, nothing will be official, no paperwork for the archives – nothing attributable. Phoebe and I have gone round and round with one another and we still arrive at the same place: stalemate. Go on, Phoebe, you tell it your way first.'

'Well, Eve, Colonel Linder has now got a whole string of Bureau people – or, as we must now say, SOE agents – graduating from the Finishing School. As you now know, SOE does secret and dangerous work. Every undercover operation behind enemy lines means danger to agents and resistance groups alike. There will be men taking on the roles of railway workers, or timber fellers, women posing as hairdressers or . . . or anything. They will be the means of contact between people *here* and people *there.* In France, there is a resistance movement, in Greece . . . and the opposition to General Franco is not dead. In Holland and Belgium there will be operations that only SOE people will be capable of doing. We're the experts, the practical people, the disruptive element. Leave special intelligence infiltration to SIS.' She took a breath as though about to dive into water.

Eve knew all this. Why was it necessary to repeat it? Phoebe and Janet had obviously planned a strategy, a double act, so she let it run without commenting.

Janet got up and propped her bottom on a desk, standing where she could watch Eve's reaction. Eve knew what Janet was doing. The second stage of the strategy was about to emerge – to test Eve's reactions. Which was why this was an informal meeting – just three women speculating. Drinking tea.

'A biscuit, Eve?'

'No thanks, Janet.'

'I see you've clung on to your thin body.'

'Slim body. I'm keeping it for the benefit of the cut of my uniform. I'm very fit.'

Phoebe plunged in. 'You've seen a fair bit of the work our boffins do – absolute geniuses at forging ID papers, disguising radios. Any one of our boys or girls who are dropped into occupied territory will have every detail of equipment authentic and perfectly disguised for their assumed role . . . and it's getting better all the time. However . . .'

Janet took over. 'No one knows better than you, Eve, that one tiny detail overlooked could easily cost an agent's life. We all worked really hard to get everything exactly right to cover you in Spain. It was a very costly operation.'

'All the time I was there I wondered whether I was value for money.'

'Finance isn't the problem – it is the safety of our people.

Did it ever occur to you that in Holland a man's shirt collar is fastened with a *vertical* buttonhole, not horizontal as here? An undercover agent in a French café orders *café noir*. Why does the Gestapo come to collect him?'

Eve shrugged.

Phoebe answered. 'Because he or she wasn't aware that there is nothing *except* black coffee in France now. The Gestapo aren't fools. The devil is in the detail. Like us, they *know*. SOE is building itself a reputation as unassailable.

'I do *know* all this. Keef's attention to detail provided me with a wardrobe of clothes fit for a millionairess, remember.'

'Because that is what you *were*,' Phoebe said.

'And because your psychology was right, the two together – your training and the props – made you invincible,' said Janet.

'So?'

'So, you were a guinea pig. I had time to spend with you. Only you and Miss de Beers to concentrate on at that time.'

'And Paul?'

'He was a gift. Except for a list of venues, he –'

'You know he's dead?'

'Of course we know. It was a very sad accident, a great loss to SOE.'

'And to his wife-to-be and their baby.' There was a silence which said that they didn't know. 'He told Wilhelmina de Beers and me a few hours before. We were a threesome.'

Janet said, 'Three SOE agents, Eve.'

'I know that, Janet. But human beings do tend to form close relationships. They end – it hurts – we deal with it – bury it along with all our other emotional trash.'

'Eve, we should talk about this. We will make a date.'

'Now,' Phoebe said, 'every few weeks trained people are coming out of our various training establishments, or being recruited.'

'And,' Janet went on, 'they come out brilliantly trained, psyched by me and my team, but vulnerable. The vulnerability matters, but more to some than others. Most at risk are those who will go into Occupied Europe to live supposedly ordinary lives – except, of course, that they will be working for us.'

There was a short silence during which Phoebe and Janet looked at one another.

'Oh, come on, please,' Eve pleaded. 'It's a bit one-sided that you have an agenda for this meeting and I don't know what the hell all this preamble is for. Tell me what you have cooked up that you want me to do, but don't like saying.'

'It is Colonel Linder's idea,' said Phoebe, 'and I think it is a good one, and so does Janet. Janet has written a paper on prostitutes. I've read it and I think it's brilliant. It's not about the obvious reasons why men use them, it is about their use as confidantes.'

Janet said, 'My study was in several countries and in many strata of various societies, and what I discovered is that a quite large percentage of men don't necessarily want sex, they simply want to talk, need to talk, and will pay the going rate for that. The need *to tell* is overwhelming. There is an element in talking that can free a man of sexual inhibitions – in short, he can get an erection that had been held back by his subconscious. And, of course, there is that very masculine trait – showing off to a woman. Even males who have no sexual problems will use prostitutes as a listening ear.' Janet smiled broadly. 'I was pleased to learn that it is usual to charge for that too.'

'The confessional, with no Hail Marys to pay,' Phoebe said. 'Some men have egos the size of Texas.'

Janet said, 'That's good in a secret agent – the attitude "I can do that!" And not *only* men – we are no different. It is your ego, Eve, your pride in yourself, knowing that you are better, more competent, are ambitious . . . your ego is one of your greatest assets. But you are not egotistical.'

'Is *my* ego the size of Texas?'

'It may or may not be with you and with me,' Janet laughed. 'I'm not so sure of Phoebe – we don't need anyone to admire our competence.'

Phoebe said wryly, 'Well, thank you very much, Dr Freud.'

'No, no . . . not Freud – the man who thought he knew what made women tick and got us completely wrong. Actually, Phoebe's ego is interesting. She has always known how good she is – hers *is* the size of Texas. However, she likes to confuse people by her scatty manner and dress. What *she* says is, "Look at me, aren't I an interesting and scatty woman?" whilst hiding her great intellect within. Now, what is interesting with Phoebe here is that when one does discover her abilities, one is overawed. Didn't you feel that when you first saw her sitting in her tricorn hat and gold lace?'

'I did, yes. Quite a transformation.'

'And very satisfying to any Texas-sized ego – right, Phoebe?'

Phoebe smiled and nodded. 'In a party-trick kind of way.'

'The thing is with Phoebe, she has no need to boast. You and I have seen both Phoebes. But what if she was, say, the canteen lady at Griffon House with a senior WRNS officer inside? She might, just might, just once, want to let one other person know. Actually, Phoebe, you wouldn't, but it makes my point.'

'Which is? If you don't mind me asking, because it's all as clear as mud to me,' Eve said.

'That even those of us who play the game close to the chest have our egos to deal with.' Eve thought of Alex, and her drinking and her pillow-talk with Duke. As far as Alex was concerned, Duke might have been anybody.

'. . . "courtesans with good manners".' Eve had missed the

start of Phoebe's sentence. 'Colonel Linder's description . . . more polite than mine. I'd call them "FiFi".'

'Please, Phoebe, put it in words that a simple country girl like me can understand.'

'Colonel Linder has asked me to see how you would react to organising a few very special trained women. They would be SOE.'

'As *courtesans*?' Eve started to laugh, then stopped short. 'You're serious? Train nice girls to become prostitutes?'

'No, no,' Janet said, 'courtesans, geishas. They need not be sexual encounters. Seduction is an art that can be taught . . . learned. If necessary, I could talk about the techniques, but we have in mind one woman who knows a lot about it. It would be your job to arrange for the man ready to go on his first operation to meet one of these women. The men will be those about whom I am not one hundred per cent confident – who might succumb to a pretty woman, who might be a pretty enemy agent.'

'Do you mind telling me why you've asked me?'

'You're the cat who walks by itself. Were you always like that?'

'I suppose I was; I never had much in common with the children I grew up with. Being the cat who walks by itself doesn't mean loneliness.'

'I know,' Janet said.

'Why do you ask?'

'I think running FiFi requires a person who can stand aside, be uninvolved but concerned. These girls must be respected for what they are willing to do, and this couldn't come from a person who doesn't respect herself. You respect yourself.'

Eve had never had a better compliment.

'This is not an assignment I could order any agent to undertake,' Phoebe said. 'Will you do it?'

'Yes, ma'am.'

'Lieutenant Hatton said that you'd agree.'

Eve left the office still warm from the glow of the compliment, but raging inwardly that David hadn't told her what to expect.

David Hatton was waiting for her in the foyer of the building, wearing the same civilian clothes he had worn yesterday. Good God, was it only then?

Stiff and erect, Eve approached him.

His smile vanished when he read her expression.

'You shit!'

He flushed and then went pale. 'Eve!' he said mildly. 'Language, language.'

'Don't you dare language me!'

He caught her elbow firmly and guided her out into the September sunshine and on to the Thames Embankment, where yellowing plane trees were shedding a first leaf or two. Jaw clenched and still stiff, Eve allowed herself to be seated outside a tiny riverside café that also served an underground station.

David laid a packet of cigarettes and a lighter on the table and went inside without asking what she wanted.

She extracted a cigarette and was shocked to see how much her hands were shaking as she lit up.

He brought out two cups of tea, plus a filled teapot, and four biscuits. 'No choice.'

Accepting the tea, she held the cup in both hands to steady the tremble.

He took a cigarette and lit it.

They had been able to let a full five minutes pass since she had attacked him with the words that had obviously shocked him.

'Now, can we discuss the problem you have with me?'

She sipped the tea. It was not only very strong. It was excessively sweet. She expressed her distaste.

'Drink it, Eve. Sugar's good for occasions like these.'

'Oh, *really*?' she said sarcastically. 'And what kind of occasions *are* these?'

'Rage on your side, anger on mine. Adrenalin high, blood sugar low.'

'Oh God, David, you are so smug!' But he was right. Within a few minutes the trembling stopped.

In a calmer voice she said, 'You poke around in my life – not for the first time – you discuss me, give people advice on how to approach me. *Don't deny it!* Your fingermarks are all over this FiFi job.'

'They need to be, Eve. In the end, I am the one who must carry the can if it fails.'

'It won't fail, David. I will see to that. I might detest setting up this little operation, but I shall set it up good.'

He tapped his cigarette nervously. He was not good at hiding his reactions.

Eve knew he felt intimidated. You'd break under questioning, David, she thought. Lancing College doesn't harden you up a quarter as much as Lampeter Street Girls' School.

'What's the joke?'

'Just us, David. "Tango Man and the Cat Who Walks by Itself."'

Looking directly at her, he said, 'You used to be Tango Girl.'

'History, David. Another place, another life.'

Janet McKenzie, Phoebe Moncke, Eve, DB, Anomie Nash, Vee Dexter and Electra Sanderson were meeting in Electra's house. These were the women who, in a preliminary sounding out by Phoebe and Keef had not rejected the notion of 'caring subversion – to protect our own.' They met at Electra's because it was private and neutral ground, and because Electra was recovering from miscarrying her baby.

It was Anomie Nash who settled the matter of how they should be referred to.

'"Courtesans with good manners?" What a blinking joke. What does he think we would do – sit around in boudoirs with peignoirs slipping off our shoulders? I'm sorry, whoever thought that up is a joke himself.'

'Colonel Linder, actually,' Vee Dexter said.

'Well, Miss Dexter, I'm sorry if it sounded rude, but it's true. Some men like to kid themselves . . . but to my mind sex for money isn't courtly.'

Eve wondered what Vee's motives for showing interest were. Had the wife of her lover, Colonel Linder, found out about her? Or was there a new woman organising his life for him? At least Vee knew something about secret sex.

'When I was in the business,' Anomie said, 'I used to call myself "a hostess". It was good, really, because being that, I was the one who had the say in how far I would go. As far as the Jimmys were concerned, they paid me for my companionship by the hour. It was a job, and it paid well. Anything extra was negotiated. A night in *my* bed, in *my* flat, didn't come cheap. But you know, you can get fed up with all that sameness, so when Commander Keifor got me a chance with Special Ops, it was the best thing that had happened to me in ages.'

'You'll have to give us a few lessons in hostessing, Miss Nash,' Electra said.

DB, in her blunt and honest way, said, 'You didn't do badly with dear old Paul.'

Electra gave a wry lop-sided smile. 'I didn't, did I?' Locking her fingers tightly, she pressed her thumbs hard against her mouth before she continued. 'Look, can I say this now and finish with it? Losing the baby soon after Paul being killed was pretty bad at the time, but that's behind me now. The only thing I seem to be able to do well is drive, and seduce a man.' Now she cupped a hand over her mouth and smiled. 'Paul and I had a fling. He didn't intend to make a mistake . . . neither did I . . . but it happened and we would have got married if . . . you know? That's it.'

'DB,' Phoebe asked, 'are *you* all right with the hostess idea?'

'Why not? I won't be spending all my time singing in foreign nightclubs. And, although I like women best, I can do men; second best, but they like what lesbians do for them. Also, I'd really like to sing in the kind of sleazy joint this seems as though it's going to be.'

'Darling Wilhelmina, I was merely thinking that the Finishing School won't be turning out all that number of undercover operatives who are lesbians.'

'Phoebe,' Janet McKenzie said, 'aren't you making assumptions? And Miss de Beers is right: men are often intrigued by having sex with a lesbian – they think that a good man can cure her of it.'

Janet and DB burst out laughing together.

'Not with you anywhere near me, Doctor.' DB leaned a shoulder into Janet.

The coffee substitute made palatable by a dash of whisky, which had been Phoebe's idea, was doing what it was supposed to do, helping them to relax and be open.

'I have been given several suggested names of likely girls, but who are not SOE, and I thought we could best discuss such a ticklish idea with women we already know, and who know at least one or two of the others. If any of you would have difficulty in working with Miss Anders, then let's talk about it. If the rest of you think you won't get along together, that's not going to matter too much.'

'I'd be fine,' Anomie said. 'We were OK at the Priory.'

DB said, 'Eve seems to be a natural leader, don't you think?' Vee and Electra agreed. 'What about Eve?'

'You realise that I won't be a FiFi – that name seems to have stuck so we may as well go with it. My role is to see that the new graduates of the Finishing School are left in the company of FiFis. Then you will take over.'

'You think it will work?'

'Of course it will work. We're Special Ops.'

Phoebe said, 'I always liked the idea of you being named FiFis.'

No matter what now, this small group of women would go down in the history books as SOE's FiFis.

The refurbishment of Griffon House was now complete. A great deal of money had been spent on it. Every bit of crisscross blast paper had been removed from the windows, and replaced by screens of fine mesh wire, so that when there was sun, it came into top rooms all day, spattering floors, walls and furniture with cathedral-window colours.

Dressed in civvies appropriate to the glamour of the rooms, Petty Officer Glasspool showed Eve round with almost proprietorial pride – 'We have done this. We have done that. Don't you think that we have restored this room wonderfully?'

'Nobody could say it looks like a tart's boudoir now it's finished.'

'I'm glad you like it, ma'am.'

'Maybe we should settle somewhere and make ground rules?'

'I thought maybe you would like to see how things might run in a small way. I mean, in the nature of a guest arriving for an informal visit?'

'OK.'

'Tea or coffee? We have the best of both in many varieties.'

'French coffee?'

Glasspool pulled a bell pull embroidered in silk and gold thread.

A young Asiatic man, dressed in wardroom whites, appeared. 'You wish for something, Miss Glasspool?'

'Nasser, this lady is Miss Anders.' He nodded a stiff little bow. 'Miss Anders is my boss-lady, which means that she is also your boss-lady.' Glasspool spoke as though Nasser might not be able to hear or to understand.

Nasser replied in soft, accented but well-spoken English, 'Good morning, Miss Anders. Is that how I should address you?'

'That would be fine, Nasser.'

'We should like some coffee – French mild roast – not breakfast roast.'

'Madam.' Nasser disappeared, his soft-soled shoes soundless on the thick-pile oriental carpet.

Eve ran a hand over its luxurious surface. 'This is beautiful. It's silk, isn't it?'

Glasspool nodded. 'Washed silk. I hope you don't mind

me saying, ma'am – it is a compliment – I had been hoping for someone who understood and appreciated what had gone into making Griffon House – and you obviously do.'

'Did you go to art school?'

'Yes, ma'am, and then for a while I worked with Phoebe and Keef in their theatre days. I have always been interested in extravagances. My ultimate delight is Gaudí. If it hadn't been for the war out there, I would have loved to go to Barcelona.'

'I have seen his work – never seen anything as beautiful – breathtakingly beautiful.'

'Don't mind me saying so, ma'am, but you don't look old enough to have been there.'

'I was there when Barcelona fell.' Eve gave a wry smile. 'Unfortunately I wasn't in a position to appreciate the Gaudí buildings fully. But I shall go back when things are better.'

'You went . . . ? I'm sorry, ma'am, I'm too inquisitive.'

'We all are when we find somebody who likes the things we do.'

Nasser returned with the coffee, and poured the aromatic blend into small porcelain cups. Eve was delighted to be reacquainted with something she hadn't tasted since staying at the Madrid Ritz. On the tray were crisp little cigarette biscuits dipped in chocolate.

'What has all this to do with SOE?' Eve asked. 'There's a war going on. Have you met the person responsible for this finery?'

'Oh yes, ma'am. He's a very handsome young man – Prince Raffi.' Glasspool made a gesture of regret. 'He isn't interested in women.'

'And Griffon belongs to him?'

'I don't think so. It's a very complicated story from what I know of it.'

'I'd like to know,' Eve smiled. '"Unattributable", as they say.'

'I only know what I have picked up from Miss Moncke. She will probably tell you more herself.' Glasspool poured more coffee and settled back in the comfortable upright chair. 'An important member of the aristocracy closely connected to the royal family, a naval officer, and Prince Raffi are very close companions.'

'Lovers?'

'I think they must be. The Englishman is married to a tobacco heiress. They have two daughters. I think you could describe them as part of the fast set. She likes the same type of lover as her husband, but not necessarily as young. They live very respectable lives, Lord and Lady of the Manor, hugely charitable, admired for everything that is publicly known about them.'

'Pillars of the establishment?'

'Exactly!' Glasspool was quite relishing this gossip, as was Eve. Having just done with one royal entanglement it appeared that here was another.

'How close to the royal family?'

'The same German ancestors. Close.'

'Who?'

'I don't think I should . . . I know you said "unattributable", but I think none the less, I ought not to say. But you can work it out for yourself. Their estate isn't a hundred miles from here. And Portsmouth is his port and Prince Raffi's, which is why Griffon is so convenient.

'All this is to conceal a member of the royal family who is homosexual.'

'I'm not sure if you would say that he was a *member*. And he has two daughters.'

'Just the same . . .' Eve gave the room a meaningful look.

'A man with a wife and a lover both rolling in it? Small

change to them. And most of the furniture and furnishing have been sent over by Raffi's father.'

'So . . . how am I to fit in here?'

'Officer Moncke suggests that Griffon shall be run very much on the lines of an exclusive club and a safe house. Beyond that, I think that it is up to you to suggest what you would like.'

Eve had known ever since she had taken on what Phoebe insisted on referring to as 'Operation FiFi' that she would find her role difficult. Phoebe, at a meeting subsequent to the one in London, had said, 'Not a pimp, Eve – that's sordid – nor a madam. You will be an agent working with women who will *willingly* undertake their roles as undercover investigators . . . under-the-cover volunteers.' Eve had smiled. Only Phoebe Moncke could come up with such a title.

Now Eve got up and wandered about the room. 'If this place is to be run on the lines of a kind of exclusive private hotel, I think the Special Ops women would fit in very well. Some of them have been part of the nightclub set: they aren't shrinking violets, and love the fast life they've been used to. Phoebe and Dr McKenzie are convinced that these young women could save lives. I hope that they are right. Between members of SOE I always want them referred to as Agent So-and-so. I think they will quite like that. It will make them feel that they are contributing to the war. Here they will be known as hostesses.'

'Yes, ma'am.'

'Is your role purely organisational?'

'It is.' Glasspool was glad of that in the circumstances.

Eve picked up the agent newly out of the Finishing School at the bus depot. Tom Seymore was the FiFis guinea pig. Smiling and extending a welcoming hand, she said, 'Mr Seymore? I have a car waiting.'

'I must say, I didn't expect to be collected.'

'I've been through the Finishing School, and I know how it feels to be let out at last.'

'It's quite bewildering in a way, but I'm eager to receive my orders.'

'You are seeing Lieutenant Hatton – tomorrow, is it?'

'Yes, at the Marine Barracks.'

'He's hoping to meet you tonight at Griffon House, the hotel where we put up some of the more specialist agents like yourself whilst they are awaiting orders.'

That evening, Tom Seymore met David Hatton and Eve in the bar. Things between David and Eve had become as they should be when two people are devising a vital plan.

'Tom, this is Lieutenant Hatton,' said Eve. The two men greeted one another. 'David, I hope you don't mind, but I have a friend staying here, and I thought it would be a nice idea if she joined us for dinner,' Eve added.

'Absolutely.'

Eve left and returned in five minutes with her friend, who was in a pretty dinner dress with necklace and earrings, and wearing dancing shoes. 'Anomie, this is Lieutenant Hatton, and this is Tom Seymore.'

David said, 'Oh, *David*, please,' standing a little closer and holding her hand a little longer than was necessary, but Anomie didn't seem to mind.

Anomie Nash was brilliant. She all but ignored David Hatton but was open-eyed with interest in Tom, asking him if she could taste a morsel of the duck from his plate. After closing her eyes with feigned passion, she said, 'I just *love* good food and wine, don't you, Tom?'

When Tom replied that he hadn't eaten anything like it for months, Anomie whispered in his ear, 'Poor, Tom. I know all about Priory food.'

Tom was now stimulated by the revelation that Anomie was part of the world of covert operations. At least that was how it appeared to Eve and David, though perhaps Tom was playing Anomie along. But for now, Tom had reacted in just the way Eve and Anomie had hoped he would.

Anomie had said earlier that day, 'What if he really doesn't want to play, Eve?'

'With all your experience, you'll soon know, won't you, Anomie?'

The Griffon dining room had the atmosphere of an expensive London hotel, pre-war – the clientele only officers in uniform, mostly naval – and women dressed prettily, as was Anomie. One needed to know what was going on to understand that this wasn't just any hotel. The young man waiting at table, dressed in white messroom waiter's uniform, did not flinch when his hand was overlaid casually by a 'customer's' hand, or his buttocks were felt discreetly as he served at table. Eve wondered why, if this was primarily a house safe for homosexuals to meet, that it was necessary for this charade, but then looked across the table at Tom, who was entranced by Anomie. Like most heterosexual Englishmen, had he seen the homosexual flirting, Tom would have regarded Griffon as a den of depravity and run a mile.

What went on in Griffon could be called vice, but it had an air of respectability. Maybe Prince Raffi and the tobacco heiress had transformed Griffon, but Eve guessed that it was even bets that the property still belonged to SOE and that they had top say in how it was to be run. Linder, Faludi, and probably Keef and Phoebe too, were powerful people, and had friends in very high places.

Now, Anomie and Tom appeared to be getting along fine, drinking just enough to break down barriers. As they were about to take coffee, a bellboy brought a note to David. He looked nonplussed and bent towards Eve. All he whispered was, 'Time to make ourselves scarce.'

Eve looked disconcerted. 'Oh dear, is it absolutely important?'

David nodded. ''Fraid so. I say, Tom, Eve and I have been called away . . .'

He looked towards Anomie, who said, 'Don't you worry about us, David. Tom and I will be absolutely fine, won't we, Tom?'

Eve said, 'I feel dreadful, leaving you two to finish on your own. Shall we be back, sir?'

'Probably not. You come to my office in the morning, as arranged, OK, Tom?'

'I'll be there.'

'Go away you two. Tom and I are going to dance, aren't we, Tom?'

David walked with Eve to her temporary accommodation a short walk from Griffon, a big Edwardian House with '13' in brass figures on its outer doors. It was being used by nurses and a few WRNS who needed a night's rest away from air raids, sleeping on cots in an enormous basement reinforced with iron girders. Eve had slept in worse places, and, as all the women were dog tired, there wasn't much talk.

'How do you think it went?' David asked as they walked along the blacked-out promenade.

'Smoothly, for a first attempt.'

'We shall see.'

'I said it would work. It will.'

She wasn't treating him well. He didn't deserve to be.

The winter of 1940–41 was Siberian. Griffon House stood as though encapsulated in a bubble of light and warmth, whilst around it the whole country appeared to be going up in smoke. Thousands of people were killed. By then, Eve had had enough of Griffon House. Electra was well able to take her place. She determined to go over David and Faludi's heads and ask Colonel Linder for something that could involve her more directly in the war.

A few days before Christmas she received a letter from him saying that she was to come to his office on 30 December.

Nobody went to London by choice, but if one was travelling out of almost any city at that time, it was a case of exchanging one blitzkrieg for another. It was hell on the railways, so Eve decided to travel up on the last Sunday of the year to give herself more time. She had been given a permit to stay in the basement of one of the Government buildings in which Colonel Linder had his London office. It was a case of arriving and taking your belongings into the basement, and staying there overnight.

That night 10,000 fire bombs fell on the centre of London. Even so deep underground, Eve could hear the crash of buildings collapsing throughout the night. It was impossible to sleep. Smoking was not allowed. Those who had foresight had brought something to eat and drink. Eve had only a screw-top bottle of lemonade and sponge cake she managed to buy at the café on the Embankment where she had rowed with David Hatton in September.

Now that the social barriers had come down, English people were talking to one another. Eve struck up a conversation with a woman who told her that she was Mrs Jago, a Jewish refugee, and that she and her little girl had recently arrived in England and she must present her papers.

'What about Mr Jago?'

'Seb was taken away – some friends say in a cattle truck, but I wasn't there.' The woman said it so matter-of-factly. 'I do not expect to see him again.'

What was there to say? 'I am sorry' was so inadequate. 'But you have your little girl. What is her name?'

'Elizabeth.' The woman stared at Eve, disconcerting her. 'May I tell you something?'

'Of course. What have we got to do except sit here and talk until the raid is over?'

'The day after we arrived, which was . . . I don't remember, after Christmas Day, we came into London Docks. After we had disembarked and were free, there was an air raid. Elizabeth tripped as we ran for shelter. Her arm was broken, not a serious break. Some people were so kind. They took us to the hospital where we were told to wait to get an X-ray and plaster.'

'So she's still there?'

'No. A nurse took Elizabeth and told me it would take time, so I should find a tea trolley and wait. The X-ray department was directly hit by a big bomb . . . nothing left but a big, big, hole. Everyone was killed.'

'Elizabeth?'

'Everyone.'

The woman's dry-eyed constraint was frightening.

'You should get some treatment yourself,' Eve advised.

'I think you may be suffering from shock. It could be bad if you don't get help.'

'Thank you.' She withdrew into herself for several minutes. 'We would have been better to go with Seb.'

All that Eve could do was to break off half the cake and offer to share the lemonade.

The last Eve saw of Mrs Jago was when the all clear sounded, and Mrs Jago took her one bag and went to queue up to use the toilet.

The world outside was unbelievable. The whole area from where Eve had spent the night to St Paul's Cathedral had been all but demolished. Elizabeth Jago was known to have been killed, but in the devastation of last night's blitz, there would be hundreds of people never accounted for.

Surprisingly, the building where she was to meet Colonel Linder still stood. It was too early for office workers, but a night guard allowed Eve to use the ladies' room and found her a place to wait until her appointment.

'They tell me my courtesans are working well.'

'They are, sir. They prefer to be known as the FiFi.'

'Ha, ha. Damned good. But I understand you want to move along?'

'There is nothing at Griffon House that Miss Sanderson can't do. The women there like working in those surroundings. But I think my brain will shrink if I stay there any longer.'

'How is Vee Dexter?'

'Very well. She certainly suits the place, and I think the place suits her.'

'If I take you away, then I should appoint Miss Dexter to your post.'

'Vee hasn't been to the Finishing School, and I thought Miss Moncke's plan was to have everybody at Griffon under her command.'

'All right, then Miss Dexter shall have the full Finishing School treatment. And Miss Sanderson shall replace you in the meantime.'

'Right, sir.'

'And what about you, Miss Anders? You must have had something in mind when you went over your two seniors and asked to see me.'

'I realised that it would be you who would make the final decision, so coming to you directly seemed appropriate.'

'Miss Anders, don't take this the wrong way, but do you ever ease up?'

'Yes, of course I do, sir. Why do you ask?'

'You are such an earnest young lady. I'm told that you have a great intellect and ability which you seem to need to use endlessly.'

'I can hardly switch off my brain, sir.'

'Do you go dancing?'

'I love dancing.'

'Tennis? Swimming, the cinema, music?'

'All of those, sir.'

'Really? Then I may have read you wrongly. I believe that it is essential that life contains an element of pleasure.'

'Satisfaction is better, sir.' She gave him a smile. 'More satisfactory.'

He nodded and smiled. 'What is it that you want me to give you permission to do? I am quite sure that you have it all planned.'

'I should like to learn to fly, sir. I know that I could do it. I have always had an affinity with anything mechanical that has an engine and moves. I can strip down an engine and put it together again.' She gave him another smile. 'I know that I would make a good pilot.'

The colonel leaned back in his chair and stared off through the netted windows, drumming his fingers. 'I believe what you say, but what would you propose to do – *if* I allowed this?'

A shiver ran through Eve, thrilled at his interest. 'There are two possibilities at the moment. One is to transport aircraft from the factories; the other is to do the channel-hopping, dropping our agents wherever they need to be dropped.'

Colonel Linder slapped his hands together briskly. 'Right! You shall have it.'

Eve raised her eyebrows high and smiled broadly. 'Thank you, sir. Thank you very much.'

'Good, now that's settled, let us get down to my reason for calling you here. Maybe it could be part of a deal between us.'

A deal? Linder was head of SOE for the entire south of England. Pike don't make deals with minnows.

'Now. Concerning Major Vladim. I, of course, know your past history with him.' He looked at her over his half-lens glasses, expecting a response, which he didn't get.

'Major Vladim has proved himself invaluable to us, more than that . . . He now has a section of his own, brought into being by him, and it is proving very, very important.'

'Yes, sir. I can imagine it would.'

'However, we have a problem. His presence here is clandestine – he's best classed as a refugee. However, his own country considers that he has no such status, but is a deserter and traitor. They demand that he is handed over to them.'

'How could they possibly know that he was here?'

'Good question. We believe that the GPU have been on his trail, but have come to a dead end *for the moment.* So they are, so to speak, flying a kite; demanding any of the likely nations who may have accepted him – Australia, Portugal, Switzerland, ourselves – to hand him over.'

'Are you saying that they don't actually know that he has come here?'

'No, as I say, they are fishing around. We, of course, don't admit to knowing who this man is, but the GPU aren't fools. Vladim himself is proof enough of their calibre, if proof were needed.'

'You can't possibly hand him over . . . sir. He would be shot as a deserter. He would have to be made an example of.'

'However – and I warn you what I am about to tell you is classified Top Secret, and I should not be telling you this if it were not for the Vladim problem – the Soviets are teetering on the brink. Which way will they jump, with Germany or Britain? Britain cannot afford to cross them with things as delicate as they are.'

'You aren't even contemplating using him –'

'No, no. Vladim must stay with us. He is crucial to the Polish cipher section. But he must disappear. He has already been registered as a refugee, Lec Podsadowski. But change of name is not enough, and he is not truly a refugee. Under international law, if his country wants him returned, then we must do so.'

Suddenly Eve felt cold. She crossed her arms over her chest and stilled her shivering hands under her arms. She knew almost nothing about international law. Even if what Linder said was a pack of lies, it was probably what would happen anyhow. Individuals could sink as long as governments swam.

Linder took two glasses from his desk drawer and poured a finger of golden spirit into each. 'Almost the last of my good brandy – go on, drink it.'

Eve took the drink and felt it burn its way down. She wondered how delicate interviews would be managed if there was no drink to smooth difficulties. It was either the teapot or the bottle of spirits. 'Thank you, sir. It's no use me saying that I can't believe this would happen, because I know that it could, and I know how guilty I should feel for my being the reason for him to have come to England.'

'You have no reason to feel that. Major Vladim came very willingly.'

'That doesn't make it any easier if he is handed over to them.'

Linder poured out the very last of the brandy. This time Eve sipped and felt her mind, which had been dull with fear, begin to function. If the Government intended to hand Dimitri over to the Russians, they would just do it, and she would never find out what had happened.

'You haven't called me here just to tell me this, have you, Colonel?'

'There is a solution, Miss Anders.'

Eve knew that there was. She stared through the glued-on nets at the windows and saw a fire reignite in a nearby building. Linder waited patiently. 'Naturalisation. If I married him, as my husband he could become a naturalised British citizen.' She turned from the window and met his gaze.

Linder nodded. 'Would you do it?'

Eve took plenty of time, then nodded. 'No need for us to do a deal, sir. Of course I will do it. But with one condition.' She never really understood the true reason behind this. 'After the official civil ceremony, you allow Major Vladim leave to come to my home and for us to be married in the village church.'

'All right . . . why not? Actually, Miss Anders, I think that a splendid idea. Could it wait a few weeks? Not the registry office ceremony, the church wedding?'

'A spring wedding in a village church – what could be more cheerful in the midst of war? Do you think I might start my flying tuition before then?'

Linder laughed. 'You press a hard bargain, Miss Anders. All right. I'll tell Captain Faludi to sort it out.'

In early January 1941, Eve and Dimitri were married at Caxton Hall in the middle of London.

For two days they felt closer than they had ever been. For both of them, it was a serious step.

Earlier that morning, Dimitri had been waiting in the foyer of a hotel in Half Moon Street, close to the Ritz but which – according to Faludi, who had reserved their rooms – had better style and service. Not knowing whether they would prefer separate rooms, he had booked two.

When Eve arrived, Dimitri was seated on the edge of a chair too small for his bulk, looking eagerly at every turn of the revolving door. She held her arms wide in greeting. He picked her up, swung her off her feet, and hugged the breath out of her.

'Look at you, you have become a sailor.'

'Better still, I am almost a pilot.'

'More beautiful – I thought that was not possible – and you are thin . . . but ah . . . very nice.' Dimitri couldn't enthuse quietly if he tried.

'And you? I didn't know that you were an army officer. I mean one of ours . . .'

'Not strictly true, but they tell me that I can have rank as major, but only when I am British subject. Which is today! Oh, Eve, my good, kind, wonderful Eve, you do this for me. I am always indebted . . . (Right?) to you. Thank you, thank you one million times.'

She put her arms round his neck and kissed him firmly on the mouth. 'You owe me nothing, Dimitri, nothing. You saved me, now it's my turn.'

'We do something special today. After we are wife and husband, eh? What you like to do? Anything. I want a day of happiness as most as I can give you, and we shall remember when we are old.'

'I'll think of something. We should go now.'

Eve had insisted that nobody from SOE should stand as witnesses, so they asked passers-by if they would be willing. It was easy. The first two people asked – an elderly man who signed himself 'R. Barfoot – Cabinet Maker' and a young woman, 'L/Cpl. Pamela Stride, ATS', agreed readily. The registrar's assistant said that it was usual to offer witnesses something for their trouble, so Dimitri had thrust a five-pound note into each of their hands and thanked them profusely. Pamela Stride thrust the note into her shoulder-bag, a little embarrassed to be taking a note of such large denomination from a complete stranger, but R. Barfoot – Cabinet Maker crackled the note and held it to the light and went off still turning it about as if not quite sure that there wasn't a catch in it.

A little group of curious onlookers stood and watched the newlyweds emerge into the daylight. 'Would anyone mind taking our picture?' Eve asked. 'My camera is easy to use.' A youth volunteered and Eve set the focus.

A soldier and a Wren – the kind of wedding that happened every day now. The groom looking smart and pleased, kissing the bride, who held a bunch of cut flowers bought from a seller on the way. Another of Dimitri's five-pound notes went into the pocket of the young photographer. Eve felt very happy.

'Do you remember what you were told about tipping?' she laughed.

'I remember well. Her name was Annie . . . no, it was Amy. She said never tip more than a shilling, ten bob was too much. But I like to give away. SOE gives me plenty. What can I do with it?'

'Take the Scottish girls on the town.'

'We are not near towns.'

'Haven't you got a girlfriend yet?'

'Of course not. I am married man.' He pulled her close. 'I have wife. No, no, Eve, don't look like that, is only a joke. There is a young woman, we go to the movies, not very many times. I like her, but it is just friendship. Maybe she scares me, she had such a sharp understanding. She is not in the Polish section, so I do not look like an idiot compared to her. Also, you know what? She has written books, very many. One afternoon when we have been to see a movie, she makes me go with her into a bookshop. "I have written these. I buy you one for you . . . will you read it and when you have read one hundred pages, stop and tell me what will happen?" So I say, of course I will read it, but why not all? She says her books are puzzles about who done the murder. She said if I had not guessed who done it, then she would think others would not. It is red herrings, hidden clues, I must find them. She is very good writer. I have read many of her books.'

'Her name wouldn't be Fran, would it?'

'Not Fran . . . is Frances.'

'Frances Haddon?'

'That is right!'

'Small world – though maybe not, considering we are all SOE. I know her. She is *such* a clever woman, and so nice.'

'She is.'

'You will tell her that we met?'

'And that you are my wife?'

'No, Dimitri. You know you can't do that. Perhaps it's better that you don't tell her at all.'

'I tell her. It makes me feel I belong more. We have same friends. Is wonderful . . . *It* is wonderful.'

'You must still be Lec Podsadowski the Pole.'

'Of course.'

'She will want to know if I told you anything else about the Scrubs team. It's a prison we worked in. Tell her that Paul was killed in a flying accident. She and Paul got on well together. He had been hoping to get into ciphering.

'He was your friend too?'

Eve nodded. 'A nice man. You would have liked him. His girlfriend was expecting their baby, but she lost it. They were going to be married.'

'Is a cruel world, Eve.'

They were walking through Piccadilly Circus, signs of war all about them. Except for the weeks in Australia, war at close quarters had always been the background to their relationship. Eve suddenly thought about there being a strange romanticism about living on the edge. Enjoy the moment. By tomorrow, Piccadilly Circus might be a bomb crater, and she and Dimitri might be dead.

Paul and Electra – Paul's death was a tragedy, yet had they not grabbed their moments, Electra might have been left with only regret.

'Dimitri, we have never danced together. Shall we do it?'

'I am good dancer.'

Eve laughed at his boast. 'How is it that we have been married for two hours and I didn't know that my husband is a good dancer. Come on, let's find a place that's open.'

With the war now in its second year, there was growing a kind of frenzy of taking pleasure where and when it presented itself. Dance halls – some of which opened early in the day and didn't close until late – were filled. Big bands played the latest music; dancers flung themselves around with unrestrained pleasure as they jived and jitterbugged.

Frequently people left with partners they may never have met until that day. It wasn't very easy to get drunk – there wasn't always alcohol available – but who needed it to dance and romance? In some dance halls the sheer numbers of people all moving in time to the rhythm of a big band could induce a wonderful intoxication.

Dimitri's boast was not false. He danced with enthusiasm, even at one point doing a bit of cossack leaping, which gained him a circle of clapping supporters. From the dance hall Eve and Dimitri walked to the same Lyons Corner House where her Scrubs friends had turned up in disguise. Eve tried to tell Dimitri about it, including how Frances Haddon had been involved, but he didn't really get it.

'Just tell Frances that you have been to the café where she dressed up as a waitress,' Eve concluded.

He nodded seriously, still puzzled about the reason for this.

'Oh, Dimitri, you do make me laugh. I'm having such a good time.'

'I am also. Maybe you would like to go to opera? A theatre?'

'Not much chance of that. I know!'

The Windmill Theatre was gaining a reputation for never closing. Even when there was an air raid there might be a bit of disruption during the worst of it, but the show would go on. Dimitri looked at Eve in surprise when he saw the kind of spectacle the Windmill was famous for: glittering dancers, and beautiful young women standing still as statues wearing tall head-dresses of feathers, high-heeled shoes and nothing else. Like every other male in the packed house, Dimitri leaned forward and waited for one of the nudes to move. None of them did. The Windmill Girls were becoming famous in every camp, airfield, and ship that went to sea.

Before darkness fell, Eve took Dimitri to see some of London's famous landmarks. They finished up walking through Green Park on their way back to their hotel with an air-raid siren whining.

'You know what to do, Eve?'

'Yes, we go to the underground station.'

When they reached it, people were moving down the steps in a steady stream. Even still held on to the flowers Dimitri had bought her, but by now they were a bit the worse for wear. She managed to salvage one each, which she attached to their uniforms. Where they were seated on a wooden bench well back from the platform's edge, other people sharing that area were cheered by the sight of newlyweds. Dimitri responded to the attention. He played up the jovial foreigner who made people laugh at his mistakes, making them warm to a big man with a funny accent. He knew very well what he was doing.

Not for the first time, Eve thought what a good, nice, generous man he was. How fortunate she had been in meeting him. In enjoying their nights – and days – of wonderful sex.

Not for the first time she watched him playing with children, charming casual acquaintances.

Every time they caught one another's eye, he would wink and smile broadly.

Why can't I be content with you, Dimitri? Eve wondered.

For hours they leaned against one another and took fitful dozes. It was four o'clock in the morning when the thin note of the all clear sounded and they could walk on to Half Moon Street.

'You like if we sleep together, wife?'

'I like very much if we sleep together.'

Eve had worried that Duke Barney might come between them. He didn't. The familiarity of Dimitri's body, his smell, his voice kept Duke well out of the bed.

In the morning she took off her wedding ring and held out her hand for his. 'You get this back at the church.'

'No, I keep them. Don't worry, I keep them safe. We will use them again in the spring. Captain Faludi, he says that it can be April.'

The small branch-line train steams along at top speed, swaying and rattling. The interiors of the compartments have gritty floors scattered with cigarette stubs, worn upholstery, ashtrays overflowing. The light bulbs either do not work or are missing; the windows are brown inside from tobacco smoke and grey outside from the steam and smoke of the engine. Most travellers hardly notice, and, in any case, 'Don't you know there's a war on?' is used to shame moaners. Most people in Britain have better things to worry them than neglected railway coaches. Many of the travellers are in uniform. Some look only inwards, some doze; others, on their way home or to embark, talk heartily and make jokes. None of them wants to look at the passing scene.

But Eve does. The last time she travelled on this line was in 1937. Then, the Southern had plenty of coach cleaners. With her forefinger she rubs a little clearing on the window and peers through. The sight of the very Englishness – Hampshireness – brings a lump to her throat. She loves her own county, always has, yet she could hardly wait to leave it when she was barely twenty years old.

She is anxious to see her family, and the place called Roman's Fields where they all now live together. Over the years that she has been away there have been times when she has missed them, but not much. She knows she couldn't last a week living within such peaceful domesticity.

She hopes that they take to Dimitri.

When she looks away from the rolling green countryside, she isn't surprised to find Dimitri's eyes upon her. He winks. With his military-style haircut and his major's uniform, he looks so much like the man she met in Spain. Again her heart is wrenched a little. Will this ploy of naturalisation by marriage be enough? She still can't believe that the GPU will not somehow get hold of him. The only hope is that Russia might come into the war on the British side.

She smiles at him warmly. She has made him a British subject, but never in a hundred years could he become British. Like her, he can put on another personality like a coat, but like her too, nature runs deep.

'We're almost there.'

He too rubs a bit of window. 'Is still farmlands.'

'Is now station.'

Eve's uncle, Ted Wilmott, has only one good arm, but he puts twice the strength in it to hug her. Then, moving back a pace to look at her, he says, 'Lord help us, Lu, you got splendid all right. I shouldn't never have recognised you. And this is your intended. I'm pleased to meet you, sir.'

'Dimitri, Ted. You call me Dimitri. This major stuff is all jacket and hats.'

Ted gives Eve a look of approval. 'Come on then, Lu. Let's get you home.'

She is always going to be Lu to everybody living on Roman's Fields land, Wilmotts and Barneys alike. She is glad that they have decided that here Dimitri should not be Lec. Lu and Lec? How many faces do they have?

Roman's Fields in Wickham has been owned by Ted and May Wilmott since May's father died. Theirs is a fertile corner of the county, close to where the landscape starts to swell and rise gently until it reaches its highest point at Beacon Hill where it swoops down again into yet more fertile chalklands and the decaying village of Cantle, and then up again to ancient hill forts.

The big, old house is alive with women's warm voices. The men are out and about – Ray at his work as signalman, Eli Barney picking on the smallholding. Ken went somewhere yesterday. He's cagey about it.

Ray Wilmott, Eve's brother, brings a good pay packet to Roman's every Friday. His wife, Bar, sister to Duke, also brings in a wage. She has gone back to work on the estate as head groom. Now that so many of the young men have joined up, Bar has brought in two of her young brothers to help her.

When this happened, Gunner, the estate agent, went to Lady Stanton-Lewis to complain: 'It's bad enough having a gypo running the stables, but she's bringing in a whole lot more.'

But her ladyship would have none of it. 'They are good with horses. That is the only consideration.'

'Give them an inch and they will take a mile, madam. I know gypos. The old man takes game birds.'

'We can spare him a few. Our woods are full of them.'

'He sells them. And so he does the snowdrops and the holly and mistletoe. He takes birch for making pegs and our willows for his wife's baskets. He practically lives off our estate.'

'His lordship's estate, Gunner.'

'And I want to protect it for him from the likes of the Barney clan.'

'Why do you have such a down on them, Gunner? There was a time before it was enclosed, many years ago, when everybody in this area was free to live off the land. His lordship's family took it, quite legally of course, but people like Barney don't see it like that – and I can't say that I blame them. Be tolerant with them, Gunner. Young Mrs Wilmott is doing such good work with the horses and with Megan.'

Megan was the only child of the Stanton-Lewises, and going through a stage where horses were central to her life.

'Yes, well, there's that too. That girl spends a deal too much time in their company.'

'So you want to give me advice on how to bring up my daughter as well? Megan's boarding school has closed, and until we find another, I am glad that Mrs Wilmott doesn't mind her hanging around the stables. I am contemplating sending her to the village school, so that I can have her close, now that his lordship has rejoined his regiment.'

Gunner was shocked. The country was going to the dogs. One thing he admired about Hitler was that he had got rid of the gypos.

'Let the Barneys be, Gunner. We owe them more than they owe us.'

'Your ladyship, that can't be.'

'Why do you have such a down on the family?'

'Because they're gypos, your ladyship. They aren't like us. They're scroungers.'

'Don't be ridiculous, man. Who around here works harder than the Barney family?'

Gunner left with rage in his heart. What could anybody do about people like that who married into the aristocracy? A woman who went around saying she was proud that her grandmother had gone to prison to get votes for women.

When Gunner had rage in his heart every past wrong boiled up. The Barney girl took days off and went out to do witchetty things. She went to the circle of stones, and the yew circle on Butser Hill. He suspected she did evil things there. When he'd told her she couldn't be spared, she'd brought in her two brothers. She'd said, 'You got your holy days and bank holidays, and I got mine.'

He was a good estate agent. Half the work he did should rightly have been done by a gamekeeper. His house was tied to the job, and he had the same fear as every man whose home was given as part of his wages. No chance to save and, in the end, no job, no home. He never complained because he wasn't a young man and he had an injured leg. Only in the safety of his four walls did he speak of his fears to Mrs Gunner.

'If my leg gets any worse, that gypo girl will have the job from under me. She put a spell on her ladyship and Miss Megan. With my own two ears I heard her ladyship call her "Mrs Wilmott".'

'That's who she is.'

'She's a damned gypo. Don't tell me you're taken in by her.'

'I don't see there's anything to be taken in over. A more open and nice girl I've yet to meet.'

Gunner rejected vehemently his wife's suggestion that he make her his ally instead of his opponent.

'So you won't be going to the wedding party over at Roman's on Saturday?' Mrs Gunner asked.

'No I won't be going to no wedding party, and no more will you. If Ted Wilmott don't mind having truck with the Barneys, I do. You've only got to see what happened to Ann Carter, a decent village girl until Eli Barney got a hold of her.'

'He never got a hold of her. She wanted him.'

'Not wed in church.'

'But wed in the olden way. If it suits Ann Carter, then it's no business of anybody else's.'

All of which was listened to by their son, Maurice, who heard everything but said very little. Maurice wasn't 'all there'. Damaged at birth, he was still, at the age of twenty, his mother's child. But to Gunner, Maurice was yet another daily reason for anger and torture: retribution handed out by his hard-hearted God for a sin he had committed before Maurice was born.

Maurice spoke. 'Miz Carter . . . she's a nice lady. Miz Carter talks nice to Maurice. I goin' to Miz Carter's party.'

Gunner thumped his fist on the draining board. 'You've been letting the boy wander again.'

'He needs to wander.'

'Not to no Barney camp, he don't.'

'It's not a camp, and you know it. They live in a decent enough place on their own bit of land. The Barneys are no different to you and me – except that they've got a bit of land and we're in a tied cottage.'

That hit where it hurt most. Mrs Gunner wasn't normally as argumentative as this. Anything for a quiet life. But she was beginning to come to the end of her tether, coping with a husband who was becoming stranger by the day in his obsession with gypsies, a grown-up son with a child's mind, and not many years to having to give up the cottage.

'Whilst we are on the subject, I let Maurice go over to Ann Carter because she is better than you or me at getting Maurice to do normal things.'

'Normal things! Normal? What normal things is that?'

'She's been showing him how to make strawberry chips. May Wilmott said she would give him something for them when he's learned. Maurice, show your dad.'

Maurice would never understand why his dad had put the chip basket into the cooking range. Only broken chips went for firewood.

Gunner would never understand how his wife came to side with Ann Carter and her queer brood got on her by Eli Barney. Even his lordship hadn't seen any danger in taking on the Barney girl for the stables. Like everybody, he had been won over by the way this bit of a girl had with his hunters.

Gunner had always been a regular churchgoer, a sidesman, a parish councillor. An upright man, as he could truthfully say. And now his wife had gone against him, siding with the godless tribe because one of them was coming back to get wed. He thumped his fist on the arm of the chair in which his wife had been seated before she went out, saying in that reasonable voice she always used when Maurice was around, 'James, if you don't put a curb on your unreasonableness with our nearest neighbours, then I shall take Maurice and go down and stop with my sister in the village. You don't never stop talking about the Barneys. To my mind, we'd all be a lot better off if you'd take as much notice of your own son as you do of them.'

'All right then, if that's what you want, clear off and take that shameful thing with you!'

Alice Gunner was stunned. The burning of Maurice's chip basket had been cruel enough, but to turn on the boy who had had no hand in his own making . . .

Maurice couldn't know that it was he who was the 'shameful thing', but he did feel his mother's hand tighten, sensed the fear that shivered through her, and wanted to be out of the house away from his father.

He couldn't know that most mothers and fathers sleep in the same bed. He couldn't know of the silent dementia that can take over a reasonable man when every night he is reminded of the sins of the flesh that had created Maurice.

Gunner craved that sin. Every night he remembered when it was not a sin, but God-given in the marriage vows. For the procreation of children. But James Gunner had bad seed. Turned bad by a single coupling with a loose woman.

He shouted after Alice and Maurice, 'Church wedding! It's a sin if any of the Barneys enter a church!'

As agent for the estate, he needed a whole row of shotguns. He selected one, filled his pockets with cartridges, and walked off into the shafts of sunlight that filtered through the trees that surrounded Keeper's Lodge in which he had spent his entire life.

Let Eli Barney cross my path, and I'll have him, he thought.

Ted Wilmott opened the heavy farm gate. Eve noticed how he had aged, how the effort the act cost him showed in the bend of his back.

Dimitri got out to shut it after Ted had driven the van into the yard.

'Eve, your home is beautiful house, big. Looks maybe a hundred years or maybe more?'

'Three hundred.'

'So important. Piece of history. I like this very much, Eve. There is sense of forever . . . ? Unchanging?'

'Continuity?'

'Yes. Maybe I now know better how it is that you can be Eve and Lu. You have two worlds in which to live. I think it is hard for you, yes?' He gave her a light peck on the back of her neck. 'Look, these must be your people coming out of house.'

Eve's spirits rose, then sank. They had come to meet Lu, but she had stayed behind in Spain with Duke.

Eve moved into May's arms and was enveloped in the warm smells of country clothes, soap-washed hair, boiled-white aprons to which the smell of baking clung.

Dimitri was introduced, openly appraised, welcomed. Walking through the yard to the kitchen door, Eve felt her senses were hit by everything that had been forgotten – the yard dust kicking up, the steaming muck heap, the low contented grunts from the pigsty, a cock and more hens than when she was last here. The smell of sun on old brick and thatch, hay, cut grass, faint whiff of the septic tank, hard soap, disinfectant, country wine, yeasty beer, stewed apples, warm pasty – not individually, but as a recognisable whole, the smell of Roman's Fields greeting her.

It ought to have felt like coming home. Instead Eve was being treated a bit like a visitor. Dimitri, with his praise and endless questions, charmed them all into warm informality as only he could.

They moved into the kitchen where May had put on a bit of a spread. 'Now come on in and sit you down. Leave your bags. They'll wait, but the food won't.'

'Oh, Ray! It's so lovely to see you. Where's Bar? Are these two yours? Dimitri, come and meet Ray.'

Ray shook hands formally. 'Nice to meet you. And I suppose congratulations are in order, seeing as how you and Lu will be getting wed.'

'Thank you, Ray.'

Ray nodded. 'This is Bonnie, and this here is our Anthony.'

Dimitri, squatting to Bonnie's level, held his finger out for Anthony to clutch. 'Is nice baby. Hey, you, Anthony, you a nice baby. You see, Lu, he likes me.'

Bonnie said, 'That's not a smile, it's wind.'

May was watching Lu's 'intended' like a hawk, liking what she saw.

But, if she could have seen what was going on beneath the surface, she would have wondered at Dimitri's distress.

From the moment Eve had emerged from the revolving door into the foyer of the hotel in Half Moon Street, Dimitri had experienced pain and pleasure in everything they did together. Except for the lovemaking, everything was for the first time as well as for the last time. First and last time dancing together; first and last time seated together watching a show. The shutters were coming down on their relationship. This was a marriage of convenience, nothing more – something Eve had agreed to to save him from extradition. Later, they would be divorced. The conditions had always been clear.

It was breaking his heart.

When, in Australia, she had miscarried a baby, he had told himself that there would be others. She would carry his children. But, as it turned out, she didn't love him. Not that she had ever pretended that she did, nor that she wanted to be married – to himself or to anyone – but in his mind there had never appeared to be anything that would separate them. Almost as though there must be a steady progression into their future. Russian literature was full of tragic love, wasted lives, ironic situations. He would try not to waste his own life, but, without her, there would always be something lacking.

The irony was that they were married, and would be confirming their union with a big family wedding. Eve had explained that she was doing the village wedding to please Ted and May, especially May. Yet Dimitri could not help hoping that a church wedding before all her family was so much more than a registry office marriage, and that she would come to see it as the tightening of their knot and not want the agreed-upon divorce.

In the kitchen at Roman's Fields, Ann Carter, Ephraim, Harry and Young Gabe – the boys looking like young editions of Duke – all stared and nodded.

Ann said, 'Bar's still over at the stables. Not much help now so many lads has joined up.'

It was Young Gabe who said what his brothers must have been thinking. 'If you're a Russian, why haven't you got long boots, like in Ma's 'cyclopaedia?'

'Is only Cossack who can have these things.'

'By law?'

'Yes, by law.' Boys understood that. 'But I do have a

winter hat made from white fox. Is very warm when there is snow.'

'Is it deep snow?'

'Very, very deep.'

'Caw, I wish I could go to Russia. We don't have hardly any here.'

In only minutes, Dimitri appeared to be more at the heart of her family than Eve herself.

'Sit yourselves down then. Go on, Lu, don't wait to be asked.'

Ted, May, Ann Carter, Ephraim, Harry, Young Gabe, Ray, Bonnie, Anthony in his crib, Eve and Dimitri.

There was an eager dive for the cheese tarts by the boys, and Dimitri, and a more sedate choice from the grown-ups. There was so much talk about the deliciousness of the food that it eased any awkwardness there might have been about the passage of time since Eve had last sat at this table.

Ken had been out when they had arrived. Suddenly he was there.

'Oh, Ken . . .'

'Hello, Lu. Nice to see you back.' A quick tight clasp around one another's neck. How brave he had been as an International Brigader. She had seen his injuries, wrapped his frostbitten feet, yet here he was looking fitter and healthier than she could ever have expected. It was a dangerous moment for both of them. It would be easy to break down and weep for what they had seen, and done, and how they had failed. But her return was to the whole family, who did not want to be reminded that two of them had chosen to leave.

Ken was more emotional with Dimitri. For a brief moment they buried their faces in one another's shoulders . . . a very un-English gesture, but a heart-stopping moment.

'*Salud*, comrade.'

Spain set the three of them apart from the rest and

could have easily made them spectres at the feast had it not been for Dimitri's adroitness. 'You see, May, we Russians are great dramatists. I think maybe it is embarrassing for English people. We Russians do not think that a book or an opera is worth anything if it does not rend our hearts in two.' He held his heart and rolled his eyes ridiculously, making the children laugh, and the adults warm to him even more.

The weather being fine and mild, the door to the yard was open. A clatter of hoofs sounded. 'That'll be her.'

Eve dashed out, calling and waving.

Bar had dismounted and was fastening the gate. Babies had thickened her figure only slightly. She pulled off her battered riding hat and the black Barney hair sprang out in its crinkly mass. The two women clasped one another cheek to cheek and searched one another's face briefly.

'Oh, Bar! You're just the same as ever.'

'I got some grey hairs and I haven't got a waist no more. Can't say the same to you. You lost a lot of weight. Where's your tits gone? And I won't say nothing about your hair – you'll go grey soon enough. Come on, help us put Fairy in her shed.'

'Is she yours?'

'Yeah, except that she's really Duke's – Fairmile Queen. Didn't he have her before you went off?'

There was this about Bar. She wasn't skirting around Eve's absence as the others had. 'You'm beautiful an't you, Fairy. The major says I can put her with his Darkie – he's a beaut – but I don't know how Duke would take to that.'

Eve took some oats and Fairmile Queen nuzzled them out of her hand. Together Eve and Bar watered and fed the dainty mare, speaking mainly to her rather than each other. Bar wasn't the same as ever. Now that the greetings were over she held her mouth in a tight line and, except to the mare, was strained in her replies, which were as short as when she and Eve had fallen out as children – a rare thing.

'What's up with you, Bar?'

'Nothin's up with me, Lu. More to the point, what's up with you?'

'Nothing. Here, let me do that.'

'Come *on* . . . what's up with you?'

'Nothing, Bar. Really nothing. Perhaps I'm trying too hard to get back together.'

'Here.' Taking Eve by the shoulders she pressed her to sit on a hay bale by the stable door. 'Fairy can wait a minute.' Taking Eve's hands, Bar looked straight in her face, her brow furrowing slightly, 'What's up with you is that you can't pretend with me. I can see right through you. You been seeing Duke.'

'Duke?'

'Yes, yes, yes, you daft thing. Look how you're blushing, and your aura's glowing like a blooming neon sign. I know you saw Duke. What were you doing going back to Spain?'

'You *know* that I was there? What was it, spirit messages?'

'Don't get sarky with me, Lu, Lady Morag lets me have telephone calls there sometimes. You been to Spain again. And you met Duke. Now, Lu, are you going to tell me?'

'I *can't* tell you, Bar. OK, you know I was in Spain, but I can't say anything about why.'

Now it was Bar who was the sarcastic one. 'Oh, so it's all hush-hush, like at Brownsea Island where they're breeding germs to spread on the Germans.' Bar laughed, running her hands through her hair in a familiar gesture. 'That's so hush-hush that people in pubs is talking about it.'

'Well, I'm not people in pubs.'

Bar took a place beside Eve on the hay bale. 'That's for sure. You're people in posh cocktail bars.'

'I'm still me underneath.'

'No. You're a changeling. As soon as I married your Ray, I was so happy. Then, to stop me getting above myself, the "Darks" come here, and what they did, they took away my best friend, Lu, and gave back Eve so I wouldn't get too cocky.'

'Don't play with me, Bar. You're too old to be talking like that now. Neither of us is twelve any longer.'

'More's the pity. When we was twelve, we was pure and innocent, and only the wood spirits was around us. Duke gave you the witchetty piece I made for him. Shows how serious he is about you.'

Eve hardly knew what to say.

'What about your chap you're going to marry? You both in the same line of work?'

'I don't know what Dimitri does.'

'He don't make your aura glow. What you marrying him for? You said you wouldn't never get married. I wanted to, but you never did. You always said that you wouldn't get tied down by no man. I was pretty shocked when your auntie got your letter. It didn't make sense, not with knowing about you and Duke.'

'There's nothing about me and Duke.'

'That's not what he thinks.'

'He can think what he likes – there's nothing between us.'

'That still don't account for you marrying this foreigner.'

'Come and meet him. You'll like him. They have all taken to him; he's a nice man.'

'You're really going to marry a nice man then?'

'Of course I'm going to marry him.'

'OK.'

'What do you mean, OK?'

'I don't know.'

'Bar . . . don't do this to me.'

'Do what?'

'I know we're not kids any more, but what we used to say about us being two halves of one person . . . doesn't it mean anything?'

'You're the half that went away.'

'I know. But that's not what's up, is it?'

Long moments of silence fell between them whilst they both stared off into the distance.

'No, if I'm honest, I was the first one to break us up when I married your Ray.'

'We didn't break, we just grew up; but that's not to say we can't talk to one another like we used to.'

'Duke's in love with you.'

'No he's not. Duke, he would never say such a thing.'

'He did.'

'He just wouldn't.'

'And why not?'

'It would make him vulnerable.'

'What d'you mean?'

'If he said he was in love with me or anyone and they didn't love him back, he'd be humiliated, you know he would. He could never stand being rejected. He's just too proud.'

'All right, he never actually said it, but I could tell. Duke and you was destined for each other.'

'For goodness' sake, Bar, people aren't *destined.* They just happen to come across one another and sometimes they hit it off.'

'Then how come you just happened to come across him in a place where none of you should rightly be? That's Destiny.'

'I gave up thinking like that ages ago. Coincidence is a common thing.'

'You're marrying to a foreigner you don't love.'

'We have been together a long time, went through thick and thin, he saved me. So, I'm going to give May the wedding she's always wanted for a daughter she never had, and I want Ray to take me down the aisle and Ken to be best man.'

Clearly changing the subject, Bar went over to Fairy and started seeing to her stable. 'What d'you think of Bonnie? An't she just the picture of a little girl?'

'She's amazing. I've never come across a child so young who could hold a proper conversation.'

'That's due to her two grandmothers. Neither of them's ever babied her.'

'And what about Anthony then? He follows everybody around with those lovely eyes. I don't know who he takes after but it will come out when he loses all that baby chubbiness. Isn't he a perfect little sweet?'

Bar didn't answer, except for an absent-minded, 'Mm . . . oh yeah.' The atmosphere changed again, but Eve ignored it. 'Well, let's hope so. If he'd been a mongol like that Maurice, I should have drowned him like a kitten in a bucket.'

'Bar! For pity's sake, stop talking so weird.'

Bar was forking hay and clattering water pails with a vehemence quite out of proportion to the minor tasks of bedding and watering a small horse. 'Don't mention nothing about Duke, Lu. It'd hurt Ma if she knew about him wantin' you and you marrying this foreigner.'

Supper was a success, laid out in the huge kitchen where the long table was covered with plain white paper held with drawing pins. Dimitri was in his element, helping the women. How he must miss his own family, Eve thought.

May's hand was evident in the splendid home-made dishes, and Ann Carter's in the little jars of summer flowers and leaves, and bowls of curd cheese and sweet goat's butter.

Mrs Gunner, whom Eve could scarcely remember except that she was the wife of the land agent and had a boy who was 'not all there', joined the family, bringing a jar of rare wild-bee honey, which she and Maurice had taken from the hollow trunk of a rotted tree.

May said to Maurice, 'You give it to this lady. She's the queen bee here.' Eve asked herself if May was nipping at her – or was she herself sensitive after the disturbing way Bar was acting? Eve thanked the boy – nobody would ever call him a man.

'Ma, she kissed me. D'you see that? I was kissed by her.'

'Now, Maurice,' Alice Gunner said, 'don't get so excited.'

Eve held the youth's hand. 'My name is Lu, if you want to call me that.'

'I will. Yes. I will call you by your name. Lu. 'Tis a queer name. You say Lu-Lu-Lu. 'Tis like a little owl.' Eve thought about what Bar had said about drowning a mongol like a kitten in a bucket. How could she think such a horrible thing when she must see this boy all the time, and know that he enjoyed life?

Bonnie demanded that Maurice took her to the honey tree.

He took her hand. ''Tis a long way, you know.'

Alice held the two hands – one flaky-skinned and red, with blunt, flat fingernails; the other like a small, pink starfish. 'Another time, Bonnie. Me and Maurice will take you there, but only when your pa says so.'

The flaky hand and the starfish settled for playing the old cross clapping game, making Alice Gunner as pleased with her son as was Ray with his knowing little daughter.

Eve watched and thought how fortunate Maurice was to have been born to such good parents who hadn't sent him to the asylum.

But neither Eve nor anyone else, except Maurice, and possibly May, had any idea of what went on in the Gunner house, and that Alice sometimes kept at home until the bruises went down. But James Gunner never touched Maurice. Roman's Fields was a haven to Alice, and May, being May, always welcomed a woman less fortunate than herself. May had a pretty good idea of what went on with Jim Gunner.

'You been all right lately, Alice?'

'Not too bad, May, not too bad.' Which May knew was a lie.

Bar, now out of her stable clothes and into a black skirt and top much as she had always worn as a girl, picked up Bonnie and said, 'How's my girl then?' Then she made a beeline for Dimitri. 'So you're the one then? I'm Bar.'

Dimitri stood hastily and shook Bar's hand, making a slight formal bow. 'I know from how you look. You are her best friend, and wife of Ray. And mother of two beautiful children. I am so pleased to meet you.'

There was something not right. At first, Eve had intuited it; now she noticed that Bar petted Bonnie, but didn't even look in Ray's direction. Eve glanced at Ray, who was watching but who quickly looked away, and fussed with the blanket covering Anthony.

Ted's wines, made from his own fruit, were easy to drink, and they drank plenty. May was constantly urging Eve to eat something: 'I made it special because you were coming' and 'I dare say you've got used to different food these days.' Although said cheerfully, there was some resentment in May's tone. Eve felt guilty and ungrateful.

Dimitri kept the atmosphere light. Ted, May and Ray were eager to hear about the Ukraine and Dimitri was happy to tell tales about his boyhood, in a place nobody had ever heard of. May told how Lu had come to them as a sick child and gone home well.

'That's because I took her to the Swallit Pool.' Bar challenged Eve with a look. 'An't that right, Lu? I showed her how to join up with the sky and she got better.'

Ted said, 'Maybe, maybe, Bar, but I reckon May's father's tonics helped build her up. And May's cooking.'

'Don't look as if it lasted. She's thin as a rake. Come on, girl, eat up. You tell her, Dimitri.'

'I? She will never listen to me, Lu knows what she wants.'

'Well,' May said, 'I hope she wants the best wedding Wickham has seen in a long time.'

Eve, knowing what May wanted, stood behind May's chair and bent down to kiss her cheek. 'I do want the best wedding, and I know it will be because the best aunt has made it.'

Alice and Maurice stayed on as late as could be, enjoying the normality of the Wilmott's, until finally, Alice said quietly, 'Could you lend us a torch, Ted? I think Maurice and me will go down to one of my people in the village.'

'If you like, I'll walk you down.'

'No, Ted, I don't want James's wrath to fall on Roman's.'

May said, 'Just let him try, Alice, just let him try.'

That night, and for many more, Alice and Maurice slept in one of the small cottages along Mill Lane. It was not as spacious as Keeper's Lodge, but safe from the man who was more mental than his son.

'He's a sick man,' Alice kept explaining to her son. 'He can't help hisself.'

The house was chilly and still smelled of wine and tobacco smoke as Eve went silently downstairs in bare feet and a cardigan over her nightdress.

She found Ray outside, sitting on a kitchen chair, feeding baby Anthony from a boat-shaped teat-and-valve bottle which allowed the baby to feed without coming up for breath.

'He's a hungry one.'

Ray looked up and nodded. 'Sleep all right?'

'Right through till the Barneys' cock started up.'

'What you planning to do today?'

'I don't know. I'll need to go down to the vicarage. We've a special licence but I have to see the vicar about the bellringers and rest of it.'

'May's seen to all that. Can't have no bells.'

'Oh?'

'Only time church bells can ring is if there's an invasion or peace comes.'

'Of course . . . stupid of me to want bells.' She held out her arms. 'Can I finish feeding him?'

'If you like. Here, put this bit of rag on your shoulder. He's a great one for sicking up when he's winded.'

He gave her the chair and seated himself on the high stone step. 'You have to keep the teat end up, else he'll take in wind.'

Enveloping the baby closely in the crook of her arm, leaning over, Eve communicated satisfaction with her eyes and the baby returned the look. She was aware of Ray watching. In answer to his unasked question, she said, 'I'm quite a professional, aren't I? You're surprised. I worked in a house full of babies and children who had lost their parents.'

He gave her a short look. Not anger. Possibly resentment or pique or injured feelings. They sat in silence until she pulled the teat from Anthony's mouth, having left only enough milk in the teat so that he did not take in air.

'There. Come on, young Wilmott, let's have a burp.' When the baby obliged she looked up and smiled at the ageing face of the man who, whilst still a boy himself, had done the same for her years ago. Her instinct was to put her arms round him. But there was too much Wilmott in Ray for that. She could do it with Ken, but not Ray.

When he had fallen in love with Bar, and had got over his initial guilt of her being so much younger, he became a changed man. Ken had gone, so the three of them had shared the old home in Portsmouth, and Ray had almost stopped feeling responsible for everyone.

'How do you and May get on – all right?'

'Pretty good. Bar wouldn't be able to run the stables if it wasn't for her.'

'I expect it suits both of them.'

'What d'you mean?'

'May having the children . . . and Bar having outside work that suits her.'

'She don't have to work.'

'I know, Ray, I just meant that it's an arrangement that suits them both. May was always mistress of Roman's, and Bar was always a favourite.'

'Not so much as you.'

'But me and May living under the same roof was never anything that could happen. You all look pretty comfortable together.'

He appeared not to come halfway to reconciliation with her. She couldn't complain. He had always put her first, but she had gone off to make a new life for herself and not returned until it suited her to.

'How about Ann and Eli?'

'They're OK. It's a bit of a funny set-up. May and Ann keeps open house to both families. Bonnie has grown up in two homes, but it's OK. It wouldn't be my way of going on – too much like the families in our old street, the kids belonging to everybody.'

'But not us. We were different.'

He flicked a look at her, not sure how to take it. 'Yes, we were. We were a cut above. It wasn't easy keeping yourself to yourself . . . being respectable.'

'I know.'

'I wonder if you do. You have to have kids to bring up, then you know. I'll tell you something, Lu, I'm not a natural-born countryman. I'm a townie. I know how to live down there, but not out here. It's like I'm living in a foreign land, but I never come to live here for me, but so that Bonnie wouldn't have to be brought up in a place like Lampeter Street.'

For Ray, that speech was an outpouring, a baring of his soul. There was nothing sensitive that Eve could say, so she turned her attention to the baby, who was nodding contentedly to the rhythm of her rocking. It was a quiet time of year for songbirds, but the aggressive twittering of sparrows carried clearly on the early-morning air. It was hard to believe that this was a country at war.

After a while, Eve said, 'Is it any good saying I'm sorry, Ray?'

'For what?'

'You know what. I thought that you and Bar with the new baby and your new job . . .'

'That I wouldn't notice that you had just upped and left us?'

'It wasn't like that, Ray.'

'It was from where I was standing. I'd been your father and mother, Lu, and you just took off and went where you was likely to get killed and I was worried sick.'

'But I didn't get killed, Ray.'

'Might as well have, for all that's left of your old self.'

'And I went without ever saying what I should have said – that I was thankful for the way you had brought me up. God, I was a self-centred little bitch.'

'You was that, Lu.'

For her, there had never been a worse moment between them.

'You wasn't thinking of coming back? I know May and Ted was hoping you would.'

She pointed to demonstrate what she was about to say. 'Look at me, Ray, as posh a London lady as ever you'll see. This is *me,* this is what I've become, this is how I intend being.' She put a hand gently on his arm and felt him flinch. 'Ray, try to understand. This person I've become is sort of built over the one with all the really decent things you taught me.

'Dimitri bought me a wooden Russian doll. It's actually a set of four of them, exactly the same, except smaller and smaller and they fit inside one another. He said the littlest one is Lu, the one that is inside all the others.'

Ray probably thought that Dimitri was as fanciful as herself, but it was the best that she could do.

'So you reckon I'm giving you away to the right man?'

'You will give me away then?'

'Yes, of course I'm going to give you away.'

'Given away' by one man to another? That was one of the things she had against church weddings. Given away and then bound by the badge of servitude – a wedding ring.

'Of course he's the right man. Dimitri is very special. He has ideals that are probably stronger than yours or mine. He's not like anyone you'll ever meet around here. You'd be better asking, am I the right woman for him.'

The morning progressed. Ray had gone off on his shift. The Barney family was about its own work and school. Bonnie was at kindergarten. The house was quiet, work in the kitchen had been done, and May was just ready to go out to the fields, wearing the same old field-hat tied under her chin that Eve remembered from years before.

May had busied herself like always. But busied herself to the extent that she hadn't taken a minute to sit down with Eve and talk. Perhaps that was still to come, except that Eve sensed that what she was seeing was not the reality of their lives now. It was almost as though they were acting, trying hard not to forget their lines. Dimitri was their prompt, filling in with his brand of jollity. He was good at it. The two of them hadn't had a moment together alone. Eve wondered what he made of them and whether he saw them as she had described them so often – or as fragmented as they so clearly were.

Was it that Ted was dying, wasting away, as he so clearly was, and nobody must mention it?

Ken was seated at a corner of the kitchen table writing.

May said, to Eve, 'Listen, love, why don't you stroll down the lane with Baby? He likes going out in his pram. Take Ken with you.'

'Where's Dimitri?'

'He's off with Ted.' May smiled. 'My dear Lord, he's no shirker. He's gone to do a stint at the winter wood.'

'Just his style, sleeves rolled up, swinging an axe.'

'Ah, yes. I'll bet he's worth a look at when he's working.'

'He'll get a handful of blisters, but that won't daunt him. He's a big show-off.' Eve felt proud of the man she had brought home. If she imagined bringing David Hatton here, as at one time might have been on the cards, or the tangle and trouble that being here with Duke would have provoked, it was too awful to contemplate. Everywhere she and Dimitri had ever been, he fitted in. His enjoyment of life overflowed and warmed other people. He deserved to be loved. Fran Haddon would be perfect for him.

May said, 'I rubbed his hands with spirits.'

'I hope you've got plenty of wintergreen, or he's going to church in a wheelbarrow.'

Ken looked up from his writing. 'I was going to suggest a tractor and trailer for him.'

May laughed, her care-worn face transformed – the old May. 'He is a size, all right, that broad and upright. What I call a real manly man.'

'Ha ... you should have seen him in his major's uniform,' Ken said, giving a mock salute.

A small thud of awkward silence. Eve and Ken exchanged brief glances.

Saying, 'I'm glad I didn't,' May left the house.

'Phew,' Ken said, 'that was a bit of an icy blast. She hates it that there are things that go on outside the family that she doesn't know about. She sees herself as the matriarch.'

'It's what she *is*. Everything at Roman's Fields revolves round her. And everybody likes it that way.'

'Except me and you.'

'I don't *not* like it, I just don't want to be drawn in. I can do without the comfort.'

'Let me just finish writing this envelope, and I'll be ready.' He blotted the page and handed it to his sister. 'Read it.'

'What is it?'

'Read it.'

The salutation stopped her in her tracks and she briefly looked up, not knowing whether she wanted to read on, but she did.

> Dear Lieutenant Hatton,
>
> Thank you for seeing me yesterday. I am pleased to confirm that I wish to apply for the training course you offer, and shall report to you in Portsmouth on Saturday, 26 April.
>
> Yours faithfully, Kenneth Wilmott.

'Ken!'

'I know, surprising, isn't it? Come on, let's walk down to the post office – don't say anything until we get away from the house.'

The walk into the village was both familiar and strange to Eve. The familiarity was the curves and bends in the road, lined by forest trees that had been there for generations. The strangeness was that she and Ken should be doing it at all, to say nothing of wheeling an old-fashioned perambulator.

The lane still showed signs of last year's fall of mulberries. It was obvious that nobody had laid out sheets to catch the fruits.

'Remember the smell of ripe mulberries? Happy memories, Ken.'

'Ted's wine? We never hardly knew wine existed until we came here that Christmas.' He turned and gave her a smile. 'Tasted a lot worse since then. God, some of that rough stuff out there . . . and some very nice stuff too, I have to give the Spaniards that.'

How different were their relationships now. When they all lived together in Portsmouth, Ray was the one Eve could tell anything to, Ken was always 'off on the razzle', interested only in having a good time. Spain had changed that.

Indicating the letter he was carrying, Eve asked, 'How did this come about then?'

'Out of the blue. I had been trying to sign on in one of the forces, but they wouldn't take me on account of my frostbite. Then a letter came,' he laughed, 'which May's been hinting at ever since. It was from him.' He indicated the letter. 'Said that he remembered meeting me, and would I be interested in seeing him to talk about how I might fit in to a new unit he was running? I was wondering if you had anything to do with it.'

'Why would I?'

Ken raised his eyebrows and shrugged his shoulders. 'Because you know each other. He's your senior officer.' Again he laughed. 'In charge of WRNS, is he? He even knows you are getting wed tomorrow because he said I should come after the wedding. He knows it's special licence, and it's Major Vladim. So he knows a lot he shouldn't if you wasn't part of this unit that he's running. I know what the unit does and what it's called – SOE.'

Eve didn't know what to say. She seemed to remember

having said something about Ken to David, but not to suggest him to SOE.

'I know him, of course I do. You first met him through me. How did he get your name?'

'He gets passed on to him the names of any Brigaders who try to join up. I was rejected because of that frostbite damage to my feet but they mark your card if you were a Brigader.'

'That's a waste of good soldiers. The training out there was as good as anywhere.'

Even now the walk back showed up Ken's limp.

'Are your feet still much of a problem?'

'Nah, I got patched up well in that hospital. Actually, I feel almost proud of my queer toes.'

As she was about to open the side-gate, he stopped her. 'I've got a kid out there, Lu.'

'Oh, Ken.'

'Yeah . . . don't even know if it's a boy or a girl.'

'What about the mother?'

'She was one of those women you just had to admire for their ideals. She was very political . . . taught me a lot, taught me the language. What she was doing was pretty much the same as Dimitri – going around reminding the troops what they were fighting for.'

'Have you talked to Dimitri?'

'A bit. He said he couldn't stomach any more Russian propaganda. Remember that poster that was everywhere – "Madrid Will Be the Tomb of Fascism"? Well, it wasn't, was it? He said he couldn't go back to Russia knowing what he knew was going on there. Two and two together, I take it that he's SOE as well.'

'Changing the subject, what's happened to Bar? She makes me afraid.'

'She makes everybody afraid.'

'She was so strange with me yesterday. One minute she was talking about drowning babies like kittens, the next she's all high spirits and acting the fool with Bonnie.'

'I don't know the right of it. What I know is from Ted. It seems that when she was expecting this last baby, she refused to admit it. Even when it began to show she got that abusive. Our Ray didn't know what to do . . . poor bugger, he still don't. Anyway, one morning, she goes over to her mother's place. Next thing, Ann comes over to Roman's and says Ray's got a son. And that's how it's been. *Ray's* got his son. She won't have anything to do with the baby – nor Ray for that matter.'

'Ray's good with him. Lucky he's got three willing women to help.'

'She behaves as though the baby don't exist.'

'She knows he exists all right, because that's how she started being weird about the baby not being normal and drowning kittens.'

'I know some women never take to their babies, but this . . . this is extreme. Do you reckon the baby's safe?'

'Oh yes, there's always somebody taking care of him. He just doesn't exist for her.'

'Poor old Ray,' Eve said. 'He brought me up because Dad good as gave up on us. Now he's got to be mother and father to another one.'

In the years since Eve was last there, the Barneys' 'encampment' had become more of a conventional home: converted outhouses with a well-cultivated cottage garden, which, in the height of summer, would be filled with rows of ferny carrots and bulb fennel, onions with their tops bent over to stop the flowering, potatoes, parsnips and other root vegetables, plus many herbs and old-fashioned flowers, for distillation into tinctures which Ann would give freely to anyone in need. Marigold, bergamot, feverfew grew, all hover fly and bee attractors.

'Ann?' she called.

'I see you coming, so I made you some of your sort of tea, seeing as you never did take to my infusions.'

'I've grown to like Earl Grey.'

'Bergamot and lemon, that is, but it an't nowhere good as mine. So I'll pick some bergamot and you can put it in if you like.'

They sat on wooden stools at a wooden table silver with weathering and age, glistening in the April light.

When Eve had been brought to May and Ted's, it had been Ann and Bar who had taken care of her mental and spiritual health. Although Ann's was not a Christian spirituality.

Ann Carter rubbed rough knuckles along Eve's jawline as she searched her face with her soft eyes. 'You'm still the girl of summer. I told Bar two years and more ago when she was frettin' that you was gone to the war that you would return before three years was up. And you would come for the summer solstice and your birth date which is midsummer – except you're a bit out.' Ann had a way of expressing herself that was like no one Eve had ever met. She was always totally aware of and focused upon whoever it was she was speaking to. She cast the runes, and read lives in hands and tealeaves. Her voice itself was confident and comforting. Ann Carter knew things that no one else knew – except perhaps Bar.

She picked up Eve's hand and casually turned it back and forth, then looked up sharply. 'Still the two babes. It's time they was here, Lu.'

'We brought two orphans out of Spain.'

'You know better than that. Only your own babes show on your hand.'

Eve sipped the aromatic black tea in which pinched leaves of bergamot floated.

'Only your own,' Ann repeated, still looking closely at the place below Eve's little finger. 'And there's two.'

'I had a miscarriage . . . in Australia.'

'My dear child, that's sad. It's why the line is so small and faint.'

Eve withdrew her hand and looked closely at where she knew children were supposed to be foretold. There was a second crease, quite clear when she clenched her fist.

'That one's not.' Ann ran her split and grubby fingernail along the little fold. 'Are you carrying?'

'No I'm not.'

Ann made a doubting grimace. 'How many times has women and girls said that?'

'I can't be.'

'Ah, if you rely on having your "flowers" to tell you that you an't carrying then you're on quaggy ground.'

It was true. With the miscarriage, she had been fooled by her menstrual cycle right up to the time when Jess Lavender had held a pail under Eve to catch the small foetus.

'Is that why you're going to marry the big fella?'

'No. I'm marrying him so that we'll be husband and wife.'

'That don't ring true. I bet Bar don't believe that.'

'Well, no, as a matter of fact she doesn't, but I can't help what you and Bar believe. He's asked me to marry him, and I'm going to. Why is that so hard to believe? You've seen him, he's a good, lovely man.'

The older woman came to stand behind Eve, gently smoothing her hair and cheeks. 'Don't take no notice of us, my darling. You know what queer ideas me and her gets. 'Tis true, he is a lovely man, and he will make you happy.' Ann grinned mischievously, and whined, 'Buy a bit o' luck from a gypsy, my dear. Cross the gypsy's palm with silver.'

Eve laughed and pushed her away. 'You're a witch-woman, not a gypsy.'

The Barneys' guard dog barked, disturbing Anthony,

who let out a squawk. Eve pressed Ann's loving hands closer and then got up from the stool and took the bottle of scalded milk from the pram. 'I'm in charge of his next feed. Can you warm this?'

Ann shook drops onto her wrist. 'It's just right for him. Do you want to let me do it? I mostly do during the day when Ray's not about. Sometimes May does.'

Eve watched as the baby suckled, his large eyes searching his grandmother's face, occasionally releasing the teat for a moment and smiling up at her. Ann gave a deep sigh, tightened her lips and shook her head.

'Is he a good baby?'

'Oh yes. Good as gold, aren't you, my little king?'

They sat in silence, watching the ever-absorbing picture of a baby suckling.

'Something's wrong, isn't it.' A statement, not a question.

'What, is it you getting the gift of insight now?'

'Ann, don't you shut me out like the rest of them. What's wrong between Ray and Bar? When I was with Ray this morning and he was feeding and changing Anthony, it seemed to me that he was being mother and father again, as he used to be with me, as though he had to make up to the baby for something, the way he used to make up for my father always being away. Am I right?'

'Yes, you're right. You can't hide a thing like that. It's Bar – she can't take to this one. Right from the day he was born, she wouldn't put him to the breast. Not like Bonnie – she kept her on for months. After that we all of us had a hand in bringing her up. Bar went back to the stables. The major put her in charge of everything, all his good horses. He told people as he'd got the best stable manager in the county. Eli says that's right. Bar can make horses do anything she wants.'

'She appeared . . . well . . . radiant when I saw her

come in with Fairy yesterday. Then, as soon as we started speaking, she went . . . I don't know . . . weird.'

'Bonnie and Fairy, Fairy and Bonnie. That was her whole world. I told her first off that she was carrying. She said no. Even when she began to show, she wouldn't have it. Then she started taking out the big hunters, galloping them cross country like she was in a steeplechase – she was trying to shake him loose.'

Anthony was now lolling over his feed. Ann jiggled the bottle and he began sucking strongly again.

'She never wanted him, poor little soul. She's as good with the herbs as I am – she could have took the penny-royal if she'd wanted to – but it was as though she thought that if she denied that she was carrying, then she wasn't carrying. Her mind was that bent. Poor Ray was half out of his mind. He wanted this baby, and she was telling him not to be so daft, because she wasn't carrying.'

'I can't believe it.'

'Oh, you can believe it, my sweetheart. She treats poor Ray as though it didn't take two to make a baby. She won't talk about it, but it's my reckoning that she won't let him near her in bed. Talking and reasoning didn't make no difference. She just said she couldn't take to the baby, she couldn't help how she feels. And now if anything's mentioned she just looks through you and gets out. She's my only girl, and she's breaking my heart. I cried all my tears, and I'm dried up. Crying dry is worse than anything.'

Eve sat and watched her little nephew smiling up at his grandmother, as he had smiled up at Ray. Tears gathered and she could not stop them.

'Want to get his wind up?'

Eve shook her head. She felt chilled to the marrow. The love affair between Ray and Bar, which had bloomed so wonderfully in the old house in Lampeter Street, had died. Not merely died, it had been done to death in a barbarous manner.

Ray had made her feel guilty that she had kept her new life from them, yet here was something far more serious that they had kept from her. The traditional family supper last night had been a sham. She hadn't given it a thought at the time, but now she recalled that Ray had fed, changed, washed the baby and then carried him upstairs already asleep in his rush crib. At the other end of the table Bar had played with Bonnie, putting little twists of flowers in her hair and feeding her little titbits from her own plate. What had appeared a united and happy little family was in two parts. No, that wasn't quite right, Bonnie was as much Ray's pride as she was Bar's, but baby Anthony was not Bar's.

'You're only here for another day, so I wouldn't say nothing. It might get all right again, you never know, so I say least said, soonest mended.'

'There's nothing for me to say. In the morning, I'll get up, get dressed, walk down to the church, and then catch the train to London.'

'You brought spare nappies with you? No? It don't matter, I keep some here.'

When Anthony was back in his pram, contentedly sucking his thumb, Eve made to leave. Giving Ann a kiss on each cheek, she said, 'Thank you, Ann. I can't ever remember leaving this yard without feeling that my thoughts had been given a good shake up and had settled down in better order.'

Ann laughed. 'You always had a way of saying things like nobody I ever knew. Look, my darling,' she took a pill box from her apron pocket, 'you know I wouldn't give it except in the spirit of love. It's sun-dried pennyroyal. You know what it does. If you don't ever want to use it, then don't. But I for one won't blame you for not bringing into the world a babe that isn't wanted. It's against the law, and Church Christians calls it a sin, but that's their affair. They haven't got no right to tell the rest of womankind how to live their lives. The women in the village know where to come, and I'm glad they do.'

The small chemist's pill box containing Ann's packet of pennyroyal rubbed gently against Eve's leg until she reached her room, when she put it in another small box that contained the Dutch cap she had last used when she and Dimitri were married at the registry office.

'It was a mistake to have come here. I should have let well alone.'

Dimitri took Eve's hand. 'These are good people . . . your family . . . is not a mistake. They all want to see their Lu with a ring on her finger.'

The church service was to take place late morning, so the house was stirring at 5 a.m.

May had everything planned, organised and written down in lists. Except for essential work to do with animals, the rest of the routine work was to be left until late afternoon. She had sent Ted and Ken down to the village hall in the van with wine, a keg of beer, the prepared food in boxes and tins, and several armfuls of flowers for the church. This left only the washing, dressing and hair-curling to be done, and May herself to be got ready in a new coat dress and hat to match.

'Now, you two go off out and be together until it's time to go. Best not wear your court shoes until it's time, so's you won't get them all muddied up. And you, Dimitri my lad, just be careful of getting pussy willow pollen on your jacket. It's just starting to fluff up and it's the very devil.' She didn't say, 'That's two less under my feet', but Eve knew.

Bonnie pleaded to go too, but was restrained by promises of hair-bows and flower baskets to be finished. Ray, not yet wearing his starched collar and new tie, was busying himself with the children, a large white apron protecting his navy-blue suit.

Bar had gone over to the stables to see the stable hands and arrange the work that was to be done whilst she was at the wedding service. Ray had pressed Bar's full-skirted black frock and hung it behind the hall door, together with the wreath of ivy and rosehip that Bar had twined herself. 'I could make you one too, and you could wear it instead of that hat, Lu.'

Eve didn't know how to refuse because Bar had already asked if there was anything wrong. There was. Now that the situation and the family cover-up of the rift between Bar and Ray had become apparent, Eve played her scenes of bride-to-be and happy families well.

Eve took Dimitri's hand. 'I know they're nice people, but everything's changed. Maybe it was never as rosy as I remember. Ted and May have grown old in a couple of years. I think if it wasn't for Eli and Ann, this place would be too much for them.'

'But they do *have* these nice Carter people, so don't give yourself worries where none need to exist.'

'Maybe you're right. But I still can't wait to get this over and get back to my flying lessons.'

Clasping her shoulders gently, Dimitri looked directly into her eyes. 'I am worried, Eve. Maybe you will fly into dangerous territory.'

'I shall be delivering aircraft from the factories to the airfields.'

Drawing her to him, he hugged her hard. 'I am very happy, Eve. Even if this will not be a true marriage, I am happy. I do not want to lose you.'

Ted, with Ken beside him in the van, slowed down when he saw Eve and Dimitri. 'Hey, you two, I thought the groom wasn't supposed to see the bride on her wedding morn.'

'A bit late now, Ted. Tell May we're on our way.'

After the van had gone, Dimitri said, 'That poor Ted, he is sick.'

'I know, I know . . . but it's like everything else that's hard to take at Roman's, nobody is going to mention it. We are having marriage celebrations. Ted's state of health must wait its turn. They all know what's happening but, like Bar's mental state, nobody wants to look it in the eye.'

Dimitri nodded.

'Those two pictures on the mantelshelf – me and Bar when we were twelve?'

'Innocent young girls, with pretty flowers and pretty clothes, painted with colour. Of course I have seen them.'

'*That's* what everybody's trying to keep going. May and her father tried to keep human problems out of Roman's Fields. They thought that the Quaker way could keep the people who live here in a kind of cocoon of goodness. To care for and be good to people was all that was needed. You understand?'

'Perhaps.'

'All that they wanted was for people to be well and happy – and to live together with generosity and care for one another. They did it. May and Mr Sawbridge lived their belief. Ted, as a young man, was their first casualty, brought in to be made well. Then Ann and Eli Barney. Gabriel Sawbridge handed over that whole plot of land and buildings so that they could live their lives as *they* wanted. Then Bar and her brother – they gave them the chance to work. Then me. Then Ken and Ray, and now the grandchildren. Gabriel is dead, but May can't stop believing that you can make people good by believing that they *are* good. Mr Sawbridge seemed to have that knack. And now May is trying to be herself and her father rolled into one. Soon it will be Alice Gunner and Maurice.'

Eve paused. 'There is a worm in the bud of the Roman's rose?'

'I think that you are right.'

'Reality is the worm. I feel so sorry for May. She sees the idyll of Roman's Fields decaying. And the only thing that *I* can do is to go away again. This time, I shall never come back.'

'You are best to do so, Eve. It is the child, Lu, who lives here, not you. Eve Anders . . . Eve *Vladim* is woman of the world. This place is too narrow for her.'

She looked up at him. 'Dimitri Vladim . . . you see, I'm right! You are a good wise man. I've been lucky that you came into my life. My life is better and happier than it would have been had I not invited you to my room that first night. Serendipity.'

'What is this? Is a word Dimitri Vladim does not know? Tell me, tell me, so that I can surprise Frances.'

A bolt of distress pierced Eve. She didn't want him to show off his new word to Fran Haddon.

'You go on up to the house. I'm going along the Swallit path for one last time with Bar.'

The pool that had once appeared so wide and clear was not what it had been. No children played here now, clearing weed and keeping the edge free of nettles.

'You came then? I thought you wouldn't.'

'It seemed the best thing to do.'

'Full circle. Nature loves a circle.'

'Finish where it began.'

Bar nodded. 'You won't come back, will you?'

'I shouldn't think so. I thought you would all miss me. What arrogance. You're OK without me.'

'Ray missed you.'

'I know. I wish he hadn't taken it so hard.'

'That's how he is, Lu. It's that kindness to people that makes me love him.'

Eve was taken aback to hear that. 'You don't love him, Bar. Anybody can see that.'

'Well,' she said fiercely, 'that's where everybody's wrong. It's because I love him so much that I can't bear to look at him. I can't, I can't, I can't.'

Bar, standing with her feet just apart and her arms dangling, looked straight ahead at Lu, not making a sound, but with streams of fat tears flowing over her cheeks and dripping off her chin.

Eve went to her and, enveloping her in her arms, rocked her back and forth, murmuring, 'It's all right . . . it's all right . . .' for what seemed ages.

'Come on. Here, wipe your face in my hanky.'

They sat on the tussocky grass as they had done years ago, arms round one another, heads close together, blonde summer and black winter.

'Now tell me what's wrong. You're scared of something, aren't you? Not Ray.'

'No, not Ray, but I'm afraid of what he would do.'

'What would he do?'

'I can't tell you, it's too bad.'

'Tell me, Bar! Whatever it is, I'm going away today and I shan't ever come back – you know that.'

'I couldn't bear him to think bad of me.'

'What have you done for him to think that?'

'*I* haven't done nothing.'

'Then tell me.'

'I'm going to cool my eyes.'

She was away at the pool, scooping water and splashing her face for several minutes. Then she came back and took up her place again.

'You remember that thing Mr Gab'rel told us, about a tribe of people who used to have a goat to take on their sins, so they could start afresh?'

'A scapegoat. Is that what you need?'

'Something like that, but it's not sins I want took away. It's secrets . . . dark ones, horrible ones.'

'Do you know what my job is now?'

Bar gave a hysterical little giggle. 'Not a scapegoat, are you?'

'Do you smoke?'

'Not much.'

'Here, let's have just one, unless it's a desecration of Swallit Wood.'

'Ray don't like to see me do it.'

They lit up. From the way Bar swallowed the smoke and blew out, Ray couldn't know how often Bar used cigarettes.

'All right then, what do you do?' she asked.

'I'm a secret agent. If I can keep a secret for the Government, I'd keep one a lot better for you. It's what I was doing in Spain – Duke shouldn't have said anything.'

'But you told *him* the secret of what you were doing.'

'No. It was the woman he sleeps with did that.'

'Lu! He never told me about her.'

'Maybe I shouldn't have, but you have to believe that you can trust me. I'd never let you down. If you want to talk about it, go on. Whatever's bothering you, you need to tell somebody, don't you? Just now, I was with Dimitri and I trusted him enough to tell him something that was on my mind. As soon as I did I felt a ton weight had been lifted.'

'And you would take this off of me?'

'Yes. Whatever it is, I will take it from you, go away and nobody will ever hear of it again.'

Bar smoothed the damp handkerchief, folded it, opened it and refolded it compulsively, then handed it back to Eve. 'My little Anthony is Maurice Gunner's half-brother.'

'Gunner raped you?'

Bar clasped her hands over her face. 'Oh, my dear Lu, how I have wronged you. I feared if I confessed it to you that you would think that I was lustful with him. I never, I swear it, Lu.'

'You don't need to swear it.'

'I couldn't tell nobody. My pa would have done for him, so would my ma. There wasn't anybody I could tell so that it wouldn't get back to Ray. It don't matter how innocent the woman is, the man gets away with it. Even if they know he did it, it's always the woman who gets blamed. People would have had it in for me because I run the stables – there was a lot of bad feeling about that . . . a *woman*, a *gypo*. You couldn't put it past her to get up to anything. And that was what he said. "Who's going to believe a witch-woman like you? Everybody knows what witches do. They're not going to believe you against a parish councillor and a sidesman of the church."'

Eve pulled Bar's head into her shoulder. 'I could kill him, Bar.'

'So could I. Every day for a year I coulda killed him. And he's right: nobody would ever believe me against him.'

'I think Alice Gunner might.'

Bar looked up sharply, then said, 'She might . . . but I couldn't trust to her wanting to protect him. I heard her last night, telling Miz Wilmott, "He can't help himself. He's not well."'

'But you *can* trust me. Do you feel better . . . even a little bit?'

Bar gave Eve a watery smile. 'Like my ma tells people – "A trouble shared is a trouble halved."'

'Your ma usually knows what she's talking about.'

They sat silently, caressing one another's hands.

'We'd best go. Don't want to be late for your own wedding.'

Eve looked at her watch. 'Plenty of time. Plenty. I'll make my way back through the woods – one last time.'

'I have to go over to the stables. Then I'll come and get myself all prettied up for you.'

'Do you feel all right?'

'A 'course I feel all right. You got the burden now and I can be Ray's wife again.'

'And the baby?'

'He's mine, I birthed him. He can't help nothing. You love your man, Lu?'

'Probably not as much as you love Ray.'

'I'll make it up to him, Lu. They'll put it down to after birthen miseries. A lot of women gets that. What they'll say is that you and me together again put everything right.'

'And so it has in a way, Bar.'

'Lu come back and everything was all right.'

When Eve returned to the house, everything was ready. Ten o'clock. Finish dressing. A slow procession down into the village, the wedding at noon, some photographs, the cake and drinks, their train, as is traditional, carrying the happy pair to a honeymoon at an unknown destination.

All doors and windows were open, sun streaming in. Bonnie was practising little tunes on the piano. Dimitri tactfully left Eve to the family, saying, 'I go scratch the pig before we go.'

'Are you packed?'

'Ted has my bag. You must remember to give him yours.' The plan was that Ted would drive them straight to Wickham station from the village hall. 'Are you OK, Eve? You look a little pale. Let me feel your hands . . . they are so cold. You are shivering.'

'Wedding nerves – all brides get them.'

'I get you a good shot of brandy.' He went, leaving her in her bedroom to get ready.

Ray came to the door. 'You all right, Lu? Dimitri said you needed a drink. Your hands is quite trembly.'

'I'm just nervous at doing a village wedding.'

'Did you see Bar on your way back?'

'Yes, she's gone to the stables, but she says she won't

be long. Now go and leave me to get dressed and have my drink.'

Ray closed the door firmly. Eve sat at the dressing table with its oval mirror and began arranging her hair into a glossy pale cap, then creamed and fluffed powder on her face. She did look pale. A touch of rouge on cotton wool. Fine pencilled eyebrow arches. Bright red lipstick, fashionable and glossy. Her hand shook as she started to make the shape. Brandy, tossed back as Dimitri took vodka. A deep breath in and slowly out. Mascara. She watched herself as she applied the lipstick, pressing her lips together and opening them into a wry half-smile. She looked into her own eyes as she brushed a shine of petroleum jelly on her eyelids – and didn't look away.

From below in the yard, she could hear them. Ann Carter: 'Why don't I give Eli a shout? He can go over and see if Bar needs a hand so she can come back here.'

Ted said, 'If Jim Gunner sees your Eli on estate soil, he won't listen to no reason. No, I'll go. Eli's got enough on his hands. She'll be here, May . . . It's probably just a thing with one of the hunters – you know how she is with them – they'm a big responsibility.'

'If she gave half as much thought to things here –' May, sounding tight-lipped with bitterness, was stopped in her tracks by Ted raising his voice.

'Shut up, May! It's nothing to do with you. I got nothin' else to do till it's time to go, so I'll go and buck her up.'

'How about if I come then?' Ann said. 'If needs be I can stop there and Ted can bring her back straightaway.'

'No, Ann, you're one of the main family. Nobody will think twice about Eli not going to the church, but if you and your boys don't then it's going to look funny.'

'Ha! Everything looks funny if you're the sort that think funny. But you're right, I should be there.'

'She's done this a' purpose.' May's voice sounded as though it might break.

Ray's voice: 'Don't say something you'll regret. Today's not the day.'

'Of course not. No day ever is the day, is it?'

Eve wanted to shut the window, shut out what they were saying, but they were just below. If she so much as moved the curtains, they would realise that she was overhearing what they had all done their best to smooth over for the wedding. God above! she thought. What made me think coming to see them again would make them happy?

Eve had never heard Ted with anger in his voice until now. 'May! You waited a long time for this day, don't go and spoil it for yourself.'

'I'm not the one who will spoil it.'

'You will if you don't shut up. I'm going.' Moments later the van was heard rattling to a start.

May said sullenly, 'He hasn't got the strength of a louse these days. He don't need to go running after her.'

Then Ann said, 'Give her time, Ray. She won't always be like this.'

'Tell you the truth, Ann, I don't know if I care any more.'

'Ray, you don't mean that.'

'Don't I? It's months now. You said give her time, I've give her time, we've all give her time. Seems to me she's on to a good thing, got a man's job, man's wages – bringing up her own baby don't seem to come nowhere in it.'

'She's my daughter and I'm sorry she's doing this to you, Ray. But not all females as has babes takes natural to them.'

'Oh yeah . . . and I've heard it all before – the calves and lambs and kids and kittens that's rejected by their mothers.'

May's voice: 'And so they do, Ray.'

'May's right, boy. I don't think my girl wanted to turn from the poor little soul, it's not as though she hasn't got the mothering instinct. Look how she is with Bonnie.'

'Yes, look how she is.'

'It'll pass, boy. Don't let it break you two up, for sake of the children.'

Eve had sat transfixed before the mirror, seeing not her own reflection, but Ray, Ann and May as they acted out their parts, said again the lines that they had so obviously said before. This wasn't a new discussion. Unbeknown to them, James Gunner had done that monstrous deed that was killing off Eve's family.

She looked into her own eyes and didn't flinch. The best she could do was to go downstairs as if nothing had happened and start the walk down to the church, and hope that when she had gone the healing would begin. Get it over with. Get back to London.

Get learning to fly.

Bonnie's piano practice had stopped and soon she was stomping her new patent-leather ankle-straps upstairs.

Eve, in black shoes whose spit-and-polish shine could only have been done by Ray, and watched by Bonnie in her flounces, put on a pancake hat with a sprightly half-veil. Bonnie breathed the hushed words, 'Auntie Lu, you look so beautiful', then rushed out on to the landing and shouted, 'Daddy, Daddy, AnnieGranny, GrannyMay, come and see the *bride*. She's betterer than Princess Marina.'

All members of the family except for Ted and Bar had now gathered in the sitting room where Dimitri was doing the honours with generous glasses of sweet port wine or whisky. At Bonnie's announcement, all eyes turned to Eve, making her feel slightly embarrassed. Everyone appeared to be so much at their ease that she found it difficult to believe what she had overheard.

Alice Gunner, glass of sherry in hand, stood up. 'Maurice made something for you. Go on, Maurice, give it to the lady.'

'Horseshoes is lucky. Paint's dry all right.'

'I think it was young Miss Megsie that told him about giving horseshoes at weddings. She give him the ribbon and that.'

'It's lovely. You're very kind, Maurice, and artistic.'

Eli Barney, from whom both Duke and Bar had got their handsome, well-boned features and black hair, came in, pardoned himself for appearing in working clothes, wished her and Dimitri luck and gave Eve a flat cardboard package about a foot square and wrapped in a piece of hessian. 'You used to go off a-field-walking with Gab'rel. Our Duke took you there. You found a bit of old crock you was so proud of. Well, what about this? We thought this'd be a good thing to give you. But don't go tellin' nobody or they'll want to come and dig the place up.'

'Good Lord. It's a bit of Roman floor, isn't it?'

'Proof that Roman's Fields holds that secret. So far only Eli and me knows its whereabouts,' May said.

The piece was startlingly beautiful, a section of tesserae broken away from what must surely be a highly decorated floor.

'I don't know what to say . . . Look, Dimitri.'

'I think I get it mounted for you in London.'

May said, 'That's all right just so long as nobody gets to know where it was dug up. I reckon it's a palace, from the quality of the work. If it gets out we shan't none of us be able to live out our lives here in peace. Just keep it, Lu, and when the time ever comes, hand it on to some museum, but for now, just have it as a piece of Roman's Fields.'

'It's a wonderful wedding present.'

'Ray and Bar's got the same. It seemed to Eli and me that it was . . . well, the thing is . . . I might as well tell you now. When Ted and me are gone, there's nobody as will want Roman's Fields. When the war's over, Ray will want to set up in Portsmouth again. Union bosses don't live in country villages. That right, Ray?'

Ray nodded. 'Nine Elms, Charing Cross, London

Bridge, if they don't get the guts bombed out of them.' He turned back to the window again, drinking deeply on the strong, dark, homemade beer.

Eve couldn't ever remember Ray having given voice to personal ambition.

May went on, 'I've willed this place to the nation. I know that sounds a bit grand, but I've left a letter with my solicitor saying about the artefacts that keep turning up. He don't know what's in it, nor the box of finds he's holding on to. Me and Ted's got a little money put by, and that will go to the grandchildren. There, now you all know how it stands. Let's have a toast to a good day, and a happy one.'

The women perched on chair arms so as not to crease pleats. Ray continued to stand by the low window, his shoulders rigid, his fingers drumming. Eve went and stood beside him, looking towards the wide gate. 'You did my shoes, Ray. Thanks.'

'Glad you noticed.'

Eve accepted a drink from Dimitri, who gave her a sly wink. Ken came in, looking at his wristwatch. 'We all right for time?'

'Ted's gone to fetch Bar,' May said.

'She's running it a bit fine.'

'All right, Ken, we're well aware of that,' Ray said, still in his tetchy voice.

Ken raised his eyebrows and shrugged his shoulders. 'I'm going out to have one last fag. You want one, Lu?'

'OK.' She followed him outside and lit up the cigarette he offered. 'I've only just realised how bad it is here.'

'People change, sis.'

'Or maybe we don't know them as well as we kidded ourselves we did.'

'Could be.'

'I just want to get out.'

'Ditto,' Ken said. 'When I put your bags in the van, I put

my own in too. Goodbyes aren't my style. Just don't lose touch again, Lu.'

These two, who were old for their years, who had seen too much in their young lives, stood in pleasant quietness, allowing the smoke from their cigarettes to drift away into the still, warm air.

'Want to go in and fetch my flowers, Ken?'

He nodded and scrunched out his cigarette.

Soon the wedding party came out of the house and, without mentioning Bar's absence, started off down the lane towards the village: Eve and Ray with Bonnie following, May with Dimitri, Ken with Ann, Mrs Gunner with Maurice.

'We're a bit straggly,' May said, 'but we'll form ourselves up when Ted and Bar comes, and we get nearer to the village. There's quite a few who know you will be there. We want to put on a proper show.'

This was the first Eve had heard about it, but now that May's plans had swung into action, there was only one thing to do and that was to go with them. There was a good forty minutes to the village. Port wine, whisky, Bonnie and Dimitri put gaiety into the conversation.

'That's Grandpa Ted's van . . . you hear? So Ma will be on time.' As the party reached the long incline into the village, Ted drew up and Bar jumped out.

Ted left the van on the roadside and stepped in line beside May. 'Where d'you think I found her?' he whispered in a voice that carried. 'At home. Said she'd just got back from Swallit Pool, said she'd been having a spiritual cleaning.'

'Don't tell me any more, Ted, or I shall say something I shall regret.'

'Lord love us, Lu,' Bar said, 'I should have never forgive myself if I didn't see you wed.' She took her daughter's hand. 'Now, Bonnie, where has GrannyMay made my given place in the procession? I wish I could walk with your pa, but he's special today, he's with the bride.' She put her hand on his shoulder and gave him a loud kiss. 'GrannyMay goes with Grandpa Ted, AnnieGranny's got Uncle Ken, so what say I walk with you and we give your Auntie Lu two flower girls?'

The change in her was amazing. Although her legs were bare, she wore shoes with heels, the full black frock that had been hanging in the hall when the party had left the house, and the Ivy and rose-hip wreath on her black hair, still glistening with water. Her hands were very clean and her fingernails white, her face fresh and glowing.

This might well be the last traditional procession the village would see. It was already considered old-fashioned. When it reached Wickham Village, a gathering of twenty or thirty people waited, ten or so wearing flowers in their buttonholes.

With churning stomach, Eve turned to May. 'My God, May! It's the Wilmotts. How did they know? Oh, May, how *could* you?'

'Don't be silly, Lu. They're your family. It'd be hurtful not to let them come. It's a family occasion, and your aunties and uncles and cousins have come all the way from Portsmouth on the early train to be here. And they've bought you wedding presents.'

Eve felt angry and miserable. Why had she thought that she would be able to pop in and then pop out of family life and not make a ripple? She had thought that she was only going to open a small door on her memories of Roman's Fields, and she had opened a lid on a great big Pandora's box.

The Wilmott aunts would pick at her like a flock of crows.

Her cousins would be full of resentment that she had 'done well for herself'.

None of them had had the guts to get out; instead, they

perpetuated the working-class girl's cycle of life of work – marriage – children – and more work. It's the way it was for women born into their level of society – the level that had been her own. Her cousins weren't dunces, yet none of them had even tried to get a grammar school place. They had called her a snob for trying. Getting above herself. Thought she was better than themselves.

And so I am!

One thing she did know about them was that they were intimidated by their 'betters'. If she had learned anything since she left, it was how to be 'a better'.

Three hours and it will all be over.

Three hours, and Dimitri and I will be on our way to London.

Three hours and I will be free.

In this way she had coped with the production-line work when she was a factory girl.

When the new wedding guests seemed about to surge forward, she said, 'For God's sake, Ray, keep going and keep them away from me.'

'Honest, Lu, I didn't know a thing about them being here.'

'Did May think I'd want a turnout of Wilmotts? They've never done us any favours.'

'Nothing to do with what anybody wants, Lu. It's the way things are done in families and villages, you know that; if families don't turn up at weddings, people think there's a scandal, something to hide.'

If only they knew.

The ceremony didn't last long. Ray 'gave this woman'. Louisa Vera took Dimitri Constantin Rudolph – *not* Lec Podsadowski, as at Caxton Hall.

Dimitri Constantin Rudolph took Louisa Vera to have and to hold.

Ray handed Dimitri the ring, and for the second time, Dimitri put it on her finger.

They were pronounced man and wife and he was told he could kiss the bride.

May was radiantly the 'bride's mother' and the provider of the Roman's Fields wedding feast that would be talked about for a lifetime.

It was a short walk to the station. At some point, Ken had taken his own and their bags and left them in the charge of a porter and bought his ticket to Portsmouth. Their goodbyes said, the bridal couple were ready to depart.

Bar clung to Eve, their cheeks wet with tears. 'You're the most courageous woman in the world, Eve. And you're the most unselfish.'

'I wish that were true, Bar, but I know different.'

Close to Eve's ear, Bar said, 'After you left me, I saw you being sick. Are you expecting?'

Eve froze. It was true she had forced herself to bring up the breakfast that May had cooked. She couldn't think how Bar had seen her. She couldn't explain to herself why she felt it necessary to do this, any more than she could explain why she ate food she really didn't want. 'Nerves, Bar. Every bride gets them.'

Bar laughed. 'I never. I was that happy I got your Ray to get married to me. Now, please, Lu, you go and be happy. Go on and have something for yourself, be blowed to ideals and duty and all that.'

The Portsmouth train arrived, to take them to Harbour station, where they'd pick up the London train. They boarded, waved and it was over.

Something good had come out of Eve's visit. Bar had returned to her old self. It had taken very little to put her life to rights.

It was still bright and sunny when the local train drew into the Harbour station. Not many local travellers were disembarking at this terminus – just the three plus a couple of workmen and a servicewoman wearing ATS uniform.

Dimitri, who was politely guiding Eve by the elbow, suddenly gripped it tightly.

She flinched. 'What's the matter?'

'Guards. *Nyet!* Not guards – police.'

'What are you so jumpy for? It's not us they want.'

But it was.

'Are you the people who have come from Wickham?'

Before Eve could answer, Ken jumped in. 'Who wants to know?'

'Hampshire Constabulary, sir. Detective Inspector Wright. Constables Weir and James.'

Sensibly, Dimitri said nothing. Eve said, 'What's wrong? Has there been an accident?'

'It would be better, ma'am, sirs, if we could talk at the police station.'

Training and experience led them to politeness and cooperation as the best policy at this stage. At the station they were asked to wait in a room that reeked of dust and old tobacco smoke.

'What d'you reckon's up?' Ken asked.

'I have no idea,' Eve said, 'but whatever it is, we just say that we can say nothing until the police have informed Faludi or David Hatton.'

'What good will that do?'

'We must not answer questions to civilian police.'

'Dimitri's right.'

When the detective inspector returned, Dimitri stood up and announced that they were with the War Office and the Official Secrets Act forbade them to make any statement without a government official present, and if the inspector would please ring any of these telephone numbers, then a suitable official would soon arrive.

This rather took the wind out of the inspector's sails. 'Right, sir. Let's hope it won't take long. I'll get somebody to rustle up a cup of tea.'

Two hours later, nothing had happened.

'I'm fed up with this,' Eve said. 'I'm going to tell them to ring Griffon House.'

In less than fifteen minutes the door opened and the inspector announced, 'A Commander Kiefor to see you.'

Then, looking amazing in army officer uniform, Keef was shown into the dingy room. Having looked at each of the three in turn, he said, 'Yes, Inspector, I can vouch for these people and . . .' He looked enquiringly from Eve to Dimitri.

Eve said, 'This is my brother who is on his way to see Lieutenant Hatton.'

'Of course. Mr Wilmott, isn't it?'

'Yes, sir.'

'Right, Mr Wilmott, I didn't expect to find you here, but who knows what to expect these days?'

Eve couldn't help but smile to herself. Keef, with not a single 'darling' or artistic gesture. He had done a good job of transforming himself into a man wearing a Sam Browne. The thing was, which was the real Keef?

Keef, driving a civilian car, had them inside the gates of Griffon House within minutes of completing the official paperwork.

The room they were taken to was the same one in which Eve had been interviewed last winter when the snow had come thick and blinding. Now, the April sun was still bright but sinking into the sea beyond the pier. It had become a very pretty room.

Keef settled in a chair behind a smart desk. 'Some drinks on their way.' Glasspool came in, nodded archly at Eve and raised her eyebrows questioningly at Dimitri and Ken. 'G & T or vodka with ice?'

When they had all settled for the vodka, Keef continued, 'Wickham Village. You were there this morning, right?'

Eve spoke. 'I imagine that you know about me and the major?'

Keef nodded. 'Something happened at Wickham today, and there are a few things to be sorted out with the civilian police. We'll deal with this as quickly as we can, but I shall need to ask you a few things about your stay in Wickham. I don't intend spending too much time on this. It's a local thing, but seeing as you may have evidence, I have to report to the Hampshire Constabulary. Drink up.'

They all emptied their glasses rather quickly and Keef refilled them generously. Eve felt the welcome burn of the vodka sliding into her stomach, where it settled on the wedding cake May had insisted she eat. The matured cake itself could have been 50% proof. The thought of all that fat and sugar and flour fermenting revolted her, and she excused herself and made a dash for the ladies' room. There, the wedding breakfast didn't need any help in being thrown up.

With her make-up repaired and her face cooled, she stood facing herself in the mirror around which were merciless light bulbs, not wanting to meet her own gaze because she knew that Lu would be there looking back. Lu's disgust. Eve's guilt.

Why do you do this?

It was May's fault, she insisted.

You're stronger than May. It wouldn't have mattered.

I didn't want to resist.

Why keep doing it? Your old body was pretty good.

Eve smoothed powder over her cheekbones that had appeared when she had completed the weeks of banting. She put her hands on her waistline and knew how super she looked in the slim-fitting WRNS uniform. She turned heads everywhere. She loved being this elegant Eve. It was worth the occasional bout with Lu to be able to walk into a room and turn heads.

But you always could.

Lu always had the last word.

Dimitri stood up at once when she re-entered the room. 'Eve, are you not well?'

'Too much excitement and vodka. I'm fine.'

Keef questioned them for a short time, asking about who was where and when, but not a clue as to why. Eve couldn't care less why they wanted to know, and was glad that Keef was able to distance them from whatever had gone on in Wickham that day.

'All right, people, leave it to me. I'll settle with the local bobbies.'

Glasspool said that as there wouldn't be a train to take them on to London tonight, she was preparing rooms for them here.

'Keep us well clear of the FiFis. The major is probably ready for something to eat so I'll ring if we want anything. However, I think that my brother might like to have a table in the dining room.'

Glasspool winked. 'I'll be glad to entertain him myself.'

Upstairs, Eve took one of the low wooden chairs on the

tiny balcony outside the French doors that overlooked the sea. Dimitri, having exchanged his shoes and socks for leather mules, and taken off his uniform jacket, collar and tie, came to stand behind her, the heat emanating from his thighs warming her back, his large hands warming her shoulders. 'Are you feeling better now?'

'I feel fine. Don't fuss.'

'OK, OK. You think maybe you like to remember today?'

'Always. And the last couple of days. I loved being with you again where there were ordinary people around. You are so much better at all that stuff than I am.'

'My own family was big. Not all easy, not all nice people, but we were Vladims.'

'Once the war is over, you will be able to go back.'

He didn't reply.

'Come and sit here and let me sit on your lap.'

Why can't I love this loving and generous man? Eve asked herself. I could tell him that I did. Not Dimitri . . . any other man but not Dimitri. He deserves a woman who really will have and hold him from this day forward, as I promised him this morning.

Wanting to comfort him, she put her arms round his neck and kissed him. 'Dimitri! Your beard is wet – have you been crying?'

He gave her a strong hug, not letting go. 'We Russians are so passionate, you know that. Emotion bursts from us, we exclaim too loud, we sing too loud, we laugh too loud. The word I think is . . . "spontaneous"?'

'Dimitri, I said, your beard is wet – have you been crying?'

'A little. I played a fantasy with your family. It felt good to be scratching the pig and carrying logs. What a man, to have tears in his beard when many people are with nothing, are killed all the time, are without food, afraid of dictators, in prison for reading wrong books, for thinking wrong thoughts. I have beautiful woman sitting with arms round me . . .' he paused and said in a loud whisper in her ear, 'and making me hard for her.'

'You always say the right thing. But I'm more hungry for food first.'

'You like that I ring bell for something?'

'No, put a jumper on and I'll take you to a fish-and-chip shop.'

'I like fish and chips. The English have this one food only that is better than any other, but your other things are rubbish.'

She laughed and jumped up. 'Russians are not only emotional and loud – they are very opinionated.'

'I agree, but our opinions are very sound. Is right word, "sound"?'

A momentary flash of him with Fran Haddon asking her 'Is right word?' – and Eve felt possessive. Logically, a woman like Fran would be suited cerebrally, like-minded they might be with their codes and ciphering, but Fran Haddon would never understand the subtlety of the whole man. In the time that they had been together, Dimitri and Eve had shared every kind of experience, had seen one another in every mood, had looked after one another.

As her head emerged from the neck of a navy-issue jumper she was putting on, his voice penetrated her meandering thoughts.

'Come on, woman, fish and chips. Stand still, I will lace your shoes.'

If they should still be together when they were seventy, he would lace her shoes, help her, care for her. He would still love her. She didn't have that kind of commitment. She was 'the cat who walked by itself'.

'You want chips now, or next year?'

'Of course now. If I don't have them, I shan't be able to stop thinking of them. Lots of vinegar. Extra bag of scraps. Come on, it's our wedding night, and chips are only five minutes away.'

The shop was full of soldiers from the barracks. Noisy. Jolly. Beery breath. Cigarette smoke and hot oil. At the rear of the shop were a few plain tables covered with oilcloth. They each had a plate piled high with thick potato chips with a slab of golden plaice, thick bread, dark tea. Eve couldn't finish hers, so Dimitri pulled her plate towards him and finished it for her.

Then they walked up and down the terraced streets, reading the names – Adair, Kassasin . . . One street had a solid wall built across it. Dimitri refused to go back until he had satisfied his curiosity about what lay beyond, and hung on with his fingertips, peering over.

'Is only more houses.'

'Better ones?'

'*Nyet!*'

'Maybe it's the people who are better.'

'People who think they are better are not better. Is true? You agree?'

'Lift me up so that I can see. The houses are all the same. But those people are not better.'

'So we agree.'

'Yes, you daft Russian.'

'I like it when we agree.'

'Have you been at the vodka?'

'I have no need for vodka now. Sometimes I have great need for vodka. We Russians also drink too much.'

'I know.' She had seen the occasions, mostly in Australia, when he had taken himself off with a bottle, and not come back until he was restored to normal. Fran Haddon wouldn't leave him in that state; she would try to cure him. He didn't need to be cured. It was how he was, how he dealt with insoluble problems.

And I eat.

This was not Lu intruding into her thoughts. This was

Eve. I eat, but I don't have the sense to sleep it off like Dimitri. That thought was a revelation. All the food in the world won't fill the emptiness, not if I keep throwing it up . . . making myself feel guilty every time . . . every time . . .

'You are very quiet.'

She searched for his hand. 'You are noisy enough for both of us.'

'That is good. I should not like to think that you were worrying about the police. Are you worrying about the police?'

'No. I was thinking about *me*.'

'That is good.'

Forced to retrace their steps, they dawdled along, his arm lightly round her shoulders like other couples making the most of the spring evening.

'Let's walk along the beach.'

'Is a hard beach, full of stones.'

'Not if you walk along the tide-line. Carry your shoes and socks, roll up your trouserlegs.'

The tide was well out, leaving a wide strand of hard sand studded here and there with large rounded boulders and pebbles. At no time was this stretch of coastline interesting or picturesque but people did find it attractive because of its unobstructed view for mile after gently curving mile. Tonight it was made quite beautiful by light from the moon playing on the small lapping waves.

'When I was a child, this was everybody's holiday place. People came from London in trainloads. I remember mothers lifting their skirts above their knees and shrieking like girls again when a wave hit them. Little girls had their skirts tucked into their knickers. Some wore old underclothes cut down for swimming. Nobody cared. We just wanted to plunge into the water. Ray bought me a proper bathing suit. Ray was good to me.'

Dimitri waited for her to continue. She thought that

she could leave her family, but he knew that she could not. Wherever she went, she would drag them with her. 'I was scared at first, but I had to honour the bathing suit. Not many children learned to swim. There's a kind of superstition in families where the men go to sea: if they don't learn to swim, then they'll never need to. Daft, isn't it?'

'Come on, we swim.'

'It's too cold. We'd die of frostbite.'

He wouldn't hear of it, but put his shoes down and stripped off his clothes.

'Dimitri! You'll get arrested.'

'Don't worry, Mr Keef will come and rescue us.'

Eve couldn't believe that she was doing this. She was right, the water was icy. She plunged under once and ran back to rub herself with her underwear and pull her skirt and jumper over her sticky skin.

'I have been swimming in colder water than this.' Even so, he was shivering. 'Was good?'

'No, was bad . . . very bad.'

'Come on, we run fast, get blood warm.'

They ran towards the pier, fast, and stopped panting when they reached it. 'You see, you are warm again.'

Suddenly, they were stopped in their tracks by a flash, followed by a deafening crump. Two people who had survived the bombardment of Barcelona, and she more recently in London, froze at the sound. Automatically, they threw their arms around each other.

The western sky burst into a red ball. The ground vibrated. The fireball expanded, yellow, orange, red, then settled into a flaring line. Again. Again.

In quick succession bombs pounded into the dockyard and the little houses around it.

Perhaps because they had been cavorting and diving into the waves, Eve and Dimitri had heard no sound of the warning siren. Now the raiders were overhead.

They could hear the throb of aircraft engines, loaded, bomb-doors open. They clung to one another watching the dockland area exploding and could do nothing.

It was all happening again.

Dimitri couldn't stop trembling, and when Eve began to cry, she made no effort to stop herself.

Huddled together, they did not move until the all clear sounded, when they climbed the pebbled slope and started back towards Griffon House.

In the street an air-raid warden shone a light on their faces. 'Are you all right?'

They nodded.

'I should get inside soon as you can. It's been a bad night. A lot of casualties.'

Eve and Dimitri realised how lucky they'd been to escape injury, but each knew how unnecessary it was to say anything.

Had it not been for last night's air raid, what had happened in Wickham might have warranted more than the line it got in the local paper. But one death would hardly be noticed among so many.

Ken was already in Keef's office when Eve and Dimitri entered, and so, surprisingly, was David Hatton, who rose politely and waited for Eve to be seated.

Looking at the notes he had before him, David said, 'There was a death in the area of Wickham Village yesterday. I shall issue a statement to the Hampshire Constabulary that will say simply that none of the witnesses questioned in Portsmouth has anything to add to their statements.'

Ken spoke up loudly. 'Excuse me, David, would you mind not speaking for us until we know what you are giving us an alibi for? We were there. However inconvenient it might be, I don't like cover-ups.'

'Did you know this man James Gunner?'

'Yes.'

'Were you in this place –' he looked at his notes – 'Swallit Wood or Swallit Pool at some time between eleven and two thirty p.m.?'

Eve went cold. Ken didn't look in her direction. Nevertheless she felt that his eyes were upon her.

'No, I was in Wickham Village then.'

'So you didn't see this man floating in the water with a blow to the head?'

'No.'

'I know that your sister and Major Vladim were with the rest of your family, on their way to the church, right, Major . . . Eve . . . ?'

'We were in a beautiful parade of many people of my wife's clan.'

'So neither of you saw anything?'

'It was as I have just told you, Lieutenant Hatton . . . sir.'

'So I may take it then, that none of you can add anything to what you told the police yesterday?' David Hatton took silence as assent. 'Good. I am glad that none of you is to be delayed any further because of some civil matter. Major, you have a train to catch and your wife has to return to Ford aerodrome.'

'Excuse me,' Eve interrupted. 'May I make something clear? I would prefer it if I was not referred to as Major Vladim's *wife*. It makes me sound as though I am a possession. You all know that I chose my own name. I wish to keep it, as you men all keep yours.' She knew that they would think her unnecessarily assertive, but bad luck!

Suddenly, Eve began to sweat profusely and feel dizzy. 'I'm sorry, but could I have some water, please?'

Only Keef did not jump into action.

As she drank, a terrible nausea arose in her and she rushed from the room, retching into an inadequate handkerchief. She blacked out and crumpled to the floor.

The next thing she was aware of was being on a cot-bed, and Glasspool wafting sal volatile under her nose.

'Did I faint? I'm sorry, I suddenly felt so awful.'

'How are you now, ma'am?'

In other circumstances, Eve might have smiled. 'I'm

fine. We had a long day yesterday and then there was the air raid. I'm all right.'

'It's probably your period. There are some stains on your stockings. I have put a hand-towel under you. Don't move. There's a doctor staying here and I've told one of the boys to fetch him.'

Suddenly Eve was convulsed by sharp pains drawing her womb up and clutching and pulsating her back. With shock and dread, she recognised the awful pains of the onset of miscarriage, and again she was dragged into blackness.

She was between sheets, with the smell of Lysol and ether hanging around her. Way, way in the distance, an echoing voice said, 'She's with us again, sir.'

She felt warm . . . grateful for feeling warm again. Thirsty, but warm feet. Woollen socks. The pain had stopped. Her neck felt limp, her head heavy, she allowed it to sink further into the pillow.

'Can you hear me, ma'am? She's coming out of it, sir.'

The voice became normal and the sir became a head in a white coat with a stethoscope hanging from his neck. He picked up her hand and felt her pulse, then pulled her eyelid down and peered closely.

'How's the bleeding, Sister?'

'Hardly anything, sir.'

Eve wanted them to go away so that she could go back to sleep again.

She remembered the extreme pain, hearing screaming and knowing that it was herself. She remembered Dimitri gathering her in his arms and carrying her down the steps and into the ambulance, and the ambulance bell ringing and ringing.

She remembered Dimitri. 'You will be fine, Eve. The doctor says you will be well. Hold on, hold on.' Then to someone else, 'No, no, I will not go outside. This is my wife. I insist to be with her. You can make all the orders you wish, but I shall not leave.'

She remembered the bright, white light, then darkness and then this hard, comfortable, warm bed.

'She can have a cup of tea, plenty of sugar.'

The nursing sister loomed over her. 'Nice cup of tea, ma'am?'

Eve nodded. Tea. Then sleep. Silence. To be on her own. No one telling her anything. No decisions to make. The pain was gone. Peace. Peace. Peace. Sweet, sweet tea and peace.

'Do you know where you are?'

'Where is my . . . where is Major Vladim . . . my husband?'

She remembered David saying, 'Major, you have a train to catch,' and visualised Dimitri seated on a train rushing away, taking him back to Scotland. Suddenly she experienced a terrible sense of loss. The emptiness and aloneness was too much to handle, and she drifted away into the temporary oblivion again. She needed help. Where was Janet McKenzie when she was needed? Tears trickled out from beneath her closed lids. For God's sake, Eve, pull yourself together. I can't. Don't want to. The cat who walks by itself.

'She is all right, but we keep losing her. She is weak, very thin and undernourished, and underweight, but nothing that a few steaks and some iron tonic won't put right. I'm surprised this didn't happen earlier. Speak to her, sir, try to get her to respond. I'd like her to drink some sweet tea.'

The 'sir' the sister addressed didn't need to speak. His smell, his breathing, the displacement of air when he moved told Eve who he was. 'Dimitri. You missed your train.' She didn't want to open her eyes in case she was mistaken.

'You see, Sister, only two days married and already she reprimands me. You go, I will attend. Come on, sit up, you have tea to drink.' He put his hands under her armpits and hoisted her up against the pillows. 'The sister is right, you are too thin. You will eat steak and like it. Now, drink tea, or I shall have it myself.'

'Russians are so bloody bossy.'

'Don't use language.'

She drank. No tea had ever tasted so good. 'I feel better already.' It was then she felt the pads between her legs. 'Oh my God! Was I pregnant? Dimitri, did I miscarry again?' She slumped back against the pillows, not wanting to know the answer. Dimitri pressed the bell and kept his thumb hard on it.

When the hubbub died down and it was decided that this was not an emergency, the doctor stood resolutely beside Eve's bed, whilst Dimitri resumed denting and creasing it and making her drink.

'Major Vladim, there is no need to panic. Your wife is a healthy young woman, rather thin but otherwise healthy, but she must –'

'Excuse me.'

The doctor withdrew his attention from Dimitri. 'Yes?'

'Oh, good. I thought for a moment I had become so thin that you couldn't see me.'

Dimitri signalled to her with a frown, but he was holding back a smile. 'I think maybe that Sub-Lieutenant Anders means that you should be addressing her as she is the one –'

'Thank you, Dimitri. You don't have to speak for me.'

Holding his palms protectively in front of him, he shrugged his shoulders at the doctor.

'This is the first I've known about being pregnant. And if I am, then please address me.' When she asked the question she was looking at Dimitri. 'Am I still pregnant?'

'Yes, Lieutenant Anders. You are carrying a baby.'

'I'm sorry I was so rude to you. Do you think I won't lose it?'

'No. I see no reason why you should not have a full-term pregnancy, and a normal birth. It was what is known as a break-through bleed. Your husband says that you miscarried once before when you were in a weakened state – a two-months foetus. However, this time, your foetus is stronger, being more advanced. Your notes show that you have experienced a great amount of trauma . . . stress. Major Vladim tells me that you were out in the incendiary raid last night.'

Eve looked questioningly at Dimitri. 'Was it last night?'

He nodded.

'How strange.'

The doctor felt Eve's pulse – 'Not much wrong there' – and pulled down a lower eyelid. 'A little anaemic. Nothing very serious.' He smiled for the first time. 'I will ask Sister to bring you some beef broth which you will drink to the very last drop. You'll see to that, Major?'

'If she will permit me.' He shook hands energetically with the doctor and said, 'Thank you, very much. I thank you for such good news . . . that my wife will be well again.'

After he had left the ward, Eve looked up at Dimitri, who looked as though he didn't know whether to laugh or to cry. 'Four months! Four months!'

'It is how many months we have been married.'

'I know, I know.'

'It was the night we made love after our marriage. You remember how good it was?'

'I used a cap and cream. It shouldn't have happened.'

Pulling back the covers, he laid his hand on her belly and gently caressed it. 'Russians have very strong sperms. Your little contraption will not stop them.' Moving close, he looked directly into her eyes with no levity in his expression, and took hold of her hand. 'We made a baby. It is not going away.'

She tightened her grip on his fingers. 'I know and I'm terrified.'

'Of this little baby?'

'Of what it will do to me.'

'Eve, what are you saying?'

'I was supposed to marry you and then get an annulment. But now there are three of us. How can we get divorced and forget the marriage of convenience with a baby?'

'Eve . . .'

'I'm sorry, Dimitri. It wasn't your fault any more than mine.'

'No, I am sorry. I forget for a moment the agreement why you married me – to make me British citizen. I forget because I love you.'

'Please, Dimitri, not now. Just leave me to get some sleep.'

The next day, the doctor came into the ward, felt her pulse, and listened to her heartbeat and that of the baby. 'You had another little bleed during the night.'

Eve nodded. 'It wasn't anything much.'

'I want you to remain here, under my care for a while.'

'How long is a while?'

'Maybe three weeks . . . a month.'

'That long?'

'We will get you through this, and you will have a fine, healthy baby. Now then, a Dr McKenzie has asked if I would give her permission to visit you. I have no objection. In fact, I believe it might be a good thing for you to talk to her.'

'Yes, please.'

* * *

'Janet, this is devastating. I still can't believe it is true. I haven't even had to alter the buttons on my uniform.'

Looking at Eve levelly, Janet said, 'You became addicted to the banting and regurgitation.'

'Please, Janet, that sounds so crude.'

'But you've been doing it ever since you were so successful at it when you went to Spain.'

'I liked the way I looked.'

'It's a dangerous practice, Eve. You are lucky your baby didn't abort.'

'Oh, thank you, Janet, I feel really lucky. If I had known it wasn't the slimming that was stopping my periods, I would have been able to make that decision myself.'

'Anger won't help.'

'Don't lecture me. Just now I need all the anger I can get.'

'You are being kept in here to stay calm and rested. If you haemorrhage again, the baby will be too small and weak to survive. Is that what you want?'

Eve stared off through the window that showed only bright April sky. 'Two or three months ago, I would have said yes. Do you know what, Janet? Dimitri always had plenty of French letters, I have had a cap for years, and I have a box of pennyroyal, and here I am pregnant.'

'I agree, that's pretty damned bad luck. But we have to talk about the situation as it is.'

'The situation is that I am terrified.'

'It's not the first time you've been terrified.'

'Terrified of being cut off behind enemy lines with only a fast-flowing river to escape by. Terrified of trying to escape with two children – yes, but this is something I have no control over. This . . . this *foetus* is just there. I'm not able to make any decisions about it.'

'Women do change when they actually give birth. Have you thought of that?'

'Absolutely! My friend utterly rejected her baby. She wouldn't even feed it.'

'She must have suffered some kind of traumatic event.'

'*This* is a traumatic event. I don't want a baby, Janet. I just don't want it.'

'OK, so talk to me about why.'

'I had never planned to be a mother. I refuse to go the way my mother went. She was a trainee teacher and she got pregnant with my elder brother without wanting to. She gave up her plans for herself. She had wanted a career . . . she had a brain, she was clever. I want to be a pilot, not a mother. I will go off my head if I have to stay at home and bring up a child. It's just not fair. Dimitri can be a father and go on doing what he wants to do, but I can't be a mother and get my pilot's licence. I can't fly our agents and drop them safely into France. It's what SOE were training me for. It's what I want to do. Is that "why" enough?'

'OK, so let us run through the options available. Adoption?'

Eve was horrified. 'No! Dimitri wouldn't agree anyhow.'

'But you agreed to marry him.'

'That's not the same. There is this third person involved here, and we can't ask it.'

'Have the child, keep it, and find someone you trust to look after it. There are thousands of children being brought up away from their mothers and fathers – evacuees.'

'Evacuate a new-born baby?'

'Mothers die at birth and their babies thrive with substitute parents.'

Eve gave Janet a wry smile. 'I had a substitute parent – he was my brother.'

'So, substitute parenting works; you grew up all right.'

'Don't make me laugh, Janet. I'm nuts, and you know

that better than anybody. I don't even know yet who I am.'

'Of course you're not nuts. And you do know who you are, Eve Anders. Not Lu Wilmott, not Mrs Vladim, not even Sub-Lieutenant Anders – you are Eve. You didn't choose that name by accident.'

'What's that supposed to mean?'

'Even if you didn't choose it consciously, you saw yourself as the first woman . . . Eve.'

'Adam's spare rib.'

'Adam was a wimp. God had to give him somebody to show him what to do. God said, "Don't you dare pick that apple." Adam was so scared, he said, "Sure thing, God. Who wants knowledge anyway?" But what did Eve say? "To Hell with that, I want to know what's going on." So she picked the damned thing and gave all the rest of us a bite. Eve is the hero of the Garden of Eden story.'

'Thank God for you, Janet. I'll be all right now. I'll stay here as long as I'm told to. I'll eat and drink, I'll get fat.'

'Listen to me, Eve. This is your friend speaking, not the doctor. I think you have had enough hungers in your life . . . your missing father, your education, and then you "banted" your family and are now hungry for them.'

'I'm not. I've just seen them. They are dropping to pieces. There is no longer any tranquillity there. My uncle is sick, but they won't talk about it. My friend was raped . . . the rapist was found dead. I don't think they wanted me. I was just the prize Aunt May wanted. I made her a bride's mother for the day. She put on this great feast, and invited half the county, just so that they could see her being the Bride's Mother. For God's sake, I'm not even her daughter.'

'Why did you go there?'

'I wanted to make up for leaving them when I went off to Spain.'

'You went off to the most dangerous place on earth at that time. Don't you think that might have worried them – just a little?'

'I know it did, but it was the only way I knew how to break away. Clean cut. Get away.'

'Now turn the whole thing on its head. You return just as suddenly as you went. But you had changed. My, how you had changed – a slim, pale-haired WRNS officer with an impressive Russian in tow. You probably scared them to death. But what does your proud aunt do? She treats you like the princess you are to her. She wants to put a stop to the rumours about why you left. She wants to show you off. It was an act of love for you, Eve. Now she could let you go into the arms of this wonderful Russian whom everybody likes.'

Eve didn't reply. She stared out at the bright blue sky until she almost drifted off into sleep.

'I'll go now. Get some rest. I'll come as often as I can.'

'Do you think the girls would come? Maybe just DB, and Anomie?'

Janet nodded, then rose and gave Eve a light, brushing kiss on the cheek. 'Eve?'

'Yes?'

'Would you mind if I went to see your aunt? Do you think she would mind?'

'Not if you give her enough notice so that she can put on a decent frock, and show you Roman's Fields at its best.'

DB came. Eve was sitting outside in the sun. DB's hair was very short and set in broad waves.

'Brought you this.' She tossed her a cardboard envelope. 'It's what they call a private pressing, a limited edition. Play it when you don't mind crying.'

Eve read the label. 'Mina de Beers – "Sophisticated

Lady".' She turned it over. 'Mina de Beers – "Strange Fruit".'

'That's super, DB. I'll have to get somebody to bring me in a gramophone.'

'You don't mind if I don't say anything about . . . you know . . . the baby?'

'I want to hear what is happening.'

'I'm off on a tour again – Cairo, hence the short hair. The "dotty" music is proving such a good way of getting information out.'

'Good luck. I hope there are enough people out there who will appreciate your voice.'

'Hey, who cares now I've got a contract to record?'

Ken wrote Eve a letter, saying that he had had the best time ever at the Finishing School.

> I can't tell you where they're sending me, but it's back where I might get a chance to look for my girl. My old skill at coffin-making will stand me in good stead. I can be a useful tradesman. If I'm itinerant, I shall be in a good position to know what is going on. I wonder how you felt going back. I shall soon know. Dimitri's a good man, Eve. Give him a chance.
>
> Ken.

When Electra came, she told Eve that she didn't think the FiFi was working. 'But I don't want to give up on it. Even if we save just one, it will be worth it. Don't you think?'

Eve guessed that Electra wanted what she was doing justified. To save just one life. Paul's.

Every day Eve had to take gentle exercise, just walking around, keeping her legs moving. After four weeks, she asked if she could leave.

'It would be safer to wait a while – make sure you and

the baby are both quite well. Why not stay with us, and let us deliver the baby?'

There came a day when the buttons of her cotton dressing gown would hardly fasten. It seemed that almost overnight, her body had taken on the figure of an expectant mother. When she took a bath, she actually looked down at herself critically. Her breasts had become swollen, her nipples large and darkened, and her belly swelled out like the dome of a silver serving dish. Running her hands over it, she felt the baby move.

My God! I really am pregnant.

Dimitri didn't write from Scotland every day, but quite often, the letters arriving in batches. She didn't write back, except for a postcard now and again, to say that the baby was well and moving. Although she had plenty of time to write, she didn't know what to say.

Then one day a nurse came to say that there was a visitor.

'May! What are you doing here?'

Giving Eve a tentative hug, May said, 'I've come to see you, you daft thing. Here, I got you a jar of malt, some honey, cod-liver oil, and some of Ted's strawberry cordial to take after it, and I've give the nurse a block of butter that's to be give only for you.'

'Oh May. I don't know what to say.'

'You don't have to say nothing. I said to Ann, "I thought there was something wrong when she wasn't eating proper. She was having the sickness and didn't want anybody to see." And Ann agreed. "You just remind her what I said, I an't never been wrong yet about girls who's expecting. It shows in their eyes." Don't they ever give a visitor a cup of tea in this place? Hold on, I'll go and ask that nurse. I give her a pot of honey for herself, so she won't mind.'

May had arrived like a whirlwind and took over. She'd gone to see the matron and asked her to see that Eve was given all the supplements she had brought in. And she'd shown her the layette she had brought in for taking the baby home. 'I want you to send me a telegram as soon as she goes into labour, and I'll come down and be with her. Don't say no, because I shall come anyway. I've brought a good many babes into the world.'

The matron had never encountered a will stronger than her own. This was her hospital, but she wasn't averse to a bit of flattery from a woman who said that she only ever wanted to be a nurse and finish up as Matron in a good hospital. 'The best in the whole county, and I know, I'm Hampshire born and bred.'

'Have you been knitting, Eve?' May asked her now, spreading out the tiny clothes for Eve to see.

'You know I can't knit.'

'I said to Ray, do you think I should go for white, seeing as we shan't know whether it is a boy or girl until it's too late to start knitting. Ray said, "Do yellow." Do you know, I never thought of it. Look, an't these just the prettiest things you ever saw? I know it seems a lot, but the first weeks they get through them like anything.'

Then she calmed down. 'You're looking just like your old self . . . I was going to say "Lu", but that Janet friend of yours said you wanted to be called Eve now. Well, I don't mind. It's you whose name it is. She explained to me that it was important.'

A wards-maid came in with a teatray set up. 'You must be somebody's fav'rite. Visitors don't usually get anything.'

'That's really nice. It's not that I was asking for any preferential treatment, but I have come a long way on the train.'

When the girl had gone, Eve said, 'And what else did Dr McKenzie say besides that I want to be called Eve?'

'Well . . . she did sound me out about how I would feel if the baby came to live with us. It's out in the country, and as safe as houses – as you well know. We don't want for nothing in the way of decent food. It's the one thing that being a smallholder has over the rest these days. You've seen for yourself how little Bonnie and Anthony are thriving. Never a want of somebody to see to them. The baby would have ready-made cousins living in the same house, and, of course, you know how much room we've got there. It could have a proper nursery – next to your old bedroom, if you like. Then you and Dimitri could come down any time you wanted.' May had been handling and smoothing the baby clothes as she had been speaking. Then she collected them together, returned them to the bag, and went silent. Eventually, looking up at Eve, she said, 'Lord, *Eve*, I've run out of steam.'

'You're amazing, May. Do you really want to take on a new-born baby at your time of life?'

'What do you mean – at my time of life? I'm in a better state of health than you, my girl.'

'I know that. It's just that you always seem to have room for one more.'

'I just happen to believe that the best thing invented is a family – the bigger, the better.'

Even though Eve couldn't subscribe to May's belief, for May it was true. And what May believed, Eve needed to get her through.

'By the way, I brought you in the *Hampshire Chronicle*. There's a piece in there about Alice's husband.'

CORONER'S COURT

The inquiry into the death of James Gunner – land agent – of Wickham took place this week.

Gunner's wife, Alice, gave evidence that her husband had been unwell in recent months and had taken to walking in woodlands other than those on the estate which was his place of work.

Readers may remember that Mr Gunner had been

discovered with a severe injury to his head, drowned in a local pond known as 'Swallit'. At first the police were puzzled by Gunner's presence at the pond, his head injury, and the fact that his clothing was in disarray. The coroner saw nothing unusual for a man working, as he did, well away from public view to relieve himself when he was about his work.

Many trees in that area had become rotten and a good number of branches had fallen at that time in the area around the pond, and it appeared likely that Gunner had been struck by one. Blood was discovered on a broken branch.

A verdict of death by misadventure was returned.

When May had gone, Eve reread the piece and wondered about the truth. At least the coroner was satisfied and the case was closed. Eve knew she would never ask Bar about that day.

EPILOGUE

France, 1943

November. A clear night. The Germans have picked up the trace as the Lysander crosses the English Channel and comes within its range. The pilot tips the nose, ducking under the radar.

The plane comes in low over the trees. Two women and one man wearing cork helmets and parachutes hang on to webbing close to the bay doors. They are waiting to pick out the signal lights. Dangerous for those signalling. Dangerous for the parachutists. Dangerous for the pilot.

The Lysander makes one more turn and then – there it is! A winking light, just where it is supposed to be. The plane goes as low as it is safe to do, the engines sounding so loud to those waiting to jump that they feel they must be alerting every guard on sentry duty. But it is a bitterly cold night. Rivers are frozen, the farmlands from where the signal flickers are frosted well below the topsoil. It is hoped that the enemy patrols are holed up, warming their hands on tin mugs of ersatz coffee. The pilot sticks a thumb up and chutes with bulky equipment are tipped out to sway down ahead of the parachutists, who follow. One. Two. Three.

This is her tenth sortie.

She pulls the stick back, watching the dials, and climbs, hoping that everything will hold together until she has crossed the English coast.

Looking at her luminous watch she sees that Dimitri should by now have ended his long journey from Scotland to Hampshire. No matter how late he arrived, he will take the stairs at Roman's two at a time and pick up Louisa from her cot and sit on their bed cradling her, observing every minute change in her since his last visit.

By morning she will be there too, listening to his running commentary on what Louisa has done, how Louisa smiled at him, how clever she is, what she did in the bath, what she did with the present he will certainly have brought for her.

Ray and Bar and the children have gone to live close to Ray's new job as a trade union official in the West Country, so, except for keeping Ted going, May has only Louisa to fuss over, and Dimitri when he pays his frequent visits, and Eve, when she can be spared.

Now she is out over the sea. Elated. Self-sufficient. Proud of herself. Confident. Successful. Alone.

Her destiny is in her own hands, as are the lives of the agents she flies in and out of Occupied France.

This, for now, is Eve Anders' private paradise.

AUTHOR'S NOTE

The Face of Eve is a work of fiction but it is based on fact.

The Priory Finishing School and The House by the Sea are modelled on various houses on the Beaulieu estate in Hampshire, which were used for the training of SOE agents.

The FiFi, or 'courtesans with good manners', existed, and although mentioned by Professor Michael Foot in a definitive history of the SOE, like so much of women's history, the detail is lost. Whilst writing this novel I discovered an ex-FiFi living in France, but she wasn't willing to talk. Who could blame her sixty years on?

There was a haven for the crowned heads of Europe in Southsea during the Second World War.

The Duchess of Windsor did express a hope that she might take up designing clothes, and when she and the Duke packed to take up residence in the Bahamas, among the items they took with them was a sewing machine.

DB's work as an SOE agent was like that of opera singer Diana de Rosso, who successfully carried message 'dots' in musical scores.

As for Dimitri's provenance – a Red Army officer did work with SOE.

Betty Burton, March 2001